T0365988

Diabolic Revelations

JILLIAN E. MARTYN

DIABOLIC REVELATIONS

This is a work of fiction. All of the characters, names, incidents, organizations, and dialogue in this novel are either the products of the author's imagination or are used fictitiously.

iUniverse books may be ordered through booksellers or by contacting:

iUniverse
1663 Liberty Drive
Bloomington, IN 47403
www.iuniverse.com
844-349-9409

Because of the dynamic nature of the Internet, any web addresses or links contained in this book may have changed since publication and may no longer be valid. The views expressed in this work are solely those of the author and do not necessarily reflect the views of the publisher, and the publisher hereby disclaims any responsibility for them.

ISBN: 978-1-6632-0878-1 (sc)
ISBN: 978-1-6632-0879-8 (hc)
ISBN: 978-1-6632-0877-4 (e)

Library of Congress Control Number: 2020920753

Print information available on the last page.

iUniverse rev. date: 11/24/2020

This book is dedicated to my best friend Carrie Anthony and my nephew Nick Martyn. Thanks for the support and all the laughs.

Introduction

From the moment Fallen had laid his eyes upon Sinah, he never once shifted his attention. His expression weakened as he stepped closer to her and removed one of his gloves. He whispered gently placing his cold pale hand on the side of her face. "…Sinah."

The moment his skin touched her flesh, Sinah made a loud gasp as oxygen rushed into her lifeless body, returning her from death. Fallen instantly doubled over as blood flooded then gushed from his mouth. While Bridger on the other hand, screeched collapsing to all fours. He frantically began to claw at his back feeling his skin burning in agony.

The soldiers nervously took a few steps back from him as large feathered wings pierced through his back then tore through his battle suit. Once they were finished freeing themselves from his flesh, the color of his wings could clearly be seen. Each feather was a pale bluey white. The tips were touched with gold.

The Director closed his eyes as a cool breeze rushed through the Launch Pad area and swiftly blew away the once stagnant air. Having never experienced it before, the soldiers looked around not understanding what was happening.

The Director's lips curled into a full smile as he looked toward the unconscious erratically breathing Sinah. "Welcome to our Lab, God."

One

Aftermath

Looming ominously in its solidarity was the final building in the facility, building Seven. Its towering presence and highest level of security made it more than just simply unwelcoming. Whispers and rumors were always heard about this particular restricted building. While most gossip was sinister in nature, most of it was true. This building was where the main branch of the Angels, Demons, God and Lucifer Labs were located. Being the final step in the process of Helix creation, vital signs, level of Helix and general health were checked here. This was also where it was decided which field would best suit the Helix. Building Seven was also a place Fallen had known only too well. The levels of pain he endured in the cells on the higher floors could make even the strongest Helix beg for a mercy death.

The Med Tech pushed the gurney with Sinah upon it as fast as her feet could take her down the singular passage into the building. Any Helix soldier in her path seemed to instinctively move out of the way. The second their eyes touched upon the barely alive Sinah, they instantly stopped what they were doing and stared. The Helixes close to mid-range or higher placed their hands upon their chests as expressions of a hurt confusion took their features.

As the Med Tech pushed Sinah toward the enclosed security booth protected by six armed Helix soldiers, she yelled out. "Computer! Alert

ADGL emergency team for operating room 3! Locate any ADGL Lead Tech and send out an emergency message: Top priority Helix in critical condition!"

The computer made a sound of acknowledgement. As the Med Tech raced through the security scanner, she glanced behind herself. Fallen had followed in her wake and was only a few steps behind her. As he tried to step through the scanner himself, one of the six armed Helix soldiers stepped in his path. "Sorry Commander, this is a restricted area even to y-"

Fallen wasn't hesitant to snatch his hand around the Helix soldier's throat and slam him against the opposing wall. This action was so fast and so aggressive the weapon fell from the Helix soldier's hands. Four out of the five remaining Helix soldiers instantly came to his aid. Every single one of them pointed their machine guns at Fallen's head. One of them spoke in a rattled tone. "C… Commander! Th...This is building Seven, it-"

Fallen snarled, turning his head toward them. "Anyone standing in my way will be ripped in two!!"

An aggressive wave of intimidation much stronger than Fallen's natural essence rushed over them. Before anyone had a chance to even attempt to reason with him, the Director called out. "Lucifer!" Out of breath and limping as fast as he could toward the altercation, he continued. "Lucifer, I know she is your natural enemy but in her current state she's-"

Fallen began to crush the Helix soldier's larynx as he spoke in a calm yet cold tone. "If I have to kill each and every one in my path to get to my counterpart, I will. Even your small pathetic life is worthless to me, Director Hart."

The Director's expression shifted to slight shock. Never had Fallen spoken to him in such a manner. As if caught off guard by Fallen's threat, he didn't question just waved his hand. "L… Let him through."

The second their weapons were lowered, Fallen released the soldier and raced down the hall in the direction the Med Tech had gone.

Murdoch had a full frown on his face as he approached the Director. The unconscious Bridger was being carried on his back. The second the Director caught a glimpse of them in his peripheral vision, he turned. "Call for an ADGL team to deal with this one."

One of the Helix soldiers sitting at the desk behind the enclosed security booth tapped the air. As he accessed the green screens, he responded. "Yes Director."

Murdoch leaned his head toward Bridger's ear and whispered. "You're about to go through hell A Helix. But no matter what they do to you, no matter what happens, you have to survive. You must survive, your God needs you."

Bridger only continued to breathe erratically.

Two

Saving Grace

The lone ADGL Tech sitting at the terminal suddenly turned his head toward Fallen as he busted into operating room 3. His expression went from shock and surprise to nervous and anxious in a matter of seconds. Fallen's attention was locked on the glass window ahead of the terminal leading into the operating room. The moment he stepped beside the ADGL Tech, he began to lock and unlock his jaw seeing Sinah. She was unconscious on the operating table and appeared more dead, then simply on the verge of death.

A team lead by Emma frantically went to work trying to keep her alive. As oxygen tubes were put up Sinah's nose and an I.V. was put in her arm, Fallen spoke. "Open line the room."

The ADGL Tech nervously nodded and did as he was told. "Yes Commander."

Emma picked up a small metal device from the table of operating tools. "Pad and clamp her for the heart rate monitor."

The Med Tech that escorted Sinah quickly began to cut the remains of the top of her battle suit off. Right before Emma pressed the device against Sinah's arm, she caught a glimpse of Fallen. The full frown on his face was pointed directly at her. Emma gave a slightly exasperated sigh then mumbled. "Oh great, this is just what we need right now."

Emma touched the device to Sinah's arm. Her body released an aggressive twitch as it instantly attached to her skin. The Med Tech wasn't shy about shooting Emma a glare. "Careful with her, she's in really bad shape!"

Emma returned the glare with a frown. "Just do as I say! Get that monitor up and running already!"

The Med Tech couldn't help but to frown in return as she approached the machine. Emma studied Sinah's pale lifeless face for a few seconds. "Hey Nash?"

Not getting an instant response, Emma blindly motioned her hand toward the operating room speaker. "Nash?"

The ADGL Tech behind the terminal named Nash, snickered a little. "We're already open lined Emma."

Emma glanced toward the annoyed looking Med Tech as she placed heart monitor pads on Sinah's chest. "I'm pretty sure this is Kid Harmond."

Nash instantly stood up from his seat in excitement and leaned toward the glass. The tone of his voice mirrored his demeanor. "Get outta here! Really?! I've watched tons of her Combat replays in the common social areas. Everyone loves watching them. She's amazing!"

Hints of a momentary smile dabbed at Fallen's lips. Emma frowned watching the Med Tech hook the heart monitor clamp onto Sinah's index finger. "Be impressed later! Why is she under top priority status? I know she's in terrible condition but-"

The Med Tech cut Emma off. "She's God."

Emma's eyes darted to Sinah in a shocked annoyance and disbelief. "What do you mean 'she's God' according to whom?"

The Med Tech approached the heart monitor and tried to turn it on. Nothing happened. She then smacked the top of the machine a few times before she noticed it just wasn't plugged in. As she picked up the plug, she spoke. "The Director said 'Welcome to our Lab, God' and then this thing happened with the air. It was like it moved on its own. I didn't know the air could-"

"That's some nerve!" Emma said with a scoff. "And since when is the Director an ADGL Tech?"

The Med Tech gave an indifferent shrug. "Why else would the Commander willingly come here?"

Emma scoffed again. "Well, we'll just see about that. Nash, pull up Kid Harmond's Helix file. Also activate the auto-sampler device."

Nash began to click on the terminal computer. "I'm on it."

Emma rudely pointed at the Med Tech and hissed. "And you! Hurry up with the monitor already!"

The Med Tech frowned pushing the plug into the power source. The minute she did, the heart rate monitor sprang to life. Everyone's eyes darted to it hearing Sinah's frantic rapid heart beep. Emma's eyes darted to Sinah's EKG line. It was only spiking wildly. "We have to slow her heart down! Her body could seize up at any second! If that happens not only could she suffer physical damage but it could also cause brain damage!"

One of the ADGL Techs wrapped a blood pressure cuff around Sinah's upper arm. "Checking blood pressure."

Emma raced over to the table of operating tools and snatched up a syringe filled with a blue liquid. "This will slow-"

The Med Tech's eyes darted to the needle then the liquid inside. "Are you out of your mind?! That has a sedative in it! She could easily just die if-!"

Emma raced over to Sinah's I.V. tube. "We have to do something fast! I don't have time for second guessing or simple Med Techs!" As she injected the blue fluid into the I.V. tube, she called out. "Nash! Has the sample results come up yet?!"

Nash went a little flush. "Uh... I... I didn't take the sample. I thought she-"

Emma tossed the empty syringe aside as she hissed. "Hurry up and turn on the auto-sampler!"

Nash gave the slightest nod as he pressed a button on the terminal. The metal device on Sinah's arm suddenly flicked on and slammed a needle into her vein. As if having a natural defensive reaction, all the blue liquid that had passed into her blood stream gushed back into the I.V. tube then into the I.V. bag. A large amount of her blood followed after.

While everyone's eyes filled with panic seeing what was happening, Emma hissed. "Son of a bitch, her body is having a massive rejection!"

The ADGL Tech by the blood pressure machine went flush reading the results. "Her blood pressure is through the roof! If we don't do something fast she's going to go into cardiac arrest!"

Emma's eyes darted to the I.V. bag as it suddenly exploded. Blood and medical solutions splattered against the floor and any ADGL Tech near it. "We need to replace-"

Emma was suddenly cut off by a loud beeping alarm followed by red flashing lights. Nash's eyes darted down to the terminal. Spotting the problem, he called out. "The operating room needs to be sterilized, everyone out!"

Emma's eyes darted to Nash. "Are you crazy?! We could lose her at any mo-"

Nash didn't glance up from working. "The sterilized field has detected a contamination. The risks of infection are almost at the maximum levels. Everyone needs to get out of there now!"

Emma glanced toward the Med Tech and ADGL Techs as they quickly left the operating room. "Did we at least successfully get a sample?"

Nash glanced toward a green screen to the right of the terminal. "It's processing as we speak. Now get out of there!"

Emma glanced toward Sinah for a split second before she too left the operating room. Once the electronic door closed behind her, the sterilization procedure was activated.

Emma didn't glance toward anyone as she began to anxiously pace the room. "Scan her body as well. I want to know if she has any broken bones or internal organ damage."

Nash gave a quick nod. "I'm on it."

A green light spread widely over Sinah's feet then slowly began to move upward. Emma sighed listening to Sinah's panicking heartbeat. "Please don't simply flat line. Please don't simply flat line."

Once the green light reached just beyond the top of her head, it gave a quick rush back over her body then vanished. Nash glanced toward another green screen as it appeared. It was displaying the outside and inside of Sinah's body. Emma's expression shifted to slight confusion looking at it herself. "No damage? Nothing? She appears to have some old burn scars but-"

Nash cut Emma off as a green light appeared on his terminal. "Field sterilization complete, everyone get back in there and-!"

Nash was cut off by a loud bang right beside him.

Three

A Calming Voice

Everyone's eyes darted in the direction the loud bang came from. Fallen had unbuckled his standard issue mission supply belt and carelessly dropped it to the floor. One of the ADGL Techs went flush as Fallen approached and rudely snatched his ID card from his lab coat. Emma's expression as did everyone else's shifted to confusion as he used the card to unlock and gain access into the operating room. As the door swished open, Fallen indifferently tossed the ID card back to its owner.

Emma quickly shook her head as Fallen walked inside. "W... Wait a minute Commander! You can't go in there!"

As Fallen approached Sinah, his features weakened a little. "…Sinah."

"Commander, you need to get out of there! We need to help h-!"

Emma instantly stopped short as Fallen aggressively tore off the top of his battle suit. Just like Murdoch and Bridger, Fallen had shinning lines on his muscular back and chest. His were glowing black veins which were quite striking against his ghostly pale complexion. Different from Murdoch and Bridger however, Fallen's veins didn't appear random, all seemed to lead to a black center point on his chest.

Fallen swiftly yet gently removed the I.V. attachment from Sinah's arm and the oxygen tubes from her nose.

Emma released a defeated sigh. "She needs those, Commander. Will you please just get out of there so we can help her? You're only exacerbating the situation."

Fallen removed the metal auto sampler as a full frown took his lips. His expression didn't change as he effortlessly crushed it in his palm. Both Emma and Nash jumped as he whipped it at the glass window. The force of his throw caused the glass to crack.

Nash's expression shifted to slightly awkward. "That's supposed to be fire proof, bullet proof, chemical proof and impact and shock resistant but I guess when it was made, it wasn't Commander proofed."

Emma watched Fallen gently move Sinah a little closer to the edge of the operating table. Once he lay down comfortably beside her, Fallen hooked his arm over Sinah's shoulders and pulled her to rest against his chest. Emma's expression shifted to confusion watching him press both their hands against his collarbone. "He... He's almost gentle with her."

Nash looked up at Emma. "What?"

Emma quickly shook her head. "Nothing."

Fallen closed his eyes listening to Sinah's wild frantic heartbeat. He gripped her hand whispering. "It's alright Sinah, I'm here. You're safe with me. I won't let anything happen to you."

Everyone's eyes darted toward the operating room window hearing Sinah's heart rate suddenly calm. Despite being somewhat weak, it still held a steady pace.

Four

God's Helix

Both Emma and Nash's eyes darted to the green screen hearing it make a beep sound. Nash glanced up at Emma. "The sample results are in."

Every single Tech in the room gasped seeing Sinah's Helix results. Emma's eyes widened in disbelief before a full smile took her lips. Sinah's Helix was a thick double Helix with many long strands attached and dangling off of it.

Emma couldn't contain her excitement throwing her arms around Nash's neck. As she tried to jump up and with him, her voice overflowed with joy. "We did it! We did it! We made God!"

Nash, who was being strangled, hacked out a comment. "Is... Isn't she A.. Amos from Combat's Kid? I… I heard she was a natural b-"

As if slapped back into reality, Emma let Nash's neck go and calmed down. "That's right. Even I heard the rumor that Kid Harmond was a natural birth and I'm almost never away from one ADGL Lab or another. Where's her original Helix file?"

Nash gave a shrug with hints of frustration. "I have no idea. I've searched everywhere for the damn thing and nothing."

Emma pressed the button on the terminal shutting off the communications open line into the operating room. "I'm guessing it might be in the Commander's personal files" Emma frowned toward Fallen as she continued. "And I highly doubt he'll willingly share it with us. If we really want it, we'll have to put in a request with the Director for access."

One of the ADGL Techs looked toward Fallen holding Sinah with a slightly uncomfortable look on her face. "Shouldn't we get the Devil away from God? I mean they are enemies right? Isn't she in danger?"

Emma clapped her hands together turning to the ADGL Techs. "All of you can leave now. Thank you ADGL emergency team but the regular ADGL Lab Techs assigned to the building will handle things from here." Emma tossed the Med Tech a slight glare and a frown. "And those not even supposed to be in building Seven should leave ASAP."

Every single Tech frowned as they began to leave operating room 3. Nash snickered a little hearing every nasty comment muttered under their breaths as they left. "You know this is why you don't have any friends, or you're really bad at keeping them."

Emma indifferently waved her hand turning her attention back to the green screen displaying Sinah's Helix. "I have a job to do, we all do. I can worry about how much people hate me later."

Nash couldn't help but to snicker again. "You know, if you just..."

"Look at it Nash." Emma's tone of voice was full of awe. "Tell me, have you ever seen something so beautiful?"

Nash glanced toward the screen himself. "I can't believe the Director was right. I can't believe beyond this simple window of glass is God herself."

Emma pointed toward the long dangling strands hanging from Sinah's double Helix. "And she's not done developing. Her Helix shows that she's going to have a massive physical change." Emma smiled softly as she continued. "We're going to see God in her holy form." Emma's soft smile shifted into a self-righteous smirk. "I knew God would be a woman."

Nash's eyes darted up to Emma. "Who thought God would be a man?"

"The Director did."

Nash shook his head in disbelief. "But that doesn't make sense. God is a creator and then there's that whole opposite of the masculine Lucifer thing and-"

Emma cut Nash off frowning toward Fallen again. "How will we get to perform any tests on her? I highly doubt he'll let us do our work without a huge fight."

Nash awkwardly swallowed looking toward Fallen himself. "Uh... Do you want my help getting him away from her? I can call in some Helix soldiers."

Emma walked toward the electronically locked operating room door and pressed her ID card against the reader. "No, I have a better idea."

Nash whispered watching her walk inside. "Be careful."

Five

Lucifer's Helix

A full frown took Fallen's lips as Emma approached them. "I'm not leaving her side and nothing, not even the Director can pry me away from my counterpart."

Emma glanced toward Sinah with a look of slight concern. "That makes things very difficult for us."

Fallen hissed protectively gripping Sinah a little tighter. "Of course it does, with me being here you bastards can't perform your sadistic experiments on her."

"Those experiments are important to our Lab. They help us understand the true strength and capabilities of the double Helix. We'll be able to discover all the potential and secrets it holds. Surely, Perfect Experiment A, surely you understand."

Fallen's hiss turned into a growl. "I won't allow that to happen to her! Get out of here before-!"

Emma cut him off with a shake of her head. "Sorry Commander but it's not that easy. As you can plainly see Kid needs-"

"Sinah!! Her name is Sinah! Now get out!"

Despite her body's natural warning of self-preservation of the immediate danger and the sweat beads running down her spine, Emma kept her composure calm and collected. "Okay then, Sinah. It would be best if Sinah stays in one spot until she recovers. As you can hear, her heart is still very shaky."

"She will recover."

Emma gave a quick and indifferent shrug. "Or she could simply die in your arms."

Fallen's eyebrows lowered as his tone of voice became firm yet somewhat threatening. "She will recover."

Emma went a little flush but continued to maintain her calm disposition. "Her body will be scanned and sterilized. You do realize because you're in here with her that you'll-"

Fallen turned his attention toward the ceiling. "Fine"

"We'll also need blood samples from her. She'll have to have an auto-sampler put on." Before Fallen could say anything, Emma continued. "I want one on you as well."

Fallen clenched his jaw for a few moments before he muttered. "… Fine."

Emma smiled approaching the table of operating tools. "Good. I'm so glad we didn't have to argue about-"

Fallen, who was quickly losing what little patience he naturally had, growled. "Hurry up!"

Emma picked up two auto samplers then re-approached Fallen and Sinah. "Are you ready?"

Fallen merely held his aggravated disposition as she attached it to his arm. As she tried to attach the second one on Sinah, Fallen snatched it from her hand. "Get out!"

Emma gave a slight nod before she quickly left the operating room. The second the electronic lock closed, Nash spoke. "I can't believe he actually agreed to be auto-sampled."

Emma let out a loud sigh of relief then a weak chuckle. "I'm just glad to be out of there." As she walked to Nash's side, she continued. "The second he puts it on Kid or Sinah or whatever he wants to call God, I want him scanned and sampled."

Nash looked toward the annoyed Fallen through the glass window. "Do you think his double Helix has changed even further?"

Emma grinned. "I bet my skills as a Lead ADGL Tech on it."

After a few moments of simply watching Fallen and Sinah, Nash spoke. "You know, looking at them is a bit sweet yet gross at the same time. Our innocent pure God is being protected in the arms of our cruel heartless Lucifer."

Emma glanced toward the group of ADGL Lab Techs as they entered operating room 3. "It's best not to think about it."

Fallen released an annoyed sigh griping the auto-sampler in his hand. "I hate these things." Once he placed it against Sinah's arm and it attached, he continued. "I hate that you have to have one on even more. I promise you Sinah, I promise this is only temporary."

Fallen pointed his index finger toward the operating room speaker. A thin metal blade shot out of his fingertip severing the line connecting the communications between the two rooms. As Fallen took Sinah's hand again, the auto-sampler on his arm was activated and the scanner began. Feeling the needle plunge into his vein, Fallen whispered. "This is only temporary."

One of the ADGL Tech's glanced toward the green screen as Fallen's body scan began to appear. "Perfect Experiment A's body scan is coming up. No broken bones. No abnormalities. No organ damage. Everything checks out fine and healthy."

Emma couldn't help but to scoff. "Of course everything checks out fine. I don't think anything can break him. At least nothing we've tried anyway. Nash?"

Nash glanced up at Emma. "Yeah?"

Emma didn't glance down at the terminal as she tapped her finger against it near a red flashing light. "Did he cut the communications?"

Nash's eyes darted down to the terminal. After a few minutes of working on it, he nodded. "I guess he doesn't want us listening in on them anymore."

An ADGL Tech glanced toward the cracked glass. "Should I repair it after I fix that?"

Emma shook her head. "Let's leave the communications down for now. I think we've disturbed the Commander enough for one day. When dealing with him, it's best to pick and choose our battles. Just patch up the glass from this side. It's better than nothing."

Both Emma and Nash's attention was suddenly stolen by Fallen's

Helix that appeared on one of the green screens. Just like Sinah's, his had thickened and many long strands were attached and dangling from it.

A smug smirk took Emma's lips. "I knew his would eventually change. All this time we were waiting for the metamorphic evolution of the L Helix. The changes from his human looking form to his Godly or rather Un-Godly form. Try all we liked to trigger it, absolutely nothing worked. Who knew, all it would take was for him to be in the presence of God."

Nash gave a slight nod. "I always wondered if the Commander's silver eyes would be the only thing that was different about him." With a shrug, he continued. "Physically I mean. I wonder if God's eyes will change. Will they go blue or… or... What color are her eyes to begin with?"

Emma turned from the window and leaned against the terminal. Her expression just screamed she had something on her mind. "What I want to know, how did two humans even manage to create God? I want Kid's or whatever's parents called in after the breakfast hour. I'll go write up the memo. Keep a close eye on her health status, Nash. I shouldn't take long but contact me if anything changes."

Fallen eyes darted down to Sinah feeling a massive drop in her body temperature. Gripping her as tightly as he could without causing her any discomfort, he whispered. "Sinah, don't allow death to take y-"

Fallen was cut off as a golden feather slowly lifted from her body. Before he could get a good look at it, it shot upward then vanished. Fallen's eyes darted through the glass window at the ADGL Lab Techs. Not showing any signs of panic or worry, it was obvious none of them had noticed what happened. Fallen's eyes darted back down to Sinah as her body temp rapidly returned to normal. As it did, many glowing golden veins began to form upon her. Different from Fallen, Murdoch and Bridger's, hers looked like delicate swirls of elegant filigree a masterful artist had painted upon her flesh.

A slight smile took Fallen's lips as he whispered. "Rest well my beautiful counterpart."

Six

Bridger's Wake-Up Call

Many floors above the ADGL Labs were the dreaded experimental Labs. A place that even talking about would make any Helix squirm and shudder in discomfort. Fallen was the one and only Helix that had experienced these single cell rooms and lived to talk about it. Each room had the atmosphere of being a torture chamber. The chains and shackles hanging from the ceiling to restrict the experiments movements, helped encourage that impression. This was the one and only place that could strike an equal amount of fear in both A and D Helix alike.

Bridger, though still unconscious, was chained in the standing position. His arms were extended away from his chest outward. His ankles, waist and throat had shackles as well. Ahead of Bridger was the one and only entrance in and out of the cell. Above it, near the left hand corner of the room was a noticeable camera. Above that, high upon the left wall was a glass window leading into a Lab.

Many ADGL Lab Techs were working at their stations, while one lone Lead ADGL Tech merely stared down at Bridger with a slightly annoyed expression. One of the ADGL Tech's glanced up from her green screen. The ID nametag on her Lab coat read Ayla. "All life signs are reading normal Revin. Should a stimulus be prepared to wake him up?"

Revin was a dark tan skinned, brown hair and dark eyed man. He had a very unwelcoming, no nonsense air about him. His slightly annoyed expression didn't change as he glanced toward the many green screens showing Bridger's body scan. "With the so called 'God' in our building, why are we dealing with..? What's the subject's name?"

Another ADGL Tech was quick to answer him. "That's Helix 7923 Bridger."

Revin's lips touched at a frown. "So Emma gets to deal with 'God' and I get this one? If Emma even tries to take all the glory for 'God's' experimentation, I'll have her head. We both worked on Perfect Experiment A and I'll be damned if I'm stuck only dealing with some cast off."

Ayla awkwardly responded. "Okay. No stimuli."

Suddenly the feather Sinah had dispelled from her body zipped up from the floor below Bridger. As if responding to it, his body gave a slight twitch. As the feather hovered a few seconds in front of his face, calm and comforting warmth began to wash over him. "Sin... ah." He quietly murmured.

As if responding to his voice, the feather suddenly produced a blinding light that enveloped his body. Ayla's eyes darted to the green screens and monitors as they frantically began to beep. "What the hell? Sudden massive energy output! Status is reading off the charts!"

Revin's eyes darted down to Bridger. His expression shifted to slightly confused and shocked seeing the blinding light rapidly diminish then vanish completely. As if slapped awake, Bridger gasped and his eyes snapped open. His gasp was followed by aggressive uncontrollable hacking.

Revin rudely snapped his fingers at an ADGL Tech. "Len, I want the surveillance of the last five minutes!"

The ADGL Tech named Len, quickly began to tap the green screens. "Yes Sir."

Revin began to impatiently tap his foot until four green screens appeared next to him. Once they formed together making a large screen, he watched the replay with an intense look on his face and a frown on his lips. Once Sinah's feather hovered in front of Bridger's face, he yelled out "Pause!"

The screen instantly locked on the image. Revin only stared at it for a few moments before he said. "Enlarge."

Both Len and Ayla stared at the feather in confusion. Ayla couldn't help but to question. “What is that? It doesn’t look like something I’ve ever seen before.”

Revin put his hands in his Lab coat pockets. “It’s probably a gift from his ‘God.’ Re-scan his body. I want to know if there are any abnormalities or signs of it.” Revin glanced toward Bridger. “I think it’s time for me to introduce myself to our next experiment. Ayla bring two low level pain stimuli and an auto-sampler.”

Ayla instantly went flush placing her hand on her chest. “Huh? What? Me?”

Revin frowned turning his attention to her. “All ADGL Lab Techs are trained in all Lab skills. Get what I asked for!”

Ayla, who looked like a scolded child, barely nodded. “..Yes Sir.”

As Revin stormed passed her, Ayla looked toward Bridger. Her expression instantly shifted to sympathetic.

Seven

Experiment Number 7923 B

Once Bridger got his breathing under control, he glanced around his cell in confusion. Due to the shackles and chains, his movements were very limited. "W... Where the heck am I?"

Not understanding the situation, he began to struggle in his restrictions as much as he could. Before his actions became too aggressive, a few pale bluey white with gold tipped feathers floated by his head and vanished before they touched the ground. Catching sight of them out of the corner of his eye, Bridger gasped in surprise and tried to jerk his head back. "What the-?!"

Hearing the beep from the electronically locked cell door, Bridger's wide and confused eyes darted toward it as it swished opened. Revin walked toward him with an indifferent expression on his face. It was more than obvious that he lacked any form of compassion for potential experiments.

Ayla followed behind him with a metal pushcart. In a tray on the top were two large needles filled with a light pink fluid, an auto-sampler and some sterilizing medical wipes. Bridger's state of shock and confusion shifted back to his normal pleasant self, seeing her. "Well, hello there. I don't think we've met. My name's Bridger."

Ayla's eyes darted to him. She couldn't help but to smile seeing his smile directed toward her. "Actually, we met in the Archives Lab."

Bridger childishly giggled. "Were you reading those books too? You know the ones. Where the man is all buff and the woman…"

Ayla awkwardly snickered as her cheeks touched at a red. "The romance novels, yeah, a lot of us-"

Revin abruptly interjected before their conversation could continue. "Auto-sampler Ayla." Ayla's eyes darted to Revin as he repeated himself. "Auto-sampler."

Ayla instantly went flush and quickly nodded. "Y… Yes Sir."

Revin turned his attention to Bridger. His tone and demeanor lacked any emotion. It sounded like these were words he had said to countless others. "I'm Revin Mintas and I'm the Lead ADGL Tech for your experimentation process. This won't be a comfortable or pleasant process. As you may or may not be aware, most Helixes don't last very long during these procedures."

The smile from Bridger's lips had long vanished. "…Experimentation process?"

Revin watched as Ayla attached the auto-sampler to Bridger's arm. "You are a double Helix and as one we-"

"What are you talking about? When we checked my Helix, it was-" Bridger stopped short as a few more feathers floated in front of his face. His expression quickly shifted back to confusion.

Noticing his expression, Revin stepped forward, reached beyond him and grabbed the top of Bridger's wing. Bridger twitched and tried to turn his head to see what Revin was doing. Thanks to the shackles, he couldn't turn very far. "What are you doing? I know you're grabbing me but it doesn't feel normal or-"

Revin suddenly ripped out a large chunk of feathers. Bridger let out a loud 'Ow!' then frowned. "Ouch! What the heck did you do pull my hair or something? That's a sick thing to do to someone who can't move."

Revin moved the fistful of feathers in front of Bridger's face. Bridger's expression instantly shifted to absolute shock. "Feathers?! Those came from me?!

Revin turned toward the metal pushcart as he spoke. "Yes, you have wings." As he placed the feathers onto the tray, they vanished. "Make a note: Collecting samples from Experiment number 7923 B may be difficult. Perhaps we'll need to try to use an unbreakable vile. Have a U.V. ready for our next session."

Bridger tried to move but yet again to no avail. "So why am I chained up?" Before anyone could answer, Bridger suddenly went flush. "Oh no, this is building Seven isn't it?"

"Yes, Experiment number 7923 B, welcome to your new home."

Nervous sweat beads rapidly began to form on Bridger's forehead. "Oh my goodness, I'm here to be tortured aren't I? Just like what happened to the Commander."

Revin picked up one of the needles from the tray then turned back to Bridger. "Perfect Experiment A went through extensive levels of the experimentation process. The likelihood that your Helix double or not, will be able to sustain such-"

"And I'm supposed to just sit here and take it!"

Revin flicked the syringe a couple of times to release any trapped air bubbles. "Thanks to the restraints, you'll just stand there and take it."

Bridger hissed and began to aggressively struggle. "To hell with that!"

Revin glanced at the needle then Bridger. "Today we will be introducing you to our first level of pain stimuli. This is to-"

"I said to hell with that!!" Bridger snarled trying his best to get free.

Ayla lifted her hands defensively and quickly shook her head. "Bridger! Bridger, stop! You have to calm down! It's impossible to break them! Calm down!"

Revin watched Bridger's pointless resistance for a few moments before he spoke. "I'll tell you what I told Perfect Experiment A. The longer you fight this, the longer the process will take."

Bridger suddenly stopped his struggling and locked his eyes with Revin's. His tone of voice was hinted with hostility. "You want co-operation? Get me Murdoch!"

Revin stared back at him in silence. As Bridger's eyes sharpened a little, Revin noticed a thin white ring around his pupil that began to glow slightly. The longer he stared at it, the brighter it began to shine. "If I agree to your demand, will you stop with this pointless resistance?"

Bridger wasn't hesitant to nod. "Get me Murdoch."

Revin lifted the syringe in his hand. As Ayla passed by him with the metal pushcart, she took it. Revin watched Bridger blink a couple of times before the bright glow in his eyes began to fade then vanish. "I'll think about it Experiment number 7923 B."

Revin didn't glance at the frowning Bridger before he left his cell. Once the electronic lock was activated, Revin called out. "Computer, access Cell Lab 6."

Once the computer made a sound of acknowledgement, Revin continued. "Len, what were the scan results, any abnormalities?"

"No Sir, everything is normal."

Revin glanced back at the cell door. "So 'God' only gave him the strength to awaken. Everything else is natural for him. I think I may just have to do a more extensive experimentation on our new experiment then I intended to do. I think I'll take my time with Experiment number 7923 B."

Ayla's expression weakened before she whispered. "Poor Bridger."

Eight

The Intelligent Team of Two

Being more than a few hours after the dinner hour, the Residential area was illuminated by the street lighting system. Alex didn't glance at the star filled artificial night sky as he passed through one of the 'outdoor' common social areas in the facility. There weren't too many people or soldiers wandering around at this time of night. Most were simply on their way home to sleep or unwind from their day.

After walking up the pathway and approaching the front door to one of the many houses, Alex gripped Dante's computer and knocked. Waiting only a few moments, Dante's mother answered. She was an older woman with short brown hair and brown eyes. "Yes?"

Alex awkwardly swallowed. "Um… Yes, good-evening Ma'am. I'm looking for Dante."

Dante's mom smiled opening the door wider. "Oh, you're a friend of Dante's? Come in! Come in! Do you work with Dante and his team?"

Alex stepped only slightly into the house, just enough for the door to be able to close. "Um… I…"

Exactly like the Harmond home and every other home in the Residential area, the kitchen and living room were an open concept design.

Different however, from Sinah's living room which was clean and tidy, Dante's coffee table was full of cords, wires and mother boards. All were connected one way or another to the large screen on the wall.

Alex gripped Dante's laptop. "Is he here Ma'am?"

Dante's mom nodded as she sat down in one of the puffy chairs in the living room area. She spoke picking up her knitting needles and yarn which sat beside her in a wicker basket. "He's just getting more of his computer junk from his room. Do you know Bridger and Murdoch?"

"Everyone knows them Ma'am. Well, about them anyway but I have met Bridger personally."

Dante's mom cooed. "Oh that Bridger, he's such a sweet talker. It's a wonder that he hasn't entered into the marriage contract with anyone." Her charmed expression faded as she continued. "But that Murdoch, he doesn't say much of anything."

Alex barely nodded but before he had a chance to say anything, Dante entered the room. He had a laptop and many different types of cords in his arms. Noticing Alex, he couldn't help but to smile. "Oh good you're here. I'm glad you made it out of the Commander's office alright."

"With all the commotion with… Well, I guess God I was able to get out of there without any problems." Alex lifted the laptop. "I wanted to return this right away but then I got called in to help fix the trouble we caused in the Launch Pad area."

Dante took his laptop then flopped down on the couch. "Did you have a chance to get some dinner? My Mom can make you something if you'd like."

Alex smiled politely and shook his head. "I'm okay, thanks though."

Dante patted the spot beside himself. "Then let's get down to work. We need to break into building Seven."

Alex's expression instantly shifted to shock. "Building Seven? But that's impossible!"

Dante's lips touched at a frown. "Actually, I-"

Dante's mom cut Dante off. "Where are your manners Dante? You should introduce us."

Dante blindly waved his hand at Alex then his mom. "Alex, Mom, Mom, Alex. Okay, now let's get down to work."

As Alex walked in front of the couch and sat down, Dante's mom spoke. "What are you two working on?"

Dante began to inter-twine the laptop Alex had returned into his computer web. "Sorry Mom but this is top secret stuff."

Dante's mom glanced up from her knitting. "So, does that mean Alex works with you and your team as well?"

"That's right. He's a member of the Commander's team."

Alex's eyes darted to Dante. "But I-"

Dante opened a laptop and placed it in front of Alex. "Welcome to our team, now let's get to work."

Dante glanced up at the large screen ahead of them. A live feed of the enclosed security booth in building Seven appeared. The six armed Helix soldiers looked very focused and diligent standing at their posts. Alex made a sound of being impressed looking at the screen himself. "Wow! You actually made it in? That's amazing!"

Dante's lips touched at a momentary proud smile. "It wasn't as hard as I thought it would be. I guess when my A Helix level increased, so did my intelligence. The only problem is I haven't been able to get any further."

Alex looked toward the single person scanner. "Is it true that even getting into the building by person is a pain?"

"I checked the protocol on the passage into building Seven. First, you need to have a special request or be a Lead ADGL or Lab Tech specifically assigned to that building. Then you need to be body scanned, manually pat down and then there's paper work. This is all by gun point mind you. I can only imagine how nerve racking that would be."

"I couldn't do it. Even with all the right paper work and everything, I'd be too nervous. They'll probably think I'm trying to break in."

Dante sighed slumping a little in his seat. "I may have control over the entrance camera but the damn thing is stationary. All we can see are those two A Helixes and four D Helixes. Even life signs disappear completely once they're beyond that booth."

"That makes sense. Building Seven has the highest level of security in the whole facility."

Dante's expression weakened as he closed his eyes. "I can feel it" Dante placed his hand on his chest. "Something's wrong. I can't just sit here and do nothing. Sinah and Bridger are in trouble, I just know they are. I have to help them, I need to help them."

Alex looked at Dante's pained expression for a few seconds before he frantically began to work on the laptop. "Well, we can't use the maintenance route again. ADGL Lab Techs are trained in all fields."

Dante's eyes snapped open and to Alex. "You're actually going to help me? You do know the consequences if we're caught right?"

Alex went flush lifting his fingers from the keys. After a split second of hesitation, he confidently nodded. "That's okay. If God's in danger, we have to help her anyway we can or at least try."

Dante couldn't help but to smile. "Thanks Alex."

"I'll do my best."

After a few moments of them working in silence, Dante spoke. "You might want to call your parents. Even getting a little bit further could take all night."

Alex awkwardly chuckled. "I… I live in the building 2 dorms."

Dante's expression went from shock to awkward in a matter of seconds. "That's the one where those without a soul or ones with a really low level soul live isn't it?"

Alex barely nodded. "My parents were killed in one of the first Synthetic tests. I was just sort of shoved there afterwards."

Dante lowered his tone of voice. It was as if he didn't want anyone to hear him. "What's it like living amongst them?"

Before Alex could answer, Dante went flush quickly shaking his head. "Sorry. Never mind. I shouldn't be asking that. Sorry."

Alex shrugged with a smile. "It's okay. I don't mind. Since they pretty much have nothing inside, they leave me alone. It's like living with apparitions. They're there but not really."

Dante's expression shifted to sympathetic. Alex, who noticed, chuckled. "It's okay, really. I'm used to it."

Dante shook his head. "That's not something anyone should get used to, especially, someone on the Commander's team." Dante's voice suddenly shifted to a resolved tone. "Okay, it's decided! Alex, you're going to live with us from now on. Mom, Alex is going to be staying with us."

Dante's mom smiled putting her knitting aside and standing up. "Okay, I'll go make you boys some cookies."

Alex's eyes darted up to her as she walked toward the kitchen. "Uh... Thanks Ma'am."

Dante's mom made a happy sound of acknowledgement. Alex looked toward Dante with a smile. "Thank you Dante."

Dante smiled himself. "Now let's break into building Seven."

Alex gave a confident nod before he went to work.

Nine

The Man in Demand

Murdoch walked through the darkened shooting range toward his and Bridger's sleeping quarters. Only the very dim emergency lighting systems kept the room slightly visible. Once he opened the door, the lights to his room automatically flicked on. Walking inside, Murdoch's eyes scanned over the wall of pictures varying in tastes. Turning toward the bunkbed, his eyes caught a glimpse of a picture of two small boys.

Murdoch sighed a little turning his attention completely toward it. The picture was of him and Bridger. Murdoch had his normal expression on his face and was dressed in military attire holding a handgun. Bridger on the other hand, had a huge smile sprawled across his face. A few of his teeth were missing and a large chunk of his hair looked like it had been burnt off. Even his regular clothing had many char marks and burn holes all over them.

Murdoch chuckled shaking his head. "Idiot A Helix, you'd think that would have discouraged your love of bombs."

Murdoch's amusement faded as he continued to look at the barbequed Bridger. His expression weakened a little as he reached his hand out toward the picture. Right before his fingertips could touch the image of Bridger he drew his hand back and clinched his fist. Releasing a loud annoyed sigh, he turned away from the wall and flopped down on the bottom bunk.

As he got comfortable crossing his arms behind his head, the computer beeped. Murdoch yawned as a woman's voice spoke. "Helix 3421 Murdoch, please respond."

Murdoch closed his eyes. "…Yeah?"

The woman made a sound of relief. "Oh good you're awake. This is ADGL Tech Ayla from building Seven. We need you to report to Bridger's oops! Sorry! I mean Experiment number 7923 B's cell ASAP."

Murdoch frowned as much as he could as he opened his eyes. "Experiment number 7923 B?"

"This is a special request from Lead ADGL Tech Reivn Mintas."

Murdoch snarled leaping to his feet. "You mean one of the sick bastards that tortured the Commander?!"

Ayla awkwardly glanced toward the annoyed yet busy Revin as she whispered. "Uh... I can't really comment on that particular Tech working only a few feet away from me."

Murdoch clinched his fists. "I'm on my way."

Murdoch held his full frown passing through the shooting range. As he approached the flap behind the counter, his eyes darted to a lone ADGL Tech standing by the entrance doorway. "The shooting range is always closed at this time of night but if you really need to shoot something then-"

The ADGL Tech quickly shook her head lifting some papers in her hand. "No actually, I'm here with request forms from-"

Murdoch hissed rudely snatching the papers from her. "That prick Revin Mintas, I know."

"Um... No. They're from Lead ADGL Tech Emma Witfeild."

Murdoch's eyes darted down to the papers in slight confusion. After a few seconds of reading, he spoke. "…Sinah's parents? Why would she want me to bring..?"

The second Murdoch paused in his sentence, the ADGL Tech excitedly chimed in. "She's God!! Can you believe it?! God is in our facility!" She gave an upward nod toward the papers. "Her parents are to be brought into building Seven, after the breakfast hour."

Murdoch carelessly dropped the request forms on the counter with a frown. "I can read."

The ADGL Tech instantly went flush and quickly nodded. "Oh! Um.. Okay then. Well, good-night."

Murdoch waited until she left before he left himself. After taking the elevator to the main floor in the 4th building, he walked through a few corridors into a large lobby. Different from all the other buildings which could be easily accessed by many other passages, building Seven had only one singular route. Murdoch frowned at the large sign which read, 'Restricted Area Authorized Personnel Only.' He frowned even more as he began to make his way down the long hallway toward the security booth.

The second the Helix soldiers guarding building Seven noticed him, they gripped their weapons. One of the two A Helixes sitting behind the enclosed security booth spoke. "We're approaching the all building shut down mode for the night. Whatever you need can wait until morn-"

Murdoch's sharpened eyes shifted to each Helix soldier. "I'm not here by choice. I was given the order to report ASAP."

The A Helix soldier tapped the air accessing the green screens. "Give me a moment to confirm the request forms."

Alex glanced up at the large screen displaying building Seven's security booth. "Hey look, it's Murdoch."

Dante, who was eating a freshly baked cookie, looked up at the screen. The minute he caught sight of Murdoch, he snapped his fingers. Cookie crumbs fell from his mouth as he spoke. "I got it!"

Alex looked toward Dante in confusion. "Got what?"

Dante rapidly began to type on his laptop. "Our way into building Seven."

The A Helix soldier gave the slightest nod. "Helix 3421 Murdoch, you have been cleared for entrance. We also have a request form here for tomorrow. You are to bring Amos and Violent Harmond here after the-"

Murdoch snipped stepping into the scanner. "I know my orders."

Once the cleared ding sound approved Murdoch, he stepped toward the D Helixes for the manual pat down. The A Helix soldier glanced toward another green screen that suddenly appeared by the others. "You also have an urgent message from Helix 2341 Dante."

Murdoch's annoyed expression shifted to confusion. "What does it say?"

"Residential area ASAP."

Murdoch glanced around the security area. Once he caught sight of the stationary camera, he gave the slightest nod. "Looks like I'm not getting any sleep tonight."

The D Helix that had patted Murdoch down handed him a clipboard full of papers. "Fill these out and we'll have an ADGL Lab Tech escort you to the upper floors."

Murdoch gave another nod turning his attention to the paperwork.

Ten

Not the Sugar Coating Type

Murdoch didn't make any attempt to hide his full frown as he followed the ADGL Tech toward Bridger's cell. Both Revin and Ayla were standing just outside the electronically locked cell door. The second Revin caught sight of him, he frowned in return. "ASAP means 'as soon as possible,' not whenever you feel like it."

Murdoch's full frown didn't fade in the slightest. "And what the hell did you want?"

Revin waved his hand dismissively at the ADGL Tech that had escorted Murdoch. Once gone, he put his hands in his lab coat pockets and spoke. "Experiment number 7923 B wants to talk to you before his experimentation process begins."

Murdoch scoffed as his eyebrows lowered. "You mean his torture, don't you?"

Revin instantly began to fume. "Experimentation is needed for-!"

Murdoch turned his head as if disgusted. "Spare me. I understand my orders. Now get the hell out of my way so I can carry them out."

A full frown locked onto Revin's face. "If you are thinking about breaking him out of here, I'd think-"

"And how am I supposed to do that? This building has heavily armed Helix soldiers hidden all over the place. Not to mention the surveillance here, there and everywhere. This building also has a protective automatic deactivation on all Combat gear except for the soldiers assigned here. Both of us will be long dead before we make it anywhere near the lower floors."

"Inform Experiment number 7923 B that his experimentation begins in the morning."

Murdoch was quick to hiss. "You mean his torture!"

Revin didn't react or respond as he left them.

Ayla smiled zipping her ID card through the electronic lock. "This will take a few moments."

Murdoch only stared intently at the closed door.

The electronic lock beeped and the red light flickered to orange. Ayla spoke as she began to type in a numerical code. "Have you seen God yet? I know she was just brought in, well, that's what I heard anyway. Have you seen her?"

Murdoch released a slightly irritated sigh but still didn't respond.

Ayla zipped her card through the lock again. "I wonder what she's like. I bet she's really nice. I always pictured God to be nice. I mean, she'd have to be, she's God."

Murdoch shifted his eyes toward her as a slight frown touched at his lips. "I haven't got all night."

Ayla went a little flush as she quickly put in the last numerical code. "Sorry."

The lock beeped and the orange light flicked to green. The second it did, and the door swished open, Murdoch's eyes darted to Bridger. He was struggling so aggressively in the chains and shackles that sweat had coated his skin and through the remains of his battle suit.

Ayla raced toward him as she defensively raised her hands. "Bridger! Bridger! You need to calm down!"

Bridger only snarled trying his best to get free. "Where in the heck is Murdoch?!"

Murdoch couldn't help but to smirk. "I guess it doesn't matter what level your Helix is, you never grow out of your temper tantrums."

Bridger's eyes darted to Murdoch. He instantly stopped struggling as a full smile took his lips. "Hey, Mean Helix."

Murdoch cautiously entered the cell as his eyes scanned the restraints.

"See." Ayla said as she began to sop up the sweat from his forehead with the sleeve of her blue and white ADGL uniform. "We brought you Murdoch. Now you need to try and calm down. Overexerting yourself will do you more damage than good."

Murdoch, who hadn't shifted his attention from the chains and shackles, frowned. "Yeah, they want to make sure you're perfectly healthy before they mangle you. I guess it's their sick way of showing mercy."

Ayla's eyes darted to Murdoch. "We... We don't want to-"

Murdoch cut her off as his eyes shifted and locked with Bridger's. "Tomorrow these sick bastards are going to start putting you through hell. Revin Mintas was one of the ADGL Lab Techs that…" Murdoch's tone of voice became angrier and angrier as he continued. "..Tortured the Commander! That sadistic prick likes to use electro-shocks to subdue his victims. He, like every other Lead ADGL Tech will blab on and on about learning about your Helix and its potential, but we all know it is just torture!"

Murdoch suddenly turned on the shocked Ayla. "There I told him, now get out!'

Ayla's shock instantly shifted to a panic. "Y… Yes!"

Both Bridger and Murdoch were silent as she left the cell.

Eleven

Optimistic Martyr

The minute Bridger heard the electronic lock activate, he smiled and spoke in a pleasant tone. "Hi Murdoch, how have you been?"

Any remaining traces of Murdoch's anger vanished as he released a slight chuckle. "...Better than you."

Bridger gave the chains a gentle rattle. "Oh this? This is nothing. Don't worry about it."

Murdoch's expression weakened a little as he turned his head and released a hesitant sigh. Before he had a chance to say anything, Bridger whispered. "I'll be okay."

Murdoch forced his features back to normal and gave a confident nod. "I know."

Bridger suddenly released an awkward chuckle. "Stop showing your nice side Mean Helix, it's freaking me out."

Murdoch scoffed stepping into his soldier at ease stance. "I'm just tired that's all."

Bridger smiled slightly. "Hey, can do you me a favor?"

Murdoch chuckled shaking his head. "I can't break you out of here if that's what you're going to ask. We'd both end up dead."

Bridger couldn't help but to snicker. "I wasn't going to ask for that. It would have been nice though."

Murdoch smirked. "Yeah it would have been."

Bridger tried to glance around the cell but the restraints prevented him. "Is there any of those green screen things in here?"

Murdoch shrugged. "I don't know. I'm one of the Commander's soldiers not some Lab Tech."

Len spoke over the communications open line into the cell. "What do you need it for Bridger?"

Bridger tried to lift his head up toward the window but again, couldn't. "A mirror."

Green screens suddenly appeared in front of him, blended together and reflected his image. The second Bridger saw his wings, he gasped. "Hey! I do have wings! Check those out!"

Murdoch couldn't help but to chuckle at Bridger's childlike excitement. Bridger tried to move his back in an attempt to move them. Again, thanks to the chains and shackles all his efforts were futile. His eyes studied them for a few moments before he smiled. "Aren't they pretty?"

Murdoch indifferently shrugged. "What do you want me to say here?"

Bridger looked toward Murdoch. "When did I get these?"

Murdoch glanced toward the green screens as they vanished. "You don't remember what happened, do you?"

Bridger's expression shifted to concentration. "I remember a bright light then this heat. It was so hot, I thought I was going to burn to death then-" Bridger's entire disposition suddenly shifted to panic. "Oh my god! Sinah! Where is she?! Is she alright?!"

Murdoch shook his head. "I don't know. Tomorrow, I have to bring her parents to operating room 3. I'm assuming she's there."

Bridger's panic didn't calm in the slightest. "By herself?!"

"The Commander followed after her so-"

"Something's wrong! I can feel it! Sinah is in danger!"

Murdoch shook his head stepping closer to him. "Watch what you say! We're being recorded and I just know that dirt bag Revin is going to re-watch this to find out what we talked about."

Bridger's features weakened as he began to whisper. "Murdoch, you have to do something."

Murdoch began to whisper himself. "If the Commander's with her then there shouldn't be any problems."

Bridger closed his eyes. "The fact that I changed so much means Sinah truly is God. She forced me into what I'm meant to be." Bridger opened his eyes and locked them with Murdoch's. The thin white ring around Bridger's pupil was brightly shinning. "I need to protect her."

Murdoch stared at the ring a few seconds before he turned his head. "You really have changed."

Bridger released a weakened chuckle. "What gave it away, the wings?"

Murdoch shook his head clenching his fists. "It's not just that. Our Helix's were basically evenly matched but now you're the stronger Helix and that really pisses me off."

"Jealous?"

Murdoch's lips touched at annoyed frown as he turned his attention back to the smirking Bridger. Before Murdoch could offer any sort of come back, Bridger's features returned to upset. "I'm worried about her."

Murdoch glanced up at the restraints again. "Worry about yourself right now. You'll be useless to her if you die during that bastards torture sessions."

Bridger forced his usual happy disposition. "This? Oh, don't worry about this. I'll be fine."

"Tomorrow, I promise I'll check on her."

Bridger's expression snapped back to serious. "Thanks Murdoch."

As Murdoch began to walk toward the electronically locked door, Bridger spoke again. "Oh, can you do me one more favor?"

"I already told you I can't break you out of here."

Bridger gave a momentary snicker before he spoke. "Could you apologize to Dante?"

Murdoch glanced back at him in slight confusion. "What for?"

Bridger's expression shifted to slightly awkward. "When I took all the blame for... Well our rebellion. Bruno stared at me with relief. He was happy I didn't get him in trouble. He's not a part of our team so he doesn't get our unity. Dante, he stared at me like I betrayed him. Like how any of us would have felt if one of us did what I did." After a sigh, he continued. "I just couldn't let him get in trouble. Everything in me felt like I had to protect him."

Murdoch gave a slight nod. "I'll tell him."

"Thanks."

As Murdoch took a few more steps, Bridger spoke again. "Got any suspenders on you?"

"Sorry."

"Damn, I feel so naked without them."

As Murdoch took another step, Bridger spoke again. "Hey? Do you know what happened to that romance book?"

Murdoch chuckled pulling it out of his back pocket to show it to him. "I got it. I didn't think you wanted any of these Techs to steal it on you."

Bridger chuckled himself. "And don't you dare go reading it. I borrowed it and... Wait, she's dead now, isn't she? I guess I inherited it that means I got first dibs."

Murdoch hooked it back into his back pocket and stepped toward the doorway. Once the electronic lock was released and the door swished open, he spoke. "You want it? Survive experimentation." Murdoch glanced back with a serious, no nonsense expression on his face. "Survive Angel Helix."

Bridger confidently smiled. "I will Mean Helix, I will."

Murdoch gave a quick nod before he left.

Twelve

Dante's Infestation

Murdoch's expression shifted to an annoyed confusion as Alex opened the front door to Dante's house. It was obvious he had no idea who Alex was or why he was even there. Alex tried his best to smile in an attempt to lighten the situation. Unfortunately, his smile looked more awkward than anything else. "Uh… Hi, come on in. We've been expecting you."

Murdoch kept his eyes locked on Alex as he followed him inside. The longer Murdoch stared at him, the more uncomfortable he became. Alex nervously motioned his hand toward the kitchen area. "M... Murdoch's here, Dante."

Dante was frantically typing on his laptop. "Give me a minute."

As Murdoch approached him, he spoke. "Sorry for the delay. I was ordered to talk to Bridger." Stepping into his soldier at ease stance, he glanced toward the large screen. It was still displaying the security booth of building Seven. "But I'm guessing you already knew that."

Alex's expression filled with sympathy. "Is he okay? I saw everything that happened in the Launch Pad area and-"

Murdoch cut Alex off with a snip. "What does it matter to you? Who the hell are you anyway?"

Before Alex could answer, Dante did. "He's Alex. He's a part of our team now."

Murdoch's eyes sharpened slightly. "What are you talking about?"

"It's exactly as I said. Alex is a part of our team."

"Did the Commander tell him to join us? Have you talked to him?"

Dante pointed at Alex then his second laptop. As they both went to work, Dante spoke. "No, I put him on our team."

Murdoch spoke in a tone that suggested utter disgust. "You put a human on the Commander's team?"

"I put a very intelligent Lab Tech on our team that helped Bridger and I find Sinah or... uh... God."

Murdoch glared as hard as he could at Alex. Feeling his disapproving eyes upon him, Alex went ghost white. Murdoch didn't shift his attention as he spoke. "So that gives you the power to put random people on our team?"

Dante looked up at Murdoch with a confident nod. "You're damn right it does!"

Murdoch's eyes darted to Dante. Seeing his insistence and determination, he released a defeated sigh and closed his eyes. "Alright fine, our team has been pretty much ripped apart anyway."

Dante lifted his fingers from the laptop keys as his tone of voice shook a little. "H… How is he?"

"That idiot A Helix is how he always is." Murdoch gave a slight shrug looking toward the screen displaying building Seven. "For now anyway. He's in the hands of Revin Mintas."

Dante gasped leaping to his feet. "What?! That's one of the people that tortured the Commander!"

Murdoch released another sigh. "Why couldn't it have been Emma? She at least treats experiments with a little dignity and respect. Revin just sees a piece of meat he can mutilate."

"He… He's going to be an experiment?"

"Experiment number 7923 B."

Dante's expression broke almost to the point of tears before he forced back his emotions to hiss. "Damn him! He shouldn't have taken all the blame! He shouldn't have..!"

"He told me to tell you he's sorry. He said he just had to protect you. And knowing what he's going to go through, I know he feels like he did the right thing. He'd never forgive himself if you experience even a bit of the pain he's going to."

Dante's expression went from angry to sympathetic to ashamed. His tone of voice broke as he turned his head. "S... Stupid Bridger."

Murdoch closed his eyes. "He's strong. We have to believe he'll survive."

Dante only gave the slightest nod in agreement.

As the silence began to fill the house, Alex broke it. "Done!" Both Dante and Murdoch's eyes darted toward him as Alex smiled. "It's ready."

As if slapped back into work mode, Dante sat back down and began to frantically type again. "Okay good. Murdoch, when are you going back to building Seven?"

"Tomorrow after the breakfast hour, Emma wants Amos and his wife brought to operating room 3."

"Is Emma the Lead ADGL Tech for Sinah?" As Murdoch began to nod, Dante continued. "She probably wants to find out how two humans could give birth to God."

Murdoch shrugged. "That's what I figured."

Dante suddenly made a sound of triumph. "Hah! There! Finished!"

Murdoch's expression shifted to confusion. "Finished what?"

Dante moved his laptop a little. Upon the table were two tiny metal spiders. They were about the size of his pinky finger nail. As Dante picked one up and placed it into his palm, he spoke. "Tomorrow, I need you to sneak this into building Seven."

Murdoch quickly shook his head. "I can't. You've seen the scanner it will pick it up right away."

Dante grinned. "Oh I know I'm expecting detection. As you step back from the scanner, I want you to drop this just beyond it. When they re-scan you, they won't find anything. If you act like it was a momentary technical glitch then I highly doubt anyone will be the wiser."

Murdoch gave the spider a look of confusion as Dante handed it to him. "What is this thing anyway?"

Dante smiled proudly. "It's my data and surveillance into building Seven. This little guy can scan and send information back to me. The feed may be a little slow due to building Seven's interference but it will give us eyes into the restricted areas."

"I can check on everyone for you, you know. I'll be damned if anyone is going to keep me from checking in on the Commander."

Dante placed his hand on his chest. "I can feel it. Something feels wrong. At least having eyes in there will give me some peace of mind."

Murdoch barely nodded. "Bridger said something feels wrong too. I think it's because your Lord, or rather your Lady is hurt."

"That's what I'm thinking as well."

"I'll deliver this."

Dante smiled. "Thanks Murdoch."

Murdoch rubbed one of his eyes. "Oh man, I really need some sleep."

Dante blindly waved his hand behind himself toward the hallway leading to the bedrooms. "You can crash in my room. My Mom won't care. She'll probably be happy to make breakfast for another person."

Murdoch shook his head as he walked toward the front door. "I have to open the shooting range first thing. There are a lot of soldiers that like to shoot things before the breakfast hour. I'll see you later."

As Murdoch opened the door, he glanced at Alex. "Welcome to our broken team."

Alex awkwardly nodded. "Th... Thanks."

Once Murdoch closed the door behind himself, Alex pointed at the second spider. "What's the second one for?"

Dante smirked looking up at Alex. "That's for you. You're going to deliver this to the Director's floor. Now let's make you a human friendly ear piece."

Alex instantly went flush as panic filled his voice. "I..! I'm going to what?!

Dante couldn't help but to snicker. "Welcome to our team."

Thirteen

A Guilty Heart

All the buildings in the facility had gone into shut down mode for the night. Only a handful of night shift Techs assigned to each build for emergency purposes only, were still working. Even with all the rules and restrictions placed upon building Seven, it also had a small group of ADGL Lab Techs. The lone ADGL Tech, who was assigned to operating room 3, sat behind the terminal. Instead of doing his job however, he had fallen asleep.

Fallen, who was staring blankly at the ceiling, gently began to caress Sinah's hand with his thumb. "I should have felt it. I should have felt you beside me." Fallen suddenly snatched her hand with a frown. "I am Lucifer! I should have felt my counterpart battling next to me! I should have known who you were! It shouldn't have mattered what your Helix level was, I should have felt you! I should have sensed you!"

Fallen's eyes darted to the ADGL Tech as he stirred a little in his sleep. Once he settled back into a deep slumber, Fallen closed his eyes. "All I felt was drawn to you."

Fallen's grip on her hand loosened as he whispered. "I thought it was simple attraction. No, not simple attraction, it was far from simple. I felt like I needed you with me, always beside me."

Fallen opened his eyes and looked down at her. "I felt like you saw me for what I truly am. You saw the evil that runs through my veins. You calmed the hellfire raging within me. Sinah, my precious counterpart, you are the one and only light within my darkness."

Sinah nor her body gave any sign of a reaction to his words.

Fallen suddenly released a loud snarl. "This shouldn't have happened! You shouldn't even be in this state! Bridger shouldn't have forced me to leave you behind! I should have been stronger than that Synthetic guck he injected into me! I am Lucifer! I am-!"

Fallen's anger was instantly disarmed by a loud rip sound. Letting Sinah's hand go, he glanced at his own. Seeing that his glove was now in shreds, his expression shifted to confusion. The small red rectangular microchip that connected earpiece and mind to weapons and equipment had long been obliterated. Fallen lifted his other hand from Sinah only to see the same destruction on his other glove. Removing one of them, his eyebrows lifted in slight shock.

Upon the top of his ghostly pale skin were single black glowing veins that ran down each and every one of his fingers almost to the cuticle. Instead of his normal finger nails, they now had the appearance of many over lapping shards of jagged black glass.

Fallen very gently ran his 'new' nails against the second glove. Without even the slightest bit of resistance, they tore to shreds like razor blades would against paper. Once his hands were completely freed, Fallen looked into his palm. In the center was a large collection of black veins. The amount that had pooled together made it look like he had a large black void like hole in his hand.

Fallen suddenly snapped his hand into a fist then opened it. A silver blade with drops of red slowly lifted from the 'hole.' Staring at it only for a few seconds, it caught fire. Fallen's eyebrows lowered before he turned the flaming blade toward the blood pressure machine. His finger twitched only in the slightest before it shot and hit his target.

The machine instantly caught a silver flame and burned to ash in a manner of seconds. Fallen's eyes shifted toward the fire detection system, anticipating it to go off. The fire however, had burned so high and so fast that it didn't even register a fire had actually occurred.

Fallen smiled placing his hand back on Sinah's shoulder. Even though, the glass like jagged nails had returned to normal, they were now completely black. As he pulled Sinah closer to himself, he whispered. "I will make this up to you my sweet counterpart. I promise you I will."

Fallen gripped her tightly, closing his eyes. "The more I change, the more sure I am that you will recover. That we will become the superior beings we were meant to be. Rest well my beloved."

Fourteen

Distraught Parents

Since Sinah's disappearance and being placed on the 'Missing Persons' list, neither Amos nor Violet had reported to their assigned Labs. Violet spent her time more often than not just sobbing. While Amos on the other hand, did everything he could to comfort his distraught wife.

Both of their eyes darted to the front door, hearing a knock. Violet lowered her tear soaked tissues from her face. "D... Do you think it's news on Kid?"

Amos quickly got up from the couch and raced toward the front door. "I hope so!"

Amos stepped back a little in confusion finding Murdoch on their door step. "Oh! Uh… Good morning."

Murdoch glanced up at the artificial sky. It was a clear day with only minimal cloud coverage. "I've been given the order from Emma Witfield to escort you and your wife to building Seven."

Amos' confusion increased with noticeable hints of discomfort. "… What for?"

Before Murdoch could answer, Violet hissed through whimpers. "I'm not going anywhere! I'm going to stay right here until Kid comes home!"

Amos looked toward his wife sympathetically. "Did Sinah go on the volunteer mission with your team?"

Before Murdoch could answer again, Violet hissed. "That bastard Commander of yours, he lured our daughter away! He tricked her into-!"

"Have either of you been in any of the common social areas?"

Amos shook his head. "No, once we found out that Sinah wasn't in the facility, we decided to stay and wait here. We hoped she'd eventually come home safe and sound."

Violet whimpered. "She shouldn't have run away from home to begin with. Your Commander poisoned her against us!"

"Then you haven't heard."

Amos opened the front door wider. "Haven't heard what? Please come in."

Murdoch gave the slight shake of his head. "I have to deliver you both to building-"

Violet cut Murdoch off with a slightly hysterical wail. "I'm not going anywhere until Kid comes home!"

Amos quickly approached his wife as she began to cry. Sitting back down on the couch, he wrapped his arms around her. "I'd hate to make things difficult for you but I think it would be best if we stayed here to wait for her."

Murdoch stepped into his soldier awaiting a command stance. "Sorry, but I have my orders."

Amos gently stroked his wife's back as she sobbed against his chest. "I understand that but-"

"If either of you two had gone to one of the common social areas, you probably would have heard the news."

Amos only continued to try and calm and comfort his wife as Murdoch continued. "Sinah is God."

Violet instantly stood up and out of Amos' grip. This action was so fast her knees hit the bottom of the coffee table knocking it over. "What?! What do you mean she's God?!"

Before Murdoch could answer, Violet questioned again. "Do you know where she is?! Is she okay?! Where is she?!"

Murdoch's lips couldn't help but to touch at a frown. "She's in building Seven."

"Why is she in that building? Why hasn't she come home?"

"The Director thought that would be the best place for her to recover."

Violet's demeanor instantly clicked into panic. "Recover?! What do you mean recover?! Did something happen?!"

Since hearing that Sinah was God, Amos' utterly shocked expression hadn't changed once. "Are you sure she's God?"

Murdoch gave the slightest nod. "Yeah, there was an incident in the Launch Pad area that proved it. Bridger…" Murdoch paused for a split second before he shrugged. "Let's just say, he had a reaction."

"A physical change?"

"A massive one."

Violet hissed wiping her drying tears from her cheeks. "Who cares what happened to him?! Take me to my daughter!"

Murdoch couldn't help but to frown. "Then let me obey my orders to take you both to building Seven without any more delays."

Violet raced toward the front door. "Hurry up and grab your jacket Amos! Kid is waiting for us!"

Fifteen

Motherly Panic, Fatherly Pride

Just as both Murdoch and Dante had predicted, the scanner had a reaction to the spider. Without hesitation, Murdoch dropped it into safety then stepped back. As he stepped forward to get re-scanned, he noticed all six of the Helix soldiers had their weapons drawn and aimed at his head. A frown instantly took Murdoch's lips. "If one of you low level Helixes accidently shoot me because of some stupid machine, you better make damn sure it's a kill shot."

One of the D Helix soldiers gripped his weapon as he calmly spoke. "We are about the same level as you and don't worry, we've been trained to ONLY use kill shots. Now step back into the scanner."

Murdoch held his frown as he re-entered. Once it made a sound of approval, all the Helix soldiers lowered their weapons. Murdoch scoffed as one of the D Helix soldiers began to pat him down. "…About the same level as me. Yeah, my foot."

The D Helix began to frown as he handed Murdoch the clipboard. "Fill this out."

As Murdoch dealt with the required paperwork, Amos and Violet went through the security process. Once finished and visitor badges were hooked onto their clothing, one of the A Helix soldiers spoke. "Do you need an ADGL escort?"

Murdoch answered walking away from them. "None of us Helixes forget where the ADGL operating rooms are."

A slight nod of agreement was passed around the Helix soldiers.

The second the door to operating room 3 was opened, both Violet and Amos raced inside. Being caught off guard by such a boisterous entrance, every ADGL Lab Tech's eyes darted toward them.

Noticing the sudden lack of work, Emma forced a loud cough of authority. Once everyone went back to their assigned tasks, Emma displayed her friendliest smile. "Good morning Harmonds. I'm Emma Wit.." Emma paused for a split second recognizing Violet. "Hey, wait a minute, I know you. Violet Harmond from Creation L-"

Violet cut Emma off. "Where is she?! Where's my daughter?!

Emma gave an upward nod toward the glass window leading into the operating room. Both Violet and Amos raced toward it. The minute Amos' eyes caught sight of her, a sense of relief washed over him. "I'm so glad she's alright."

Violet hissed seeing Sinah in Fallen's arms. "What the hell is he doing in there with her?! He's probably the reason she got hurt! How can you let that happen?!"

Emma awkwardly laughed. "Well... The Commander didn't really give us much of a choice in the matter."

Violet turned quick on Emma with a growl. "Choice?! To hell with his choice! Get him out of there! Get him away from her!"

Emma defensively lifted her hands. "You need to calm down. I don't want to have to sedate you." As she lowered her hands, she continued. "Now listen, I understand that you are upset and angry but-"

"But?! But?! But what?!"

Amos hadn't shifted his eyes from Sinah. "Are you positive she's God?"

Nash pointed toward the green screen with Sinah's double Helix displayed on it. "Yeah, check it out."

As Amos looked toward it, Violet pushed by Emma so she could see it as well. The second her eyes caught sight of the green screen, all of her anger was instantly defused. "Th... That's Kid's Helix?"

Nash pointed toward the second green screen displaying Fallen's double Helix. "And that's the Commander's."

Violet's temper flared up as fast as it was extinguished. "That's all the more reason to get him away from her! She's God! Something so pure, so innocent shouldn't be anywhere near a monster like him!"

Amos smiled proudly at Sinah's double Helix before a slight chuckle escaped his throat. "Heh! I always thought it was just a fatherly thing."

Nash glanced up at him as he continued. "I always thought our little girl was special. She never once got into trouble. She never made anyone angry. She was always willing to help out anyone who needed it. And now to find out our daughter, our girl, our Sinah is God. This is amazing. I can't believe it."

Nash couldn't help but to smile at Amos' beaming pride. "I wouldn't have believed it either if I were you. I saw her Combat replays. Who knew God would be so kick butt."

Violet hissed at Nash and Amos. "Who cares about that right now?! Get the devil away from my-!"

Amos cut Violet off turning to Emma. "Is there any chance I can talk to her?"

Emma slowly shook her head. "I'm sorry but she hasn't yet regained consciousness."

"Please, I would just like to see for myself that she's okay. I promise to be careful."

Emma thought about it only for a few seconds before she gave a slight nod. "Alright but be very brief. She's still in critical condition."

Amos gave Emma a soft appreciative smile. "Thank you so much."

As he walked toward the electronically locked door, Violet tried to follow. "I want-!"

Emma wasn't hesitant in snatching her arm. "Not you! I can't have any kind of stress going in there. The last thing we need right now is you screaming at the Commander."

Violet struggled aggressively in Emma's grip. "I won't! I-!"

Emma frowned rattling her a little. "This is the last time I'm going to warn you about sedation."

Amos smiled toward Violet. "Don't worry I'll make sure she's alright."

Violet's eyes filled with tears as she nodded. "...Okay."

Emma nodded herself letting Violet go. "Good. Okay Nash."

Nash glanced toward Murdoch. He had been standing by the electronically locked door the entire time. "Is there something you need?"

Murdoch gave the slightest nod. "I need to talk to the Commander."

Nash glanced toward Emma. Once she gave an approving nod, he pressed a button on the terminal releasing the lock for the operating room.

Sixteen

Protective Lucifer

Violet's eyes were transfixed on Fallen and Sinah. "Could you open line the room please?"

Nash shook his head. "Sorry but the Commander wrecked the communications."

"Why hasn't it been repaired?"

Emma closed her eyes releasing a loud defeated sigh. "When dealing with the Commander it's best to pick and choose your battles. Trust me."

Amos nervously stood just past the operating room doorway. After listening to Sinah's heartbeat for a while, he spoke. "I'd hate to bother you Commander but may I see my daughter?"

Fallen lifted his hand from her shoulder in slight acknowledgement. "Make it quick."

Amos' nervous disposition didn't falter as he walked to Sinah's side of the operating table. His expression was a combination of sympathy and happiness. His eyes couldn't help but to gaze in awe at the intricate designs of her golden glowing veins. "I still can't believe it." He said removing his jacket and placing it over her naked shoulder.

Fallen didn't shift his attention from the ceiling as Amos questioned. "What happened to her?"

Fallen closed his eyes. "It doesn't matter."

As Amos reached his hand out to touch Sinah, Fallen's grip tightened. "You've seen that she's fine. You can leave now."

Amos drew his hand back but didn't move from his spot. "I'm just happy to know she's safe and sound. I... I know Sinah is God but.." Amos paused for a split second looking at Sinah's features. "Will she be alright?"

Fallen's grip relaxed a little "She'll recover. I'll make sure of that."

Amos let out a sound of relief but then released a sigh of disappointment. "And when she does, the ADGL Lab Techs will begin their experimentations."

Fallen's lips were instantly consumed by a full frown. "I'll never allow that to happen! My counterpart is far too precious to have any human filth come anywhere near her."

Amos' eyes darted to Fallen. "But she is God and..."

"And God is a superior being."

Murdoch, who was standing near the bottom of the operating table on Fallen's side, spoke. "I'd be more worried about you and your wife right now, if I were you."

Amos' eye darted to Murdoch. "What are you talking about?"

Murdoch gave the slightest shrug. "Your wife gave birth to God. I don't know what type of tests that are performed on humans but..."

Amos cut Murdoch off as his expression weakened. "Then everyone will know."

Murdoch glanced from Amos to Fallen. "Know what?"

Amos reached out for Sinah again. Despite Fallen's sudden tightening grip on her, Amos wasn't going to be discouraged. He softly brushed his knuckles against the side of her face. "We're not her biological parents."

Fallen calmly turned his head toward Amos and spoke in a firm serious tone. "It's time for you to leave."

Amos' eyes darted to Fallen's. Only seeing his own reflection off of Fallen's sunglasses, he couldn't quite read his expression. "But I-"

Fallen's eyebrows lowered. "Sinah needs to focus on recovering right now, nothing else. I don't want her thinking about something she may not even know about. Especially something that could upset her." Fallen's voice abruptly shifted to hostile. "Now, get out!"

Amos felt an aggressive wave of intimidation rush over his body. It was so forceful, it caused him to shudder and stumble over his words.

"Y… Yes. Th... Thank you for letting..." Amos swallowed heavily before he got his fear under control. "Thank you, Commander, for allowing me to check on her."

Fallen turned his head back toward the ceiling as he gave a slight nod.

Amos gave a slight nod himself before he approached the electronically locked door. Once it opened and Amos left the operating room, Violet raced toward him. "How is she?! Is she okay?!"

Amos took his wife's hands. "I never thought I'd say this but she couldn't be in safer hands." As Violet opened her mouth to say something, Amos leaned close to her ear and whispered. "We're going to have to explain some things we tried our best to hide."

Before Violet could question, Emma clapped her hands. "Alright Harmonds, let's get some samples."

Violet turned to Emma with a slightly confused look. "…Samples?"

Emma smiled motioning her hand toward the exit. "Let's go to operating room 5."

Violet's lips touched at a frown. "I'm not going anywhere. I want to be here when Kid wakes up."

"This won't take long."

Violet continued to protest. "I told you I'm not-"

"I want to know how two humans managed to give birth to God."

Violet's eyes darted back to Amos as he barely nodded.

Seventeen

Loyal D Helix

Murdoch cautiously glanced around the operating room. Fallen, who noticed, spoke. "You're free to talk Murdoch. I've cut the communications."

Murdoch barely nodded as he walked into Fallen's line of sight. "I've spoken to both Bridger and Dante."

Fallen softly began to rub Sinah's shoulder with his thumb. "What is Bridger's status?"

Murdoch's features slightly weakened. "He's being prepared for the experimentation process. Revin is the Lead ADGL Tech."

Fallen's eyebrows lowered slightly. "Revin is going to try and break him."

Murdoch closed his eyes and released a weak sigh. "Double Helix or not, I don't know if Bridger is strong enough to handle that much pain."

To both Fallen and Murdoch's surprise, Sinah's heart rate suddenly became rapid. Murdoch's eyes darted through the glass window seeing a few ADGL Techs running toward the operating room door. Fallen gripped Sinah and whispered. "Calm down Sinah. You need to worry about healing before anything else. Everything will be alright."

Before the ADGL Tech's could release the electronic lock, Sinah's heart rate seemed to calm and return to its weak yet steady pace. Murdoch waited until the ADGL Techs returned to their stations before he spoke.

"He's worried about her. Both him and Dante say they feel like she's in danger."

Fallen shifted his eyes toward Murdoch. Glints of the crimson red around his pitch black pupil flashed against his silver iris. "The other A Helixes must be feeling it as well."

Murdoch stepped into his soldier at ease stance. "I guess they would be. After all, it's not like they can do anything for her right now. All of them must be feeling pretty useless."

Fallen's lips touched at a frown. "Now that we both exist, what are the Director's intentions for us?"

Murdoch's expression shifted to a confused concern. "Commander?"

"Even before I breathed life he has been trying to create my counterpart. Now that she's here, what are his plans for her?"

"I always thought his main goal was to create a better world."

Fallen was quick to scoff. "For who? Our facility and the other Labs we've attacked have all managed to continue life without either of us. The reproductive and death cycle that had once stopped has now been resolved. Even the never ending day and night doesn't seem to bother any of them. The artificial seasons and scheduled 24 hour spans of time creates an acceptable illusion."

Fallen turned his attention toward the ceiling as he continued. "Only those in the World of the Lost Souls are suffering. Yet even then, they've done what all humans do, they adapted. We're not truly needed in this world, so why was it so important that we were created?"

Murdoch's confusion seemed to increase by the second. "Commander, are you questioning the Director? We normally obey his orders without hesitation."

Fallen pulled Sinah closer to himself. "I'm feeling the danger as well. Not just for her but for myself as well. I know I need to do something to protect us. I just don't know what needs to be done."

Fallen's temper was suddenly sparked. "He said she was my natural enemy!"

Murdoch's eyes darted to Sinah in disbelief. "The Director said that? But that can't be! She's a part of our team and…"

"We all thought Sinah was just a high level A Helix. She might have even thought that herself. Now that she is God, her thoughts and feelings might have changed completely."

Fallen closed his eyes as he continued. "She could truly see me as her enemy. And once we make the world into whatever the Director wants, he may order her to end my life. My use will be over and she'll be under his control."

Murdoch quickly shook his head in disbelief. "Commander, you can't believe that!"

Fallen opened his eyes and released a sigh. "Perhaps we're merely needed as weapons, something simply to be used to destroy our current world. Then re-create another for the Director to rule over as a God. A world where he can-"

Murdoch suddenly cut Fallen off kneeling down before him. Fallen's head shot toward him as he lowered his head and spoke. "Commander Fallen Hart, Lucifer, my Lord. I am loyal to you and you alone. I won't allow some human to simply use you for what they want. This world belongs to you and her. Whatever I can do to assist you, command it of me and it will be done."

Fallen's lips touched at a momentary smile. "I knew I was right in choosing you for my team."

The second he finished his sentence, he reached his hand out and placed it upon Murdoch's head. Murdoch gasped feeling a rush of cold almost freezing air rush over his body. As Fallen removed his hand, Murdoch looked up at him.

The slight smile re-took Fallen's lips seeing Murdoch's eyes. The black of his pupils had become so wide, it covered not only the dark color of his iris but all of the sclera surrounding it. After a quick blink, Murdoch's eyes had returned to normal. Only a very thin almost unnoticeable pitch black ring remained around his pupil.

Fallen placed his hand back on Sinah's. "You and Dante are the remaining members of my team that isn't trapped within these walls. Make sure it stays that way."

Murdoch slowly stood up. As his mouth passed Fallen's ear, he whispered. "Dante has managed to get surveillance into this building."

Fallen's slight smile increased. "With the arrival of my counterpart, all of our Helixes are improving. It's obvious his has as well."

Murdoch looked at his hands. "I don't feel any different."

"If I were to force your Helix to become a double Helix like Sinah did to Bridger, you would be in the same situation he is. I need you to keep me updated on Dante's reports. I want to know every inch of this building and where the hidden soldiers are."

Fallen turned his head toward the glass window as he continued. "I want to know the best way for us to escape."

Eighteen

Sympathy for Bridger

Revin glanced toward the upset looking Ayla. "Give me two of our low level pain stimulus."

Ayla awkwardly looked at the six syringes on the tray sitting on top of the pushcart but didn't reach for them. After a few seconds, Revin rudely snapped his fingers at her. "Now ADGL Tech!"

Ayla shook her head closing her eyes. "B... But.. I... I.."

Bridger smiled toward her. "Hey."

Ayla's eyes darted up to him. Holding his smile, he spoke in a soft comforting tone. "It's okay."

Ayla's expression weakened almost instantly. "I... I'm so sorry."

"It's okay."

Ayla picked up the two needles filled with a light pink liquid and offered them to the frowning Revin. Right before he took them, he suddenly shook his head. "Actually no, instead of a low level, let's increase the dosage to a medium level."

Ayla's weakened expression didn't change as she put the two back and picked up a different syringe. This one was filled with a darker pink liquid. As she offered it to Revin, he spoke. "Inject it into his blood stream ADGL Lab Tech."

Ayla's eyes darted to Revin in shock. "What?! Me?!"

"I am the Lead on this experimentation process! You will stop questioning me and do as you are ordered to do!"

Bridger's lips touched at a slight frown. "Wow. The rumors about you were right, you really are a dick."

Revin hissed. "I said do it now, Ayla!"

Ayla's expression broke almost to the point of tears. "...Yes Sir."

As Ayla began to clean a spot on Bridger's arm with a sterilizing pad, she whispered. "I'm sorry about this Bridger, I really am. You're one of the nicest Helixes there is and-"

"Stop talking to Experiment number 7923 B and administer the injection!"

Even though Ayla was jabbing the needle into his flesh, Bridger didn't lose his smile. "Aw that's sweet of you to say."

Once all of the fluid was forced into Bridger's blood stream, Revin dismissively waved his hand. "Return to the cell Lab."

As Ayla wheeled the pushcart toward the exit, Revin spoke. "If this refusal to obey a Lead Tech happens again ADGL Lab Tech, you'll be transferred out of building Seven. Am I making myself clear?"

Ayla gave the slightest nod before she left.

Revin walked toward the corner of the cell under the window leading into the Lab. As he tapped the air to access the green screens, he spoke. "The reaction time of the stimuli effects vary with each individual. Give it a few moments."

Bridger only began to frown.

The second Ayla stepped into the Lab everyone looked toward her with the same sympathetic expression she had plastered on her face.

Len suddenly got up from his seat and turned from his terminal. "I can't watch this! I like Bridger. He doesn't deserve to go through this!"

Ayla closed her eyes. "I know that but we have to do what we have to do."

"But it's Bridger!"

"We all worked really hard to be building Seven ADGL Lab Techs."

Len ran his hands down his face releasing a loud defeated sigh. "I know. I know. We're the second highest ranking ADGL Techs in the whole facility. We're the only Techs with the potential to become Leads. B... But it is Bridger, you know."

Ayla barely nodded. "I know. He treats us all like equals. He talks to us like we're all the same, like he doesn't care if we're human or Helix or even what field we're in. He treats us like we're friends."

Len closed his eyes. "Some friends we are."

Every single ADGL Tech cringed as Bridger suddenly released an agonizing ear piercing screech.

Bridger aggressively struggled in the shackles and chains as an overbearing fire like sensation enveloped his entire body. It felt as if flames were trying to not only burn him but escape his body from within by any means possible. Bridger released another screech as the burn rapidly shifted to a razor scraping sensation against his skin.

Revin looked Bridger with an indifferent expression. His eyes shifted toward the green screens every few moments looking at Bridger's body scan. Every single one of Bridger's pain receptors was flashing an orange color. His heart rate was climbing by the second as was his blood pressure.

Before the pain could become unbearable, Bridger released a loud gasp then lost consciousness. Revin's eyes darted to him than the green screens in confusion. Any sign of Bridger being in distress had vanished completely. "That's it?"

Revin's lips touched at a frown. "I was expecting so much more from a double Helix"

Revin tapped the green screens to access the scanner. As Bridger's body began to get scanned, he muttered. "What a sad pathetic experiment."

Revin's expression suddenly shifted to shock as Bridger's internal body was displayed. All of his veins were shining a blinding gold. Any sign of the pink fluid that had been injected into him was rapidly being destroyed.

Revin's lips touched at a smile. "Your body is fighting it. Good. This hasn't been a total loss."

Revin stepped back from the green screens. As he walked toward the cell door, they vanished. "Once you regain consciousness we'll continue."

Nineteen

The 2nd Spider

Many soldiers, Helix soldiers, Techs and civilians went about their business in the lobby of building 6. Nobody seemed to pay attention to the lone, anxious looking Lab Tech. His brown eyes darted to each person while nervous sweat dampened his dirty blonde hair. It was obvious he wasn't used to his external ear piece, for he kept trying to make sure it was on right.

A young man's voice spilled though the ear piece. "You can do this Alex."

Alex nervously responded back. "..No, no I can't. I can't do this Dante. It... It's the Director."

Dante clicked over to the lobby surveillance cameras in building 6. He could see Alex's panicked disposition. "Okay first things first. You need to calm down. You haven't even done anything yet and you already look suspicious."

Alex forced himself to nod. "Okay."

Dante watched Alex take a few deep breathes before he spoke again. "Just follow our plan and everything will go smoothly."

"Okay."

"I would have done it myself but the Director's receptionist knows everyone on the Commander's team. I can't exactly pretend I made a mistake going there when I'm always the one who hands over the mission reports."

"Okay."

"Luckily for us, she doesn't know about any new members."

"Okay."

Dante couldn't help but to snicker. "You keep saying 'okay.'"

Alex went a little flush. "I... I do?"

Dante glanced toward another surveillance feed. "Head to the elevators now, it looks like a decent amount of people are waiting for them. You'll easily blend in unnoticed."

Alex quickly nodded. He looked more frantic rather than simply agreeing. "Okay."

Alex raced toward the group of people then into the elevator with the others. As each floor was highlighted, he began to feel knots forming in his stomach. Whenever the doors opened and people stepped onto their desired floors, Dante whispered. "You can do this Alex. You're a member of the Commander's team. You can do this."

Alex was the only person left in the elevator as it passed the 10th floor. Once the doors opened for the 11th Dante's tone of voice shifted to forceful. "Go! Get out!"

Alex mustered up all of his nerve and calmly walked toward then beyond the reception desk. Noticing him, the receptionist's eyes darted up to him in confusion. "Um... Excuse me. Can I help you?"

Alex dismissively waved his hand. "No, no I'm good. I just..." Alex suddenly faked a forced confusion as he looked around. "Wait a minute. Where the heck am I?"

The receptionist sighed in disappointment like a displeased parent would for their disobedient child. As she motioned her hand in front of her desk, she spoke. "Where are you supposed to be young man?"

Alex approached the front of her desk. As he pressed himself against it, he dropped the spider. "Umm... The 5th floor."

Dante smiled typing on his laptop as the receptionist began to nicely lecture Alex. The spider raced toward the closed Director's office doors and easily slipped under it. It raced along the edge of the room toward one of the many book shelves. Once it climbed to the top, it settled into a stationary stance amongst the slight layer of dust.

The reception sighed again. "..So next time pay attention to what floor you're trying to get to."

Alex awkwardly nodded. "Yes Ma'am. Sorry Ma'am. I really didn't mean to come up here."

The receptionist motioned her hand toward the elevators. "That's alright. Now go off you go."

Alex quickly nodded. "Yes Ma'am."

As Alex entered the elevator, Dante spoke. "Success! Great job Alex! I knew you could do it!"

Alex pressed the lobby floor button. Once the doors closed, he responded. "Is it in a good spot?"

Dante looked at the surveillance the spider was displaying. Dante could see the Director's entire office. He was merely sitting at his large desk filling out paperwork. The dim blue light from the eclipsed sun and moon from the ceiling to floor windows reflected slightly off of the spider's camera. "A perfect spot if you ask me. The Director rarely uses the automatic cleaning systems and unless someone's really looking for it, nobody will find it."

"Good and the live feed?"

Dante moved the spider back and forth a little. The surveillance moved with it. "It's just as it should be. I knew only building Seven would have a time delay."

As Alex passed through the lobby of building 6, he spoke. "I should be back there real soon."

"I knew you could it. Great job Alex."

Alex's cheeks hinted at an embarrassed flush. "W… Well I am on the Commander's team now."

Damn smiled. "Damn right! I'll see you when you get back."

Alex smiled proudly as he went on his way.

Twenty

Emma's Choice

Violet raced back into operating room 3 and called out. "Is she awake?!"

Nash's eyes darted up to her as she raced to his side. The second she saw Sinah and Fallen still together, she hissed. "He's still in there with her?!"

Nash smiled slightly until he noticed a flashing light on his terminal. "Yeah, I don't think he intends to go anywhere until she recovers."

As Emma and Amos re-entered the lab, Nash spoke. "Emma, the hole the Commander made is causing the sterile field to act up."

Emma shrugged approaching another ADGL Lab Tech. "Access all information from operating room 3. And Nash, just sterilize the room whenever the field is contaminated."

Nash leaned forward and knocked on the glass window. Both Fallen and Murdoch's eyes darted toward it. Nash pointed at Murdoch then in the direction of the electronically locked door.

Murdoch gave a slight nod then looked back toward Fallen. "I will report back the second I have any information."

Fallen turned his attention back to Murdoch. "Don't let me down Murdoch."

Murdoch confidently nodded. "I won't."

Once Murdoch left the operating room and the door relocked, Nash activated the sterilization system. "Sorry about that but I didn't think you wanted to be sterilized."

Murdoch shrugged. "I was going to leave anyway. Emma, are you finished with the Harmonds?"

Emma, who was tapping the green screens, spoke. "Let's just see the results firs-" Emma suddenly stopped short as her expression shifted to confusion seeing Sinah's D.N.A strands then Amos' and Violet's. Emma's eyes darted to Amos. "They're not even close."

Amos, who was staring back at her with a slightly awkward and upset look, barely nodded. "I know."

Emma lowered her hands from the green screens and quickly approached him. "Where the hell did she come from then?"

Amos whispered. "…The World of the Lost Souls."

Emma snatched Amos' arm and dragged him away from anyone else who could potentially hear them. The tone of her whisper was full of shock. "God was born out there?"

Amos barely nodded. "…Yeah."

Emma glanced back at the ADGL Techs. All of them were too busy working at their assigned stations to pay any attention to anything else. "Does she know?"

"I don't think so. We found her when she was really young. She was on the verge of death and-"

Emma lifted her hands and shook her head. "Don't tell me this! Here, I'm thinking that two regular people gave birth to God and now I find out she could have been born from two Helixes. But that in itself doesn't make sense."

Amos gave her a confused look. "What do you mean?"

Emma rubbed her temples as if a sudden headache had begun to form. "The reproductive issues that affect humankind are completely different from a Helix. Their body's skill to create off-spring isn't there. It's completely absent. They're not flawed or anything. Their bodies are exactly like ours and they have all the proper functioning reproductive organs. They just don't produce the eggs or semen needed for reproduction. It's like that is not their purpose, so it isn't needed. Humans were created in God's image not angels or demons."

Amos looked toward Murdoch. He was standing in his soldier at ease stance watching everyone work. "Then how can two Helixes give birth to God?"

"That's what I want to know!"

Amos turned his attention back to Emma. "But there can't be any Helixes in the World of the Lost Souls."

"Are you sure? I mean how would we know? We're in the safety of the facility. We don't know if Helixes from other Labs decided the World of the Lost Souls was a world they'd prefer to live in. Did one of them just..?" Emma paused for a shrug. "I don't know get 'selected' to give birth to God?"

"Why would they just abandon her then?"

Emma looked toward Violet. She hadn't once moved her eyes away from Sinah. "That's a very good question. That Helix had to have known it was God within her. But even if God needed a passage into our world, why would it be a simple Helix?"

Amos chuckled a little. "Why would you believe it would be a simple human?"

Emma looked back at Amos. She stared back at him only for a few moments before she questioned. "How many other people know about this?"

"Violet and I did our best to hide it. Only you, the Commander and Murdoch know."

Emma gave a slight nod. "Okay good, then this will be the last time we ever say anything about it."

Amos opened his mouth to say something but Emma spoke first. "Where God came from isn't all that important. If it says in the reports that you and Violet are her biological parents and all the tests are completely conclusive on that fact, then nobody will question."

Amos swallowed heavily. "Won't the Director wonder how two humans gave birth to God?"

Emma smiled slightly. "We've all been taught that God is supposed to make miracles happen. Let's just say this is one of them."

Amos shook his head as his expression weakened a little. "Say what we like. If he checks into her D.N.A then..."

Emma's slight smile shifted into a smirk. "Leave that to me. Now are you and your wife staying or heading to your Labs?"

Amos shook his head in disbelief. "Why would you hide this? Don't you need to report the truth?"

Emma's lips touched at a frown. "Why just because I'm a Lead ADGL Tech?" Emma scoffed walking over to the section she was originally at. "God is in critical condition right now. That's all anyone needs to worry about."

Amos couldn't help but to smile as much as he could. "Thank you and if it's okay we'd like to stay."

"Sure, just try not to get in anyone's way."

Violet's eyes darted to the smiling Amos then to Emma. Her expression shifted to a shocked relief seeing Emma changing hers and Amos D.N.A. patterns to match Sinah's.

Emma glanced toward Murdoch. "The Harmonds will be staying with us for a while. Murdoch, you're welcome to stay as well."

Murdoch gave a slight shake of his head. "I have other things to deal w-"

Murdoch was cut off as the door to the operating room swished open. A frown instantly took his lips as Revin calmly walked inside.

Twenty-One

Offering Nothing

The second Emma saw Revin, she rapidly began tapping on the green screens. Nash's eyes darted down to his terminal as she began to override and lock it down.

Before Revin even had a chance to open his mouth, Murdoch hissed. "Did you kill him already?

Revin glanced over his shoulder at Murdoch and gave an indifferent response. "Experiment number 7923 B hasn't regained consciousness yet. His rapid healing capabilities seem to be defective."

Murdoch growled. "I'll show you defective you son of a bitch!" As Murdoch thrusted his hand out to snatch Revin's Lab coat, Emma spoke. "You can go now Murdoch. I'll handle things from here."

Murdoch frowned pulling his hand back. "…Fine."

As he began to turn, Revin caught a glimpse of Murdoch's fully black demon eyes. "Wait!"

Murdoch glanced back at him with a full frown and a glare. "What?"

Revin stared at Murdoch's normal looking eyes for a few seconds before he said. "I'll need a blood sample from you."

Murdoch scoffed before a condescending chuckle caught his throat. "You want it?" Murdoch's tone and demeanor suddenly shifted to aggressive. "Come and get it! I don't think anyone will miss you."

Emma walked toward Nash as she dismissively waved her hand. "Thanks Murdoch."

Murdoch gave a slight nod. "I'll be back shortly."

Revin didn't remove his eyes from Murdoch as he left.

After a few long moments of merely hearing the sounds of the room, Emma spoke. "What do you want Revin?"

Revin turned and walked toward Nash's terminal. "I want a sample of that Helix's blood. Next time he's here, I want you to collect one."

Emma snickered a little. "You heard him. If you want one, go get it. I have far more important things to deal with then to run an errand for you. Not that I was going to anyway."

Revin looked through the glass window at Sinah and Fallen. "I heard the rumors."

Emma shrugged. "So?"

Revin's lips were instantly consumed by a frown. "Is that supposed to be the high and mighty God?"

"You would think after working on him you'd know he's Perfect Experiment A."

Revin's eyes sharpened and shifted to Emma. "I meant the girl."

Emma gave another shrug but didn't say anything. Revin looked back toward Fallen and Sinah. He spoke ignoring the full frown Fallen was sending him. "It's rather foolish of you to let Perfect Experiment A in there with the supposed 'God.' We were taught they are natural enemies. Perhaps the rumors weren't true after all."

Emma released a rude, almost forced yawn. "Maybe you're right. Maybe she's just some girl."

Revin growled under his breath as he began to attempt to access the green screens. "Stupid, useless…"

Revin stopped his insults not getting a computer response. Revin tapped the air again. Both Emma and Nash smirked at his annoyed confusion. Different from Emma however, Nash did his best to try and hide it his amusement.

Revin shifted closer to Nash and began working on his terminal. After a few moments of nothing responding, he tossed Emma a glare. "You've locked the system down."

Emma wasn't shy in her response. "Yeah, I know. This is a restricted area with restricted information."

Revin's anger was instantly charged. "I am a Lead ADGL Tech! Information is-"

Emma cut him off rolling her eyes. "You're not this project's Lead ADGL Tech, I am. So save your 'information on any project is not limited' speech. Access is prohibited and denied."

Revin's glare shifted to Amos and Violet. "Yet you're allowing a couple of civilians in here."

Violet frowned toward him. "We're not civilians. We're-"

Emma lifted her hand to stop her from continuing. As she lowered her hand, she spoke. "Amos Harmond is from Combat and Violet Harmond is from Creation. They're not simply civilians."

"Nor are they building Seven ADGL Lab Techs. They shouldn't be anywhere near..." Revin stopped talking for a split second before he nodded. "They are the girl's parents aren't they? Did you check the D.N.A.? Were there any abnormalities in the Creation process? What amount of G Helix was introduced to the specimen? Why are we just discovering this now? An important Helix like this wouldn't have just slipped through the cracks. We would have kept her in the experimentation process from birth like we did with Perfect Experiment A. Just where exactly was this girl created?"

Emma gave a short and indifferent shrug. "Sorry, but that's restricted information."

Revin hissed almost instantly. "Lead ADGL Techs get access to any and all restricted areas and information."

"Didn't I just tell you not to bother with that speech? You're not getting anything from me or any of my ADGL team. Now please leave before I have a Helix soldier take you out of here." Emma suddenly nodded. "Actually, that's a good idea. Computer! Have two Helix soldiers report into operating room 3, ASAP!"

The computer made a sound of acknowledgement and within a blink of an eye, two Helix soldiers raced into the room. Their weapons were drawn and ready for combat. Emma smiled toward Revin. "Please leave."

Revin frowned as much as he could. "Well, we'll just see what the Director has to say about this."

Emma lifted her hand and forced an obvious false happy tone. "Bye-bye."

As one of the Helix soldiers tried to leave with Revin, he hissed. "I don't need an escort!"

Emma couldn't help but to chuckle as Revin hissed again, only this time toward her. "This isn't over Emma!"

Once the door swished closed behind Revin, he spoke. "Computer access cell Lab 6, Ayla?"

Ayla responded back. "Yes Sir?"

As Revin began to storm down the hallway, he spoke. "Has Experiment number 7923 B, regained consciousness yet?"

Ayla looked through the window down at Bridger. He was wide awake and aggressively trying to get free from his restraints. Closing her eyes, she answered. "Not yet."

"Fine, alert me the minute he does, I need to speak the Director."

Twenty-Two

From Boy to Man Helix

Alex's expression shifted to slight confusion. "Uh... Dante?" Dante, who was frantically typing on his laptop, spoke. "What is it? Did you find something?"

Alex lifted his hands from the key board. "Someone from building Seven is using a lock down system from my old Lab."

Dante continued working. "Put it up on the main screen."

Once the information appeared on the large screen, Dante gave it a quick glance then turned his full attention toward it. "This is a basic Lab Tech lock down numerical sequence."

Alex nodded with a chuckle. "It's the fastest code we can put in when we don't want to get caught looking into files we shouldn't." Alex's amusement shifted to confusion. "But why would someone from building Seven, use something so simple."

Dante smiled tapping on his laptop keys easily breaking the lock down codes in seconds. "It's actually quite smart. Someone from building Seven would never think to use easy codes to protect information. They would automatically assume it would be complex and try using only high level techniques to break it. Whoever did this, did it fast and did it knowing that."

Alex watched Dante effortlessly break code after code in seconds. "The second they notice the lock down is being hacked, I bet those advanced codes will be activated."

Dante smiled. "Yeah but access to building Seven is on a time delay which means extracting info should be the same. We might only get a little of whatever is being protected before the system detects us and installs the stronger level of security, but we'll take what we can get. Now I need you to keep an eye out for any system tracking interference. The last thing we want is to get caught because we didn't notice the warning signs."

Alex quickly nodded as he went back to work. "I'm on it."

After a few more moments of working, Dante's computer suddenly paused. He couldn't help but to chuckle as he leaned back on his chair. "Did they detect us?"

Alex shook his head a little. "No but I don't recognize these security codes that are coming up."

Dante stretched his arms up into the air and released a slightly achy groan. "We've been blocked. Get out of that system and let's see what we got."

Dante stood up from the kitchen table and walked toward the back of the couch. As he leaned against it, he looked toward the large screen on the wall. Information from operating room 3 began to slowly load. Once Alex was finished working, he looked toward the screen as well.

Dante tilted his head slightly as two unlabeled D.N.A. strands displayed on the screen. Once the third appeared, tons of unusual information followed after. Alex's expression shifted to confusion. "I don't understand what I'm seeing."

"Me neither. But according to the info, they seem to be tampering with D.N.A. patterns. Now why would they do that?"

Not having an answer, all Alex could do was shrug.

Dante crossed his arms staring at the unusual codes and commands. "I... I think whoever is altering them is trying to make them link up."

Alex stood up from the kitchen table. "You mean like a bloodline connection?"

Dante gave the slightest nod. "Exactly, but what would be the point in doing something like t-?" Dante suddenly stopped short as Sinah's Helix was displayed on the screen.

Dante uncrossed his arms and clutched his hand over his heart. It was as if a ball of fire suddenly wielded up from inside in his chest. "Ah!"

Alex's eyes darted to Dante. "Dante?"

Dante suddenly collapsed to his hand and knees, squeezing his eyes tightly closed in pain. As his nails pierced through his shirt then his skin, he released a loud groan.

As Alex began to bend down to help Dante, there was a knock at the door. Rapidly filling with panic, Alex yelled out. "C... Can you come back later?!"

Alex's expression shifted to relief as the front door opened and Murdoch stepped inside. "Sorry but I have my-"

Murdoch stopped short seeing the distressed Dante. As he raced over and knelt down in front of him, Dante released another loud groan. "What the hell happened?!"

Alex shook his head with a look of sympathy. "I don't know! We were looking at some stuff we got from building Seven and-"

Murdoch looked up at the large screen. Once he saw Sinah's Helix, his demonic pupils widened and the black consumed all the white. Murdoch placed his hands on Dante's shoulders. "It's your change Dante. You've seen the Helix of your Lord. Don't fight it."

Dante's breathing became labored as he muttered. "I... I don't w... want to... to be like Bridge... Bridger. He... He..."

As Dante's sentence trailed off into another sound of pain, Murdoch spoke. "I don't think you will, but fighting is going to make it worse."

Dante's free hand grabbed Murdoch's arm. "H... Help... Mur... Murdoch."

Murdoch barley nodded. "Just focus on your breathing Dante. The pain will pass."

Dante tried his best to breathe normally. It was obvious he had low tolerance to pain for every few seconds he'd make a sound of discomfort. Murdoch made his breathing sound much louder than normal giving Dante something to focus on and try to match.

After a few minutes of doing this, Murdoch spoke. "You've been given an order by the Commander. You need to get a full surveillance layout on building Seven."

Dante only continued to try his best to breathe at a steady pace as

Murdoch continued. "He wants to get Sinah out of there and needs to know where all the soldiers are."

Dante's head suddenly shot up to Murdoch. His breathing snapped back to completely under control. "He wants to escape with her?"

Murdoch smiled seeing the same white ring around Dante's pupil that Bridger had around his. "Yes, he says it's dangerous for both of them there."

Dante stared at Murdoch's demonic eyes for a few seconds before he whispered. "Do you feel any different?"

Murdoch shook his head. "No. Do you?"

Dante shifted himself to sit comfortably on the floor as he looked at his hands. "No, but the pain's gone."

Murdoch gave the slightest nod as he got to his feet. "I don't know if your change is supposed to be painful or if it's just this way because Sinah is in bad shape."

Dante watched Murdoch's eyes return to normal before he spoke. "So Bridger's change could have been caused by Sinah's body suddenly being brought back to life? Like a pain reaction?"

Murdoch shrugged. "I wouldn't know."

As Dante opened his mouth to say something, a very angry voice spilled through one of his laptops. "Director Hart, I want access to the supposed G Helix!"

Twenty-Three

Eavesdropping

While Murdoch and Alex's eyes darted to the laptop on the kitchen table, Dante sprang to his feet and raced toward it. "That's the second surveillance!"

Before anyone could say anything, Dante accessed the spider's live feed and put it up on the large screen. Murdoch's expression shifted to confusion looking at the Director. "You bugged the Director's office?"

"I must and will get any information I need, consequences be damned."

A slight smirk took Murdoch's lips. "It looks like all of us have lost our loyalty to that simple human."

Dante's eyes shot to Murdoch in shock before he hesitantly said. "..You have become different."

Murdoch stepped into his soldier awaiting a command stance. "When you have a spare moment, maybe you should question where your loyalty lies as well."

Before Dante had a chance to respond, the angry voice spoke again. "This is nonsense that Emma is the Lead on this!"

Dante clicked a few keys on his laptop. The camera shifted slightly to see who the angry person in the room was. It was Revin. He had his hands on his hips and his demeanor just screamed outrage. Both Murdoch and Dante began to frown. Alex, on the other hand gave a slightly confused look. "I don't recognize him. Who is he?"

Murdoch instantly piped up. “An asshole.”

Dante followed after. “A total asshole.”

Alex’s eye darted toward Dante and Murdoch at their shared dislike.

The Director calmly flipped through some of his paperwork. “I haven’t received any reports on the G Helix yet. I’m assuming she’s recovering.”

Revin’s anger was disarmed by slight disbelief. “With such an important being in our facility, I would think you’d want minute to minute updates. I’ve seen the girl’s condition, she could simply die.”

The Director smiled slightly. “She won’t.”

“How can you be so sure?”

“I have faith.”

Revin’s whole demeanor shifted to bewilderment. “…Faith?”

The Director dismissively waved his hand. “A Lead ADGL Tech was randomly called to oversee the ADGL emergency team that tended to God’s injuries. Emma was selected merely by chance.”

Revin’s lips touched at a frown. “If that girl truly is God then she shouldn’t be in the care of only one Lead. With Perfect Experiment A, we were the underlings for five Leads.”

The Director flipped through another pile of papers. “Times and circumstances were different back then. All of us were expecting God to be our first successful creation. Besides, until she regains consciousness there’s nothing that anyone can do.”

“Fine but I want access to her files. Until I see the progress of the G Helix with my own eyes, I won’t believe that girl is God.”

The Director looked up from his paperwork and leaned back in his leather bound chair. “The world had a reaction to her. It may be moving unnoticeably slow but the world itself is recovering with her. Only God can cause such a massive effect upon a dead world.”

Revin looked through the ceiling to floor windows at the eclipsed sun and moon. “If the world is beginning to move merely with her presence alone, why would she even need to regain consciousness?”

The Director only responded by tenting his fingers. After a few seconds of silence, Revin spoke again. “Lead ADGL Techs are supposed to have access to any and all Helix information. I want access to her files.”

The Director released a slightly annoyed sigh. “If Emma found it necessary to put restrictions on God’s progress then so be it. I won’t over turn her choice. This is the most important Helix in all of existence. This is the one and only Helix every Lab has been trying to create since this all started, since the very beginning. This is the one and only Helix that has the power to change the world completely."

The Director dismissively waved his hand again and returned to his paperwork. "Your request is denied. Now I don't have time to be dealing with petty squabbling among my Leads. Get back to whatever you were working on."

Revin's lips touched at a frown. "I'm in the beginning stages of the experimentation of Experiment number 7923 B."

The Director gave an indifferent nod. "That's one of Lucifer's A Helix soldiers right?"

"Yes."

"I expect a report on my desk sooner rather than later."

"I'm also here for another request."

The Director glanced up at Revin. "And that would be?"

Revin didn't hesitate to answer. "I want permission to perform the experimental process on his other soldier, the D Helix."

Twenty-Four

Disposable

Both Alex and Dante's eyes darted to the frowning Murdoch. He had placed his hands on the back of the couch and clenched his muscles. The strength in his hands began to crush the wooden frame that held it together.

The Director leaned back on his chair. "Why?"

Revin put his hands in his lab coat pockets. "With Perfect Experiment A being so close to God, his Helix must have changed. If it has, then more than likely his D Helix soldier has as well."

The Director's eyebrows lowered slightly. "What do you mean 'being so close to her'? Is he still in building Seven?"

Before Revin had a chance to respond, the Director spoke again. His tone reflected his annoyance. "With God recovering, she won't have the strength to protect herself against him. She'll be easy prey."

Dante's expression shifted to bewilderment. "I don't get it. Why would Sinah have to protect herself from the Commander to begin with?"

Alex's expression mirrored Dante's. "He's talking like they're enemies. But if that were true, the Commander wouldn't have even bothered to bring her back to life."

Murdoch frowned as much as he could. "The Director says they're natural enemies."

Dante shook his head in disbelief pointing at one of his laptops. "That can't be right. Alex access the Archive Lab and check out the ancient times history."

"I'm on it."

Dante looked back toward the Director. "We've seen them together Murdoch, there's no way they're-"

Dante was cut off by the Director. "She needs to be at full strength to get rid of him once and for all."

Revin questioned, not believing what his ears were hearing. "You want God to kill Perfect Experiment A?"

The Director stood up from his chair, grabbed his metal walking stick and approached the ceiling to floor windows. As he looked up at the eclipsed sun and moon, he spoke. "So long have I been waiting for this moment. So much time just waiting for positive results, only to always come up empty. Hoping for success, yet being overwhelmed by doubt. Finally, finally after all this time, we have a chance to end the world of all its suffering. God will usher in a new world and wipe away all of our sins. Only those worthy enough to stand in her presence should be allowed to live. Lucifer isn't worthy of that honor, he is nothing but suffering."

"Do you really think she'll kill him?"

The Direct glanced back at Revin with a slight smile. "Oh I know she will. It's in the Divine's nature to destroy evil. If Lucifer's Helix is changing, it's probably awakening a crueler more vicious side. The stronger he gets, the closer he becomes like the original owner of the L Helix, the being of absolute pure evil. Something only God herself must annihilate."

"What about the D Helix soldiers?"

The Director gave an indifferent shrug. "Without Lucifer, all of them are useless. It will be up to God to decide if she simply wants to dispose of them or not. If she doesn't, I will order them to report to the ADGL Labs. Let them deal with them however they see fit. I couldn't care less."

The Director suddenly frowned. "That is, of course, assuming Lucifer doesn't strike her down before she recovers. I'll just deal with this right now."

As he limped toward his office door, Revin questioned. "What about my request?"

The Director shook his head opening one of the double doors. "Not at this moment. I still may have one more use for his team. After that, I will grant you your request."

Revin followed the Director out of his office with a smile. "Good."

Twenty-Five

Logic

The second the lights turned off in the Director's office, Murdoch stormed toward the front door. Dante's eye's darted to him in shock and confusion. "Where are you going?"

Murdoch instantly hissed back at him. "Where the hell do you think I'm going?! The Commander thought the Director was going to have Sinah kill him and he was right! I need to let him know!"

Dante quickly nodded. "I agree, but not now."

Murdoch stopped in his tracks and tossed Dante a glare. "What the hell do you mean 'not now.'?!"

Dante lifted his hands defensively. "Murdoch, you need to calm down."

Murdoch turned on Dante with a snarl. "Calm down?! Calm down?! The Director wants Sinah to kill my Lord! And we D Helixes, we're just useless disposable soldiers?!"

Dante barley nodded. "I know what he wants but that's not going to happen."

Murdoch's hostile demeanor didn't waver in the slightest. "How in the hell do you know that?! What makes you so damn sure?!"

Dante went a little flush lowering his hands. "U… Uh... Well, I don't think Sinah and the Commander can live without the other."

"The Commander was around long before Sinah was even-"

"Are you sure?"

Murdoch's anger touched at confusion as Dante continued. "None of us know how long Sinah has been alive. It's not like she can speak to tell us. What if when his Helix was created, hers breathed life too? There has to be a reason why her God side stayed dormant. Maybe she needed to be in his presence, just like the Commander needed to be in hers to develop enough to awaken your D Helix capabilities. I think despite what the Director says or wants they need one another. Her Holy and his Un-holy forms need each other, like light needs dark and vice versa."

Murdoch's anger began to simmer down. "But if the Director commands her to kill him, she might just obey. All of us are… or were loyal to the Director."

Dante smiled slightly. "All of us have been Lab created. We owe our existences to him. Sinah is different, she was naturally born and…"

Dante suddenly turned his head back toward the large screen. "Alex, could you put up those D.N.A. patterns again?"

Alex clicked off of the Archive files to do as Dante asked. After a few moments of Dante studying them, he nodded. "Ah, I understand now. Whoever was tampering with these were trying to make them link up with Sinah's. Her parents aren't her real parents are they?"

"I don't know the whole situation but Amos said they're not."

"I still don't think Sinah was Lab created, at least not by our Lab anyway. If she was, they would have definitely known she was God at birth. Not being from here, she shouldn't have any loyalty to the Director."

Murdoch stepped into his soldier at ease stance. "How can you be so sure? Loyalty aside, what if they are natural enemies?"

Dante shook his head in disbelief. "They're not! They're-"

Alex cut Dante off. "According to the ancient history text, they are. The original two were constantly battling over the fate of the human soul."

Murdoch barely nodded. "See, I-"

Dante cut Murdoch off with a forceful hiss. "No! I refuse to believe that! Sinah and the Commander are not just some re-creations of what God and Lucifer once were! They are not just repeats of the past!"

Dante rudely thrusted his index finger toward Murdoch. "And the D Helixes are not just useless disposable soldiers!"

Murdoch couldn't help but to snicker at his assurance. "Thanks Dante, but this doesn't help stop the Director's plans for us."

Dante frantically began to work on his computer. "I don't care what the Director's plans are. It's arrogant to think he can control God. I'm getting the Commander and Sinah out of there come hell or high water."

Murdoch's lips touched at a smile. "Then let me get back to building Seven and let the Commander know."

"You should wait until the Director leaves. It might appear suspicious if you were to suddenly bust in there pissed off."

"Fine, but the minute he's back in his office, you contact me Dante."

"I will."

As Murdoch walked toward the front door, Dante spoke. "My loyalty is with Sinah and the Commander, Murdoch. Whatever loyalty or gratitude I once felt for the Director has been replaced with my contempt."

Murdoch smiled a full smile as he nodded. "I feel the same A Helix."

Dante confidently nodded as Murdoch left.

Twenty-Six

Bickering Leads

The Director stood in the operating room with an expression of utter shock and disbelief. His widened eyes were locked on Sinah in Fallen's arms through the glass window. "I don't believe it."

Emma frowned at Revin as she muttered. "I'm still not sharing any information with you."

Revin returned the frown. "With the Director here, you can't stop me from trying to look into her files."

Emma smirked. "Oh yes I can. Those two A Helix soldiers have been ordered to shoot anyone who tries to touch anything."

Revin couldn't help but to grimace glancing back at them. Both were diligently standing by the entrance to the room. "If the Director decides to access the information and I happen to look over his shoulder then..."

Emma scoffed. "Moron, the Director doesn't care about the scientific side of things. He just wants results and he's looking at them."

Revin's lips were instantly consumed by a full frown. Before he had a chance to say something unpleasant, the Director spoke. "How long has he been in there?"

Emma turned her attention to the Director. "He showed up not long after she arrived."

"And you just allowed this?"

Emma went a little flush. "He didn't really give us much choice."

Fallen shifted and sharpened his eyes toward the Director through the glass window. Noticing his glare out of the corner of Fallen's sunglasses, the Director's lips touched at a frown. "Have you collected any samples from him? Where is his Helix display?"

Emma's eyes darted to Revin as he snickered. "It looks like he does care."

Nash glanced back at the frowning Emma for approval. Emma gave the slightest nod. "Only Perfect Experiment A's."

Nash pressed a few buttons on his terminal. The second Fallen's double Helix was displayed Revin's eyes darted to it. "So there has been a change to the L Helix, I knew it."

The Director looked toward Fallen's Helix as well. "Why hasn't there been any reports sent to my office?"

Emma gave a slight shrug. "God is our top priority. In the condition she's in, something that trivial just slipped my mind."

Revin frowned as much as he could. "Trivial? Perfect Experiment A's Helix developing beyond our expectations, is trivial to you? This is why there should be more than one Lead ADGL Tech working on this project! When one of them is too stupid to remember something so apparently trivial, the other would know of its importance."

Emma hissed at Revin. "I'd rather subject myself to our most extensive experimentation than work with the likes of you."

Revin hissed back. "The knowledge of God is beyond you, Emma!"

"Don't you ever shut up, you zealous twit!"

Before Revin could snap back, he noticed the Director accessing more files on Fallen. As the Director studied them, he spoke. "It's obvious his Helix is developing in defense against the pending danger. So why would he put himself directly into the fray?"

Emma looked toward Fallen. He hadn't once removed his sharpened eyes from the Director. Flipped through a few more files, the Director questioned. "And how does God's Helix look?"

Emma indifferently shrugged. "Like a Helix."

The Director looked toward Emma with a slightly annoyed yet confused look. "Can I see it?"

Emma looked toward the grinning Revin. She frowned for a split second before she forced a grin herself. "…Nope."

The Director's eyebrows lowered slightly. "…And why not?"

Emma rudely pointed at Revin. "Sorry Director Hart, but that information is restricted from your irritating shadow."

The Director glanced back at Revin. "Return to your experiments"

Before Revin even had a chance to protest, one of the A Helix soldiers stepped toward him with their weapon raised. "You need to leave Sir."

"I am a-"

The A Helix soldier finished Revin's sentence in a harsh no nonsense tone. "Deadman, if you don't leave, now."

Revin looked toward the Director. He was flipping through Fallen's files again. His eyes shifted to the smirking Emma. Before his lips could send her a frown, the A Helix soldier poked him in the ribs with his machine gun. "I won't tell you again."

Emma lifted her hand and spoke in a forced happy tone. "Bye-bye."

Revin tossed her a glare before he was escorted out.

Emma snickered before she turned her attention back to Nash. "Display our collected data on God."

The second the Director saw Sinah's double Helix, his eyes instantly lit up. "So this is what the Creator's Helix looks like."

Emma gave a slight nod. "The development appears very similar to Perfect Experiment A's. Both should start showing signs of a physical change very-"

"I knew it would be our Lab that would be successful in creating God."

Emma glanced back at Amos and Violet. "Actually, the Harmonds-"

"Her original Helix isn't in these files, where is it?"

Nash shrugged. "We can't find it. I've searched every buildings Lab files and nothing."

The Director looked back toward Fallen. "Perhaps Lucifer is hiding it, but why would he do that?" A frown took his lips as he continued. "How is God supposed to make a full recovery with Lucifer looming over her?"

The Director walked toward the electronically locked door holding his frown. "Open this, I'll handle Lucifer myself."

Emma pressed a button on the terminal and the door swished open. The moment it shut behind him, Emma spoke in a sarcastic tone. "Oh yeah, this is going to go real well."

Twenty-Seven

Attempting Doubt

Fallen pulled Sinah protectively closer to himself as the Director approached them. "Lucifer, you're doing her more harm than good by being in here. Let the ADGL Lab Techs deal with her recovery."

Fallen instantly began to frown. "I'm not going anywhere."

Though the Director was standing on Fallen's side of the operating table, his eyes were locked on Sinah. "I'm saying this for your own good you need to leave her to recover on her own."

Fallen's eyebrows lowered. "And I'm saying this for your own good you need to leave us be."

The Director leaned on his metal walking stick. "With her natural enemy being so close, her body is probably only focusing on protection. She needs to focus on healing."

Fallen shifted his silver eyes toward the Director. Glints of the crimson red around pitch black pupil could clearly be seen. "Sinah isn't my enemy."

The Director stared dumbfounded at Fallen for a few moments before he spoke. "You truly believe that don't you?"

Fallen instantly hissed. "It isn't what I believe! It's what I know!"

The Director weakly sighed shaking his head. "Then you're not listening to your natural instincts. You're not sensing the pending danger right in front of you."

Fallen's eyes sharpened as the crimson color began to bleed into the silver. "I am well aware of everything my instincts are telling me."

"Then you should separate yourself from her. When God awakens, she could simply kill you. She may be a merciful being but you are her natural..."

"Sinah isn't my enemy!!"

The Director stumbled backward a little as a suffering wave of intimidation slammed against his body. His widened and confused eyes darted to Fallen.

Fallen's tone of voice suddenly became calm, yet forceful. "Sinah won't kill me."

The Director released another sigh only this one was louder. "Your instincts astound me, Lucifer. You of all the Helixes should know only too well the evil that courses through your veins. She is compassionate, kind and merciful. You are cruel, sadistic and heartless. Why would someone so pure, so good, waste her time keeping something like you alive?"

Fallen's grip on Sinah loosened ever so slightly. The Director released another sigh as he continued. "God shouldn't be protected by the Devil. The Devil should fear her. Your darkness is doing her light more harm than good. Now I think its best if you-"

"No."

"No?"

Fallen tightened his grip on Sinah again. "No, I will continue to guard my counterpart. I won't let her be harmed or experimented on or whatever else you or those Techs have planned for her."

The Director shook his head in disbelief. "Lucifer, you're putting yourself in danger by staying here with her."

"And by doing so, I'm keeping her safe from everyone else."

The Director's lips touched at a frown. "If I have to order you then..."

Fallen let Sinah's hand go then snapped his hand into a fist. Before Fallen could do or say anything else, loud beeping noises and flashing lights flooded the operating room. As the Director's eyes darted around in confusion, Nash knocked on the glass window. Once the Director looked up at him, he pointed toward the electronically locked door.

The Director gave a slight nod as he limped toward the exit. "Consider what I've said Lucifer. Deep down, you know that my words are the truth."

Once the door swished closed behind the Director, Fallen snapped his hand open. His nails had become the overlapping jagged shards of black like glass. He looked toward them as he spoke. "Consider yourself lucky Director Hart."

Nash pressed a button on the terminal. "Sorry Director, the sterilization system keeps acting up. You can go back in there in a few moments."

The Director shook his head. "That won't be necessary. I have other things I have to deal with. I want the results on both God and Lucifer sent to my office ASAP."

Emma gave a slight nod. "Yes Director."

Twenty-Eight

Pain in the Bridger

Revin accessed the green screens just below the window in cell 6. Despite Bridger's full frown directed toward him, Revin only glanced up when Ayla entered the cell with the pushcart. On top were three syringes. Two exactly like the first injected into Bridger and the third was filled with a very dark pink almost red liquid. Ayla looked toward Bridger sympathetically. "Here are the pain stimulators."

Revin gave the slightest nod of acknowledgement as he continued working. "…Fine."

Ayla only stared at Bridger for a few moments before he noticed. The minute he did, he smiled softly. Ayla's expression weakened as she mouthed the words. 'I'm sorry.'

Bridger only held his smile. The second Revin noticed them, he frowned. "That will be all Ayla."

Ayla gave a quick nod. "Yes Sir."

Once Ayla left, the full frown found its way back onto Bridger's lips. "What pisses you off more, the fact she has sympathy for me or the fact she isn't a cruel bastard like you?"

Revin ignored Bridger's question accessing his body scan. "I've put in a request for that other Helix on Perfect Experiment A's team."

A wave of panic washed over Bridger's features. "What other Helix?"

Revin glanced beyond the green screens toward Bridger, hearing the panic in his voice. "You sound almost worried Experiment number 7923 B."

Bridger forced his expression back to normal the best he could. "I couldn't care less. If you want to waste your time with those low level Helixes, be my guest."

A chuckle caught Revin's throat. "You wouldn't even protect that other A Helix?"

Bridger clenched his jaw and gave a quick. "Nope."

"Interesting, he's the intelligence factor on Perfect Experiment A's team, isn't he?"

Bridger swallowed heavily. Despite wanting to hold onto his normal expression, worry began to seep into his eyes. "..I guess."

Revin began to check the fluctuation of Bridger's heart rate from his pain tolerance session. "I tend to wonder how his A Helix is changing. Does his level of intelligence have an effect on its development?"

Bridger tried to shrug but the restraints held him in place. "I wouldn't know."

Revin glanced toward Bridger again. He could clearly see the uncomfortable state he was in. As a slight smile took his lips, he spoke. "It looks like I'm going to have to put in a request for him as well."

Bridger made a quiet sound of relief before he suddenly chuckled. "I bet you get denied."

Revin's lips touched at a frown. "Oh? And why would that happen?"

"I'm guessing the Director is more concerned about Sin..." Bridger paused for a split second before he corrected himself. "..About God right now to even listen to you. I bet you already tried to get those two and he just brushed you off."

Revin's slight frown increased as he walked over to the pushcart. "I will have Perfect Experiment A's D Helix soon enough."

Bridger chuckled. "Yeah, good luck with that. Why you'd want either of those low level Helixes, I'll never know. It's not like either of them are changing. With Sin.. God and the Commander's Helixes being pretty much useless right now, I'm sure-"

"Perfect Experiment A's Helix has changed! More than likely this has caused his D Helix soldier to develop further as well!"

Bridger's lips couldn't help but to curl into a cocky smirk. "Thanks for the update."

Revin's expression shifted to momentary shock before it became annoyed. "You're a lot more clever than I thought Experiment number 7923 B."

Bridger chuckled trying to shake his head but again couldn't. "No, not really, I just know Lab Techs are chatterboxes. They can't help it. You chat with them long enough and they'll tell you everything."

Bridger's chuckle became louder. "And they say I talk too much."

Revin snatched up one of the medium level pain stimuli. "Well, how about I shut you up right now?"

"You better, if you don't, who knows what else you'll tell me."

Revin slammed the syringe into Bridger's vein then forced the liquid into him. Bridger closed his eyes anticipating the sudden rush of agony. After a few long moments of nothing happening, Bridger opened his eyes. He looked toward Revin, who had returned to the green screens. "That, was supposed to shut me up?"

After a few more long moments, Revin called out. "Len, check the scanner."

Len was quick to respond back. "Okay."

Bridger didn't react as the green wave ran up and down his body. Revin frowned a little seeing Bridger's updated body scan. Despite having injected the fluid into him, there wasn't any sign of it.

"The scanner is working just fine Sir. It's running like normal."

Revin frowned as much as he could as he walked back to Bridger. "So it looks like your Helix has adapted. I must say I'm quite surprised."

Bridger mirrored Revin's expression. "No you're not. You're probably pissed that you never got to see me suffer again."

Revin picked up the syringe filled with the dark pink almost red liquid inside. "Oh don't worry, I will."

Before Bridger could say anything else, Revin injected the contents into him. Different from the medium level ones which had a pain reaction delay, this one was instantaneous. Bridger released an ear piercing screech of agony. Sweat rapidly gushed from his pores and tears flooded his eyes. Even though all his muscles had suddenly been forcibly tightened, his body was trembling uncontrollably.

Before Revin could take even a single step back from him, Bridger lost consciousness. Revin's expression instantly shifted to annoyance. "Again, you simply black out?!"

Revin stomped over to the green screens and looked at Bridger's body scan. Just like before, his veins were shinning a blinding gold destroying all the pain stimuli. Frowning as much as he could, Revin glanced back at Bridger. "I'm going to have to figure out how to keep you conscious through our experimentation process Experiment number 7923 B. One way or another, your Helix will experience this."

Twenty-Nine

Calling Out

Alex glanced up at the large screen as the Director's office lights flicked on. As the Director approached his large desk, Alex spoke. "The Director's back. Should I contact Murdoch?"

Dante didn't glance up from his frantic clacking on the keys of his laptop. "Give me a moment."

Before Alex could respond, Dante's mother did. She was drying her hands after just finishing the dishes. "Dante, are you peeping on the Director?"

Dante went a little flush. "It's called surveillance Mom. Geez, the way you say it, makes it sound perverted."

Dante's mom placed the tea towel onto the counter then looked at the large screen. "Why are you watching him to begin with?"

"It's complicated. Now Alex and I really need to work so…"

"I hope this doesn't get you in trouble."

Dante lifted his hands from his key board and looked at his mother with a very serious expression. "I really don't care what happens to me, I have to help God and the Commander anyway I can."

Dante's mother looked toward him. The second her eyes locked on his, she could see the glowing white ring around his pupil. After a hesitant nod, she whispered. "Be careful Dante. I don't want to lose you too."

Dante responded in a confident tone. "You won't Mom."

Dante's mother gave another hesitant nod. "Well... Okay then. I have some errands I have to run. Now, you two boys don't get into any trouble, while I'm gone."

Dante only gave a brief acknowledgement while Alex politely said. "Good-bye Ma'am."

Once she left, Alex turned his attention to Dante. "She's really protective of you."

"We lost Dad in a Lost Souls raid. Since then, she's always been worried something might happen."

Before Alex could offer his condolences, Dante pressed his ear piece. "Murdoch?"

"Is the Director back?"

As Dante opened his mouth to say something, the Director spoke. "Computer, unlock communications to all Labs."

Dante's eyes darted to the large screen. "What the..?"

"…Dante?"

Dante pressed his earpiece. "Hang on Murdoch. The Director is doing something. I'm going to open line my ear piece okay?"

The second Dante opened lined his earpiece so that Murdoch could listen, the Director spoke. "Voice recognition: unlocking system: Director Walter Hart."

Alex glanced toward Dante. "I didn't know the Director's first name was Walter."

Dante dismissively waved his hand at Alex. "Shh!"

Alex went flush covering his mouth with both hands.

The book filled bookshelves to the left of the Director's desk began to rumble and shake. Coats of dust and filth poured to the floor and got released into the air from the aggressive movements. It was obvious nobody, not even the automatic cleaning system, had been anywhere near these shelves.

Dante slowly stood up from his kitchen table, hearing loud unfamiliar grinding noises. It sounded almost like the mechanics were running on an old gear and cog system. Dante's expression shifted to confusion as the bookshelves split down the center then moved into hidden slots in the walls.

Murdoch, who could hear the noises, questioned. "Dante, what the hell is that sound?"

Dante slowly shook his head. "...I don't know. I don't know what's happening."

Once the shelves locked into place, nine large black screens moved forward replacing the wall of bookshelves. The Director reached into his desk and pulled out a black box. As he dusted the layer of filth from lack of use off of it, he spoke. "Computer, lock my office door and draw the curtains."

The computer beeped and did as it was told. Black flaps closed over each of the ceiling to floor windows and the lock to his office snapped shut.

Both Dante and Alex watched in anticipation as the Director opened the box to retrieve a small rectangular item with buttons on the top. Once the Director pressed one of the buttons, all of the screens, flicked a couple of times then turned on. Each one of them was displaying a different Lab number.

Dante stared at the screens in bewilderment. "This looks like some ancient technology. I've never seen anything like this before."

The Director sat comfortably in his leather bound chair before he called out. "Any remaining functioning Labs, this is Director Walter Hart from Lab 1. Respond."

None of the screens changed. The Director chuckled a little. "Come on now, we all made a pact from the very beginning."

The screens still didn't change. The Director held his pleasant tone and called out again. "I repeat. Any functioning Labs this is Director Walter Hart from Lab-"

The Director was cut off as two screens began to flicker.

Thirty

Lab Two and Eight

A man appeared on the Lab 2 screen. He had dark hair and an eye patch covering his second brown eye. A woman appeared on the Lab 8 screen. Her blonde hair and brown eyes complimented her olive skin tone. The one side of her face was marred with heavy scarring.

The Director smiled toward them and spoke in a friendly familiar tone. "Chris, Isadora, it's been so long! How have you been?"

Chris frowned almost instantly. "You have a hell of a lot of nerve contacting us, you murderer."

Isadora hissed right after. "Traitor! Thanks to you turning against us, we had to make soldiers and warriors instead of Angels and Demons! We had a chance to wipe out even the thought of war from our planet and you made us have to recreate it for our own protection!"

The Director indifferently waved his hand. "We all do what we have to."

Chris released a loud scoff. "Ha! And I bet in your eyes that justifies it for you doesn't it, you murderous son of a bitch!"

The Director glanced at the other Lab screens. "Where is everyone else? I know Lucifer and his men didn't destroy all their Labs."

Isadora frowned. "They're probably ignoring the contact signal, just like I should have."

The Director returned the frown. "All of us scientists made a pact.

If this form of communication is used, we respond. It doesn't matter the situation or the circumstances."

Chris crossed his arms. "Yeah, we all made that pact but none of us were expecting some lunatic to turn on us. Wiping out the world's governing powers made perfect sense back then. The world had a chance to start anew and become a better place with peace and freedom at its forefront. None of us were expecting someone who shared our goals to start killing us. That's just barbaric!"

The Director tented his fingers and leaned back on his chair. "We needed more samples. My Labs progress was much further along than anyone else's. We weren't going to be slowed down merely because we lacked the necessary components."

Chris scoffed shaking his head. "...The audacity of some people. Listening to you is like losing my eye to our beginning experimental stages of Helix comprehension all over again. It hurts like hell, scarred me for life and though necessary, I wish I never did it. Now I'm done listening to your attempts to justify your acts of sin, I'm leave-"

"I need both of you to send a message to the remaining Labs."

Isadora gave a look of utter disbelief as she brushed her hand against her facial scars. "We all have suffered damage from our work, but none of it has made us stupid. Did you inject some Synthetic crap into your brain or something? There's no way any of us are going to do anything for you."

The Director ignored her and continued his thought. "All Lab Directors and their finest creations are invited to Lab 1.Our perfectly functioning facility will welcome all of you with open arms."

Chris released a weak chuckle. "Tired of having the Devil and his men hunt us down? You'd rather we make things easier for you and have all of us executed in one spot? Now where's the fun in that?"

Isadora shook her head. "I'm not bringing my creations to a slaughter! I'm not going anywhere near your Lab. You haven't been able to locate a few of us and I'm going to do everything in my power to make sure it stays that way."

The Director frowned getting up from his chair. As he snatched up his metal walking stick and limped toward the screens, he spoke. "I expect you and all the remaining Labs here in five 24 hour cycles."

Isadora gave a quick laugh. "They're called days, traitor."

Chris shook his head. "Actually, since the sun never sets or rises, the day never begins or ends so-"

"Are you really thinking about technicalities at a time like this?!

Before Chris could react, the Director spoke. "If any of you or the other Labs, choose to ignore my demand, Lucifer and his men will be sent out to collect you."

Chris scoffed. "Or kill us."

Isadora chimed in right after. "You'll have to find us first!"

The Director smiled tapping the air accessing the green screens. "Nobody is going to be killed. The ADGL samples are useless to me now. Eventually, you'll notice that they're unusable in your creation process as well."

Isadora spoke in a voice full of hesitation. "We... Our Lab... Creations have come to a sudden stop."

The Director held his smile. "And I know why."

The Director accessed Sinah's Helix and displayed it on the Lab screens. "…This is why."

Chris suddenly sat up straight uncrossing his arms. He stared at Sinah Helix in shock and awe. "A double Helix with metamorphic possibilities, is this what the L Helix has become?!"

The Director's smile softened as he looked at Sinah's Helix, himself. "No fellow Scientists, this, this is the Helix of God."

Thirty-One

Denying the Divine

Isadora was instant in her disagreement. "This is some sort of trick! God doesn't exist! He..!"

The Director cut her off. "You can see for yourself that the Helix is different."

Chris' eyes were transfixed on Sinah's Helix. "Your Lab was successful in creating Lucifer you could simply be showing us a variation of his Helix."

Isadora was quick to voice her opinion. "Or this could just be a fake Helix created just to lure us to your Lab."

The Director chuckled tapping the air accessing another green screen. "Such distrust in your fellow Scientist."

Both Chris and Isadora weren't shy about expressing their outrage as many curses poured from their lips. Once the Director displayed Fallen's Helix over the Lab screens, Chris paused in his profanity. "This is the Devil's?"

"That's right."

Isadora quickly shook her head. "Chris, don't be fooled by this nonsense! His Lab didn't create God!"

Chris leaned back in his chair shaking his head. "I don't think so either. God wouldn't allow himself to be created so close to his enemy. He's not stupid."

The Director pointed at Sinah's Helix. "Then what do you call this? A fake? A lie? I wouldn't be wasting my time contacting you in this way if it was."

Isadora hissed. "Yes, you would have! I'm sure you'd use any method you can think of to try and locate our Labs!"

Chris' eyes shifted from Sinah's to Fallen's. "They're similar. But how do we know these are authentic? You could have simply altered Lucifer's Helix enough to appear convincing."

"I wouldn't put it passed him to do such a crooked thing."

The Director suddenly hissed. "Our Lab created God!"

Isadora shrugged. "Where's your proof? A Helix display isn't good enough. I want hard evidence to prove it."

The Director's eyebrows lowered. "You want proof? Check with your temp regulators."

Both Chris and Isadora's expression shifted to confusion. The Director forced a smile through his anger. "Or better yet, go outside."

Chris held his look of confusion. "Go outside?"

Isadora turned her attention off screen and key typing sounds could be heard. "Why? Did you already send your soldiers to-?" Isadora suddenly stopped short.

The Director couldn't help but to genuinely smile. "Notice it?"

Chris quickly questioned. "Isadora?"

Isadora shook her head in disbelief. "Impossible, this can't be true."

"Isadora, what is it?"

Isadora turned her attention back to Sinah's Helix. "Access your Lost Soul's camera, if you have one."

Chris turned his head calling out. "...Camera 91!" After a few moments of staring at another screen, he crossed his arms and leaned back in his chair. After a few more moments, he released an impatient sigh. "Waste land, waste land, waste land. So what else is new? I don't-"

Chris suddenly sat up straight uncrossing his arms. "...Wind?!"

The Director couldn't help but to chuckle. "The world is starting to breathe again."

Chris' eye darted to Sinah's Helix in disbelief. "It... It could just be a coincidence."

Isadora closed her eyes, shaking her head. "We're Scientists we don't believe in such things."

"This can't be true! You can't have created God! He can't have been created in a Lab full of monsters!"

The Director chuckled again. "Whether you believe it or not, God has been created and the world is recovering."

Isadore released a defeated sigh as she slumped in her seat. "He's going to kill us the minute we step into his Lab."

Chris leaned back in his chair again. "But if we ignore him, Lucifer and his men will kill us first."

"I have to believe we won't be found. I have to believe we're safe. He hasn't found us yet, so we can keep hiding!"

The Director leaned more of his weight on his metal walking stick. "Do you really think I don't know where each and every Lab is located?"

"I know you don't or we would have been wiped out a long time ago."

The Director limped back toward his leather bound chair. As he took a seat, he spoke. "Perhaps I just ignored you because you used up too much of the ADGL samples in our early years of creation. There wouldn't be any point in attacking the Labs that have only trickles of what we needed."

Isadora hissed. "My Lab showed the very first signs of a successful Helix creation."

The Director placed his metal walking stick on his large desk. "And my Lab created both Lucifer and God. Now let's stop dwelling in the past shall we?"

Chris slowly shook his head. "This can't be possible. God can't have been created in your Lab."

The Director tented his fingers. "You'll be able to see God with your own eyes in five 24 hour cycles. I expect you to send word along."

Chris hesitantly gave the slightest nod. "..Fine, I'll be there."

Isadora shook her head in disbelief. "…But Chris-!"

"If I'm killed at least my Lab will keep moving forward. If I don't show up, Lucifer will kill everyone. We don't have any choice but to deal with this son of a bitch head on"

Isadora hissed as loud as she could into the screen. "I hate you Walter!! I hope one of your creations rips out your eyes!!"

Once both Lab screens went blank, the Director chuckled under his breath. "It was so nice seeing them again."

Thirty-Two

Following Protocol

The second the wall of screens returned to behind the bookshelves and the Director went back to work, Dante stepped into action. "Alex, I need you to only focus on collecting building Seven's schematics. Murdoch, I need you to get over to the Commander and let him know the situation."

Murdoch wasn't hesitant to respond. "Understood."

Dante sat back down and clicked on his laptop keys as fast as his fingers could move. "We have less than five days to get Sinah and the Commander out of there, we need to hurry up!"

Alex quickly nodded as he went to work. "I'll get you those schematics for you in no time."

Dante gave a confident nod. "We won't fail them!"

Murdoch raced passed many soldiers, Helix soldiers, Helixes and civilians as fast as he could toward building Seven's lone passage. As he raced toward the security booth, the Helix soldier's eyes darted toward him. Without hesitation, every one of them gripped their weapons preparing to shoot.

Before Murdoch could simply pass through the scanner, two out of the four D Helix soldiers stepped in his way. One of the two spoke, while the other aimed his machine gun at Murdoch's chest. "There is a certain protocol you already know about when entering building Sev-"

Murdoch cut him off by snatching his arm. This sudden action made all the other Helix soldiers shift their weapons target point to Murdoch's head. The D Helix soldier Murdoch had grabbed, frowned looking up at him. His frown instantly vanished, seeing Murdoch's fully black demonic eyes.

Before Murdoch could say anything, the D Helix soldier whispered. "He's in danger, isn't he?"

Murdoch, who was taken back by such a question, asked one in return. "Do you feel it?"

The D Helix soldier stared at Murdoch for a few moments before he hesitantly responded. "It… It doesn't matter what I feel, I have my orders and I must follow them. There is a protocol that must be followed when entering building Seven."

Murdoch scoffed releasing his arm. "Coward D Helix, your loyalty lies with the wrong person."

The D Helix soldier turned his head with a slightly upset look on his face. Murdoch stepped in the scanner. As it scanned him, one of the A Helix soldiers tapped the air accessing the green screens. "I don't see any request forms that requires you to be here."

Murdoch frowned as much as he could. "Nobody will stop me from seeing my Lord."

The A Helix soldier shook his head. "Without the proper request forms, entrance into this building is restricted."

Before Murdoch could hiss, the D Helix he had grabbed spoke. "He doesn't need a request."

The A Helix soldier frowned. "Yes he does. Protocol says..."

"The two he escorted here this morning are still in the building. His request order will remain active until they leave with him."

The A Helix soldier's frown faded. "You're right. Please fill out the necessary paperwork for passage."

As Murdoch impatiently thrusted his hand forward for the clip board, the D Helix soldier gave an upward nod down the hallway. "Go."

Murdoch's eyes darted up to the D Helix soldier as he gave another upward nod. Murdoch placed his hand on the D Helix soldier's shoulder and gave it a quick squeeze. As he bolted down the hallway, the D Helix soldier looked at the other three D Helix soldiers. All of them were staring back at him. Once eye contact was made, all four of them shifted then sharpened their eyes toward the two A Helix soldiers.

Thirty-Three

A Blood Trade

Emma's eyes darted to Murdoch as he busted into the operating room. "Murdoch, I was just about to contact you. The Harmond's need to be-"

Murdoch cut Emma off as he approached the electronically locked door. "I need to see the Commander."

Before Emma could agree or disagree, Murdoch hissed. "Now!"

Nash glanced back at Emma for approval. Simply staring at Murdoch for a few moments, she said. "I want a blood sample."

Murdoch instantly began to frown. "If I didn't give one to that sadistic prick, what makes you think I'll give one to you?"

Emma smiled slightly. "I'm the only one that can grant you permission to you see your Commander."

Murdoch frowned even more. "You will let me see him."

Emma watched as the whites in Murdoch's eyes were consumed by the black. Nash, who had watched it as well, shifted further away from him. "What the hell?!"

Emma nodded approaching Murdoch. "You have no idea how right you are Nash."

Murdoch frowned as much as he could at Emma. "Nobody will stand in my way to see my Lord."

"I don't have any intention to. I just want to know how far your Helix has developed."

Murdoch's eyes sharpened. "I won't become an experiment, Emma. I won't become like Bridger."

Emma whispered glancing toward the two Helix soldiers by the exit. "It won't be reported, just like I didn't report them. I hate to admit it but Revin had a good idea about checking the Helix status. Both God and Perfect Experiment A's double Helix are developing. It would make sense that the A and D Helixes would be as well."

As Murdoch glanced toward the Helix soldier's himself, Emma took his wrist to check his pulse. "I'm thinking yours is developed much faster than theirs."

After a quick blink, Murdoch's eyes returned to normal. "Don't stand in my way Emma."

Emma smiled letting him go. "Your heart rate didn't change when you got your anger under control. Does it increase like it does for humans when you get angry?"

Murdoch's expression shifted to confusion as he shrugged. "It's just normal."

Emma glanced toward Nash. "If you want unlimited access to your Commander, I want a blood sample."

Murdoch's lips touched at a frown. "A permanent request needs to be put in at the building access point."

"Of course, as long as the building isn't on shut down mode then..."

"No."

Emma's eyes darted to Murdoch with a slightly annoyed expression. "This is a good trade Murdoch. Any other Lead ADGL Tech would just have you taken to the experimental cells."

"I want an entrance request without restrictions. Whether the building is on shut down mode or not, I want to be able to talk to the Commander."

Emma stared back at Murdoch for a few moments, really contemplating the trade. "Do you promise you'll only enter this building to see Perfect Experiment A?"

"No."

Emma's expression shifted to confusion. "What could you possibly want to see on the other floors? You'll get yourself killed wandering around."

"I know but I'll do what I have to do when I have to do it."

Emma's confusion increased. "And what is it that you have to do?"

Murdoch merely shrugged.

Emma closed her eyes and released a defeated sigh. "Alright, fine, deal."

As Murdoch turned toward the electronically locked door, Emma spoke again. "There's a lot more dangers in this building then you think Murdoch. Getting yourself killed is the easiest thing you can accomplish here."

Murdoch couldn't help but to scoff. "Oh yeah? Then how come the experiments haven't been able to save themselves and get mercy killed?"

Before Emma could answer, Murdoch spoke again. "You'll get your sample after I talk to my Lord."

Emma barely nodded as she motioned her hand toward Nash.

Thirty-Four

Suspicions Confirmed

Murdoch raced to Fallen's side in a panic. "It's exactly as you thought Commander, the Director intends to have Sinah kill you. He claims it's in her nature to want to destroy evil."

As Fallen softly caressed Sinah's hand with his thumb, he sighed. "So my counterpart is to be my executioner."

Murdoch continued with his report. "The Director contacted the remaining Labs and invited all of them here. He has-"

"Probably to not only view upon God in all her majesty, but also brag that she's in our facility."

Murdoch stepped into his soldier waiting a command stance. "The Director said if they don't show, he'll order you and your team to collect them."

Fallen couldn't help but to chuckle a little under his breath. "Leaving Sinah defenseless against their experimentations, he's foolish to think I would just abandon her. His pathetic attempt to separate us was unsuccessful and commanding me won't be either."

Murdoch looked toward Sinah's face. Despite the weak yet steady heartbeat and lack of any signs of improvement, her features were very calm and serene. "Commander, what if Sinah..? What if she really is..?"

Fallen turned his head toward Murdoch. "If Sinah chooses to obey the Director then I won't stand in the way of her choice."

Murdoch shook his head in disbelief. "God or not, I won't let her kill you!"

Fallen released a chuckle. "I won't allow her kill me either." His amusement vanished as he continued. "But I won't directly attack her either. Enemy or not, my counterpart means more to me than even I ever thought possible."

Murdoch closed his eyes. "Then we have to keep believing she isn't your enemy."

Fallen turned his attention toward the ceiling. "Faith isn't something I'm familiar with. We need to wait until Simah recovers before we'll know the truth."

"Yes Commander."

As the room filled with silence, Fallen looked toward Murdoch out of the corner of his eye. "...Anything else, Murdoch?"

"The other Lab Director's and their creations are due to be here in five days."

Fallen's eyes sharpened a little. Glints of the crimson red around his pupil could easily be seen. "That doesn't leave us much time. How is Dante's progress?"

Murdoch glanced up at the glass window leading into the operating room. All the ADGL Techs looked like they were getting ready to call it a night. "His A Helix has improved. Just like Bridger's, it was painful."

Fallen's eyebrows furrowed sympathetically looking down at Sinah. "The way they are changing probably wasn't in Sinah's plans. I'm sure she would have eased them into their development. I tend to wonder if the other A Helixes are showing any signs of change or is it just those on our team."

"Those close to her."

"If Sinah is unaware that she's awakening the true capabilities of their Helixes, she could be subconsciously trying to strength our team. She could be trying to protect the weakest link without even realizing it."

Murdoch's eyes darted to Sinah's forehead as a few golden veins began to form. Just like the rest of her veins, they appeared like elegant filigree. Symmetrical swirls began to appear on either side of her forehead and stopped just before reaching center point. It now looked like Sinah wore an elegant crown.

Fallen's lips touched at a smile at her newest change. "My counterpart may currently be our weakest link but not for very much longer."

Murdoch barely nodded. "Dante is working as fast as he can to locate any and all hidden cameras, Helix soldiers and whatever other dangers we need to be worried about."

"Keep me posted."

"Yes Commander."

Fallen's eyes darted to Murdoch hearing him pick up something from the table of operating tools. Once he saw that Murdoch was drawing a small amount of blood into a syringe, he questioned. "Murdoch?"

Murdoch removed the needle. "It's my payment to have constant access to this building even during shut down mode."

Fallen's eyebrows lowered slightly. "Don't become an experiment Murdoch. If you do, you're as good as dead to me. I didn't begin the awakening of your D Helix capabilities for those damn Lab Techs. Even if you have to lose your life in the struggle, don't you dare allow yourself to get captured, understand?"

Murdoch gave a confident nod. "If they try, I'll end as many lives as I can before my death my Lord. I promise you that."

"Good. Keep me posted."

Murdoch quickly nodded. "Yes Commander."

Thirty-Five

Turn of Tide

Murdoch handed Emma the syringe with his blood in it. "Is that enough?"

Emma looked at the small amount with a smile. "That's plenty. I knew you wouldn't back out on our deal."

Murdoch gave only the slightest nod.

Emma looked toward the exhausted looking Harmonds. "I need you escort them home."

Violet instantly began to protest. "No! I'm not going anywhere! I want to be here when she wakes up!"

Amos took his wife's hand. "I'm tired, you're tired, I think it's time we head home and get some rest. I'm sure we'll be allowed to come back as soon as the buildings are off of the shutdown mode."

Emma nodded in agreement. "Of course you are. Murdoch will escort you here just like he did today."

Violet looked toward Sinah through the window. "But... But..."

"Don't worry. I have work I have to do on the higher floors and will be in the building all night. The night shift will inform me directly if there are any changes in her status. The minute I know something, I'll contact you."

"But..."

Amos softly ran his hand against his wife's arm. "We need some rest

Violet. She's in good..." Amos paused for an awkward chuckle. "..She's safe."

Violet barely nodded before she hesitantly walked toward the exit. As she passed by Emma, she whispered. "Do you promise to call us if anything changes?"

Emma nodded with a smile. "I promise. You don't need to worry."

Violet barely nodded again. "Okay."

Emma glanced toward Murdoch. "Make sure they get back to Residential safely."

Murdoch gave a sight nod leading them toward the exit. "Understood."

As they walked toward the security booth leading them out of building Seven, sudden sounds of machine gun fire could be heard. Without hesitation, Murdoch snatched Violet and Amos' arms and pulled them out of that hallway into another.

Amos' eyes darted up to Murdoch. "Was that gunfire?!"

Murdoch cautiously peeked around the corner trying to see the security booth. "Yeah, now shut it."

Both Amos and Violet went flush. Despite hearing a few more shots, Amos forced a smile gripping Violet's hand. "It's okay. It's okay. Everything will be okay."

Violet, who looked terrified and confused, only stared back at him wide eyed.

Murdoch's eyebrows lowered. "Is someone trying to escape building Seven?"

Before that question even had a chance to be considered, a male voice spoke from behind them. "Wandering building Seven is…"

Before he could finish his sentence, Murdoch turned and hooked the Harmond's protectively behind himself. The person who had spoken was another D Helix soldier. Despite being unarmed, Murdoch's entire disposition looked prepared to fight and dominate the battle. "There was gunfire at the entrance point."

The D soldier gave a slight nod. "…I know."

Murdoch's expression shifted to slight confusion. "You know?"

"Yeah, now building Seven is reaching the shutdown mode, so I highly suggest you..."

"I'm not leading them directly into danger! That wasn't my order!"

The D Helix soldier shook his head. "They're not in danger and you, Sir, you're definitely are not in any danger."

Murdoch's expression remained confused as he studied the D Helix soldier's features. He looked very calm and collected. His dark eyes didn't show any signs of distress or anger. Murdoch's eyes shifted to his machine gun which he held against his chest. The barrel of the weapon was producing a very small amount of smoke suggesting it had been fired very recently. Murdoch's eyes slowly shifted beyond the D Helix soldier. Upon the floor in a pool of blood, was a dead A Helix soldier. Despite being covered in bullet holes, the one through her forehead looked like it was the kill shot. Her expression was a combination of shock and confusion.

Murdoch slowly began to back up. As he did, he put his hand behind himself encouraging the Harmonds to do the same. "We're leaving."

The D Helix soldier gave a slight nod. "Try not to wander again. There are many dangers in building Seven. You'll end up getting yourself killed."

Murdoch barely nodded keeping his eyes locked on the D Helix soldier. The second they were on the one path leading them toward the security booth, Murdoch spoke. "Keep up."

Before either Amos or Violet could respond, Murdoch bolted down the hallway. Even though they gave chase as fast and they could, Murdoch easily put them in his dust. Every few seconds he would stop short, cautiously glance around then mutter. "Clear."

As Murdoch reached the security booth, his eyes darted to the Helix soldiers. Only three of them were still breathing. Both A Helixes had been killed in the booth in front of the green screens. Bullet holes had hit every unprotected point on their bodies. Blood was splattered and sprayed in a chaotic mess. It appeared more like a frenzied attack rather than a strategic kill.

Murdoch glanced toward the three D Helix soldiers. They were standing over their fallen fellow D Helix soldier. It looked like at any moment, they were going to start crying. Once Amos and Violet finally caught up with Murdoch, he gave a slight nod. Keeping his eyes locked on the D Helix soldiers, he waved his hand toward the exit. Without hesitation, Amos and Violet raced through the scanner then quickly continued on their way out of building Seven.

Murdoch didn't' shift his stare as he passed through the scanner himself. Once he took a few steps toward the exit, one of the three D Helix soldiers spoke. "You've been granted access to building Seven at any point even during shut down mode. You won't have any more trouble coming and going."

Murdoch only gave the slightest nod before he raced down the hall and out of the building.

Murdoch clenched his fists fully expecting to be greeted by bloodshed as he raced into the corridor. Not seeing anything amiss, his expression shifted to confusion. Both A and D Helix, soldier or not were acting normally around one another. They socialized and went about their business completely unaware of what had just occurred.

Murdoch looked toward the equally confused Harmonds before he frowned and pressed earpiece. "Dante, What the hell's going on?!"

Thirty-Six

Shock

Dante didn't shift his attention from working on his laptop. "Did you tell the Commander? What does he-?"

Murdoch cut Dante off. "Have you been recording anything from building Seven?"

Dante pressed a few keys accessing the view from the stationary camera showing the security booth. Before Dante could even glance at it on the large screen, Alex gasped. Dante's eyes darted to him then the screen. The second he saw the massacre, Dante lost all color in his face. His eyes widened as his mouth dropped. "Wha..? What..?"

"I'm heading over to Residential. Once the Harmonds have been returned to their home safely, I'll be heading over to yours."

Dante only stared traumatized at the carnage of building Seven.

"Are there any other attacks I need to be aware of or is it just isolated to building Seven?"

Dante didn't move or respond his eyes were transfixed on the aftermath.

"…Dante?"

Dante still didn't respond.

"Dante!"

Alex clicked on a few of his laptop keys then awkwardly responded. "Um... Murdoch, can you hear me?"

"Where's Dante?"

Alex began to check all the surveillance videos in the facility. "He… Uh…"

Alex glanced toward Dante in sympathy for a few moments before he went back to work. "He's temporarily unavailable. I've checked the facility surveillance and everything seems to be running normally."

"Alright, contact me if you notice any changes and Dante, FOCUS!"

As if being slapped across the face, Dante suddenly turned his head back toward his laptop. "O... Okay."

Alex flipped from one camera feed to another. "I'm going to keep one step ahead of you Murdoch, just in case."

Dante licked his drying lips. "I'm going to check on building Seven's spider."

Alex's eyes darted up to Dante. "But..!"

Dante swallowed heavily. "I need to know what happened. Access the replay from the stationary camera for about… Hm. I guess about twenty minutes ago."

Alex's features weakened a little. "Dante, are you sure you want to see this?"

Dante hesitantly nodded. "I need to be strong for the Commander's team. I have to know what happened."

Alex barely nodded. "Yeah but shouldn't we wait for Murdoch?"

Dante shook his head clicking on the keys of his laptop accessing the spider in building Seven. "I'm the Data, Information and Surveillance soldier on our team. It's my responsibility to keep on top of any and all information."

Alex nodded with a weak smile. "…Alright."

Dante began to tap his finger impatiently against the kitchen table. A sigh matching his impatience escaped his lips waiting for the spider's surveillance to upload. The minute it did, Dante displayed it on the large screen.

Most images were of empty hallways and hidden camera locations, while others were horrific scenes of absolute brutality. Blood and bullet holes were randomly scattered in a frenzied chaotic manner. In most cases it was the D Helix soldier that was the victor. Any surviving A Helix soldier looked beyond confused and a tad scared. They had their weapons gripped so tightly, their knuckles had gone white. Despite the battle they had just endured, none of the A Helixes moved from their designated locations. The D Helix soldiers on the other hand, were cautiously moving around. It was as if they were looking for something.

"They're hunting." Dante whispered watching them. "They're hunting the A Helixes. What happened? Did their Helixes just snap?"

Alex glanced up from his laptop. "The surveillance is ready Dante."

Dante took in a large amount of oxygen and got to his feet. As he approached the back of the couch, he clenched his fists. After he loudly released his breath, he spoke in a tone brimming with assurance. "Put it up on the screen."

Thirty-Seven

The Slaughter

Nothing seemed out of the ordinary with the six Helix soldiers. All stood diligently at their posts guarding the passage into building Seven. Dante's eyes quickly and repeatedly studied each any every Helix soldier looking for any sign of a sudden abnormality. All looked completely focused on their orders.

Alex glanced at the surveillance cameras ahead of Murdoch and the Harmonds, everything still looked normal. As he looked back at the large screen, Dante gasped.

Dante's eyes locked onto one of the D Helix soldiers as his hand slowly unclenched then found its way onto his chest over his heart. His expression shifted to sight confusion as he hesitantly whispered. "…I …I can feel it. My fellow A Helix brethren are in danger."

Suddenly one of the A Helix soldiers lifted his head. It was as if he had felt it too. His eyes slowly shifted to the D Helix soldier Dante was staring at. Suddenly all three D Helix soldiers turned their heads toward the A Helix soldier in unison. It was as if all of them were hearing a silent command from within. The minute the second A Helix soldier followed suit, the gunfire began.

Dante's feature weakened watching his fellow Helixes that once lived contently with one another, suddenly turn on each other like they had become savage. Dante's eyes couldn't help but to fill with tears watching the madness unfold.

Each Helix soldier being proficient in combat held their own against the other. It was a stray bullet from one of the A Helix soldiers that went clean through the eye of one of the D Helix soldiers that made him fall. The second he went down, the other A Helix soldier focused all of his gunfire only on the fallen. It was as if he was ensuring his death. Watching their fellow D Helix soldier die, something suddenly clicked in the D Helix soldiers. Their entire dispositions shifted to calm and collected. All of their wild frenzied attacks became focused and completely accurate. The A Helix soldiers were killed in a matter of seconds.

Dante suddenly turned his head as a few tear escaped his eyes. Before Alex could say anything, there was a knock at the front door. Alex turned his attention toward it and called out. "That should be Murdoch. Come in!"

The instant Murdoch stepped inside, his eyes darted to the large screen. The three D Helix soldiers were standing over their fallen fellow Helix. Murdoch looked toward Alex and motioned his head toward the large screen. "Is this what's happening now?"

Alex shook his head. "No, we just watched what happened."

Murdoch turned his attention to Dante. "Was it a Helix snap?"

Dante shook his head as his voice trembled a little. "N... No, this.. This wasn't a snap. All knew exactly what they... They..." Dante slapped his tear off of his face not wanting to show any signs of weakness. "They knew exactly what they were doing."

Murdoch stepped beside Dante and placed his hand momentarily on his shoulder. "Was there any warning signs or anything?"

Dante crossed his arms but refused to turn his head toward either Murdoch or Alex. "I felt that the A Helix soldiers were in danger. Then they showed signs that they felt it too. Then the D Helix soldiers showed signs and-"

"What are they doing now?"

Dante closed his eyes. "Alex, go back to the 'real time' surveillance feed."

"I'm on it."

Once the normal feed was back on the large screen, the three remaining D Helix soldiers appeared. They looked very busy calmly cleaning up the mess. Their expressions suggested they were simply cleaning up an everyday spill as opposed to a slaughter.

Before Murdoch had a chance to comment, Dante spoke. "Murdoch, let's head over to building Seven."

Both Murdoch and Alex's eyes darted toward him. Dante locked his eyes with Murdoch's as he lowered his eyebrows. "There won't be a better opportunity than this to free Sinah and the Commander."

Alex quickly shook his head in a panic. "But you just saw what happened to the A Helix soldiers Dante! You're putting yourself in danger!"

Dante kept his eyes locked with Murdoch's. "And if I can successfully make it into building Seven, I can access information there and send it here. We'll be able to tamper with the surveillance timelines to show that the Commander and Sinah just vanished. The ADGL Lab Techs watching the surveillance will think that during the Helix soldier massacre, they managed to escape. The might even think that during the commotion, they did it to save themselves."

Alex shook his head in disbelief. "B… But you could be killed before you even make it into the building!"

"I know the risk."

Murdoch stared at the glowing white ring around Dante's pupil. "Are you sure about this?"

Dante gave a confident nod. "I am."

"Then let's head over to the shooting range for some Combat equipment. It will automatically be deactivated when we step into building Seven but it should at least get us beyond the security booth."

As Murdoch and Dante walked toward the front door, Alex spoke. "Be careful you two and good luck."

Dante glanced back at him with a smile. "We're members of the Commander's team, failure isn't an option. Keep track of us as far as you can then wait for the information I send."

Alex barely nodded. "Okay."

Dante turned his attention back to Murdoch. "Let's go."

Thirty-Eight

In the Artificial Night

Fallen, who was staring blankly up at the ceiling, softly began to run his thumb across Sinah's knuckles. Before he could release a contented sigh, listening to her rhythmic weak heart beeps, they suddenly shifted to rapid.

Before Fallen could react, Sinah's body began to twitch and shake. All of her movements seemed like minor muscle spasms. Fallen's eyes darted down to Sinah as he gripped her tightly. "Calm down Sinah, I'm here."

Sinah's body and heart rate didn't change nor did it show any signs it intended to. Even her face began to twitch.

Fallen's attention shifted through the glass window at the lone sleeping ADGL Lab Tech as the emergency alarm went off. After a few moments of the blaring sound flooding the rooms, the ADGL Tech suddenly jerked awake. At first, he looked disorientated and seemed like he didn't know where he was. Once he regained his composure, he began to tap on the terminal to find out what was going on.

Fallen's eyebrows furrowed in confusion as the two A Helix soldiers guarding the room quickly yet silently moved up behind him. Once the ADGL Tech released the electronic lock, one of the two A Helix soldiers slammed the butt of his machine gun against the side of his head, knocking him out. Neither of the two A Helix soldiers reacted as the ADGL Tech slid off the chair and flopped to the floor.

Fallen's expression didn't change as the two A Helix soldiers moved toward the operating room doorway. The closer they got, the more aggressive Sinah's body began to twitch and shake. It was almost as if she was trying to struggle free from Fallen's grip.

Fallen lifted his head a little to look down at the two A Helix soldiers. Both had their weapons drawn and locked on his head for a kill shot. Fallen's eyebrows lowered as he frowned. "What the hell do you two think you're doing?"

One of the two A Helix soldiers hissed. "Get away from her!"

Fallen's frown increased as much as it could. "And if I refuse."

The second A Helix soldier snapped back. "You were told to get away from her!"

Fallen gripped the aggressively struggling Sinah the best he could. "Nothing will tear me away from my counterpart! Especially not some low level A Helixes."

"We will shoot you L Helix!"

Fallen growled, his severely angered tone made sweat beads form on both of the Helix soldier's foreheads. "I am the Commander! You will address me as such! Now get the hell out of here!"

Despite the suffocating waves of intimidation thrashing against the A Helix soldiers, neither moved nor did they lower their weapons. The first of the two spoke again, this time his tone was noticeably less confident. "W... We only obey the G Helix."

The second tried his best to resist his body's overwhelming desire to tremble in fear. "We need to protect her! You need to get away from her or be killed!"

A smirk touched at Fallen's lips. "And you think your pathetic little bullets will end my life?"

Suddenly both Helix soldiers snatched hold of their nerves and confidently gripped their guns. The first hissed. "We will kill you!"

The second A Helix soldier followed after. "Get away from the G Helix! She, herself doesn't want you near her! She's obviously trying to escape you!"

Fallen glanced down at Sinah, she was still struggling in his grip. Her resistance had become so extreme, she begun to dig her nails deep into his collarbone. The expression on her face just screamed anger.

Noticing her expression, the first A Helix soldier spoke. “You know it’s true L Helix you can probably feel it yourself. She shouldn’t be anywhere near you!”

Fallen’s expression shifted to hostile. “I am the Commander! I won’t tell you again!”

The second A Helix soldier hissed. “Get away from her!”

Fallen’s tone of voice suddenly became very calm yet had noticeable hints of anger in it. “No, nothing and nobody will-”

Fallen was cut off by the clicking sounds of machine guns.

Thirty-Nine

Of One Mind

A barrage of bullets shot toward the A Helix soldiers from outside the operating room. Without hesitation, they turned their attentions and began to shoot back. Fallen's eyes darted through the glass window before he protectively covered his and Sinah's head with his arms. Three D Helix soldiers had entered the room and opened fire.

Neither A nor D Helix soldier said or yelled anything. All of them just kept their focus on killing the other. Suddenly one of the D Helix soldiers tossed his weapon aside and raced toward one of the A Helix soldiers. He managed to avoid each and every bullet as he leapt onto him, knocking them both to the floor.

The A Helix soldier didn't react as the D Helix soldier savagely bit into his jugular. Nor did he react as blood sprayed across his focused features. The A Helix soldier merely reached toward the side of his army attire to retrieve his standard issue military army knife. Once he got a good grip on it, he slammed it into the side of the D Helix soldier's head easily piercing through his skull into his brain. The D Helix soldier tossed his head back and released an ear piercing screech.

Fallen's expression shifted to a confused concern as Sinah's movements became so aggressive she began to rattle the operating table itself. Lifting his arm slightly so he could see what was happening, Fallen began to watch the battling Helix soldiers.

The second the D Helix soldier stopped screeching and breathing, Fallen felt a sudden sharp pain in his chest. His eyebrows furrowed until he heard a weak whimper from Sinah. Fallen shifted himself away from her a little to see her face. Even though she was still unconscious, a few tears had escaped her closed eyes. Despite her upset disposition, she hadn't stopped struggling. Fallen turned his attention back to the Helix soldiers.

The A Helix on the floor had stopped breathing and the other had lost his life by lowering his guard. In that split second that he had glanced down at his fellow fallen A Helix, the D Helixes calmly unloaded bullet after bullet into him.

As they stepped into the operating room, they focused their shots on the A Helix soldier with the ripped open jugular ensuring his death. Once they were satisfied both were dead, they turned their attentions to their fellow fallen D Helix soldier. Both of their expressions weakened almost to the point of tears.

Fallen's features weakened a little as he looked back at Sinah. "We felt their deaths."

Sinah only continued to struggle in his arms. Fallen's demeanor shifted back to angry as he hissed toward the D Helix soldiers. "What in the hell is going on?!"

Both D Helix soldiers turned their attention to Sinah and Fallen. As they raised their weapons and pointed them at Sinah, one of the two calmly spoke. "Please move away from the G Helix. We need to end her life while she's in this weakened state."

The second of the two nodded in agreement. "We don't want to accidently hit you L Helix."

Fallen instantly snarled. "I am the Commander!"

The first gave an indifferent shrug. "If that's what you want prefer to be addressed as L Helix then…"

"That's not what I prefer! That's what I am! Now get the hell out of here!"

The second released a slightly exhaustive sigh. "No disrespect L He... Commander, but she needs to be dealt with. Most of the A Helix soldiers are dead. Don't worry, we will find and kill the remaining few soon enough. Now the G Helix needs to die as well."

Fallen continued to try and hold the resisting Sinah. "Do you really think I'm going to let anyone harm my counterpart?"

The first one mirrored the seconds sigh with one filled with frustration. "Your mind has been clouded by the human who runs this facility. Our minds are clear Commander. We'll handle things until you're ready to lead us."

Fallen's lips were instantly consumed by a full frown. "Whether I'm ready or not, killing off the A Helixes or my counterpart wasn't something I ever would have wanted."

The second D Helix soldier's lips touched at a frown in return. "If the G Helix wasn't in the shape she is in now, the A Helixes would have killed us all. Without her strength to fuel them, they are at a disadvantage. They are confused and hesitant. We have the upper hand, now is the time to-"

"I will not allow this execution to continue! Lower your weapons and stand down!"

The first D Helix soldier shook his head. "Sorry Commander but we need to end them while we can."

The first glanced at the second. "Try not to hit the Commander."

Fallen's angered disposition suddenly shifted to calm. His tone of voice mirrored his demeanor as he opened and lifted his hand toward the ceiling. "I promised my counterpart safety…"

Fallen suddenly snapped his hand shut. Both D Helixes gasped as they were forced to drop their weapons and fall to their knees. It was as if an invisible force had pulled them downward to the floor.

Fallen turned his fist toward them as he finished his sentence. "..And safety is what she will have."

Fallen suddenly opened his hand. Two silver blades with red spots shot from the 'Hole' in his palm into the D Helix soldier's forehead. Before either had a chance to respond, their heads exploded in a bloody mess.

The second both of their headless bodies flopped to the ground, Sinah instantly stopped struggling. Fallen turned his attention back to her as he lowered his hand. Sinah's features had returned to normal and her heart rate returned to its weak yet steady beat.

Fallen closed his eyes pulling her closer to himself. "Even unconscious your body was trying to protect us from danger. Sinah, let me protect us, you need to focus on healing."

Fallen didn't react as the alarm for the contaminated field began to blare.

Forty

Into Madness

Murdoch frowned shaking his Combat gloved hands. The rectangular microchip on the top that connected mind to Combat equipment kept flickering on and off. "What the hell is wrong with these stupid things?!"

Dante looked at his own gloves. They were doing the exact same thing only his took a much longer amount of time to shut off. "I think because we've changed, the Combat gloves are having a hard time connecting to our minds."

Murdoch pointed toward the lone corridor leading into building Seven. "Then how the hell am I supposed to get you into the building safely." Murdoch withdrew his gun as he continued. "This is pretty much useless without bullets."

"I guess we'll have to bluff our way through."

Murdoch's eyes darted to Dante. "What happens if they just open fire when they see you Dante? You might be able to get a few defensive rounds off with your gun but you're far from an expert in combat."

Dante awkwardly chuckled. "No, I probably won't come even close to hitting anyone. But what choice do we have? We have to get to the Commander and Sinah."

Murdoch released a frustrated sound. "I'm responsible for your safety. This is too dangerous of a risk."

Dante confidently removed his gun from its holster. "My safety is nothing compared to theirs."

After a short defeated sigh, Murdoch spoke. "Alright, let's go. Stay as close to me as possible Dante."

Dante gave a quick nod. "Okay."

The second the two of them cleared the passage and approached the security booth the D Helixes soldier's eyes collectively darted to Dante. As if sensing the danger, Dante's free hand snatched the back of Murdoch's Combat suit and whispered. "They intend to attack."

Murdoch locked his eyes on the D Helix soldiers as he spoke. "We're both going through."

As the D Helix soldiers all gripped their machine guns and tried to take aim at Dante, one of the three spoke. "You're the only one with unrestricted access into building Seven."

The second glared at Dante as he nodded. "That A Helix needs to be dealt with. Please move aside so we can handle him."

Murdoch pointed his gun at the D Helix soldiers. "If we have to enter by force then so be it."

The third D Helix soldier shook his head with a slight frown. "If you would just step aside and let us handle him then you will be free to go."

Murdoch growled gripping his gun. "We're both going into building Seven!"

The third shook his head again. "He doesn't have clearance and needs to die. Move aside and let us deal with the A Helix."

Murdoch's eyebrows lowered and the white in his eyes were consumed by the black. "We'll be going in together!"

Dante's eyes darted up to Murdoch then the D Helix soldiers. All of their expression appeared suddenly confused. They went from being prepared to kill Dante, to long amounts of hesitation. Dante gave a slight nod before he whispered again. "It's your Helix level."

Murdoch didn't glanced back as he questioned. "What?"

"You're the higher ranking soldier to them. You're the closest to the Commander, the L Helix, which means you outrank them and can give orders."

"Are you sure about this?"

Dante couldn't help but to release a weak chuckle. "Not in the slightest.

But if I remember the ancient text correctly, Lucifer ran things in a military way. I, of course could be way off on my theory though."

"Well, let's hope you're right." Murdoch's tone of voice suddenly shifted to authoritative. "Drop your weapons!"

None of the D Helixes soldiers obeyed, they merely held their looks of confusion.

Murdoch hissed. "That's an order D Helix soldiers! Drop your weapons!"

The D Helix soldiers hesitantly placed their weapons on the floor in front of themselves.

Murdoch kept Dante behind him as he moved toward the security booth. As they entered the scanner, it made a sound of disapproval from all the Combat equipment. As if in an automatic response, the D Helix soldiers reached down for their machine guns. Seeing this, Murdoch hissed again. "Are you trying to disobey an order given by a higher ranking soldier?!"

All of the D Helix soldiers stopped reaching for their weapons and meekly responded with a "No Sir, sorry Sir."

The second they were clear from the security booth, Murdoch glanced back at Dante then bolted down the hallway. "What the hell made you think it was my Helix rank?"

Dante, who could barely keep up with Murdoch's speed, responded. "I felt it! At first I felt the danger from them but then the strength of your D Helix drowned that feeling out. It sounds weird I know but..." Dante shrugged. "I don't know. It's hard to explain."

Murdoch cautiously glanced around for any signs of danger. "Can't you move any faster Dante?"

Dante panted out of breath. "I... I'm running as fast as I can!"

Murdoch suddenly stopped short. Not expecting it, Dante slammed into him. Turning quick to Dante, Murdoch's lips touched at a frown. "I guess Bridger really did know what he was doing about this."

Before Dante could question, Murdoch tossed him over his shoulder. "Hey! Put me down goddamn it! I'm not some-"

Murdoch cut Dante off as he raced down the hallway. "Shut it."

Dante went flush before he released a defeated sigh then went limp.

Forty-One

Influence

Busting into the operating room, Murdoch and Dante's ears were greeted by the blaring alarms. Once Murdoch placed him on the floor, Dante raced over to the terminal to shut the emergency and sterilization alarms off. Murdoch on the other hand, raced toward the operating room.

Murdoch stopped in his tracks seeing the dead Helixes in the doorway. A sudden wave of panic washed over him as he called out. "Commander, are you alright?!"

Fallen released a slightly irritated sigh. "There seems to be some discord amongst the Helixes. They've begun to turn on one another."

Murdoch barely nodded stepping over their bodies and approaching the operating table. "I never thought they would have come in here."

Fallen looked through the glass window toward Dante. He was frantically working on the terminal. "I wasn't expecting the danger I was feeling to be from the other Helixes. With Sinah in the condition she's in and my strength increasing, the balance between A and D Helix is off. It's causing the Helixes to frenzy. Without both of us, they can't seem to adapt."

"That's why we're here to break you both out Commander."

"How is his Helix adapting?"

Murdoch looked toward the busy Dante. "He feels the danger from the other Helixes but it hasn't taken him over like it did with the others."

Fallen gave a slight nod before he called out. "...Dante!"

Dante's eyes darted toward the window. Murdoch gave a quick 'come here' motion with his hand. Dante quickly approached the doorway but paused for a split second looking at the bodies. As he nervously stepped over them into the operating room, he spoke. "Yes Commander?"

"How much time do we have before the buildings are off of shut down mode?"

Dante, who was looking at Sinah with a weakened expression, answered. "Not long Commander. That's why I'm working as fast as I can. Luckily for us the emergency alarm was isolated only to the operating Lab and not to the rest of the building. Nobody knows what happened in here."

Fallen gently moved Sinah away from himself then sat up. As he hooked his legs over the table edge and stood up, he nodded. "Then there's no time like the present to escape."

Dante's eyes didn't shift from Sinah. Fallen, who noticed, questioned. "Dante?"

Dante's eyes darted up to Fallen as he quickly nodded. "Oh! Um... Yes Commander."

Before Dante could leave the room, Fallen questioned again. "What is it Dante?"

Dante looked back toward Sinah as his features weakened. "I keep thinking about when Bridger and I found her, how horrible she looked. I'm nervous that she won't ever recover. I'm feeling worried and a little scared. I know my mission but I feel somewhat lost and... and in danger."

Fallen turned his attention to Murdoch. "Perhaps that's what all the A Helixes are feeling. Though Sinah is recovering, her Helix isn't producing the strength needed to comfort her A Helixes."

Dante swallowed heavily. "Will... Will she be alright Commander?"

Fallen gave the slightest nod. "Yes, but it's safer for all of the Helixes if we leave this place. The World of the Lost Souls has only humans in it. They're not affected by our Helixes one way or the other. Hopefully with us gone and our Helix's overwhelming influences away from them, they can balance themselves out and calm."

"Then I suggest you get a move on Commander. I'll stay here and do what I can about covering up any signs of your escape."

Murdoch's eyes darted to him. "I need to make sure the Commander and Sinah make it out safely. I can't stay here and protect you."

"I know that and that's okay."

"Dante, you'll be in direct danger."

Fallen tore off the auto-sampler from his arm. "He may not be. Any Helix in the area will sense me and my counterpart moving around. They will be drawn to us. Once we are out of the facility, if I'm right, then their Helixes will return to normal."

Dante nodded. "That's what I'm counting on. I'll fake a Director approved request for a vehicle Commander so you shouldn't have any trouble getting them. You just need to get to the Launch Pad area."

Fallen removed the pads from Sinah's chest, her finger clamp and the auto-sampler. Once he hooked her arms in Amos' jacket and zipped it up, he scooped her up into his arms. "Get out of here as soon as you're finished Dante. Don't get yourself captured. You'll be useless to her if you're caught."

Dante looked toward Sinah then confidently nodded. "I won't let either of you down Commander."

Fallen turned his attention to Murdoch. "Let's go."

Murdoch gave a quick nod. "Yes commander."

As Fallen carried Sinah passed Dante, he whispered. "Good luck out there Commander. Please protect her."

Fallen gave the slightest nod "No harm will come to my counterpart."

Dante barely nodded as they left operating room 3.

Forty-Two

The Escape

Murdoch's eyes shifted cautiously up and down the hallway. "The passage to the Launch Pad area with least amount of security is through Residential Commander. Should we-?"

Fallen shook his head. "No, we'll take the direct route. I'll deal with any problems we have along the way. The sooner Sinah and I are out of here the better."

Before Murdoch could give any type of response, Sinah suddenly began to twitch aggressively in Fallen's arms. Fallen lips touched at a frown. "Six D Helixes have sensed us and are now approaching."

Murdoch's eyebrows lowered as he stepped in front of Fallen and Sinah. "I'll deal with them."

A quiet snicker left Fallen's throat. "Your Helix hasn't woken up enough for you to be a true threat Murdoch, hold onto Sinah."

Murdoch turned to Fallen. An awkward expression took his features as Fallen placed Sinah into his arms. Once her twitches and spasms became much more aggressive, Murdoch's expression went from awkward to trying his best not to drop her.

The six Helix soldiers raced toward them with their weapons drawn and ready to shoot. Fallen calmly and protectively stepped a few feet in front of Murdoch and Sinah. The second they stopped running, all of them pointed their weapons beyond Fallen directly at Sinah.

One of the six spoke with a frown. "L Helix, move aside so we can deal with the G Helix. We don't want to accidently shoot you."

Fallen clenched his fists. "I am the Commander and I've heard this before. If you want to get to her, you'll have to get through me first."

Another of the six spoke. "L Hel... Commander, we know that your mind has been clouded by being in the presence of the G Helix. She has affected your judgement and confused your senses."

Fallen shifted himself in an aggressive ready to fight stance. "I'm not the one who is confused. Either leave us or prepare to die. Either option is fine by me."

All the D Helix soldiers released a unified defeated sigh. Before any one of them could speak, Murdoch hissed. "You're in the presence of your Lord! You will stand down!"

The D Helix soldiers didn't have a change in their demeanor. Murdoch frowned as much as he could. "You were given a direct order! You will stand down or-!"

One of the six cut him off. "Sorry Sir but we don't take orders from anyone until the G Helix is dealt with. We are only doing what's best for the L Helix to clear his confusion."

Murdoch frowned as much as he could. "I said-!"

Fallen lifted his hand cutting Murdoch off. "You're wasting your time Murdoch. It's pointless to try and convince them of anything while the balance of the Helix strength is off."

One of the six gripped his machine gun as he spoke. "This will be the last time we ask you to move before we open fire."

An ugly sneer captured Fallen's lips. "You have no idea how right you are."

Fallen snapped his hand open widely. His nails instantly changed into the over lapping jagged shards of black looking glass. Before any of the D Helix soldiers even had a chance to take a breath, Fallen raced toward them and went on the attack.

Not a single one of them managed to get a shot off before Fallen slashed his nails clean through their machine guns like a hot knife through butter. They only had a split second to be dumbfounded before Fallen went on the attack again.

Fallen effortlessly slashed his nails across one of the D Helix soldiers throat. The slash was so deep her spinal cord could be seen as her head flopped backward. Fallen ignored the sharp pain in his chest from her death as he turned on another.

Despite Murdoch's overwhelming feeling of loss for his fellow D Helix, he didn't once shift his attention from the fight. Fallen slammed his hand straight through another D Helix soldier's chest. Different from before when he would attack this way, the enemy would simply fall dead. This time the D Helix soldier caught a silver flame. He didn't pull his arm back from the body as it instantly burned to ash.

One of the remaining four yelled out in a panic. "The L Helix has snapped! We need to subdue him!"

Fallen chuckled effortlessly snapping another's neck. "I haven't snapped nor has my judgement been clouded. I will protect my counterpart with my life. So your lives are just in our way."

Murdoch looked down at Sinah. She was still aggressively twitching and struggling. One of the remaining D Helix soldiers raced toward them. "She needs to die!"

Murdoch didn't even have a chance to react before a silver blade shot into the back of the D Helix soldiers head and half way out of his eye. Murdoch stared at him wide eyed as he stumbled forward then fell dead.

One of the final two leapt onto Fallen's back and wrapped his arms around his neck. "L Helix, You need to calm down! You need to let us kill her!"

Fallen chuckled snapping his hands shut. "What I need to do is free her from this place."

The other D Helix soldier slammed his weight against Fallen hoping to knock him down. Fallen, who was very sturdy on his feet, didn't even stumble. The D Helix soldier on his back tightened his grip on Fallen's throat. "We have to knock him out!"

Fallen suddenly snapped open his hands. Thick silver blades with red spots shot from his back. The D Helix soldier was thrown then slammed into a wall. The blades that had pinned him in place instantly caught a silver flame.

Fallen didn't acknowledge the burning to ash D Helix soldier as he grabbed the head of the last. With a quick close of his hand, the final D Helix soldier's head was crushed effortlessly like an overly ripe piece of fruit. Fallen carelessly tossed the dead aside and flicked the blood, brains, skull and other biological goo from his hands.

Murdoch's eyes darted down to Sinah as her struggling came to a sudden stop.

"Let's go." Fallen said glancing back at them.

Murdoch gave a quick nod before he raced through the carnage.

Forty-Three

Releasing Heaven and Hell

As they raced toward the security booth, Fallen called out. "Run straight through Murdoch! Meet me at the elevators!"

Murdoch wasn't hesitant in obeying his order. He quickly caught up with Fallen then easily passed him. A slight smile touched at Fallen's lips as Murdoch zipped clean through the scanner. He had moved so fast, the scanner it didn't even have a chance to register that a person or people had even gone through. "I wonder if you're even noticing the changes in your D Helix."

Once the D Helix soldiers guarding the entrance into building Seven caught sight of Murdoch, they raised their weapons. One quickly left the booth and gave chase. He could only take a few steps before Fallen raced up beside him and slapped him upside the back of the head. The seemingly light force he used still caused the D Helix soldier to crash to the ground.

Once Murdoch carried Sinah out of the building, it was as if a switch from within the D Helix soldiers was activated. They instantly lowered their weapons and began to apologize. The one on the ground got to his feet apologizing as well. "Sorry Commander, We didn't mean to draw our weapons. We were just following orders."

Fallen's lips touched at a frown as he looked toward them. "What orders?"

The D Helix soldiers looked toward one another with a slightly confused expression. It was as if they didn't understand the question he had asked. One of the three shrugged. "..Our orders to protect building Seven."

Fallen gave the slightest nod before he left them.

Murdoch's eyes darted to anyone who stepped into the area of the elevators. Still being somewhat late, the amount of people was very scarce. Most gave a quick glance at him and Sinah then went about their business. The ones that would lock their eyes upon them were Helixes. Their expressions were a combination of hurt and confused.

The second Fallen stepped into the area with them, their expressions shifted to a confused hostility. Fallen, who noticed, stepped protectively closer to Murdoch and Sinah. "Press the elevator call button Murdoch and ignore the Helixes."

Murdoch quickly nodded and did what he was told. "Yes Commander."

The few Helixes in the area suddenly shifted their attentions to a Helix soldier as she walked into the corridor. Her eyes darted to the Helixes as if they had silently called out to her. She gripped her weapon, turning her attention to Fallen.

Once the doors opened, Fallen wasn't hesitant to push Murdoch into the elevator and slam his hand on the close door button. Murdoch's eyes darted back to the closing elevator doors hearing rapid gun fire.

As Fallen took Sinah from his arms, Murdoch spoke. "So it's not just the Helixes in building Seven."

Fallen gave a slight shake of his head. "If we would have just stayed put, eventually all the Helixes in the facility would have felt it and turned on each other. Then we would have a hell of a lot more dead Helix blood on our hands."

As the elevator doors opened, Fallen spoke. "This is as far as you go Murdoch."

Murdoch shook his head in disbelief as he followed after him. "But Commander, I..!"

Fallen glanced toward the security booth that was only a few feet ahead of them. "There can't be any evidence that you helped Sinah and I escape."

"But Dante-"

"You need to go back to building Seven and get Dante out of there."

Murdoch stepped into his soldier awaiting a command stance. "Then we follow after?"

"No, you and he will return to your normal daily routines."

Murdoch's features weakened a little as he looked toward the ground with a slightly hurt expression. "C… Commander, are you abandoning us?"

Fallen couldn't help but to chuckle a little. "No, I'm just convincing Director Hart that he's still in control."

Murdoch looked up at Fallen with a look of confusion. "… Commander?"

"If both of you act like you're still loyal to the Director, he won't think twice about sending you two out to find us and bring us back. And when he does, the moment you drive out of the facility, tell Dante to scan the hummer for tracking devices and deactivate your earpieces. Soon your mind to equipment devices will become completely useless and your Helix's natural strengths will flourish."

Murdoch looked down at the Combat gloves. The microchip was still flicking on and off. "But what if they activate the tracker on your hummer, Commander?"

"I know where it's located. I'll remove it before we leave the garage. Now go."

Murdoch swallowed heavily. "B... But Commander, how will we find you?"

Fallen smiled slightly glancing down at Sinah. "Your Helix will find me. Trust your instincts Murdoch."

Murdoch barely nodded as Fallen walked toward the security booth. "Yes Commander."

The security guard's eyes darted to Fallen then his naked chest, then Sinah. "Uh… Commander?"

Fallen's lips touched at a frown. "Has the use of a vehicle request come down yet?"

The security guard tapped the air accessing the green screens. Once he saw the request, he nodded and picked up the clipboard. "Yes Commander, you just need to fill..."

Fallen couldn't help but to hiss. "And how exactly am I supposed to do that?!"

The security guard went flush as his eyes darted down to Sinah. "B... But you need… to… to..." He suddenly shook his head and waved his hand. "Don't worry about it Commander. I'll fill them out."

Fallen gave a slight nod walking toward one of the hummers. As he opened the door to the backseat, he spoke. "It's a good thing most of the security booths are manned by humans Sinah. They only understand obeying human protocol. We shouldn't have any difficulties leaving here."

Murdoch's expression weakened watching Fallen gently place Sinah into the vehicle. He then reached under the hummer and tore out the tracker. Carelessly tossing it aside, Fallen climbed into the driver seat and drove out of the garage.

Forty-Four

No Time for Tears

Murdoch had only a split second to feel upset and lower his head before the frantic Alex spoke over his earpiece. "Emergency alarms are going off in building Seven!"

Murdoch's expression instantly snapped back to normal as he pressed his earpiece. "Has Dante returned?"

"No, and the information he was sending suddenly stopped! Do you think something happened to him?!"

Murdoch turned back toward the elevators. "I'm heading back there now. What is the situation outside the building?"

"About twenty-five soldiers... I... I don't know if they're Helixes or not. A few people have been killed. I don't know what happened. Sh.. Should I check it out?"

Murdoch stepped into the elevator and jabbed the button. "No, just keep watch, I want to know if the situation changes."

"Okay."

Murdoch looked up at the highlighting numbers. "So even though the Commander and Sinah were there for only a few minutes, the Helixes still reacted. The Commander was right, it was better for Helixes that the two of them escaped."

Once the elevator doors opened, any Helix soldier in close proximity instantly directed their weapon toward Murdoch. Simply ignoring them, he tried to race passed. Without hesitation, five D Helix and seven A Helix soldiers stepped in his way with a full frown.

Murdoch returned the frown before he hissed. "Get the hell out of my way!"

As the whites in Murdoch's eyes was consumed by black, the Helix soldiers nervously stepped back then moved aside. Without missing a beat, Murdoch took that opportunity to bolt down the passage into building Seven.

None of the D Helix soldiers even glanced up as Murdoch raced through the scanner. As he ran toward operating room 3, his eyes darted to Dante. He was on his knees with his hands raised in surrender. Two D Helix soldiers stood on either side of him with their machine guns ready to shoot.

Murdoch's eyebrows lowered as he hissed. "Let him go, you son of a b-!"

Before Murdoch could finish his sentence, Emma stepped out of the operating room with a full frown. Right before she said anything, Dante noticed Murdoch and spoke in a forced panicked tone of voice. "They're gone! Sinah and the Commander are gone! I felt it and had to come here to be sure!"

Murdoch tried his best to mirror Dante's fake panic. "Uh... Yeah. Yeah! That's why I came here too!"

Emma held her frown. "How did you get in here to begin with?"

Dante looked back at Emma. "Didn't you see the surveillance? The Helixes were too busy killing one another to notice me slip in. When I found out Sinah and the Commander was gone, I hid in here hoping they wouldn't find me."

Dante suddenly forced a full frown. "Do you really think I'd sneak in here for fun?! This place is beyond dangerous!"

Dante forced a loud sigh of relief. "I'm just lucky I wasn't killed."

Murdoch frowned at the two D Helix soldiers. "Lower your weapons! He is a member of the Commander's team and deserves to be treated with respect!"

As the D Helix soldiers lowered their weapons, Dante got to his feet, raced to Murdoch and snatched his arm. "What do we do Murdoch?! They're gone! They're gone!"

Emma gave Dante a look of distrust. "Did you tamper with anything in there?"

Dante glanced back at Emma. "In where?"

Dante pointed at operating room 3's door. "In there? Why would I tamper with anything?"

Emma held her expression. "Am I really supposed to believe that the Commander's Data, Information and Surveillance soldier didn't take any information from a restricted area?"

Dante's eyebrows lowered. "And just what the hell are you implying?! Do you really think I care about information at a time like this?! The Helixes were killing each other, the Commander and Sinah... No, God are gone, do you really think I give a damn about information right now?!"

Before Emma could answer, another Lead ADGL Tech did. "That's exactly what I would be thinking."

Murdoch was the only one that didn't look in the direction of the speaker. He merely frowned as Revin spoke again walking toward them. "You're right to think that Helix would extract information from our restricted building Emma."

Dante's eye sharpened as he pointed at his foot. "Hey, see my Combat boot? How about I shove that up your-"

Murdoch cut Dante off with a quiet snicker. "You people obvious don't know anything about A Helixes."

Both Revin and Emma began to frown as Murdoch stepped into his soldier at ease stance, continuing. "A Helixes lack the capability to lie. They can't help but to be anything but perfectly honest. Now if you'll excuse us, I need to take Dante to the Director to report his actions."

Dante's eyes darted to Murdoch in shock. "What?!"

Emma's frown faded as she shook her head. "You're right Murdoch, A Helixes can't lie. I've spoken to enough of them to know that firsthand. I don't see any reason why you should report him. I understand his actions were just an A Helix reaction to the loss of his God."

Revin's eyes darted to Emma. "God's dead?!"

"No, you imbecile, she and the Commander-"

"Incompetent Lead, you lost them didn't you?"

Emma hissed. "Do you even know what happened?! Why don't you go watch the surveillance footage on the Helix snaps before you...?"

Revin's expression suddenly shifted to curiosity. "There was a Helix snap?"

Before Emma could answer, Revin spoke again. "I wonder if Experiment number 7923 B felt it. Better yet, I wonder if his Helix knows where God is. I'm sure with the right amount of motivation he'll answer anything I ask him."

Dante suddenly released a snarl very uncharacteristic for his A Helix as he leapt toward him. "Bastard!!"

Without hesitation, Murdoch snatched hold of him. His as well as Emma's expression was in absolute shock. Murdoch quickly turned the struggling angry Dante away from Revin as he spoke. "Sorry Emma but it's my responsibility to report the situation to the Director."

Emma barely nodded watching Dante trying his best to get free from Murdoch's grip. "...Alright."

As Murdoch began to pull Dante down the hall, Dante locked eyes with Revin. The white ring around his pupils began to shine. "You'll get yours, mark my words you son of a bitch, you'll get yours!"

Revin stared at Dante's eyes for a few seconds before he said. "I want a sample of your blood."

Dante frowned pointing at his foot. "See my Combat boot?!"

Murdoch continued to drag Dante down the hallway. "Come on."

Once they were out of sight, Revin spoke. "Let's just see what happened with the Helixes."

As Emma walked away from Revin, he called out. "Computer, alert my ADGL Techs from cell Lab 6 for an emergency meeting."

Forty-Five

Half Truths and Lies

Murdoch chuckled pressing the elevator button for the 11th floor. "Well, I have to say I wasn't expecting that from you."

Dante ignored Murdoch and pressed his ear piece. "Alex, did all the information make it?"

"Thank god you're safe! Are you alright?"

"Yeah I'm fine. Did you get anything?"

"Yes, I've also altered the surveillance the best I could."

Dante glanced up at the highlighting floors. "I know. I saw it and fixed up any minor problems as fast as I could. Now I need you to set off the self-destruct system on the spider in building Seven."

Murdoch's eyes darted to Dante, while Alex was quick to question. "Are you sure?"

"Right after they watch the surveillance footage, they're going to do a thorough scan of the building. They're going to check security, maintenance, air quality and everything else they can think of hoping to find out what exactly happened. Make sure you disconnect our stationary camera feed as well. Remove any and all traces that we were ever in there."

"I'm on it Dante."

Dante responded with an 'okay' then turned his attention to Murdoch. "I can lie."

Murdoch snickered as the elevator doors open. "Come on, we need to deal with the Director."

Dante's eyes darted to the Director's receptionist. "You were serious about reporting me?"

"Come on."

Dante swallowed heavily as he followed after him. As Murdoch passed by the receptionist's desk, he spoke. "This is an emergency and we need to speak to the Director."

The receptionist never got a chance to say anything before Murdoch and Dante walked into the Director's office.

The Director's eyes darted up to Murdoch and Dante in confusion. "...Members of Lucifer's team?"

Murdoch stepped in front of the Director's desk before he stepped into his soldier awaiting a command stance. "Director, we're here to report that the Commander and God have escaped the facility."

Dante, who nervously stood beside him, gave the slightest nod.

The Director's demeanor instantly shifted to panic. "WHAT?!"

He stood up so fast he knocked some papers and his metal walking stick to the floor. Once his eyes darted down to it, Murdoch nudged Dante's arm then gave an upward nod toward the Director. Dante barely nodded then raced toward the side of his desk.

The Director spoke as Dante picked up his metal walking stick and handed it to him. "What do you mean God is gone?! She couldn't have just got up and left!"

Murdoch shook his head. "She didn't Director. Since the Commander is gone as well, we assume he took her with him."

"Lucifer took-?"

"There was a tragic incident in building Seven. We wanted to search for them right away but we know we need to receive orders from the top before we are allowed to act. We know and follow protocol to a T, right Dante?"

Dante awkwardly nodded. "Uh... r... right."

The Director tapped the air accessing the green screens. As he frantically began to work, he spoke. "Computer, access the security booth in building..."

"I wouldn't suggest that Director. The Helix soldiers are the reason for the incident."

The Director looked beyond the green screens at Murdoch. "…A snap?"

Both Murdoch and Dante gave a shrug almost in unison.

"She can't be gone! He can't have taken her! Unless..! Lucifer must be intending to kill her outside the safety of the facility. Here, the ADGL Lab Techs can call in A Helix soldiers to protect her. Out there, she's completely helpless."

Murdoch watched the Director work for a few moments before he questioned. "…Orders, Director?"

The Director dismissively waved his hand. "Return to your daily routines until I've seen what has happened. I need you both to be on standby at a moment's notice."

Murdoch gave a quick nod. "Yes Director."

Once he stepped out of his soldier awaiting a command stance, he turned heel and left the Director's office. Dante followed after him with a full frown. Once they were both in the elevator, Dante turned on him. "Traitor!"

Murdoch pressed one of the elevator buttons glancing toward the fuming Dante. "I'm only following the Commander's orders."

Dante's anger shifted to confusion. "The Commander wanted-"

"I was ordered to get you out of building Seven and wait until the Director gives us the orders to find them"

"So that the same thing doesn't happen if another Helix team is sent out to find them."

Murdoch gave him a confused look. "What do you mean?"

"If you would've just got me out of building Seven and we followed after them, the Director would have sent out another Helix team. If they managed to get anywhere near the Commander and Sinah, their Helixes might have reacted as they did in building Seven."

Once the elevator doors open, Murdoch stepped out. "They'd just kill each other?"

Dante nodded following after him. "Exactly, in a sense, the Commander really is protecting the other Helixes in the facility. I think he knew that the Director won't have any other choice but to send the best to find the most important beings in existence. We are the best team our Lab has."

Murdoch stepped into his soldier at ease stance. "That's why the Commander ordered me to act like I was still loyal to that simple human."

Dante's expression shifted to apologetic. "I'm sorry I called you a traitor Murdoch. It just caught me off guard how you were being with the Director."

Murdoch shook his head. "Don't worry about it. Hopefully, he was tricked as well. I'm heading over to the shooting range if you need me."

Dante's expression returned to normal. "I'll sort through what I've got from building Seven."

Murdoch gave a brief nod before they went their separate ways.

Forty-Six

Home, Sweet Home

Fallen pulled the hummer up to a large lone run down house surrounded by a great deal of empty wasteland. Before the fall of Heaven and Hell, this might have been a flourishing farm, surrounded by fields to harvest and lush greenery. Now, just like everywhere else in the world, it was just another dead mass of land.

Once Fallen turned off the engine and climbed out of the vehicle, he spoke. "This place isn't anywhere near close to being good enough for you Sinah but you need a place to recover comfortably in."

Fallen opened the door to the back seat and scooped her up into his arms. As he took a few steps, he heard a sound very unfamiliar to his ears. It was a soft tingling almost ringing noise. It wasn't constant but it occurred every few moments. Fallen's eyebrows furrowed slightly walking toward the house. As he stepped onto the dilapidated porch, his eyes darted to a mangled wind chime. Only three metal cylindrical tubes were left dangling from the main base. Every few moments a breeze would rush pass them causing the tubes to lightly tap together.

Fallen's eyes shifted from the chimes down to Sinah. Every time she released air from her lungs, a gentle breeze brushed against him. Fallen's lips touched at a smile watching the timing of her breathing and the wind move in complete unison. "You're breathing life into our world my sweet counterpart. You're giving such a wonderful gift to those unworthy of it."

Fallen's lips suddenly shifted to a frown. "The Lost Souls are just a waste of human breath. We should just end them and be done with it." Looking up at the front door, his frown faded. "Shall we?"

The second Fallen opened the unlocked door, a wave of filth, grime and general age rushed out of the abandoned home. The pungent smell was so overwhelming he had to turn himself and Sinah away from the entrance.

Fallen released a slight sigh as he left the porch and returned to the hummer. As he placed Sinah back into the back seat, he spoke. "I'm sorry Sinah. I wish there was a Lab that I knew about nearby. I'd wipe out the facility and you would have a nice sanitary place to recover in."

Fallen closed the vehicle door then turned his attention back to the house. "Rest as well as you can while I will deal with the mess."

Fallen returned to the house and went straight to work. He tossed broken pieces of furniture, old empty bottles, empty food cans and anything else he considered to be garbage out of the open doorway. Even though he was very busy cleaning, he would go out of his way to pause and check on Sinah. Once he was sure she was okay, he would go right back to cleaning.

After the final bits of debris were removed from the main floor, Fallen opened the windows welcoming the breeze inside. Thanks to the cross wave of air rushing into the house the overpowering scent began to dissipate. Fallen released a slightly annoyed sound as he grabbed hold of a once white or off white lace blanket covering a couch. Having an unknown amount of years of time and neglect upon it, the actual color was impossible to determine

Once he tore it off, his expression shifted to confusion. The lace blanket hid a plastic covering which protected the couch from dirt and stains. As Fallen pulled it off, he questioned. "What is this thing for? Why would someone willingly sit on..?"

Fallen stopped short noticing the area around his grip was now completely clean. Dropping the plastic cover, he looked at his hand. It caught a black flame for a split second then returned to normal. He stared at it for a few moments before he placed his hand on the disgustingly filthy coffee table. All the grime and dirt around his hand caught a black flame for a split second then vanished taking the filth with it.

Fallen shifted his attention back to his hand as it again caught a flame. Fallen glanced down at his naked chest, pants and Combat boots, by all rhyme and reason, there should have been some evidence that he had been cleaning. Yet there was nothing, his skin, clothes and boots were completely dirt free.

Fallen ran his hands all over the coffee table. Within seconds, it caught flame then became was perfectly clean. A slight smile took Fallen's lips. "It feels like a pointless skill in my Helix but I suppose it has its uses."

Fallen looked out the open doorway toward the hummer. "This won't take long Sinah. You'll be resting comfortably in no time."

After he was convinced she was still okay, he ran his hands on anything and everything in his path. Eventually, he found himself upstairs in the two story house. On this floor were three bedrooms and two bathrooms. One of the bedrooms was the master. Inside was a queen sized bed, matching furniture, an open linen closet and a door leading into a bathroom.

Fallen didn't waste any time opening windows, ripping all the bedding off and clean burning everything in sight. After he burn cleaned the mattress and pillows, he replaced the bedding with freshly burn cleaned sheets and blankets.

Fallen didn't bat an eye seeing the awful mess in the bathroom. Long dried blood was on top and inside the sink. A razor coated in rust and crusted dry blood was lying on the floor. Despite signs that someone had either cut themselves, took their life or cut or took someone else's life, there wasn't any sign that a body had actually been in there.

Fallen ran his hands against everything burn cleaning the room. As his fingertips brushed the faucet, the pipes began to rumble. His expression shifted to confusion as he turned on the taps and the pipes produced a few loud knocking sounds. Suddenly a brown sludge oozed from the faucets. After a couple of sputters, clear water gushed forth and the tap ran normally as it was designed to. Fallen's simple expression of confusion shifted to shock. "How is this possible?"

Fallen shifted his attention to the shower and turned it on. The results were exactly the same as in the sink. "Clear water?"

Fallen shut off the taps then turned his attention to the disgusting toilet. He placed his hand on the top of the tank then closed his eyes. Instead of the burning flame being isolated to such a small area around his hand, the entire toilet caught flame and was cleaned. As Fallen opened his eyes and lifted his hand, the tank rattled. The toilet suddenly made a gurgling sound then filled with clean, clear water.

As Fallen stepped back from it, he whispered. "Perhaps... Perhaps the world isn't as dead as we thought it was."

Fallen left the master bedroom, walked down the stairs, passed through the living room then left the house. As he approached the hummer, he spoke. "Perhaps the world needed us to awaken before it could do the same."

As Fallen opened the door to the backseat, he smiled softly. "This may not be much my precious counterpart but this is only the beginning for us."

Fallen scooped Sinah up into his arms, carried her into the house then closed the door with his foot. Fallen didn't shift his slight smile from Sinah as he passed through the living room, climbed the stairs and entered the master bedroom.

Fallen drew back the covers and gently placed her upon the bed. Once he lay down comfortably beside her and pulled the covers over them, Fallen instantly fell into a deep sleep.

Forty-Seven

You Can't Break Me

Ayla averted her eyes from the surveillance replay, witnessing another death of an A Helix soldier. "…How horrible!"

Len watched with a slightly bewildered expression painted on his face. "This doesn't seem like a normal snap."

Revin put his hands in his lab coat pockets and looked beyond the combined green screens down at Bridger. He was frantically trying to free himself. He seemed more like he was in a panicked frenzy as opposed to just trying for freedom.

Revin shook his head. "I don't think it was a snap. Notice how the D Helixes suddenly become calm before they kill. No, I think this is just the natural order of things. Good against evil."

Len couldn't seem to tear his eyes from the massacre. "That makes sense, from what I've heard, God is still in bad shape. Without God's help, the A Helixes wouldn't stand a chance."

"Both God and Perfect Experiment A have escaped the facility."

Every single ADGL Lab Tech's eyes darted to Revin. Len shook his head in disbelief. "How did they manage to get out of building Seven? Our security is-"

Ayla cut him off. "You saw what happened! Obviously, they weren't paying attention to protecting the building at that moment."

Revin walked toward the exit. "Ayla, bring two of our highest level pain stimulators. I want to know where they went and I'll get my answer from Experiment number 7923 B one way or another."

Ayla went flush white as she barely nodded. "Yes Sir."

Bridger hissed rattling the chains and shackles as aggressively as he could. "Come on! I need to get out of here! Break, damn you break!"

The instant Bridger heard the door to his cell unlock, he stopped struggling. Once Revin stepped inside, he questioned. "Experiment number 7923 B, where is God?"

Bridger didn't move nor respond. He merely stared back at him. Revin's expression shifted to irritation at his lack of response. "Where is God?"

Bridger only continued with his silent treatment. Revin instantly began to fume. "Where's God?!"

Bridger simply blinked in response. As if sensing that Ayla was approaching with the pushcart, Revin turned quick and snatched up one of the needles. The fluid inside was a dark red. "You will tell me what I want to know!"

Bridger's lip touched at a smile but he still remained silent. Revin frowned as much as he could. "Where is God?!"

Bridger only held his slight smile in silence. Revin suddenly hissed. "Answer me Experiment number 7923 B!"

Ayla looked toward the silent Bridger with a combination of sympathy and concern. "Bridger, if you just tell him what he wants to know, you'll save yourself some pain, a… at least for today anyway."

Revin dismissively waved his free hand back at Ayla. "You can go."

Ayla gave the slightest nod. "Y… Yes Sir."

Revin waited until he heard the cell door close behind him before he said. "You're wasting your time resisting. Now, you will tell me where God is. How much pain you'll have to endure before you give me the information is up to you."

Bricker couldn't help but to snicker. "You're acting like you don't enjoy watching people suffer. When we both know that's not true. You love torturing the helpless. That's why you chain your so called experiments up. You're too cowardly to face them head on. You can't deny your sick sadistic nature."

"Where is God?"

Bridger only responded with a blank stare. Revin hissed again. "Answer me!!"

Bridger just continued with his silent treatment. Revin snatched up the second needle then locked eyes with Bridger. "You asked for this!"

Bridger's eyebrows lowered. "Yeah, that's exactly what I would expect a sadist to say."

Revin jabbed one of the needles into Bridger's arm vein. "I will get what I want."

The pain of the stimuli was instantaneous. Instead of screeching out in sheer agony, Bridger locked his jaw, clenched his fists and braced his feet firmly on the ground. Sweat gushed from his pores and all his muscles tightened.

Revin watched Bridger's resistance for only a moment before he questioned. "Where is God?"

Despite the repetitive twitching of his entire body, Bridger only forced a defiant smirk. Revin frowned pressing the second needle against his arm. "Answer me! Don't make me inject the second needle!"

Bridger released a shaky chuckle. Spit and drool gushed from his mouth as he calmly spoke. "G... Go to h… hell."

Revin hissed. "You won't survive this Experiment number 7923 B! Even Perfect Experiment A barely survived it!"

Bridger forced a chuckle and spoke in a sarcastic tone. "Y... yeah sure he did. You didn't b… break him and y… you won't break me."

"Where is God!?! Answer Me!"

The defiant smirk once again took Bridger's lips. Revin frowned as much as he could as he forced the contents of the second needle into Bridger's blood stream. "Your death doesn't make any difference to me"

Bridger's entire body instantly locked up. Every single one of his muscles felt like a heavy weight was not only trying to crush the flesh but also twist it away from his bones. Bridger locked his jaw so tightly it looked like he would shatter his own teeth at any moment. Not only was the sweat amount escaping him increased but also tears poured from his squinted eyes. His fists were clenched so tightly his nails pierced his flesh and blood dripped through his knuckles.

Revin calmly stepped a few feet back from him. "Where is God?"

Bridger opened his eyes and locked them with Revin's. The white ring around his pupil was blazing so brightly, it was hard to see the natural color of his light blue eyes. His eyebrows lowered as much as they could. Even though his salivation had massively increased, he managed to mutter. "Is that the best you got?"

As if thrown into an utter rage, Revin stomped over to the corner of the cell and accessed the green screens. He hissed before he tapped on one of them. "Where is God?!"

An aggressive electrical current raced through the chains and struck Bridger. Bridger let out a scream of absolute agony.

Revin's lips touched at a smirk until Bridger's screaming turned into broken chuckles. "Is that all?!"

Revin hissed and hit the electrical current again. This time Bridger only made a loud restricted groan sound. Revin tapped the screen increasing the voltage. "Where is God?!"

Bridger forced a condescending snicker. "So that's what it's like to be bitch slapped by a spineless coward."

Revin hit the electrical blast over and over again. The chains themselves rattled and hummed from the higher electrical currents he used. Between each hit, Bridger forced a chuckle. It went from a forced amusement to an insane cackle. "Is that the best you got!?!"

Revin turned the voltage up to maximum. Before he had a chance to press the button Len's panicked voice spoke over the communications. "Sir, stop! That current is too high! That level is supposed to only be used for mercy kills!"

Revin ignored Len and hit the activation button. Blue and white electricity raced down the chains and violently struck Bridger. The impact caused blood to gush out of his mouth, his feathers to explode off of his wings and various points of his muscles to split clean open.

Bridger screeched so loudly, it sounded like his throat was being ripped apart. Once the current ended, tons of black smoke rose from his shaking body. Bridger's dim eyes shifted up to Revin. The weakest smile touched at his lips as he whispered. "..Is that the best you got?"

Before Revin could react, Bridger's eyes rolled back in his head and he went limp. Revin activated the highest level of electrical currents a couple more times. The only thing it did was rattle Bridger's already fried body.

Revin scanned Bridger's body to check his status. It barely showed any signs of life. His heart beat was very weak and one of his wings had been completely obliterated. Even though it still maintained its shape, all the feathers had been charred to a black crisp.

Revin stepped back from the green screens. As they vanished, he spoke. "If you recover Experiment number 7923 B, we'll continue." Without saying another word, he left the cell.

Forty-Eight

A Light in the Dark

Sinah's eyes snapped open as she jolted upright. Her entire demeanor was full of panic as a single word escaped her lips. "Bridger."

After several moments of merely staring straight ahead, Sinah looked around the master bedroom. Her expression was beyond bewilderment. Catching the scent of fresh air, Sinah glanced toward the open windows. A breeze was flowing into the bedroom in perfect sync with her breathing. As her eyes shifted around the room that was only illuminated by the dim blue light, she heard breathing.

Sinah's eyes darted to her side feeling slight movement. Seeing the sleeping Fallen, a soft smile took her lips. As she reached her hand out to touch his face, she caught a glimpse of Amos' jacket. Sinah's expression returned to confusion as she unzipped it. Her cheeks instantly touched at an awkward blush seeing that she was only wearing a brazier. Her reddened cheeks began to burn brighter as she glanced at Fallen's naked chest. A soft smile took her lips as she brushed her fingertips against his nudity. "..Fallen?"

Sinah's voice was very soft and feminine. It was a gentle voice that didn't have any signs of negativity or malice. "..Fallen?"

Fallen's eyes suddenly snapped open. Once they focused and locked on her, he slowly sat up and whispered. "…Sinah."

Sinah smiled softly as Fallen cupped her face in his hands and whispered again. "…Sinah."

Before Sinah had a chance to respond, he softly pressed his lips against hers. Sinah's eyes widened for a brief second before she closed them. As their kiss deepened and lingered, her hands found their way onto his face. Once her fingertips touched the sides of his sunglasses, she lifted her lips.

Fallen didn't react as Sinah slowly removed them from his face. His silver eyes with the crimson ring around his pitch black pupil locked with her normal blue eyes. As Fallen stared deeper into her eyes he noticed a small golden dot in the center point of her pupil. Despite it being not noticeable in the slightest, it held his gaze. The longer he stared at it, the more he realized it wasn't just a simple dot but something very similar to a four point star. As if transfixed, Fallen's brows furrowed as many points in the dot began to form and overlap. As the final bit of black was covered and Sinah's golden eyes began to glow, a wave of discomfort washed over Fallen.

Fallen's hands fell from her face as he closed his eyes. "To view upon the power of creation isn't something meant for my eyes."

Sinah quickly turned her head from him. "..I'm sorry."

Being taken back by hearing Sinah's voice, Fallen quickly shook his head. He gently took her chin and turned her head back toward him. "No, don't be. It's an absolutely breathtakingly pure sight. A forbidden sight not a single being in existence is worthy enough to view upon."

Sinah closed her eyes. "All I see in your eyes is annihilation."

Fallen took Sinah's hand. "I would have been surprised if you saw anything else."

As Fallen brought her hand to his mouth, Sinah looked up at him. Her eyes had returned to normal. "Fallen, I am not your enemy."

Fallen's eyes darted up to hers as he lowered her hand slightly. "And Sinah I am not yours."

Sinah couldn't help but to blush as he brought her hand to his lips again and began to kiss her knuckles. Despite his intense gaze, his contact was very gentle and sweet. Sinah smiled softly at such a tender loving gesture. As she reached her nervous hand out to his face, Fallen lifted his lips and leaned the side of his head into her palm.

Sinah smiled even more before she closed her eyes, leaned forward and pressed her lips against his. Between each momentary separation of their mouths, Fallen would murmur Sinah's name. As their kisses began to linger and become more passionate, Fallen's hands slipped into Amos' jacket onto her naked sides.

The second his cold pale skin touched her warm skin, Sinah's eyes snapped open. Her surprised expression instantly relaxed seeing Fallen's utterly contented features. Placing her hands on his shoulders, she gently pushed him back from her. This action caused Fallen's eyes to snap open and for him to remove his hands from her flesh. "Sorry Sinah, I..."

Fallen stopped short as she smiled and removed the jacket. As she placed it at the bottom of the bed, she spoke. "It's okay. Let me just get this out of the way."

Fallen's lips couldn't help but to touch at a smile. "Thank you."

Sinah's eyes scanned the glowing black veins upon Fallen's chest before she reached out to touch them. Fallen closed his eyes as her fingertips began to trace each one of the veins to the center point that had the appearance of a black hole in his chest. Whether he wanted to or not, quiet restricted sounds of delight escaped his voice box. Each time he made such a sound, his brows would furrow in slight confusion. It was as if the sensation was not only new to him but strange.

As she began to trace another, Fallen's hands slipped back onto her sides. Before her fingertips could reach center point again, Fallen pulled her body firmly against his. Sinah closed her eyes as his mouth began to taste and enjoy her throat. Slipping her hands onto Fallen's shoulders, she murmured his name. As she leaned her head back to allow him more access to her neck, Fallen took that opportunity to slowly lean her backwards to lay her down.

Once he was comfortably upon her, Fallen brushed a few strands of hair from her face and whispered. "Sinah, you are my salvation."

Sinah smiled softly up at him and whispered back. "And you Fallen, you are my damnation."

Fallen smiled himself before his lips passionately locked with hers.

Both of their breaths shook as hands slowly began to explore, mouths began to taste, needs began to express themselves and unfamiliar desires demanded their attention. After the room fell silent of gasps of delight, moans of pleasure, murmurs of satisfaction and whispers of appreciation and happiness, both fell into the inevitable contented sleep.

Forty-Nine

Evolution

Dante tapped his index finger off the kitchen table sifting through the collected data from building Seven. "Most of this is just Sinah and the Commander's blood work. Nothing really all that..."

Dante paused for a split second as his expression shifted to slight confusion. "…Hm."

Alex glanced up from the laptop. "What's wrong?"

Dante clicked over to the Creation Lab files. "I need to find the original G Helix blood work."

Alex clicked on a few keys to see what Dante was looking at. "Do you think hers and the original God's are different?"

"That's exactly what I'm thinking. It never made sense to me that the A Helixes weren't naturally drawn to Sinah. We A Helixes should have subconsciously wanted to be near her, in her presence. And I don't believe for a second that her Helix level should have mattered. She's God. Why didn't we sense her? Bridger sure did but..."

Dante's features weakened as he lifted his fingers from the key board. "..Bridger."

Alex glanced up at Dante sympathetically. "Sorry we didn't extract any info on his experimentation as well."

Dante forced back his emotions and began to work again. "I didn't have enough time. I was caught before I was able get anything. It… It's probably for the best though. I don't think I could focus on the task at hand knowing what they're doing to him."

Dante swallowed heavily trying to keep his emotions in check. "If I don't know, then I won't worry."

Dante clicked on the laptop keys for a few moments before he muttered. "...Too much."

Alex opened his mouth to say something but Dante spoke first. "Here's the original, let's link it up with Sinah's and-"

Dante stopped short seeing the comparison between Sinah's Helix and the original G Helix. They weren't anywhere near close to matching each other. Dante clicked over to Fallen's then compared it to the original L Helix. It was completely different as well.

Dante's expression shifted to confusion. "..That can't be right. I know for a fact that the Commander was created in our facilities. Helix Lab Techs and ADGL Lab Techs had to have a full understanding of his creation and its progress."

Dante checked the progress and development of Fallen's L Helix. It progressed normally then in the recent blood samples, it showed a slight shift from the original then there was a sudden spike and a full change.

Alex stared at the blood sample comparisons in confusion. "Whoa! What happened there?"

Dante studied it for a few moments before he responded. "Sinah happened. That's why we weren't drawn to her. Our Helixes were waiting for the original G Helix to be created. We never once thought that God would create herself in her own way. We don't need the originals in our current world so there wasn't any reason for them to simply be reborn. The more I discover about Sinah, the more I realize just how much of a mystery she truly is."

Alex studied Dante for a few moments before he questioned. "Does that mean your Helix is different from the other A Helixes?"

Dante bolted from the table to the kitchen counter. Alex went flush as Dante grabbed a butcher knife from the knife block. "I was just asking!"

Dante made an 'ow' sound as he used the knife to jab the tip of his finger. He couldn't help but to chuckle a little as his wound instantly healed. "Well, my rapid healing skill hasn't changed."

Dante returned to his laptop and smeared the small amount of blood onto the table. "Due to the restrictions of computer access in Residential, I won't be able to use the same method as before."

Alex watched Dante in anticipation as he scanned his blood with his Combat glove. Dante smiled as he began to transfer the information from his glove to his laptop. "I'm glad Murdoch didn't ask for these back. They may not be working at 100 percent but I'll take what I can get."

Alex spoke in a voice full of excitement. "How are you so calm?!"

Dante's eyes darted up to Alex. "What do you mean? Why wouldn't I be calm?"

Alex smiled as much as he could. It looked like any minute he would burst from giddiness. "Your Helix could have become something completely different from the other Helixes! Something so much more amazing! I could be sitting here working with a new type of Helix!"

Dante glanced toward his blood as Alex continued. "Despite what we humans say, our physical natural evolution isn't really moving forward. But yours, it's like we were only given the basic tools in Creation. Once your Helix is ready, it evolves into something beyond simple Angels or Demons. Beyond what the ancient texts spoke about, something we as humans could never possibly fully understand."

Dante indifferently shrugged as he went back to work. "I never really thought about the steps in the evolutionary chain before. Besides my Helix could be exactly the same as it was before."

Alex could barely contain his excitement. "I thought Bridger had just become a full Angel but what if his Helix has completely changed as well?! Wow! This is so amazing!"

Dante awkward chuckled. "Uh... Okay calm down. If it had changed, then Murdoch and I would have probably been brought into building Seven for experimentation. A new type of Helix would…"

Dante paused midsentence then slowly shook his head. "…But then again, maybe not. If they checked Bridger's blood when he got into building Seven but didn't bother to check the past Helix process reports, they might not even know there was a complete change. They probably just think his new form is just the natural progress of his A Helix. To put it simply, his Helix is and was just his Helix. Intellectually wise, those are some pretty damn lazy ADGL Lab Techs to just let him slip through the cracks like that."

Dante leaned back in his chair waiting for the results to load. "It makes you wonder though."

"Wonder what?"

Dante shrugged. "Is that the real reason why the D Helixes turned on the A? The D Helixes had changed from the human created variations to their proper natural forms and the A Helixes hadn't yet. Maybe they began to see the undeveloped A Helixes as flaws or weaknesses. Evolution is all about abandoning the unnecessary. Perhaps to them they thought the A Helixes weren't worthy of Sinah or the Commander and were deemed unnecessary."

Before Alex could offer his opinion, the computer made a ding sound. Dante's eyes darted then widened seeing his A Helix displayed on his laptop. It had definitely changed and looked more similar to Sinah's then his original. Dante stared at it in shock for a few moments before he gave an upward nod. "It... It has changed. Look."

Once Dante sent the results to Alex's laptop, his eyes instantly lit up. "This is so amazing! A new type of Helix! Oh my god! Aren't you excited?! I can't believe this!"

Dante ignored Alex's enthusiasm and pressed his ear piece. "Murdoch?"

"Have orders been sent yet?"

Dante glanced at the large screen. The Director was hobble pacing around his office with a shocked yet panicked look on his face. "No. I need you to cut yourself and send me the scanner results."

"Repeat that."

"I need you to cut yourself and send me the scanner results."

After a few moments of silence from Murdoch, Dante spoke again. "Did you hear me?"

Murdoch hesitantly responded. "..Yeah I heard you."

"Okay good, whenever you're ready."

".. And why am I sending you my blood?"

Before Dante could respond, the Director yelled out. "Send messages to Lucifer's team! I want them in my office ASAP!"

Dante smiled slightly. "No time to be curious! The Director is about to call us in. Murdoch, I'll meet you by the elevators."

Murdoch was instant in his response. "Make sure you bring your laptop with you like you would for a normal mission. I'll bring a new Combat suit for the Commander."

As Dante stood up and began to disconnect his laptop from the cords and mother boards, he spoke. "Bring one for Sinah too."

"Understood."

Dante glanced up at Alex. "When my mom gets home, can you tell her I was called out for a mission?"

Alex nodded with a smile. "No problem. Is it okay if I continue to look through what we collected from building Seven? I can't help but to be curious."

Dante glanced toward one of his other laptops as the emergency order to report to the Director's office appeared. "Sure, contact me if you find out anything interesting."

"I will. Good luck."

Dante gave a quick nod before he snatched up his backpack and left.

Fifty

Abandon All

The second Murdoch caught sight of Dante approaching the elevators, he questioned. "What the hell was that blood thing about?"

Dante looked toward the Combat suits and basic supply packs in Murdoch's hands. As he unzipped his backpack, he answered. "My Helix has changed."

Murdoch stuffed the supplies into the bag and nodded. "It should have increased and…"

"No, you're not hearing me. It changed! I mean changed completely. It doesn't even look like it belongs to me anymore."

Murdoch's expression shifted to confusion. "So you wanted to find out if mine had changed completely as well?"

Dante nodded hooking his backpack over his shoulders. "We're different from the others. I just wanted to know how much more different."

Murdoch glanced toward the D and A Helixes going about their days. Any D Helix that made eye contact with Murdoch quickly looked away. "Now that you mention it, the other D Helixes at the shooting range seemed really nervous around me. Especially when one made a bad shot, he seemed almost panicked like he disappointed me."

Dante pressed the call button for the elevator. "I think their Helixes are warning them about you."

As they stepped into the elevator, Murdoch questioned. "That my Helix is different?"

Dante shook his head. "No, that it's much stronger than theirs and you could be a danger to them."

Murdoch jabbed the 11th floor button. "I'd never harm my fellow Helix. Not unless given order by the Commander."

"I know that and you know that, but they don't know that."

Murdoch looked up at the highlighting floor numbers. "Do you think that's what happened in building Seven? The D Helix soldiers changed."

Dante nodded. "That's my theory but it's not like we'll ever find out for sure what happened. Heck, they themselves might not even know what happened."

Murdoch glanced toward Dante as the elevator doors opened. "Did you just say 'heck'?'

Dante went a little flush as Murdoch walked toward the reception desk. "I meant hell!"

Murdoch waited until Dante was at his side before he spoke. "The Commander's team reporting as requested."

The receptionist stood up and approached the Director's double doors. The second she knocked, he yelled out. "Yes! Send them in! Send them in!"

Once the Director caught sight of Murdoch and Dante, he spoke in a panicked tone of voice. "You need to find them! You need to bring them back! They need to be in our Facility! The minute the others know about this, they're going to send out their Helixes to find them! We can't let that happen!"

Dante shook his head. "I don't think they'll send-"

Murdoch cut Dante off stepping into his soldier awaiting a command stance. "We won't fail you Director."

The Director began to wring his hands before he finally slammed his hands on his large desk. "She is our top priority! I don't care what you have to do or how many lives you have to take! Bring God back to us!"

Murdoch's lips touched at a full frown. "Mission understood Director. Bring the Commander and God back by any means possible."

The Director pointed toward the office doors. "Well, what are you waiting for? Go!!"

Murdoch turned heel and left the Director's office. Dante wasn't hesitant to follow closely behind him. As Murdoch stepped into the elevator, he frowned. "I hate how we need to bring them both back but God is our only priority."

Dante watched Murdoch press the floor button as he spoke. "Don't stress about it Murdoch. It's not like we're really going to bring either of them back here."

Murdoch waited until the elevator doors open before he spoke. "It's not like any of us are going to come back here."

Dante, who was following closely behind Murdoch, stopped in his tracks. Murdoch, who hadn't noticed, continued on to the security booth. As the security guard handed him the clipboard with the paperwork, Murdoch glanced toward Dante. His expression shifted to confusion seeing his upset disposition. "…Dante?"

Dante's eyes darted up to Murdoch. After a slight nod as he quickly approached him. "Sorry."

Once all the paperwork was finished and they both were in the hummer, Murdoch questioned. "What's wrong?"

Try all he liked to hide it Dante's features couldn't help but to weaken. "We're never coming back."

Before Murdoch could say anything, Dante continued. "I'm leaving my Mom behind and I just made a new friend who's smart and... and..." Dante closed his eyes as his words trailed off into nothing.

Murdoch drove into the Launch Pad area. "What did you think we were going to do? You know the Commander and Sinah can't stay here."

Dante's expression became upset as he looked out the hummer window. "I don't know what I thought. I guess it never really occurred to me that we'd have to leave everyone behind."

Dante's tone of voice suddenly shifted to panic as his head shot to Murdoch. "Wait, What about Bridger?!"

Murdoch's expression weakened ever so slightly. "..There's nothing we can do for him."

Dante couldn't protest fast enough. "So we're going to just abandon him?! He'd never do that to us! We... we can't just..!"

Murdoch brought the hummer to an easy stop at the last bit of road before they were into the World of Lost Souls. "This isn't something I wanted to do either but I have my orders and you have yours. The

Commander wants you to scan the hummer for any tracking devices then disconnect our earpieces."

Dante pulled out his laptop and began to work. "So our exact location will be impossible to track."

Murdoch gave a slight nod. After a few moments of merely listening to Dante clack on his laptop keys, Murdoch reached into his pocket and pulled out something that looked like a piece of paper. Cupping it in his palm, he pressed it against his chest. As he peeked under his hand, Dante discreetly glanced toward it. His expression instantly weakened seeing that it was the photo of Murdoch and Bridger as children. Before Murdoch could notice him, Dante quickly averted his eyes and went back to work.

After staring at it for a few moments, Murdoch put the picture away then spoke. "Dante, you don't have to leave here if you don't want to. The Commander may have given the order but he's my Lord not yours. Your loyalty lies only with Sinah."

Dante looked toward Murdoch for a few moments before he pressed his earpiece. "Alex, take good care of my mom."

Before Alex had a chance to respond, Dante disconnected both his and Murdoch's earpiece. Having severed the connection from mind to Combat equipment the rectangular microchip on Dante's Combat gloves instantly flicked off. Dante glanced in the side view mirror at the facility before he whispered. "Good-bye Bridger."

Murdoch waited until Dante put his laptop away and nod before he began to drive again. Murdoch glanced toward the rear view mirror as the facility slowly disappeared behind them.

Fifty-One

Waking Up in the Dim Blue Light

Sinah slowly awoke to an empty bed. Her expression shifted to confusion as she quickly sat up. Her features instantly relaxed seeing Fallen standing naked by the open windows. His arms were crossed and his attention was locked on the eclipsed sun and moon. Sinah's cheeks touched at a red as her eyes scanned the perfection of his muscular body in the dim blue light.

Sinah pressed the blanket against her chest hiding her nudity as she leaned against the headboard. "Have you been awake long?"

Fallen turned his head toward her with a slight smile. "For a while now, I didn't want to disturb you with my restlessness."

"Why were you restless?"

Fallen didn't make a single attempt to hide his nudity as he approached the side of the bed. "There are a lot of things on my mind. But I also wanted to apologize to you."

Sinah gave him a confused look. "Apologize, for what?"

Fallen released a slight sigh. "There are many things, but for now my most recent mistake. I was just so relieved that you had recovered that

I wasn't thinking as I should have. I want to apologize for us doing this wrong."

Sinah glanced toward the bed then instantly went flush. "Th... This? Um… Well... I... I've never.."

Fallen quickly shook his head at her awkward disposition. "No.no, not in our actions but in the order we choose to approach things. We're supposed to enter into the marriage contract first before the needs of the flesh."

Sinah's eyes darted to Fallen as he kneeled down before her. "My beloved Sinah will you do me the absolute honor of entering into the marriage contract with me?"

Sinah smiled softly before she patted the top of the bed. "Please sit down."

Fallen got to his feet and sat down beside her legs. Though tempted, Sinah didn't glance at his naked body before her. "Of course I will, Fallen. But you didn't even have to ask. I've known for a while now that I would follow you onto death and beyond. I've probably known this before I was even Kid Harmond."

Fallen's eyes darted to her. "Sinah, did you know you were God?"

Sinah hesitantly gave the slightest shrug. "I might have at one point but most of the time I just felt slightly different than everyone else. Everyone that is, except you. Something about you felt familiar and I couldn't place what it was. All I knew for sure was I had to be near you. It wasn't until that Synthetic creature was strangling the life out of me, did I realize it."

Fallen's eyebrows lowered as his tone of voice became annoyed. "I shouldn't have left you behind. If Bridger hadn't-"

Sinah cut him off. "He would have been disobeying something I asked him to do."

Fallen's anger was instantly disarmed as his features shifted to shock. "You asked him to get me out of there?"

Sinah smiled slightly. "When I was a child and I was on the verge of death, I felt something within me cry out in pain. It wasn't my pain but it hurt far worse than the cruelty I had been experiencing. Worse than anything I could ever imagine. I knew I had to get as close as I could to where the feeling was calling out from. I had to get as close as I could before I could die peacefully, heal then resurrect into this."

Sinah paused looking at the glowing veins on her arms. "In this form, I would have been strong enough to help whoever was suffering, whoever was calling out to me. Unfortunately, thanks to my parent's kindness that's not what happened. Since I didn't die and become my stronger self, my development became a little detached. I think that's why I... What did Bridger call it? Phasing?"

Sinah gave a quick shrug. "Any way, I'm not quite sure what the effects were or how exactly it happened. But all the feelings of suffering and the memories of needing to become this form had vanished. That is until my life was ending in that sewer."

Sinah softly brushed her hand then rested it against Fallen's cheek. "As I felt my life slipping away, I suddenly felt that pain again. Fallen, it was your pain."

Fallen's expression shifted to confusion. "...My pain?"

"Your need to try and break through the bars to save me caused your Helix to react. It cried out to mine as it did all those years ago. All the memories long forgotten suddenly rushed back into me. Right there and then I knew what had to be done. I had to save you. That's why I called out to Bridger. I had to follow my original path to become this form. I needed to die, heal and resurrect."

Fallen placed his hand over hers on his face. "Sinah, you mentioned you were experiencing cruelty, what happened to you?"

Sinah's features weakened a little. As her hand fell from her face, Fallen questioned again. "You have the rapid healing skill yet you have burn scars on your ribs. Why haven't you healed? Why haven't you spoken to me until now? Sinah, why...?"

Sinah leaned forward and softly touched her lips to his cutting him off. Once she lifted her lips, she whispered. "It's in a human's nature to try and destroy what they don't understand."

Fifty-Two

Sinah's Sad Past

Sinah released a defeated sigh as she pressed her naked back against the headboard. "I was born in the World of the Lost Souls from two humans. It was a hard birth and the woman who carried me died during it. The man, who was helping her with the birth, didn't take it so well. Not that I expect anyone to take the death of someone they cared about well. He sat there for hours merely holding her, sobbing. I didn't cry at birth, so at first, I assumed he thought I had passed away as well. That changed when he stood up with her in his arms. He looked directly at me, frowned then left the house."

Fallen lied down beside Sinah and wrapped his arms around her waist. She couldn't help but to smile slightly as she began to stroke his hair. "I could hear him outside digging her grave. When he came back into the house, he threw me a quick glare and left me in the pool of birth blood then went off to bed."

Sinah glanced toward the open windows. "For some reason, he always left the front door wide open. I think because of that, he was hoping I would simply die from neglect. My Helix obviously had other plans and my body quickly began to develop. I pulled out the umbilical cord from my belly button, the placenta and after birth was still attached to it. I rolled onto my stomach, got onto all fours and began to crawl around exploring my surroundings."

Sinah closed her eyes. "I'll never forget his reaction to seeing me crawling. At first, he only looked at the bloody mess of my birth and nothing else. His expression was indifferent, almost relieved. I assume he figured I had been taken by another Lost Soul or that some stray animal had carried me off as a meal. Either way, once he did notice me watching him from the doorway, he screeched, grabbed a chair and tossed it at me. That was my very first encounter with violence."

Fallen's grip on Sinah tightened a little as she continued. "It got worse as I got older. I don't recall a single day that I wasn't struck or yelled at for something. He rarely spoke to me and when he did, it was usually after he had hit me and I cried or made a sound of pain. He would always yell 'I told you to never make a sound! You're to be seen not heard!' And then he would smack me again only this time with much more force. I guess that stuck with me when I became Kid Harmond."

Sinah opened her eyes as her features weakened. "I remember so many nights waking up screaming or crying when I was first at our facility. The nightmares were unbearable. My mom would always bust into my room and try her best to comfort me. She would hold me and ask what was wrong? But I..."

Fallen finished her sentence. "Your body was installed with the condition that words or sounds led back to cruelty and violence."

Sinah barely nodded. "So I never spoke."

Fallen whispered softly, glancing up at her. "Did he cause your rib scarring?"

Sinah swallowed heavily. "When he went out every day with some other Lost Souls to find food or supplies, I used that time to explore the damaged world outside. I would find small animals, ones you really don't notice, mice, mostly. One day he caught me with one. Snatching it out of my hands, he broke its neck with his thumb. As he carelessly tossed it aside, he began to yell at me. Instead of being upset or even listening to him, I approached the dead mouse and picked it up. I held it in my hands and closed my eyes. It took only a few seconds before its neck shifted back into place and its heart began to beat again. When I placed it on the ground and it ran away, something inside him snapped."

Fallen closed his eyes as his expression weakened a little. "He saw the power of Creation."

Sinah weakly nodded. "And it sent him into a scared rage. He dragged me into the house and beat me far worse than he ever did before. One aggressive back hand cross the face sent me toward the floor. As I fell, the side of my head smashed against the kitchen table, after that, only darkness."

Sinah smiled slightly running her hand deep into Fallen's hair. "Within that darkness I heard your pain cry out to me. I felt an overwhelming urge wield up within me. I had to make it as close to you as I could. I knew I was going to die but it wasn't going to be there. Not so far away from where I was needed."

Sinah's smile faded. "I opened my eyes and all I could smell was gasoline. He was splashing it all over the kitchen and me. He kept saying the world doesn't need monsters like me. He should have killed me at birth and creatures with freak powers need to be burned to death."

Sinah closed her eyes. "And with that, he struck at match and dropped it on me. I caught fire and that overwhelming urge took over. He never even got that chance to react to me standing up before I snatched my hand around his throat and crushed his windpipe. As he fell to his knees, I left my birth place to burn to the ground. I didn't once glance back as I dragged my mangled body toward the one who truly needed my help."

Sinah opened her eyes and softly smiled down Fallen. Her hand slipped from his hair onto his cheek. "Thank you Fallen. If it wasn't for you, I wouldn't have had the strength to survive."

Fallen released a slight sigh. "I would say 'you're welcome' but I didn't realize my Helix was even doing it. I wonder if it was through the sadistic experimentation that it called out."

Sinah shrugged. "I wouldn't know. All I do know is that your Helix saved mine. Fallen you saved me."

Fallen sat up and slowly reached into the covers hiding Sinah's nudity. Her cheeks couldn't help but to blush and her breath couldn't help to tremble as his hand brushed the side of her breast then rest upon her ribs. Fallen locked his eyes with hers before he whispered. "You have suffered such a horrible past. But my dear sweet counterpart, you're not that abused lost little girl anymore. You are God and it's time you allow yourself to forget the pain you have endured and heal."

Sinah barely nodded. "I think that's what was going to happen if I had died and resurrected like I was supposed to. I think my mind and body was going to awaken with a clean slate. That was of course, before everything got interrupted."

Fallen whispered again caressing her skin. "Then why not let yourself heal now?"

Sinah placed her hand upon his and closed her eyes. Fallen's lips touched at a smile feeling a soft warmth radiate from her body. Once she lifted her hand, she whispered. "Let us start anew together."

Fallen lifted his hand. Once he saw that the burn scars had vanished, his smile increased. "Yes, let this be our new beginning."

Sinah gave Fallen's mouth a quick kiss before she said. "After a little more sleep."

Fallen couldn't help but to chuckle as Sinah got more comfortable on the bed.

Fifty-Three

On the Missing Persons List Again

Violet hissed at the three D Helix soldiers at the security booth in building Seven. "What do you mean I can't go inside?! My daughter is in there!"

The D Helix soldier sitting behind the enclosed booth merely shrugged. "We don't have any request orders in for a Violet or Amos Harmond."

Violet's eyes darted to Amos. "What's going on? Emma said we could come back."

Before Amos had a chance to even open his mouth, Violet hissed toward them again. "You have no right to keep us from our daughter! Let us in before-!"

The two D Helix soldiers by the scanner gripped their weapons. One of the two spoke. "This is building Seven. Nobody gets in without a request or under special circumstances. Neither of you have either of those requirements, please leave before you are forcibly removed."

Amos calmly lifted his hands. "Okay, okay, everyone just needs to calm down."

The D Helix soldiers glared at Amos as he protectively stepped in front of his wife. "Is Emma Witfield in the building?"

The D Helix soldier behind the booth tapped on a few green screens. "Yes, Lead ADGL Tech Emma Witfeild is here."

"Is it okay if we have her paged? We really need to talk to her."

"If she refuses your request, you are to leave this building immediately."

Amos gave a quick nod. "Yes of course."

Violet instantly shook her head. "No! I won't leave until I see-!"

Violet frantically shook her head as Amos took her hand and pulled her a few feet away from the booth. "I'm not leaving Amos! I'm not leaving Kid to-"

Amos cut her protest off. "I think the situation here is much worse than we thought."

"What do you mean?"

Amos glanced at the frowning D Helix soldiers. "We were supposed to wait for Murdoch to bring us back here after the shutdown mode. He didn't show up and when we checked the buildings status, it's still on shutdown mode."

Violet swallowed heavily. "Do you think it has something to do with what happened when we were leaving?"

"It has to. They wouldn't have just forgotten to remove the shutdown system. Did we run through some sort of altercation? Maybe there was a lot more fighting then we-"

Violet cut Amos off flipping into panic mode. "Oh my god, do you think they attacked Kid?!"

Before Violet had a chance to rip free from Amos' grip and rush toward the security booth, Emma passed through the scanner. "…Harmonds."

Within a blink of the eye, Violet turned on Emma. "Is she hurt?! How did this even happen?!"

Emma released a defeated yet frustrated sigh. "Trust me this wasn't something any of us expected."

Amos looked toward the D Helix soldiers. "Was it a snap?"

"We've been trying to figure that out but all signs point to no. When a Helix snaps, they lose control. It's like a frenzied chaos, like a momentary loss of sanity. It wasn't like that at all."

Amos barely nodded. "Is everything fine now? You do know that building Seven is still on shut down mode right?"

Emma pointed toward the lone passage leading away from building

Seven. As Amos began to follow and pull Violet with him, she resisted and hissed. "Where are you two going?!"

Violet pointed toward the security booth as she continued. "Kid is that way!"

Emma slowly shook her head as an awkward expression took her features. "That's what I need to talk to you two about."

Both Amos and Violet's eyes darted to her. Violet instantly flipped into a full on panic. "Did they attack her too?! Is she hurt?!"

Emma's expression shifted to confusion. "Attack her too? Wait a minute! Here I've been talking to you two like you know what happened, do you know what happened?"

Amos licked his lips. "Not in any detail. When Murdoch was escorting us out of the building we heard gunfire."

Emma instantly began to frown. "And he didn't report it?"

"Two or was it three? I think it was three of the Helix guarding the booth, were killed."

Emma stomped down the passage like a child having a temper tantrum. "Why wouldn't he report the incident? Or even activate the full building emergency systems. He knows the protocol better than anyone else. He's a Helix soldier that-"

Emma suddenly stopped short in both words and in movement. Her mouth slowly dropped open in shock and realization. "...No. ...That little son of a bitch."

Amos gave her a look of confusion. "Who?"

Emma's demeanor instantly shifted to royally ticked off. "The Commander's Info, Data, Surveillance and sneaky little A Helix soldier must have altered the security videos!"

"Why would he do that?"

Emma frowned as much as she could. "I've seen the videos more times than I can count, just trying to see if we missed something. I never realized it until now that Murdoch never left the building. We were so focused on the other Helix soldiers that I didn't even think to look for him. I saw him coming in but not going out."

Both Amos and Violet stared at Emma in bewilderment. Amos gave a blind wave of his hand behind himself. "Doesn't that mean he's still in the building?"

"No, he and that little surveillance bastard have been sent on a special mission to find God and Perfect Experiment A. They must have planned this all along. They didn't just disappear, this was planned escape."

Both Amos and Violet clicked into a state of utter panic. Violet freaked out first. "They escaped?! Kid's gone?!"

Amos wasn't hesitant to follow after. "Escaped where, the building, or the facility?!"

Emma released a loud long defeated sigh as she pointed down the passage. "Come on Harmonds, let's get some coffee and I'll explain everything."

Fifty-Four

Plan A

Fallen's eyes snapped open hearing the front door to the house open. Sitting up, his eyebrows lowered. He could hear a muffled conversation and footsteps on the main floor below them. Fallen's eyes shifted down to Sinah. She was still fast asleep with a contented serene look upon her face. A soft smile couldn't help but to take his lips as he raised the blankets higher upon her shoulder. "Rest well my sweet counterpart. I will deal with the intruders."

Carefully, Fallen shifted off the bed trying his best not to disturb her slumber. The second his bare feet touched the floor, his eyebrows lowered. Once dressed, he approached the night table on Sinah's side of the bed. He smiled softly looking down at her. "I will kill anyone who tries to get in our way. These Lost Souls are just vessels of flesh, blood and bone that need to be crushed."

Fallen snatched up his sunglasses, put them on then left the master bedroom. As he swiftly yet silently moved down the stairs, his angry demeanor vanished. Once he stepped onto the main floor, he looked toward Murdoch and Dante. It was the two of them that had entered the house.

The second Murdoch noticed Fallen he stepped into his soldier awaiting a command stance. "Commander."

Fallen put his hands on his waist. "Did you have any difficulty finding this place?"

"No Commander, whenever I tried to turn down a road leading away from here, I instantly felt like I was heading the wrong way."

Fallen turned his attention to Dante. "Good. Dante, have you disconnected any and all devices that could track us?"

Dante unhooked his backpack and placed it on the coffee table. As he unzipped and removed the new sets of Combat gear, he spoke. "Yes Commander."

As Dante placed the garb onto the coffee table, he whispered. "Um... Is... Is she alright?"

Fallen's lips touched at a gentle smile. "She's asleep upstairs. She should be awake shortly."

Dante's eyes lit up in both happiness and relief. "She's recovered?! Oh thank God!! …or …uh …thank ...um."

Fallen cut Dante's fumbling words off. "Dante, can you locate the other Labs without exposing our current location?"

Dante quickly nodded retrieving his laptop from his backpack. "That shouldn't be a problem Commander. All I have to do is activate a scrambler on my laptop and my location will jump all over the place. They won't be able to pin point exactly where it's coming from."

Fallen picked up his new Combat suit and began to change. "Good locate them and send out a message. Inform them that the Director wants them to arrive at our Lab ASAP."

Murdoch's eyes darted to Fallen in confusion. "Why would we want that Commander? Each Lab is going to bring their strongest Helixes or successful Synthetic Helix creations with them."

An ugly sneer took Fallen's lips. "Yes I know, that's exactly what we want them to do. Their days of obeying the human filth are coming to an end. Sinah and I are ready to take our places as their Lords. We are ready to take full control over this worthless world."

Dante glanced up from his laptop with a slight look of concern. "But she just recovered Commander."

Fallen held his sneer, clenching his fists. "Once those other Labs show their faces, they will see my true strength. They will know my true form"

"And Sinah?"

Fallen glanced up at the ceiling, his sneer became a soft smile. "When I have dealt with everything and everyone, I will show her our new world, a world truly worthy of us."

Fallen turned his attention back to Dante as his smile faded. "Now Dante, I want you to stay here with Sinah and keep her safe. Murdoch and I are heading back to the facility."

Dante shook his head as Murdoch left the house. "B... But Commander, I haven't finished-"

Fallen cut him off approaching the open doorway. "Keep working. By the time we've collected the needed supplies and I've awakened the true strength and potential of the D Helix soldiers, they should be arriving."

Fallen glanced up at the ceiling again, with a soft smile. "Rest well my beloved counterpart."

"...But Commander?"

Fallen cut him off grabbing the door knob. "Get it done Dante!"

Dante gave a slight nod as Fallen closed the door behind himself. Hearing him step off the porch, he whispered. "But what will happen to the A Helixes?"

Fifty-Five

Plan Bridger

Dante frowned a little frantically clicking on his laptop keys. "Ugh, this Lab's security is so annoying."

Dante released a frustrated sigh combined with a hiss as he dropped his head. "Damn it, Kicked out again!"

Dante's eyebrows lowered as he rolled up his sleeves. He gave his laptop screen a confident nod before he began to work again. "You just don't know who you're dealing with! I am Dante, a high level A Helix that is different from all the others! An A Helix who is the master of..."

Dante paused for a split second then made a sound of annoyance. "Damn it!"

Dante lifted his hands from the keyboard, cracked his knuckles then frantically began to type. "Alright, you son of a bitch! What if I did this and then this and maybe a little that and…"

Dante paused for a split second before the laptop made a sound of approval. Dante suddenly made a sound of triumph. "Ha! Ha! Ha! See! Dante the master of Information, Data, Surveillance and everything else wins again!"

Dante proudly leapt to his feet. Before he could do a childish victory dance, Sinah walked into the room. Dante instantly went bright red, both in embarrassment and the fact Sinah only had a blanket wrapped around her, hiding her nudity.

Dante turned his head from her and sat back down on the couch. "I... I... Uh... I'm glad you recovered Sin… Uh… God? Um..."

Sinah smiled slightly looking around. "Sinah is fine."

Dante's head shot back to her in shock. "You can speak?!"

Sinah held her slight smile and nodded. "I just needed to fully recover and awaken in this form. Tell me, where is Fallen?"

Dante released an awkward chuckle. "I've never heard the Commander called by name before. It's a little weird."

Sinah shifted her eyes to Dante. The second she made eye contact with him, Dante gasped. A strong wave of strength washed over him. Different from Fallen's overwhelming and smothering air of intimidation, Sinah's air was soft, warm and almost comforting. Dante couldn't help but to stumble over his words a little. "H... He wen... He went back to the facility for supplies and to awaken the D Helixes."

Sinah's expression shifted to concern. "What about the A Helixes, they're going to panic without me being there. They could easily turn on the D Helixes merely in a misguided self-defense."

Before Dante could say anything, Sinah spoke again. "We need to go back. We need to return to the facility."

"But the Commander…"

"Probably wants to deal with everything himself."

Dante barely nodded. "He wants to show you a new world."

Sinah's expression weakened a little. "One based solely on destruction. I can't let that happen, too many people will be killed."

"Then what do we do Sinah?"

Sinah smiled slightly. "I get some clothes on and we go save Bridger."

Dante's eyes lit up as a full smile took his lips. "Really?!"

"I am grateful to both you and him for finding my dead body." Sinah respectfully placed her hand on her collarbone then bowed. "Thank you from the bottom of my heart Dante."

Dante instantly went flush as he awkwardly shook his head lifting his hands. "No, no it's okay! It's okay! We're a team. I'm just happy you've recovered."

Sinah's features weakened as she closed her eyes. "I never meant to hurt him. When I was resurrected, it was by Fallen's strength and not by my own. My body just panicked and forced Bridger's A Helix to fully awaken."

Sinah gripped the blanket tightly. "Poor Bridger, the suffering his Helix has experienced is…"

Sinah opened her eyes and looked up at Dante. He had a very upset look on his face. Seeing his expression, Sinah forced a smile and a happy tone. "We'll get him out of there soon enough."

Sinah gave an upward nod at the Combat gear sitting on the coffee table. "Are those for me?"

Dante's eyes darted to the gear before quickly nodded. "What? Oh! Yeah, yeah."

Sinah scooped them up with a smile. "I'll get changed and we'll get going."

Fifty-Six

A Minor Issue

Dante gripped his backpack straps standing on the porch. Once the fully clothed Sinah joined him, he spoke. "Are you ready?"

Sinah smiled and nodded. The second she stepped off the porch, her features weakened and her smile vanished. A powerful wave of the world's emotions rushed over her. Placing her hand on her chest, she looked up at the eclipsed sun and moon. "...So much suffering."

Dante, who didn't quite hear her, questioned. "What?"

Sinah forced back her upset expression and shook her head. "... Nothing."

Both Sinah and Dante walked toward the hummer, he and Murdoch arrived in. An awkward chuckle escaped Dante's throat as they both reached for the passenger side door handle. "Umm… I can't drive."

Sinah's eyes darted to Dante. "You can't? Neither can I."

Dante gave Sinah a confused look. "You can't? But you're God."

Sinah snickered a little. "And that means I can drive?"

Dante shrugged. "Well God's supposed to be all knowing and all powerful."

Sinah couldn't help but to snicker again. "And apparently being all knowing and all powerful gives me the skill to drive?"

Dante walked a few feet back toward the house. "Damn, it's too far to make it back there by foot, by the time we arrive all hell could have broken out."

Dante released a weak chuckle. "…Literally."

Sinah looked at the hummer then back toward Dante. "We need to get back there Dante."

Dante released a frustrated sigh. "I know. If only the Commander didn't have me disconnect my earpiece, I could've at least asked Alex for help."

Dante approached the porch as he unhooked his backpack. "I'm sure I can find the basic instructions on how to use a vehicle, give me a few moments."

Sinah took a few steps toward him as she questioned. "Why did he have you disconnect them?"

Dante pulled his laptop out of his back pack and began to work. "Our earpieces can be used as tracking devices. The Commander didn't want anyone to find you."

Sinah reached for her earpiece. Not only was it missing but there wasn't any sign that something had been pierced in her ear to begin with. "We're going back to the facility anyway so I don't think it's going to make any difference. Besides, once your Helix awakens completely, it will naturally disconnect and become useless. If your friend can help us then ask him."

Dante's eyes darted up to Sinah. "But the Commander said..."

Sinah gave a shrug as she smiled. "He isn't here."

Dante chuckled a little shaking his head. "What am I even thinking? I'm an A Helix, my loyalty is to God. I'm supposed to listen and obey only you."

Sinah's smile faded as she barely nodded. Dante chuckled again as he went back to work. "I'm not sure what I was expecting when God was successfully created or arrive or whatever they were supposed to do. But it never even once crossed my mind that you would be God. I thought Bridger was crazy when he said it. But he was right and here you are."

Sinah barley nodded again. Dante clicked on a few more keys. "And you're definitely not what I was expecting. To me, you still feel like Sinah, one of the Commander's team. Sometimes you felt a little different but I always thought that was because you were a higher A Helix then-"

Sinah cut Dante off. "Um… We need to get going."

Dante instantly went flush before he frantically began to work. "Oh! Yeah, right, Sorry!"

The second Dante's earpiece turned back on, he pressed it. "Alex? Alex, can you hear me?"

Alex's panicked voice responded. "Yes, I'm here! Are you okay? The way you said good-bye sounded like you were never coming back."

"Yeah I know, sorry about that, what's the status there?"

"Building Seven is still on shut down mode and a state of caution has been declared. Everyone has been ordered by the Director to stay in the location they were when the announcement was released. I've been paying attention to the surveillance feeds. The Military and the Helix soldiers seem to be looking for something. They've been moving around in groups and in a more tactical way."

Once Dante told Sinah of the situation, she took a few more steps toward the porch. "Fallen might have just busted in there without hesitation. They could be searching for him."

Dante nodded slightly. "That's what I'm thinking too. Alex, I'm going to open line my earpiece."

"What for?"

Dante smiled looking up at Sinah. "I'm here with God."

A loud gasp could be heard from Dante's earpiece. "She... She's okay?"

Dante smiled even more. "Ask her yourself."

Alex's tone of voice was full of nerves. "Uh… Um… H... Hello God."

Sinah gave a quick 'hello' in return. Dante snickered at Alex's nerves. "Hello? That's it?"

Alex's nerves shifted to panic. "I… I don't know what to say to God! She's God! I... I-!"

Sinah cut him off. "It's fine. How do you drive?'

There was a noticeable pause in Alex's response. "…Drive?"

Dante shifted his attention back down to his laptop. "I can't drive and neither can she, can you?"

"Yeah but how can I help with that, here?"

Dante clicked on a few keys. "I have the basic instructions in front of me but I think someone walking us through it will be easier."

"Okay, no problem. I'll do my best. First you need to-"

Sinah suddenly cut Alex off. "We have something else to deal with first."

Dante's eyes darted to the frowning Sinah. His eyes then shifted beyond her toward the hummer. A Lost Soul stood by the passenger side with his handgun raised and aimed at the back of Sinah's head.

Fifty-Seven

Desperation

Dante frantically withdrew his gun from its holster and stood up. As he raised his weapon, the Lost Soul hissed. His tone of voice sounded not only angry but somewhat panicked. "Don't be stupid boy or I'll blow a hole through the back of your girl's pretty little head."

Sinah turned toward the man. He was dressed in filthy rags and looked like bathing wasn't a luxury he had in his hard life. "He's not the danger you should be concerned about."

The Lost Soul scoffed gripping his handgun. "I'm not concerned about either of you. I have no problem killing you both to get what I want."

Dante swallowed heavily seeing the microchip on the top of his Combat glove suddenly shut off. Despite the fact his gun was now being completely useless, he didn't lower it. "And what is it that you want?"

The Lost Soul back kicked the hummer's tire with the bottom of his shoe. "This. Now be good little children and just stay there."

Sinah walked toward the Lost Soul with a slight frown. "That's ours, we need it."

The Lost Soul growled. "Stay where you are! I will kill you!"

Sinah stopped walking just inches in front of his weapon. The Lost Soul shifted his nervous eyes from Sinah to Dante. "Lower your weapon! Do it now Boy!"

Sinah calmly lifted her hand. "Do it Dante."

Dante's eyes darted to the back of Sinah's head. "But..! But he's going to kill you!"

Sinah snickered quietly. "He won't get the chance."

The Lost Soul's expression shifted to confusion until Sinah continued. "Besides, his weapons are useless against me."

Before the Lost Soul had a chance to respond or even blink, Sianh slashed his gun clean in half. She then slammed him against the hummer and hooked something razor sharp under his chin against his jugular. The Lost Soul's shocked and traumatized eyes darted to the large golden circle that had appeared behind Sinah's back then the golden feathers falling around it. All looked more like images of gold light as opposed to something physical. They quickly faded from his vision as Sinah spoke. "Ending your life won't mean anything to me either."

The Lost Soul gasped feeling his skin begin to split from whatever Sinah had placed under his chin. Suddenly a woman's panicked voice called out. "Please don't kill him!"

Sinah didn't move or even glance toward the back of the hummer where the voice came from. "Show yourself."

A woman slowly came out from hiding. Another, much younger woman was leaning against her. She was severely wounded and had to be dragged to move. Both were dressed similar and appeared to have suffered the same hardships as the first Lost Soul. Tears poured down the woman's face as she spoke. "Please don't kill him. We're just trying to save our daughter!"

Dante's eyes darted to the woman in shock. "Daughter?! But the reproduction system shouldn't be functioning correctly or at all for that matter."

Sinah lowered her eyebrows. "Dante, see what you can do."

As Dante ran toward the two women, the man tried to protectively lunge forward. "No! Stay away from them!"

Sinah slammed her weight against him forcing him to stay still. "I will kill you."

The Mother of the wounded woman slowly helped her daughter lay down on the ground. As Dante knelt down to them, he glanced toward Sinah and the man. In each of her hands was one of the golden feathers. The one hooked under the man's throat had his blood on it. These seemingly beautiful feathers of light were being used as daggers.

Dante turned his attention back to the wounded woman. She had a lot of bloody material wrapped around her stomach. Dante lifted the edge a little to see the severity of the wound. It was a large oozing bloody gash. By all rhyme and reason, this type of wound should have killed her. Dante gently lifted her wrist and checked the sickly pale woman's pulse. It was very weak and slow. The wounded woman stared back at Dante with eyes brimming on vacant.

Dante placed her wrist back on the ground then looked up at the sobbing Mother. "What happened?"

The Father of the wounded woman hissed trying to move again. "It doesn't matter what happened! Let me go! Get away from her and-!"

Sinah cut the father off by pushing the feather harder against his throat. Blood began to not only slowly cover the feather but also crawl down Sinah's hand. "Understand me If I tell you again, I will decapitate you."

The Father's eyes darted to Sinah's. His expression shifted to shock seeing the unnoticeable four point star in her pupil. As it began to gain more points, he quickly turned his head. "You're one of those demon creatures those damn Labs make."

Sinah gripped the feather. "…Not exactly."

The Mother stroked her daughter's forehead. "There was an explosion. We weren't anywhere near it but we heard it. Some of the pieces began to fall from the sky. We ran for cover but when I looked back..." The mother's sentence trailed off into incoherent sobs.

The Father's expression weakened a little. "There's this doctor. She says she used to be in one of those Labs. She helps everyone she can, but for a price. She saw our daughter and said, for how bad she is she needs a working vehicle as payment."

Both Dante and Sinah's lips touched at a frown. Dante glanced toward Sinah. "Well, that's a sick thing to do. That Lead Med or simple Med Tech is giving false hope. What's the likelihood a Lost Soul would even come across a working vehicle?"

The Father frowned looking toward him. "We have! Now just hand it over and we'll be on our way!"

The Mother clasped her hands together and lifted them in front of her face in a pleading manner. "Please, please I beg of you. We don't want to lose our daughter. Please just let us have it and save her."

Dante's expression weakened looking at her tear soaked cheeks. "I hate to say this but it's a miracle she's even alive now. Even if we didn't need the hummer and let you have it, she's probably going to be dead by the time you-"

"Let's make a trade."

Everyone's eyes darted to Sinah. The Father frowned shaking his head. "Whatever you're trying to pull, we're not-"

Cutting him off, the Mother spoke. "What type of trade?"

Sinah glanced toward her. "We can't drive and we need to get back to our Lab."

Fifty-Eight

Bargaining With Mercy

The Father frowned as much as he could as he clenched his fists. "What the hell does that have to do with anything?! We don't care!" Sinah glared back toward him. "We will gladly give you the hummer if you drive us to our Lab. After that, it's all yours."

The Father couldn't help but to scoff. "Are you out of your mind?! We're not going anywhere near those places!"

The Mother looked down at her daughter as more tears began to fall. "Even if we agreed, your friend is probably right. Our daughter might not even make it to the doctor. She's losing a lot of blood and we can't seem to stop it."

Dante shook his head. "And you wouldn't be able to. The combinations of bombs he used were-"

The Mother's eyes darted up to Dante. "The bombs he used? You know what happened?"

Dante's expression weakened to awkward and slightly apologetic. "Well, we-"

Sinah cut him off. "Will you drive us to our Lab?"

The frowning Father hissed. "Are you stupid or something?! He just said our daughter probably won't make it and thanks to all this blabbing we've done, she probably won't last much longer."

A few tears escaped his watering eyes as he hissed again. "All you bastards had to do was let us have the goddamn vehicle! We could have saved her! We could have-!"

"I will save her."

More tears fell from the Father's eyes as he growled at Sinah. "There's nothing you can do! There's nothing anyone can do!"

Sinah released the Father and began to walk toward the wounded woman. Without hesitation, he snatched her arm. "Don't you dare touch her!"

Sinah didn't shift her attention from the wounded woman on the ground. "You're her father right? Do as a father should and save her life."

The Father gripped Sinah's arm tighter. "My daughter is-!"

"About to die. Now if you don't allow me to help her..." Sinah paused as her eyes shifted back to him. Sinah's pupil was now completely covered by the bright glowing gold light. Her tone and demeanor was very calm as she finished her sentence. "..Her blood will be on your hands."

The Father only calmly stared into Sinah's eyes for a split second before he turned his head and began to retch. As he doubled over like he was going to vomit, he let Sinah's arm go. Once Sinah walked over to the others and knelt down, the Mother spoke. "W... What did you do to him?'

Sinah glanced back at him. Not a single drop of sickness left his body. He was merely aggressively dry heaving. She looked back toward the wounded woman. She appeared to be a few years younger than herself. "Nothing, he just saw something he shouldn't have."

Dante glanced toward Sinah then the Father. He was sweating like crazy and looked like it took all of his effort not to collapse. "He saw something humans are never meant to see. Something their immortal souls are not worthy enough to view upon until death."

Sinah snickered quietly. "You sound like Fallen."

Dante instantly went flush looking back at her. "I didn't mean to!"

Sinah didn't shift her eyes from the wounded young woman on the ground. "I can save your daughter but we need to be driven back to our Lab. If we don't make it back, many more lives than you can even imagine will be taken."

The Mother looked down at her daughter then up to Sinah. "If you save her, we will take you anywhere you need to go, I promise."

Sinah gave a slight nod before she used the feathers in her hands to slash away the material covering the wound. Once it was exposed to the air, she released the feathers then slammed her hands into the gaping wound. The wounded woman made a loud sound of discomfort at the pain Sinah's actions were causing.

Dante's eyes darted to the worried and panicked looking Mother. It looked like any minute, her motherly instincts would kick in and she would shove Sinah away to protect her kin. Dante quickly shifted himself over to her and wrapped his arms around her shoulders. He began to whisper the words 'it's okay' over and over in a comforting manner. The Mother barely nodded gripping his arm.

Sinah smiled softly and whispered. "This is going to hurt. You have some remnants of the explosion still inside you."

Even though the light in her eyes had almost completely gone out, she gave the slightest nod of her head. She whispered again. "What the bomb was created out of is slowly deteriorating your organs."

The Father, who was panting out of breath now that the retching had stopped, hissed. "Why in the hell are you telling her that?!"

Sinah only held her soft smile. "The pain is going to be excruciating. It may be too much for her to handle. If she's aware of it, she'll fight harder to get through it."

The Father couldn't help but to frown. "That's just sick!"

Sinah closed her eyes. "No, that's the strength and determination of the soul."

The large golden circle appeared behind Sinah's back and another smaller one appeared behind her head. Both of the wounded woman's parents stared at Sinah in both shock and awe. Sinah opened her golden eyes and locked them with the wounded woman's eyes. "Are you ready?"

Once Sinah was given the slightest nod in acceptance, the large golden circle behind her began to spin. Tons of feathers were expelled from it but didn't fall to the ground. They simply levitated all around Sinah. The Father, Mother and even Dante's mouth dropped wide open at such a sight. Sinah lowered her head and closed her eyes. As if being pulled by a magnet force, every feather shot toward the gaping wound.

The wounded woman's eyes widened as much as they could. Suddenly all of her muscles tightened and her back arched. Her fingers and toes spread widely as she began to scream. The more feathers that flooded into her injury, the more agony filled her screams became. Once they reached the level of ear piercing, the Mother tried to break free from Dante grip. Despite her struggling, Dante only continued to whisper 'it's okay' in a comforting tone of voice.

The Father on the other hand, seemed locked in place. Even though he wanted desperately to rush over to his family, his body wouldn't seem to let him. It was as if his feet had been shackled to the ground. All he could do was stare helplessly at what was happening in absolute shock and sympathy.

As more and more feathers rushed into the wound and began to over flow it, they quickly began to lock together covering her body. Once the last feather landed in place, Sinah tore her hands out of the wound. As the blood on her hands faded, so did the golden circles. The wounded woman only continued to screech feeling an overwhelming burning sensation rush violently all over her body.

The Mother struggled as hard as she could in Dante's arms. "My baby, you're hurting her! Stop! Please stop! Let me go!"

As Dante gripped her tighter, he glanced up at Sinah. She had a look of utter distraught upon her face. Without hesitation, Dante questioned. "Sinah, are you alright?"

Seeing his look of concern, Sinah forced a smile. It was very weak and even though her eyes had returned to normal, they seemed to reflect a great sadness. Before Dante could say anything, Sinah waved her hand in a slightly dismissive manner. Dante, who thought she was trying to brush him off, opened his mouth to say something again. Before any words could pass his lips, the Mother gasped.

Dante's eyes darted down to the wounded woman. All of the feathers had turned black. The Mother instantly stopped her resisting as many strong gusts of wind hit all of their bodies. Dante's grip loosened in shock as the black feathers suddenly turned to ash. Every time the wind stuck them, more and more of the ash simply blew away. As it did, more and more of their daughter's perfectly healed clean skin became exposed.

Once the last bit of the feather ash blew away, the once injured young woman stopped screeching. Light once again filled her eyes and any looming moments of death had long vanished. She blinked a couple of times as her hands slowly found their way onto her stomach. Her expression shifted to a confused disbelief as she slowly sat up. "Mama, what happened?"

The second Dante let the Mother go, she snatched her daughter into an aggressive hug. As she began to cry profusely, Sinah stood up and walked a few feet away from them. Dante's expression shifted to a confused concern as Sinah wrapped her arms around herself.

Fifty-Nine

From Pain to Blame

Dante didn't glance toward the Father as he ran to his family. His attention was solely locked on Sinah. As he approached her, he began to feel a numb pain in his chest. The closer he got, the more intense the feeling became. It wasn't a physical pain by any means it was more like an emotional one.

The second Dante stepped in front of her, his expression weakened. A few iridescent colored tears fell from Sinah's eyes. As he reached out to console her, she spoke. "When I was disconnected I never felt the world's pain, its unbearable cruelty, the savage acts, the pointless killings. Why? Why did the world resort to violence? Why didn't they become stronger? Why didn't they pull together and become stronger as humankind?'

Sinah closed her eyes as more tears fell. "Why does it feel like Fallen is right and they should all be wiped out? They should all be forsaken."

Before Dante could open his mouth to say something, the Daughter yelled out. "Wow! Look at that!"

Dante's eyes darted toward the sky in the direction she was pointing. Her parents gasped in shock while Dante's expression shifted to confusion. In the sky was a decent sized dark grey cloud. Even though the wind was moving with Sinah's breath, the cloud remained still. It was as if it was locked in place.

Dante's eyes darted to Sinah as she whispered. "The world is beginning to awaken."

Before he could question what she meant, Sinah began to walk toward the hummer. "We need to get back."

Dante quickly nodded then ran back toward the family. The Daughter stared up at the cloud with a smile. "What is it?'

The Mother shook her head. "I don't know. I've never seen anything like that before."

The Daughter giggled a little. "It looks beautiful and fluffy. I bet it would be soft to touch."

As the Mother smiled and nodded, Dante spoke. "Okay, now we need you to keep your end of the bargain."

The Father frowned up at him protectively gripping his family. "The hell we…!"

The Mother cut him off as she got to her feet. As she helped her daughter to hers, she spoke. "We're happy to help."

The Father only held his frown. As they walked toward the hummer, Dante spoke. "Alex, are you still there?"

Alex was instant in his response. "Yes, I'm here! Is everything alright? I was going to ask earlier but I didn't want to be a stupid distraction."

The Lost Soul family looked around in confusion hearing Alex's voice. Dante looked toward Sinah as she climbed into the back seat. "Have you caught sight of the Commander in any of the surveillances?"

A few key board clicking sounds could be heard before Alex responded. "No but the latest report says, if anyone sees the Commander, they are not to engage him but to contact the military or Helix military immediately. He's on the traitors list."

Dante glanced at the Lost Soul family. All of them were staring at him in confusion. "Okay Alex, if you see the Commander or Murdoch, I want you to report it to either military. Don't tell them where they really are or anything, just give them a false report."

"Mislead them away from their location."

"Exactly, then tell us where they actually are, got it?"

"I'm on it. See you when you get back."

Dante gave an upward nod toward the hummer. "Hop in everyone. I just need to get my stuff."

As the two women walked toward the vehicle, the Father spoke. "Who were you talking to?"

Dante shrugged. "Someone from our Lab, don't worry about it."

As Dante took a few steps toward the porch, he questioned again. "How are you talking to them? Where's your walkie-talkie?"

Dante chuckled pointing to his earpiece. "Those types of devices are cumbersome, so we use modified internal devices."

"What does that mean?"

Dante's lips touched at a frown as he looked back at the man. "It means get into the hummer already."

The Father frowned in return then stomped away from him. As Dante scooped up his backpack, he scoffed under his breath. "'What does that mean?' Stupid Lost Soul."

The two women sat in the back seat with Sinah. Both of them couldn't say 'thank you' enough. Sinah merely nodded keeping her attention locked on the outside world. Once the Father climbed into the driver's seat, he fixed his mirror to face Sinah. "So you really are one of those monsters from the Labs."

The Mother instantly hissed toward him. "How can you say that?! She just saved our daughter's life!"

The Father didn't glance toward Dante as he climbed into the passenger's side and rested his laptop on his lap. "I think all those Labs should be burned to the ground."

Dante frowned tossing him a glare. "And if they were, your daughter wouldn't be alive right now."

The Father chuckled shaking his head. "Yes she would. That explosion probably wouldn't have even happened to begin with. I bet my life that it was that underground Lab that exploded. Probably one of those freaks broke free and went crazy or maybe-"

The Mother cut him off. "That's enough. We're grateful and thankful. There aren't any words that I have that are good enough to tell you how grateful we are."

The Father turned on the engine and growled. "Grateful? Oh yeah, we're grateful alright. We're so grateful that we live in this hell hole and-"

Dante cut him off with a snip. "Head East. And every single month, the Labs offer everyone a safe place to live. We offer food, shelter and training in-"

The Father couldn't help but to cut Dante off with a scoff as he began to drive. "Yeah and at what cost? To be experimented on? To have our baby making bits tampered with? No thank you. I don't care what anyone says about our messed up systems, we didn't have any trouble getting pregnant."

Sinah closed her eyes. "That's because I had been born and the flow of Creation had begun again."

The Father's eyes shifted up to Sinah. "…Flow of Creation? What in the hell are you talking about?"

The Mother gripped her daughter as an excitable yet nervous smile took her lips. "Y... You're God aren't you?"

A full frown instantly devoured the Father's lips as his eyes sharpened toward Sinah's reflection. "You're God?"

Sinah opened her eyes but didn't answer nor did she shift her attention from the window. The Father began to violently wring the steering wheel with both hands. "How the hell could you let the world get this way?!"

Sinah's features weakened a little as he hissed again. "We're struggling out here just to stay alive! We're lucky if we live long enough to go to sleep and even luckier if we wake up in the morning! We could be killed by anyone at any time! How could you let this happen?! Why aren't you protecting us?! God is supposed to protect us! Why in the hell haven't you been protecting us?!"

Not getting a response from her, he growled. "Answer me damn it!"

Dante spoke in a calm yet firm voice. "What exactly is she supposed to protect you from, yourselves?"

The Father's eyes darted to Dante. "What's that?"

Dante glanced at his laptop then pointed through the windshield. "Make a right at the second intersection."

Once he did, Dante continued on his train of thought. "It wasn't God who made all of you forget the kindness in your hearts and become selfish. Nor was it her who made you forget the capability humanity has to pull together and take care of one another. All of you simply ignored what should have come naturally."

Dante pointed again. "Take another right and you're blaming the wrong person for what happened. Maybe you Lost Souls should take a hard look in the mirror now and again and recognize your own sins."

The Father held his frown as Dante continued. "You made the choice to take the dark paths and justify all your actions whether they were right or wrong. Take a moment to realize just who you should be mad at, just who really is to blame."

A few iridescent tears escaped Sinah's eyes as she whispered. "Thank you Dante."

Dante gave the slightest nod then said. "Turn left."

Sixty

Back to the Facility

The Father didn't speak another word for the rest of the ride. It wasn't until the facility could be clearly seen in the distance before he spoke. "This is as far as we go."

Before Dante could say anything, Sinah spoke. "This is close enough. Thank you."

As she climbed out of the hummer, the Mother quickly did the same. She ran as fast as she could around the vehicle to Sinah. Before Sinah could question, the Mother wrapped her arms around her shoulders. "I don't know why you took so long to get here God."

Sinah's features weakened a little until the Mother finished her thought. "Even if we are being punished for something we did or didn't do. Just knowing that you exist in our world has given us so much hope. Thank you so much, not just for saving our daughter but for making all of us believe we can become better people. That the world still has the chance to be saved."

The Mother released Sinah from a hug then cupped her cheeks in her hands in a motherly manor. "Please be careful in there God. You're the light of hope in our darkness."

Once the Mother lowered her hands, Sinah walked toward the front of the vehicle where Dante stood. As she passed by the open driver's side window, the Father muttered. "Sorry God."

Sinah stopped short as she shook her head. "If I was waiting for someone to protect me and never showed up, I'd be mad too. But then I would begin to realize I have the strength to protect myself."

Sinah glanced at the two women in the back seat as she continued. "And the strength to protect those I love."

The Father was silent as Sinah joined Dante. Neither of them glanced back hearing the hummer do a three point turn then drive away.

As they walked toward the facility, Sinah released a slight sigh. "I can't be mad at them for blaming me for the condition the world is in. It is my responsibility to take care of it."

Dante's lips touched at a frown. "Yes you can. It isn't your fault it became this way."

Sinah smile softly. "Thank you Dante for standing up for me."

Dante quickly shook his head. "I was only telling them the truth."

Sinah smiled even more. "Well, thank you."

Dante glanced toward her. Once he saw her warm welcoming smile, he smiled himself. "You're welcome Sinah."

As they got closer to the facility, Dante began to feel a knot forming in his stomach. "I'm worried we're going to get grabbed by the Military the second we step into the Launch Pad area."

Sinah barley nodded. "Then we need to come up with a plan."

Dante gripped his backpack straps. "Alex, any sign of the Commander?"

Alex chuckled a little. "I was just about to contact you two. He and Murdoch have just entered his office."

Sinah snapped her fingers with a full smile. "I got it! Dante, do you still have your gun?"

Dante's eyes darted to her as he withdrew his gun from its holster. "Uh... Yeah."

"Good, you're going to need it. You just found the escaped G Helix and you're bringing her back to where she belongs."

Dante went flush. "I am?"

Sinah nodded as she picked up her pace. "Just keep your gun on me the entire time. If we get hassled or anything, you just tell them, you need to escort me to the Director."

Dante barley nodded catching up to her. "Well... He did order

Murdoch and I to head out into the World of the Lost souls to find you and the Commander."

Sinah smiled. "Then you can just tell everyone to get out of your way, you're following top orders. I don't really think we're going to have any trouble anyway. I'm sure everyone is just going to be surprised to see that I've recovered and walking around."

"And as long as I have my gun withdrawn, they're going to think I've taken you into custody."

"Making it easier for us to go where ever we want without any worry."

Dante couldn't help but to smile. "That's a pretty good plan."

Sinah shrugged. "I'm sure you would have come up with something better given the time."

Dante's cheeks touched at an embarrassed flush. "W... Well I am a Data, Info and Surveillance soldier."

Sinah couldn't help but to smile.

Sixty-One

A Reunited Team

Any soldier, be it Helix or not, stopped Sinah and Dante for questioning. After a short while of this happening, Dante began to snip at them. "You have a problem, go talk to the Director! I have my orders to follow! Now get out of our way!"

Sinah on the other hand, kept completely quiet. Whenever they were stopped by an A Helix soldier however, the conversation went quite differently. They would respectfully lower their heads and ask if they needed them to do anything. Even though Sinah didn't respond, the A Helix would place their hand upon their chest, give a slight nod then go on their way. It was as if something in their Helix told them to leave them be.

As they approached Fallen's office, the door opened. Fallen, who was giving Murdoch orders, didn't notice them as he stepped into the hall. The second Sinah saw him a full smile took her lips. Dante couldn't help but to smile as she ran toward him. As Fallen turned his attention to the quickly approaching footsteps, Sinah snatched him into a hug.

Without hesitation, Fallen wrapped his arms around her. After a few moments of simply holding the other, he spoke. "What happened?"

Sinah's head shot up as her eyes darted to his. "What are you talking about?"

Fallen shifted his hand from her back to the side of her face. "I can feel your sadness."

Sinah's eyes couldn't help but to fill with tears. She shook her head trying to maintain her composure. "It's nothing really. I just never felt so much pain and suffering before. I never knew the world itself was in such agony. I guess that was another thing my disconnected self didn't want me to experience."

Fallen gently kissed her lips then whispered. "Don't worry my dearest counterpart, we'll make things right."

Fallen's expression shifted to confusion as her hands fell from his body. "…Sinah?"

Sinah weakly smiled as she stepped out of his grip. "I know what I am but…"

Sinah looked away from Fallen as she continued. "You gave me the name Sinah. A gift I was honored to receive. When you call me 'counterpart' it feels not only indifferent but also like you're trying to take back what's rightfully mine."

Fallen took her hands. "Sinah, that wasn't my intention. I am the one that feels honored that you accepted the name that I have selected. I'm happy to know that it was worthy enough for our precious God."

Sinah nodded slightly. As she opened her mouth to say something, Fallen spoke again. "Please forgive me Sinah, it will never happen again."

Sinah smiled before she leaned forward and gave his lips a soft kiss. "I forgive you."

Fallen brushed his thumb over her knuckles. After a momentary smile, he frowned. "Now what the hell are you two doing here?"

Sinah snickered while Dante went flush. As Fallen let her go, he shifted his attention toward Dante and frowned even more. "You were supposed to keep her safe."

Dante lost all color in his face. "Y... Yeah but.. but..."

"The other Labs could be arriving at any moment! They will have their strongest Helixes with them! They may even bring any successful Synthetic creations!"

Sinah lips were instantly consumed by a full frown. "Those sins against me will be ripped to shreds."

Everyone's eyes darted to Sinah as she clenched her fists. "I will not allow those made through the manipulation of Creation to exist in this world. They will pay for all those A Helixes that lost their lives to the Synthetic destruction."

Before anyone could say anything, Sinah finished with. "Even though it was for the greater good and I reconnected with my true self, it still pisses me off that the Synthetic overpowered me."

Sinah snorted. This sound was far from a noise they were expecting to hear from God. "…Bastard."

All three men couldn't help but to chuckle. Sinah brushed off her annoyance with a shake of her head. "Besides, I need to be here to awaken the A Helixes. If you woke up the D Helixes, my angels might panic."

Murdoch licked his lips. "Or the D Helixes might attempt another massacre like in building Seven."

Sinah's eyes darted to Murdoch. "What?!"

Before Murdoch could say anything, Alex reacted. "Dante, soldiers are closing in on you fast! I tried giving another false report but they've locked onto your earpiece!"

Frowning, Fallen pointed into his office. "Why the hell did you reconnect it?"

Dante went flush again until Sinah placed her hand on his arm. "It's a long story."

Once everyone was inside, he shut and locked the door. "Shut it off!"

Dante quickly did as he was told. "Yes Commander."

Fallen turned his attention to Sinah. "Sinah, you should head to the Launch Pad area. Murdoch and I will send any A Helixes we encounter to you. I'll join you as soon as..."

"Bridger is my priority."

Murdoch's eyes darted to her. Fallen sighed slowly shaking his head. "Sinah, I understand how you feel but building Seven is-"

Sinah cut him off with a firm tone of voice. "My priority."

Fallen hesitantly gave a slight nod. "Guard her with your lives."

Both Murdoch and Dante gave an instant nod. Before anyone could say anything else, there was a loud pound on his office door. "Open up, now!"

Fallen gave an upward nod toward the wall beside the door frame. Both Dante and Murdoch quickly moved in that direction. After a long lingering kiss, Fallen let Sinah go then gave an upward nod again. Once

Sinah joined the others, Fallen ripped open his office door and hissed. "What?!"

Being such a sudden and hostel action, all the soldiers stepped back a little. Fallen wasn't hesitant to growl. "Answer me!"

One of the soldiers stumbled over his words. "Uh… C... Commander. Um... Y... you need…"

Fallen's hand clenched the side of the door as he hissed. "Spit it out!"

As if slapped across the head, the soldier spoke without any signs of nervousness. "Commander, we're here to take you into custody under the orders of the Director. Come with us now or we'll have to open fire."

Fallen's lips quickly became consumed by a full frown. All the soldiers gripped their weapons anticipating his resistance. After a few seconds, a unanimous sigh of relief fell over them as Fallen suddenly gave an indifferent shrug. "…Fine."

Before he could take his first step forward, another soldier spoke. "Where is the other?"

Both Sinah and Murdoch remained calm while Dante went flush. The soldier gripped his machine gun. "We followed the word of a witness and a tracker on an earpiece. Where's the owner of the tracker?"

Fallen opened the door widely. "There's nobody else in here look for yourself."

Thanks to Fallen telling the three of them to stand by the doorframe, the open door hid them completely. The soldiers standing in the front of the team gave his office a quick glance. Not seeing anything out of the ordinary, they gave a shrug. One of the soldiers glanced back at the others. "All clear, it must have been a glitch or something."

Fallen held his full frown. "Are we leaving or what?"

The soldiers all nodded and moved aside so he could pass them. Fallen gave a slight nod as he left his office closing the door behind him.

Sixty-Two

Not Meant For War

Once Sinah was convinced all the soldiers had left the area, she walked toward the front of Fallen's desk. Dante followed after as he spoke. "Okay, we need a plan to save Bridger."

Murdoch walked toward Fallen's black leather bound couch then stepped into his soldier at ease stance. "Building Seven won't be easy to sneak into. Near next to impossible I would say."

Sinah smiled looking out the ceiling to floor windows at the eclipsed sun and moon. "I have no intention of sneaking in."

Both Dante and Murdoch's eyes shot toward her. Dante quickly shook his head. "Sinah, you can't just walk into building Seven."

Sinah glanced back at Dante with a look of determination. "Watch me."

"But Sinah..."

"Murdoch and I will use the same tactic we used to get into the facility."

Murdoch glanced toward Dante with a slightly questioning expression. "What tactic?"

Dante shook his head. "But... But you could be taken into custody."

Sinah turned to the two men as she clenched her fists. "I will save Bridger and nobody will stand in my way."

Realizing that there wasn't any chance that Sinah was going to budge from her decision, Dante released a loud defeated sigh. "I think this is a suicide mission but I'll do my best to protect you."

Sinah gave a slight shake of her head. "Dante, I want you to head over to Residential."

Dante's eyes darted to Sinah. "What? But why? What about Bridger?"

Sinah glanced toward Murdoch. As if sensing up and coming orders, he stepped into his soldier awaiting a command stance. "Murdoch and I will handle building Seven."

Dante instantly protested shaking his head. "But I can help! Please let me help Sinah! I want to be useful to you! Let me help!"

Murdoch glanced toward Dante and muttered. "Remember your respect for your Lord Dante."

Dante lost all color in his face as he awkwardly looked toward the floor. "Sorry Sinah, I... I was just..."

Sinah smiled softly as she shook her head. "That's alright. I know that we all want to save Bridger."

Dante responded in a tone that sounded like a sulking child. "So then let me help."

Sinah held her smile and nodded. "You can help by going to Residential and evacuating everyone from the facility."

Both of their eyes darted to Sinah in shock. Before either could question, she continued. "When the other Labs get here, there may just be an out and out war between the Helixes. One that will unfortunately take many lives. It's in the nature of an A Helix to protect the defenseless but that doesn't mean they can ensure their safety."

Sinah closed her eyes. "I don't know about you but I don't want my parents killed or anyone else that isn't involved for that matter. They need to be taken into safety."

Dante shook his head. "Such a large amount of people can't just leave the facility unnoticed."

Sinah opened her eyes as she gave a slight nod. "I know that. Your mission is to take my parents, your mom and anyone else you care about into the World of the Lost Souls. Take them to the house that I recovered in. It's clean and they'll be safe there."

"Okay, so when I come back..."

Sinah gave Dante a slightly weakened smile. "I need you to stay with them and protect them. There shouldn't be any trouble but I don't want any Lost Soul attacks."

Dante quickly shook his head. "But... But what about everyone else in Residential, won't they be in danger?"

Sinah glanced toward Murdoch. He was staring at Dante with a slightly weakened expression. "I will be sending other A Helixes to continue with the evacuation."

Dante shook his head again, only this time in disbelief. "...But what about you? If there's a battle I need to be here. I need to help protect you, help fight."

Murdoch closed his eyes and gave a brief shake of his head. "Dante, your combat skills are-"

Sinah cut him off. "You're not meant to be a fighter Dante. Even when your A Helix reaches its final stages of development and you've fully awakened, your skills in combat won't improve."

Dante's whole world seemed to crumble as his entire disposition became upset. "Oh."

Sinah quickly shook her head approaching him. "It's not a bad thing Dante. That's just not your purpose."

Dante gave the slightest nod but his demeanor didn't change in the slightest. Sinah smiled softly as she placed her hand on his shoulder. "Dante, when your A Helix fully awakens you will be my most intelligent Angel."

Dante's eyes darted to Sinah in shock as she continued. "You are my Data, Info and Surveillance undeveloped Arch Angel. Now please, I'm asking you, please save our families and protect those we care about."

Dante's cheeks burned bright red in embarrassment. "A... Arch Angel? According to the ancient texts, the Arch was the most important Angels to God."

"You are very important to me Dante. We are a team."

Dante's lips were consumed by an awkward, childish, giddy smile. "I'm an Arch Angel. I can't believe it! This is so great! I can't believe it!"

Sinah snickered removing her hand from his shoulder. "Okay Arch Angel Dante, please go help our families escape."

Dante quickly and confidently nodded. "You can count on me!"

As Dante ran toward Fallen's office door, Murdoch called out. "Hey, wait! What tactic did you use to get into the facility?"

Sinah glanced toward him with a smile. "Got a gun?"

Sixty-Three

Difference in Power

Murdoch glanced at his Combat gloves with a slight frown. Even though he had his handgun in his hand, the microchip on the top remained black. "I won't be able to use this, you know."

Sinah laughed a little as they walked into the lobby leading to the lone passage into building Seven. "Well of course you won't. The strength in your D Helix has become too much for that Lab created weapon. Your natural skills are-"

Sinah suddenly stopped midsentence and turned quick. Three A Helix soldiers were fast approaching with their weapons drawn, ready to attack. Hearing their footsteps, Murdoch turned to them as well.

Once the A Helix soldiers were in close enough range, all of them raised and aimed their guns at Murdoch. One of the three hissed. "Step away from her you lowly D Helix!"

Murdoch frowned almost instantly. "Listen here, you self-righteous-"

Sinah shook her head cutting him off. "That's enough. This isn't the time for petty fighting."

Another of the three spoke. "Then come with us G Helix and we'll take you somewhere safe. We need to keep you away from those dangerous D Helixes."

Before Sinah could say anything, Murdoch hissed. "There's no way in hell I'm going to let what happened in building Seven, happen right here!"

Murdoch snatched Sinah's wrist preparing to pull her protectively behind him. However, the second his skin touched hers, an aggressive wave of power slammed then overwhelmed his body. It felt like he had been struck by a phenomenal blast of pure energy. Not having any possible way to counteract such a force, his body crumbled to all fours and he began to vomit.

Sinah didn't shift her attention from the A Helix soldiers as her expression weakened. "I am so sorry my recovery took so long. I didn't mean to cause an unbalance amongst the A and D Helixes."

All three A Helix soldier's expressions shifted to sympathetic. They quickly shook their heads as Sinah continued. "I don't know what happened in building Seven but I feel so many deaths. I know these deaths could have been prevented and I know that I indirectly caused them."

One of the three spoke. "It wasn't your fault G Helix, it was theirs. It's those evil D Helixes and that L Helix. Once we wipe them out, we can-"

Sinah weakly smiled. "I see now. The unbalanced caused your Helixes to revert back to good vs evil, as if they are your enemies."

Another of the three nodded. "They are our enemies!"

Sinah closed her eyes. "No, the A and D Helixes are all equal just like Fallen and I are. Your appearances and skills may be different but all of your power is one in the same. Now…"

Sinah lifted her hand in front of them and finished her sentence. "..Awaken."

All three gasped as a wave of warmth splashed against them and enveloped their bodies. The large and small circles appeared behind Sinah's head and back. Murdoch, who had begun to wretch, began to feel a fire like burning sensation emanating from Sinah's body. As he began to shift away from her, Sinah snapped her hand shut. The golden circles instantly vanished and the burning sensation dissipated.

As the warmth died down on the A Helix soldiers, the rectangular microchip on their Combat gloves flickered then shut off completely. After a few blinks of confusion, one of the A Helix soldiers noticed Murdoch. Without hesitation, she approached then knelt down to him. "Oh my goodness, Are you okay?"

Murdoch's expression shifted to confusion as he looked up at her. "What?"

The A Helix soldier placed her weapon aside then offered her hands out to him. "Here, let me help you up, are you hurt?"

Her expression suddenly shifted to sympathetic. "Did we hurt you?"

Murdoch cuffed her hands away from him as he got to his feet. "Do you know what's been happening?"

All three A Helix soldiers looked toward the floor as if ashamed. Murdoch stared at their expressions for a few moments before he shook his head. "It doesn't matter now."

The A Helix soldiers turned their attentions to Sinah. She had a very upset look on her face staring toward the lone passage into building Seven. Murdoch looked toward her as well. Once he saw her expression, he questioned. "What's wrong?"

Sinah didn't shift her attention. "Head over to Residential and find Dante. He'll give you your orders. If you can't find him, start getting the innocent out of the facility."

All three A Helix soldiers gave a bow, a quick 'yes God' then went on their way.

After a few moments of silence, Sinah spoke. "Are you alright?"

Murdoch gave a slight nod. "I'm fine."

Sinah barley nodded. "You're lucky I didn't just destroy your D Helix."

Murdoch's lips touched at a frown. "I have to remember that you've drastically changed from that mute girl."

Sinah couldn't help but to snicker. "Awakening in my true from will do that. D Helixes can't touch me just like A Helixes can't touch Fallen. My light and his Dark are too much for the opposing Helixes to handle."

Murdoch gave a slight nod but before he could say anything, Sinah glanced back at him. Her tone of voice had become very firm as she locked eyes with his. "Do it again and I will not show mercy."

An aggressive wave of warmth and purity very uncomfortable to Murdoch's body washed over him. Murdoch didn't have the slight bit of hesitation as he quickly nodded. "Understood."

Sinah suddenly smiled. "Then let's go."

Murdoch gripped his gun as they continued on their way.

Sixty-Four

Eye for an Eye

Murdoch chuckled tossing his gun aside on the floor in one of the many hallways of building Seven. "I can't believe that worked. Leave it to Dante to come up with such a strange plan like that."

Sinah didn't respond only continued walking. Murdoch, who was walking ahead of her, cautiously glanced around every few moments. "Not that we needed it at the security booth anyway, all of them seemed paralyzed with fear when they saw you. I'm guessing they could sense the danger of dealing with..."

Murdoch stopped in his tracks not hearing Sinah walking behind him anymore. The second he turned, his expression shifted to slightly sympathetic. Sinah's hands were clasped and pressed against her chest. Her eyes were closed and her features looked devastated. "…So much pain."

As Murdoch approached her, she whispered. "So much suffering, so many of our kin lost their lives here."

Once Sinah opened her eyes, they instantly filled with tears. "…So many were carelessly killed."

Murdoch held his sympathetic expression as he released a weak sigh. "I don't even pretend to understand humans or what they're thinking. But I'm sure somehow in some way they believed they were doing the right thing."

A few iridescent tears fell from her eyes. Even Murdoch, who never thought twice about the beauty of things, couldn't help but to stare at them in awe. Sinah whispered again. "This has to stop. They have to be stopped."

Before Murdoch could try his best to offer whatever comforting words he could muster, Sinah unclasped her hands and clenched her fists. "Nobody will kill anymore of Fallen and my Helixes."

Murdoch's expression shifted back to normal as he gave a confident nod. "Let's save Bridger then set the rest free."

Sinah's lips touched at a frown as she began to walk again. "No, let's save Bridger, empty the building then destroy it."

Murdoch's eyes shot to the back of her head and within a blink of the eye, he caught up with her. "You want to destroy building Seven?"

Sinah noticed an elevator at the end of one of the halls. As she walked towards it, she answered. "I want to obliterate it."

Murdoch couldn't help but to chuckle. "You're definitely not that mute girl anymore."

"No, I'm much stronger now."

Once they reached the elevators, Murdoch pressed the call button. As they waited, Murdoch's expression weakened a little. "..Bridger."

Before Sinah could say anything, Murdoch quickly regained his composure and spoke. "I don't know the condition he's in, so brace yourself."

Sinah weakly smiled as the elevator doors opened and they walked inside. "Are you telling me that or yourself?"

Murdoch pressed the floor button. "Both I guess."

Sinah closed her eyes. "He's critical onto death."

Murdoch's eyes darted to her. "WHAT?!"

Sinah released a weak sigh. "His Helix is only releasing the faintest cry for help. This is the main reason I didn't want Dante to come here. His Helix would have felt it and it would have broken him. Besides, I needed someone to help my parents escape."

Murdoch forcefully jabbed the floor button with his index. "Come on! Come on!!"

Sinah opened her eyes and stared at the closed doors. "Prepare yourself for whatever happens, Murdoch."

Murdoch jabbed the button more aggressively. "COME ON!!!"

The second the elevator doors opened, Murdoch bolted down the hallway. Sinah's eyes darted to him in shock before she snickered. "I guess he's really prepared."

Murdoch zipped down hallway after hallway. Once he turned the corner leading to Bridger's cell, he caught sight of Revin and another Lead ADGL Tech. Both were casually talking to one another. Without hesitation, he raced toward them and slammed his fist across Revin's jaw.

Revin crashed to the floor yowling in shock and agony. The other Lead ADGL Tech ran away from them screaming. "There's a snap in the Helix! Help! Help! Set off the building emergency systems!"

Within a blink of the eye, Murdoch caught up with him and effortlessly snapped his neck. "Nobody is calling anybody."

Revin held his chin wailing. "You broke my jaw! You broke my jaw!"

Murdoch turned quick and snarled. "That's not all I'm going to break on you, you son of a bitch!"

Murdoch zipped up to Revin and snatched the collar of his Lab coat. As he lifted him up and raised his fist, Sinah spoke. "Let him go."

Murdoch shot Sinah a glare. "For all the things he's done to the Commander and to Bridger, you're going to just let him go?!

Sinah looked toward Murdoch with a soft smile. "Please Murdoch."

Murdoch snarled careless dropping Revin to the floor. "Son of a bitch!"

Sinah didn't glance toward Murdoch as he slammed his fist into the wall beside Bridger's cell. Sinah knelt down next to Revin who was groaning in agony. "Here, let me help you."

Revin hesitantly lowered his hand from his jaw. He instantly winced and whimpered as Sinah placed her hands upon it. Sinah lips curled into a pleasant welcoming smile as she spoke. "Yeah, I bet that hurts."

Tears poured down Revin's face until Sinah locked her eyes with his. The change in her eyes was almost immediate as she spoke. "You helped kill so many of mine and Fallen's kin. You helped destroy so many precious lives."

Revins's eyes widened and became absolutely traumatized staring directly into Creation. "G… God… Pl... Please show mercy.'

"Tell me, when did you show mercy to the others?"

Murdoch glanced back at Sinah. Despite her smile, the grip on his jaw tightened. Even though her tone of voice was calm and gentle, sweat beads began to form on Revin's forehead. "Did you once listen to their cries of pain? Did you once hear their pleas for mercy? Do you know the pain you've inflicted upon them?"

Revin tried to speak but Sinah's grip was too tight. Leaning close to Revin's ear she whispered. "Oh don't worry, you will."

The large golden circle appeared behind Sinah's back. Revin's eyes darted up to it in awe until two feathers slammed into his eye sockets. Sinah released Revin as two more slammed into his ears, shoulders and palms. Even though his mouth was wide open like he was screaming in absolute horror, no sound escaped from his voice box. His muscles suddenly locked and he fell onto his back.

Sinah stood up and stared down at him with a cold expression. "You will re-live and re-experience every single moment of cruelty you bestowed upon them. You will know their agony until your life is taken with the destruction of building Seven."

Sinah's expression returned to normal as she glanced up at Murdoch. "That is unless, you just want to kill him."

Murdoch quickly shook his head. "No, the wrath of God is a much better and more befitting punishment."

Sinah lifted her hand toward Bridger's cell door. Feathers shot from the large golden circle and rapidly shredded the door to pieces. Once it was completely obliterated, Sinah's features weakened seeing the mangled Bridger.

Sixty-Five

Goodnight Bridger

Murdoch didn't wait for Sinah to enter the cell before he raced inside. His expression instantly broke seeing all the damage Bridger's body had sustained. As if not being able to handle such a sight, Murdoch turned his head.

Sinah calmly walked toward Bridger with a look of sympathy. "Keep it together Murdoch."

Murdoch clenched his fists and swallowed a few times trying to keep his emotions in check.

The second Sinah placed her hand on Bridger's cold cheek, his eyes slowly opened. It took him a few moments for his eyes to actually register that someone was in front of him. Once he finally did see Sinah, his split dry lips formed into a weakened smile. "H... Hi."

Even though her eyes reflected sympathy, she smiled softly. "Hi, thank you so much for finding my body."

As Bridger weakly chuckled a little, blood spewed from his mouth. "That's… That's the... the voice I heard in my... my hea... hea..."

Bridger didn't finish his sentence as his breathing became labored. It was as if, even speaking took all of his effort. Sinah nodded. "You heard my plea to save Fallen and I'm glad you didn't ignore it. Thank you."

Bridger's lips only lifted upward in the slightest. Sinah's eyes shifted from Bridger's wounds up to the chains and shackles that bound him. "This shouldn't have happened."

Murdoch suddenly turned on him with a snarl. "Damn it A Helix! You were supposed to be stronger than this!!"

Bridger slowly shifted his eyes to Murdoch. "S... sorry Me... Mean Helix. I... I tried."

Murdoch's angered expression weakened a little as he turned his head again. Bridger chuckled a little before it quickly turned into coughs. Once he finished trying his best not to choke on his own blood, he whispered. "A… At least I… I'm… a... alive."

Bridger closed his eyes. "But not for m... much... longer."

Murdoch's eyes darted to Bridger. "What do you mean 'but not for much longer'?!"

Murdoch's attention darted to Sinah as he questioned again. "What does he mean 'not for much longer'?!"

Sinah's expression weakened before she whispered. "..He's dying."

Murdoch instantly shook his head in disbelief. "He can't be! He has the rapid healing capability!"

Bridger tried to shake his head but he was too weak and the shackles restricted him. "B... Broken. I… I've been like... like this for... for…"

Sinah finished his sentence. "...For a long time now."

Bridger slowly opened her eyes. "It... It's not d... doing any... thing."

Bridger weakly smiled at Sinah. "B… But at least I… I got... to see... I knew... I knew you were... G... God."

Bridger closed his eyes and his body began to tremble uncontrollably. Sinah shook her head. "Shh... Try not to talk."

Blood and drool dripped from his open mouth as his breathing shook. Murdoch hissed advancing on Sinah. "Heal him! You're God, heal him already!"

Sinah slowly shook her head. "I can't. The damage done to his Helix is-"

Murdoch cut her off with a growl. "You're supposed to be his Lord! You should be able to do something! Save him, damn it!"

Sinah weakly smiled. "It doesn't work that way. There are many things that-"

Murdoch clenched his fists. "So you're just going to let him die! He's an A Helix it's your responsibility to protect them! You're his Lord! His Savior! Save him already!"

Sinah slowly shook her head and closed her eyes. "I can't."

Murdoch snarled as he thrusted his hand out to grab her. "I'm not asking you, I'm telling you!"

Right before he caught Sinah's arm, Bridger's eyes snapped open and he yelled out. "No! You can't touch her!"

Murdoch stopped short and hesitantly drew his hand back. He looked toward Bridger as his features weakened almost to the point of tears. "I can't lose you A Helix. All we have is each other."

A few tears escaped Bridger's dimming light blue eyes. "Th... There's that k... kind heart again. S... stop it Mean… Helix, it... it's freaking m… me out."

Murdoch stepped close to Bridger and pressed his forehead against his. "Bridger, I… I…"

Bridger whispered. "It... it will be o… okay."

Murdoch placed his hands on the sides of Bridger's head. "You can't leave me Bridger, you can't."

Bridger's expression weakened seeing a few tears fall from Murdoch's eyes. "Th... This, this is nothing. It… It will be... It will be okay. Tr... Trust me. I... I need to die. Let... Let me go."

Murdoch's grip on Bridger's head tightened. "No, no this isn't happening! This isn't going to happen! You're not going to die Bridger! I won't let you!"

Bridger whispered again. "P... Please let me go M.. Murdoch."

Murdoch squeezed his eyes tightly shut as he yelled. "No, I can't! No! No!"

Bridger's breathing suddenly slowed down. "It's... it's time. Good... Good-night Mean H… Helix."

Murdoch quickly lifted his forehead and frantically began to shake his head. "No! No! No!"

Bridger closed his eyes, released a final breath of air then went limp. Without hesitation, Murdoch released an ear piercing screech gripping Bridger's head. "NOOOOOO!!!"

Murdoch frantically began to shake him. "Wake up! Bridger, wake up! Damn you! Bridger! Bridger!!"

A very upset voice spilled over the communications into the cell, it was Ayla's voice. "I'm… I'm sorry but all life signs have ceased."

Murdoch snatched Bridger's shoulders and rattled him so aggressively the chains and shackles were rattled as well. "No! Wake up! WAKE UP!!"

Ayla spoke again. "The two of you are intruders into building Seven. I'd hate to do this but I have to set off the building emergency system."

Murdoch snarled as his eyes darted up to the glass window. "If you dare touch that button, I'll rip you in two!"

Sinah glanced up at the window herself. "If you feel you have to set off the alarm then do it."

Murdoch's head shot to Sinah. "You! You didn't even try to save him! You did nothing but watch him die! We never should have come here!"

Murdoch let Bridger go then turned to Sinah with a full frown. "He would have died and we never would have known! Did you want to see him die?!"

Murdoch advanced on her as he continued. "What type of sick twisted God are you?! You didn't even bother to help him! You just watched him die! You wretched-!"

Sinah cut him off. "You didn't prepare yourself for what happened very well."

Murdoch clenched his fists and jaw. "I didn't think his God would just let him die!"

Sinah didn't flinch as the blaring alarm of the buildings emergency systems was activated. "You said your piece now get out of my way."

Murdoch snarled again. "I'm not going any-!"

Sinah cut him off with a sudden hiss. "I said move!"

Feeling an aggressive wave of warmth and purity, Murdoch moved aside. Whether he wanted to or not, his body obeyed Sinah's command without hesitation. Sinah smiled toward Bridger as she approached his dead body. "And from death comes rebirth."

Sixty-Six

Arch Angel Dante

Dante frantically raced around his home collecting everything and anything he thought he might need. As he ran into the living room, his eyes darted to one of his laptops hearing loud beeping. "Where has the building emergency systems been activated?"

Alex, who was still sitting at the kitchen table working, answered. "Building Seven."

Dante's expression shifted to a concerned panic. "Sinah and Murdoch could still be in there."

Alex gave a slight shrug. "Without any surveillance, I..."

Dante swallowed heavily gripping a mother board in his hands. "They could be in danger."

Dante released a slight scoff. "What the hell am I saying? I know they're in danger."

Alex went flush as his eyes darted to the large screen in the living area. It was displaying the corridor just outside the lone passage leading into building Seven. "It looks like the first wave of soldiers has arrived."

Dante quickly began to stuff his backpack. "We don't have much time before the entire facility goes into a state of top level emergency shut down mode. And we both know if that happens."

"Every electronic device will cease to function and go into lock down mode. Even the elevators won't work."

Dante scooped up some cords. "That's why I have to pick up the pace."

Dante suddenly yelled out. "Mom, are you almost ready?!"

Dante's mother responded from her bedroom. "Do you know how long we're going to be away for?!"

"Um… Not long!"

"Where are we going?!"

Dante released a weakened chuckle. "Um… S... Somewhere safe!"

Alex gave Dante a confused look. "Why haven't you told her that you're taking her to where God told you to?"

Dante sighed before he whispered. "Ever since my Father was killed in a Lost Souls raid my Mom acts like the World of the Lost Souls doesn't even exist. I don't know where she pretends I go when I'm on a mission. I remember how hard it was for her to except that the Commander wanted me on his-"

A loud knock on the front door cut Dante off. Both his and Alex's eyes darted toward it. Without hesitation, Alex quickly began to type on the laptop keys accessing the Residential surveillance cameras. His expression shifted to nervous seeing three soldiers just outside the house. They were the same three Helix soldiers that had confronted Sinah and Murdoch. Alex whispered after the door was pounded on again. "Oh no, they must be here to…"

Alex stopped short as Dante closed his eyes. Tiny golden flickers of light began to flash around Dante's head. After a few seconds, his eyes snapped open and his expression shifted to confusion. "I was trying to sense if they were Helix soldiers or not. I swear I just saw three A Helix soldiers on our front door step."

Alex couldn't help but to smile as his eyes lit up in disbelief. "That was amazing! There are three soldiers on your doorstep! I don't know if they're Helix or-"

Alex was cut off as the pounding on the door became louder. Dante's lips touched at a frown. "I'll handle this."

Dante mustered up all of his strength and ripped open the front door. Despite his attempt at being intimidating, the A Helix soldiers just stared at him like he had opened the door without even the slightest bit of aggression. One of the three spoke. "We're here to receive orders."

Dante placed his hand on his chest in confusion. "Huh? What? From me?"

All nodded and another of the three spoke. "God has sent us."

Dante only stared back at them with the same expression before he mumbled. "Um... Okay. Uh… Come on Dante, focus."

Dante suddenly gave a confident nod. "Okay. We need to extract as many people from Residential out of facility as possible. It would have been better to do it in small groups but the building Seven emergency systems have been activated. It's only a matter of time before everything shuts down."

Dante looked beyond them at the three facility jeeps parked in front of his house. Dante pointed at one of the A Helix soldiers. "I need you to head over to the large vehicle garage. We're going to need one of the monthly supply trucks. After you get it, head over to the Launch Pad area and wait for us."

The A Helix soldier shook his head. "I can't just walk in there and take a truck. The monthly supply and recruitment rations are not scheduled until-"

Dante cut him off glancing back at Alex. "Alex?"

Knowing exactly what Dante wanted, Alex quickly went to work. "I'm on it."

Dante turned his head back to the A Helix soldier. "All the necessary paperwork will be there by the time you arrive. If they have any issues, tell them to contact the Director. Most vehicle areas are protected by human soldiers. The thought of disturbing the top over something so petty usually makes them nervous and they'll let you through. Say the same thing in the Launch Pad area as well. Trust me, you shouldn't have any trouble."

The A Helix soldier nodded before he saluted. "You can count on me Sir."

Dante's lips touched at a slightly proud smile as the A Helix soldier raced toward one of the jeeps. "Sir… I like that."

Dante shook off his pride then turned his attention to the other two. "Now, I need one of you to head over to the singular security booth on the Residential path to the Launch Pad area. The soldier or soldiers need to be dealt with so we can get through there without any trouble."

Both A Helix soldiers stared at Dante in shock. Dante, who noticed, frowned. “We can’t have any more delays. I need one of you to go now!”

One of the two nervously spoke. “S… Sir, I don’t mean to question your orders but I don’t think that it’s right to kill-”

Dante went flush as he lifted his hands and shook them in a panic. “No, No! I didn’t mean ‘deal with’ as in kill them! I meant knock them out or tell them you’ve been ordered to replace them to give them a break or something.”

Dante chuckled as the A Helix soldiers released a sigh of relief. “We’re Angels, we don’t kill without reason.”

Both nodded then one of them spoke. “I’ll handle it Sir.”

As she ran toward the jeep, Dante spoke to the third. “I need you on standby. Sinah… Uh… God has ordered me to get a certain group of priority people out of the facility first. Once I’ve grabbed them, I need you to drive us to the Residential security booth. We’ll drop you off and continue on. Both you and the other A Helix will return back here to extract the others.”

The A Helix soldier nodded. “Yes Sir. Orders understood.”

Dante glanced back at Alex. “Once you’re done with that Alex, I need you and my mom outside for pick up.”

Alex’s eye darted to Dante. “Me? But I thought God only ordered her family and yours to be taken out of the facility.”

Dante chuckled a little. “You live here, you are my family now. So hurry up we’re running out of time.”

Alex couldn’t help but to smile. “Thanks Dante.”

Dante yelled out. “Mom, Hurry up already!!”

Dante’s mom simply made a sound of acknowledgement. Dante sighed shaking his head before he turned his attention back to the A Helix soldier. “Let’s go get the Harmonds.”

Sixty-Seven

No Nonsense

Dante gave a confident nod before he knocked on the Harmond's front door. Within a blink of the eye, Amos swung it open. His worried expression shifted to confusion with traces of shock. "Emma said that you, Murdoch and the Commander took Sinah and left the facility."

Dante gave a slight nod. "Yeah, we did but-"

Violet cut Dante off with a hiss as she stepped beside Amos. "Why the hell did you take her from building Seven?!"

Dante's lips touched at a frown as he rudely pushed passed both of them into their house. "I won't allow God to be experimented on. I really don't care what any human says to justify their actions. There are certain things in this world not meant to be known about. The Creator is one of them and I'll be damned if I let God get mistreated!"

Despite Amos' slight smile at Dante's need to protect, his expression still appeared worried. "I understand how you feel, but the World of the Lost Souls isn't exactly any safer."

Violet quickly agreed. "If they find out that Kid is God, they're going to probably attack her. They'll think it's her fault their world is in the state it's in."

Dante gave a slightly confused look. "…Kid? Oh yeah, I forgot Sinah used to have that stupid basic name."

Right before the frowning Violet had a chance to say anything, Amos spoke. "We heard the announcements about the Commander being back at the facility. That means Murdoch is the only one protecting her. I'm not questioning the strength of one of the Commander's team or anything, but the Lost Souls are unpredictable. Not to mention, there are vast amounts of them. Murdoch could easily become over run, leaving Sinah defenseless."

Dante smiled. "Sinah is fine. She's here too. She's breaking Bridger out of building Seven as we speak."

Both Amos and Violet's eyes filled with an ecstatic relief. Violet stepped forward and took her husband's hands. "Oh thank god!"

Amos smiled. "Thank Sinah!"

Dante blindly motioned his hand behind himself. "Now we need to get both of you out of here."

Violet instantly shook her head in protest. "I'm not going anywhere! You said Kid is in building Seven? Well, then that's where we're-"

Dante cut Violet off. "Sinah herself has given me the order to take both of you and my family to safety out of the facility."

Violet shook her head again. "Didn't you hear us? The World of Lost Souls isn't a safe place."

Dante's lips touch at a frown. "Once the other Labs arrive, it's going to be-"

Amos' eyes darted to Dante. "Why are the other Labs..?

Amos paused for a spilt second before he answered his own question. "The Director probably wants them to see that God has been created."

Violet's entire disposition filled with panic. "Then we need to protect her! Those other Labs are going to want to take God for themselves! We can't let that happen!"

Dante stared at Violet for a few moments before he said. "And what do you think you can do?"

Both Violet and Amos' eyes darted to him. Dante stared back at them with a plain almost indifferent expression. "What could two humans possibly do against the Helixes or even the Synthetic Helixes? I know your instincts as parents are telling you to protect her. But you'll be killed long before you even have a chance to speak. This won't be some human battle. This will be a Helix war. I have my orders and my mission is to get you two out of here."

Violet frowned. "I'm not going anywhere! Kid needs-"

"Sinah doesn't need to be worrying about your safety. You either willingly come with me or I send in that A Helix soldier out there to come in and get you."

Dante shrugged. "The choice is yours, but I will get my way."

Amos looked out the open doorway at the lone A Helix soldier by the facility jeep. He was cautiously glancing around the area. "Let's go Violet."

Violet's eyes darted to Amos in disbelief. "What are you talking about? I'm not going anywhere. Kid is-!"

"He's right Violet. If the other Labs start a war and Sinah knows we're here. Not only will she worry but we may be taken hostage or even killed just to hurt her. We need to go with him. It's the best thing we can do for her."

Violet vehemently shook her head. "No! No! No! I'm not leaving! I'm not going any-!"

Dante cut her off with a snip. "We're running out of time! The emergency system could lock everything down at any minute! We need to go!"

Violet shook her head again. "No, I won't leave her here!"

Dante frowned releasing a frustrated sigh. "These are the times I wish I had Murdoch or Bridger's strength. I could just toss you over my shoulder and cram you into the jeep."

Amos began to pull on Violet's hand. "We need to go!"

Violet began to try to pull her hand back from him. "I can't just leave her! She could get hurt or-!"

Dante suddenly yelled out. "A Helix!"

The A Helix's eyes darted to Dante. "Sir?"

Amos shook his head snatching his wife's arm. "Violet, we need to go! If being away from here helps our daughter than that's what we have to do. We need to wait for her in the World of the Lost Souls."

Violet's features weakened before she hesitantly nodded. "..Okay."

Dante glanced back at them with a full frown. "Then let's get a move on already."

Both Amos and Violet barely nodded.

Sixty-Eight

Rebirth

Sinah closed her eyes placing her hands upon Bridger's cold pale cheeks. Murdoch watched on anxiously until he heard the sounds of military equipment rattling from the hallways. Within a blink of his eye, he was at the open cell doorway. As he cautiously peeked around the corner, he spoke. "That sounds like the first wave of soldiers. They should be here any moment."

Sinah lifted one of her hands and turned it behind herself. Once the large golden circle appeared, many feathers shot toward the doorway. Murdoch gasped as he leapt to his side narrowly avoiding getting hit. His lips couldn't help but to touch at a frown as he muttered. "You could have warned me."

The feathers quickly flooded then overlapped one another forming an impenetrable seal. Sinah then shifted her hand toward the window. Once the final feather covered and sealed the glass, all sounds except for the noises within the cell, were muted. Sinah smiled softly returning her hand to Bridger's cheek. "We can't have anyone disturbing us, now can we?"

Murdoch looked toward the chaotic mess of feathers. Despite them looking just like a huge pile of fluff, they produced a soft glow every few seconds. As if compelled to by some unknown force, Murdoch reached his hand out toward them.

"It won't be worth the pain you suffer if you touch it."

Murdoch pulled his hand back and frowned at it. "I didn't even want to touch it."

Sinah smiled as Murdoch returned to the spot he was originally standing. "It's your D Helix's desire to touch the forbidden. It's the same with A Helixes and Fallen's powers. Light draws dark and dark draws light. They are the opposite yet they are the same."

Murdoch barely nodded glancing back at the seal. "Is that solid?"

"It will keep everyone out, don't worry."

Before Murdoch could say anything else, the large golden circle shifted to the ground. Murdoch's eyes darted down to it in confusion as it moved under Bridger. As Sinah lifted her hands from his cold skin, a blinding light engulfed her completely. Murdoch narrowed his eyes trying his best to see within the bright shine. The golden circle below Bridger seemed to resonate with Sinah as small flashes of light began to sparkle around him. Suddenly Sinah opened her arms widely and the light encasing her vanished. Murdoch's eyes widened and mouth dropped seeing Sinah in her ethereal form, her true form.

An elegant long white gown adorned with beautiful iridescent almost transparent jewels appeared upon her body. Gold filigree matching her glowing veins complimented the flowing delicate material. The design upon her forehead had widened and at the center point was a reflective jewel in the shape of a tear drop. Despite it actually being a part of Sinah's body, it looked more like the finishing touch to an elegant crown. Behind her ears was a large plume of golden feathers. Behind her back was a huge set of four wings, two large at the top and two smaller ones at the bottom. Even though they were wings, they appeared more like blinding images of light. The gold filigree like veins around her eyes enhanced the beauty of her gentle welcoming features, while her golden eyes reflected a complete and utter understanding of anything and everything in existence. Sinah was the perfect image of good, purity and what most envisioned God would look like.

Overwhelmed by Sinah's appearance and the fact her body was emanating a power far beyond anything Murdoch could ever dream of, he couldn't help but to nervously back way from her. Everything in his D Helix was screaming his life was at an end.

Snapping her hands shut the golden circle below Bridger began to shine brighter and brighter. Sinah looked at the ceiling before she whispered. "Awaken."

The second that word fell from her lips, the golden circle blasted a flow of energy upwards. The powerful blast smashed clean through each floor destroying the falling rubble the destruction caused. Within moments, it broke through the roof and into the dim blue sky.

Even though the energy had destroyed the chains and shackles that once restricted Bridger's movements, he still remained on his feet. Feathers lifted from the golden circle and floated around Bridger as each one of his wounds rapidly began to heal. Murdoch watched in awe as Bridger's once destroyed wing began to reform and pull feathers from the air to replace the ones he had lost. Color slowly began to return to his skin and a beat of his heart had returned to his chest. Bridger released a loud gasp as breath filled his lungs and life returned to him. As his eyes opened, Sinah gave a slight nod and the golden circle below him vanished.

As the golden energy around him began to fade, Bridger couldn't help but to chuckle looking at the absolutely shocked yet relieved Murdoch. "See Mean Helix, I told you this was nothing."

Without hesitation, Murdoch hissed, raced over to him and punched him across the jaw. Bridger didn't stumble in the slightest as he chuckled again. "Aw what a sweet love tap. I missed you too."

Murdoch growled clenching his fists. "You stupid, goddamn son of a-!"

Bridger turned his attention skyward. Through the hole, he could see a dark grey cloud in the shape of the golden circle that had broken through the ceiling. Bridger lowered his head and looked toward Sinah. Her expression was slightly weakened and her eyes were locked on the floor.

Bridger stepped forward and knelt down in front of her. He lowered his head and began to speak. "My Lady, I am more than grateful and appreciative that you saved me from the emptiness of death."

Murdoch's eyes darted to Bridger in absolute disbelief. Bridger was the last person he thought would even know how to be proper and formal. As Bridger reached out for the bottom of Sinah's gown, Murdoch noticed his hands. In the center of his palm, it looked like all his blue glowing veins had pooled and became a blue glowing crystalized circular jewel. Upon each of his fingertips were smaller variations of the same thing.

Bridger gently pulled some of her delicate gown to his lips. After a soft kiss, he looked up at her and whispered. "My Lady, I know the pain of the damaged world wears thin upon you. Now that I am strong and healthy and I shall gladly take any and all burden you wish to place upon me. Please my Lady, please do not suffer alone."

Sinah's eyes shifted to the brightly shining white ring around Bridger's pupil. A soft momentarily smile took her lips, before she lost consciousness. As she fell, she flipped out of her true form. Without missing a beat, Bridger lunged forward and caught her before she hit the ground.

Sixty-Nine

Useless

Bridger smiled softly down at Sinah as he gently stroked the side of her head. "Wasn't she breathtaking in her true form?"

Murdoch shrugged glancing at the feather seal in the cell doorway. "…I guess."

Bridger continued on with his train of thought. "An absolutely perfect image of good, purity and what God should be. She is far more beautiful than anything I've ever seen before or could even imagine."

Bridger chuckled a little. "I feel almost unworthy to gaze upon such an exquisite vision." Bridger couldn't help but to release a soft contented sigh. "I'm just glad that she's alright."

Murdoch began to pace the cell like an animal caught in a cage. "You should be glad that you're alright."

Bridger didn't shift his attention from Sinah. "I'm not going to lie. I was a little worried I was going to die here in this cell. But then I realized my stubborn A Helix wasn't going to let me. It was going to hang on until I saw for myself, that my Lady had recovered."

Bridger glanced up at Murdoch as a bratty smile took his lips. "So… Did you wail like a baby when I actually died?"

Murdoch's eyes darted then sharpened toward Bridger as he clenched his fists. "We'll just see who wails like baby after I beat the hell out of you."

Bridger chuckled with a shrug. "There is no hell in me, Mean Helix."

As Murdoch opened his mouth to respond to Bridger's childishness, Sinah's eyes suddenly snapped open. They went from changed to normal in a few blinks. As she sat up and out of Bridger's arms, she spoke. "Sorry."

Bridger quickly shook his head. "That's alright. Are you okay?"

Sinah barley nodded getting to her feet. As Bridger did the same, Murdoch questioned. "What happened? Why'd you pass out? I thought God was supposed to be a superior being. You didn't last long at all in your true form."

Bridger's lips touched at a frown. "Careful Mean Helix, she may not be your Lord but she is mine and I won't allow her to be disrespected."

Sinah shook her head. "It's okay Bridger. I can't maintain my true form for long. It needs to draw upon an outside source for strength."

Murdoch's expression shifted to confusion. "…An outside source?"

Bridger crossed his arms. "You know like the good, kind, and selflessness of the world. All the positive things the world lacks."

Sinah nodded slightly. "Both Fallen and I need to draw upon the faith and energy of everything and everyone in existence to release the ultimate strength of our true selves. Without it, we can only have very short flashes of what we really are, but it drains us. That's why I momentarily passed out."

Bridger moved his wings a little as if he was trying to lay them comfortably against his back. "For how the world currently is, the Commander could maintain his true form without a drop of effort. Pain, anger and everything else bad is in abundance right now."

Sinah closed her eyes as her features weakened. "We need them as much as they need us, yet he just wants to wipe the world clean."

Both Bridger and Murdoch's eyes darted to Sinah. Murdoch was first to question. "Wipe the world clean of the Lost Souls?"

Bridger was quick to question after. "Or of everyone and start the world over?"

Sinah opened her eyes and shook her head. "We don't have time to worry about this right now. Bridger, we need to go to the Director's office to get to Fallen."

"Yes my Lady."

Murdoch looked back toward the feather seal. "Are we just going to fight our way through the soldiers?"

Bridger chuckled looking at the crystalized circular jewels in his palms. "I'll handle them."

Sinah shook her head. "You won't have to do anything. Their Helixes A or D will obey me whether they want to or not. Murdoch, your Helix at the level it is now, gives you the skill to order lower D Helixes to obey you."

Bridger's eyes darted to Murdoch as he smiled. "You can boss other D Helixes around? That's a neat skill!"

Murdoch chuckled. "I guess."

Sinah smiled herself. "Both you and Dante can do it too."

Bridger smiled even more. "Oh Yeah? Neat! I can't wait to start telling people what to do. You! Go get me some suspenders!"

Both Sinah and Murdoch couldn't help but to snicker. Sinah glanced back at the feather seal as her amusement ended. "Murdoch, I need you to order the D Helixes to assist in the evacuation of the building. Leave any Synthetic creations where they are. I have no intentions of allowing those abominations to live."

Bridger nodded in agreement. "Those sins shouldn't have even been created."

Sinah turned her attention back to Bridger. "Bridger, I need you to set up some bombs. I want this building destroyed but we need to make sure everyone is in safety first."

Bridger jumped up and down clapping his hands like an excitable child. "Yay!! Bombs!!"

Murdoch chuckled as Bridger ran over to one of the cell walls. His amusement vanished noticing Bridger's foot speed had slowed since his change. "Are your wings heavy?"

Bridger pressed his palm for a split second against multiple spots on the wall. A blue jelly like orb instantly attached as he lifted his hands. "No, it doesn't feel like I have anything on my back, why?"

Murdoch shrugged. "You run slower."

Sinah walked toward the feather seal. "He's much faster in flight."

Bridger's tone of voice filled with giddiness. "I'm so excited about trying to fly. I hope I'm good at it because I really suck at flying a helicopter. I know it's not the same but-"

"It will come naturally, don't worry."

Bridger opened his wings widely. A few pale bluey white with gold tipped feathers fell then vanished before they hit the floor. "I wonder how much weight I'll be able to carry in flight. These things are pretty huge. They have to be strong."

Sinah smiled looking at his large wings. "They are very strong. Not only are they beautiful but they are remarkably deadly."

Bridger sent Sinah a flirtatious smile. "You think they're beautiful?"

Sinah couldn't help but to giggle. "You know they are."

Bridger folded them against his back. "I just really like hearing you say it, my Lady. So Murdoch, do you think they're beautiful too?"

Murdoch rolled his eyes. "Can we hurry up with this plan already? We need to get to the Commander."

Sinah's eyes darted to Murdoch. "...We? Only Bridger and I are going to the Director's office."

Murdoch's eyes shot to Sinah. "What are you talking about?"

"I need you here to make sure the building is clear."

"Once I give the orders the other D Helixes will-"

"You'll be helping them."

Murdoch instantly protested. "The hell I will! I'm going with you two to the Commander!"

Sinah slowly shook her head. "I understand your need to be in the presence of your Lord but I don't intend to enter the Director's office quietly."

Murdoch shrugged. "That's fine with me. We'll bust in there and-"

"Fallen has awakened your D Helix and its developing at the proper speed. But until your Helix reaches its final form, you're pretty much useless. Yes, you can order lower level D Helixes to do as you command and as you develop so will that skill. And yes, you can move faster than anyone else can, again a skill that will improve. But neither of those skills are enough for you to be valuable to us right now. Especially, if the other Labs arrive here and just want a battle."

Bridger looked toward Murdoch with a look of sympathy. Murdoch's expression was a combination of anger with minute traces of hurt. As Sinah reached her hand out to touch the feather seal, Murdoch hissed. "Well God! I really don't give a damn what you say! You're not my Lord and I'm going to get to the Commander whether you want me to or not! And if there is a war with the other Labs, then I'll stand by my Lord and-"

"And you'll what? Your physical strength is fine but without a weapon, you won't last long."

Murdoch made a snarl sound very befitting of a demon. "The hell I won't!"

Sinah lowered her hand and turned to Murdoch. "You're useless to Fallen this way."

Murdoch growled clenching his fists. "Say whatever the hell you want! I won't disappoint my Lord!"

A soft calming smile took Sinah's lips. "No and I won't let you."

Sinah suddenly lifted her hand toward Murdoch. The large golden circle appeared behind her then moved in front of her. Before either Murdoch or Bridger could react, a barrage of feathers began to rapidly zip passed Murdoch cutting deeply into his flesh.

Seventy

Pound of Flesh

Murdoch hissed firmly planting his feet on the ground and shifting his arms defensively in front of his face. "What the hell are you doing?!"

Sinah merely held her soft calming smile continuing her attack. Bridger's expression was a shocked sympathy watching as more and more blood poured from Murdoch's wounds. Try all he liked, Murdoch couldn't seem to get the upper hand and his rapid healing skill couldn't work fast enough.

Sinah suddenly snapped her hand shut and a powerful blast of energy was released from the golden circle, straight into Murdoch. The force slammed him so aggressively against the wall that the foundation of the cell began to crack. Luckily, neither Murdoch nor the wall damage triggered any of Bridger's bombs. Any resistance Murdoch once had, now had completely vanished. His angered and determined dark eyes dimmed as his limp body slid down the wall into a pool of his own blood.

Even though Sinah's attack had ended, Bridger instantly panicked and tried to rush to Murdoch's aid. Sinah lifted her hand causing him to stop in his tracks. "Relax Bridger, he isn't dead."

Bridger didn't look away from Murdoch. Not only were his eyes full of worry and panic but also filled with nervousness. "M… My Lady, he'll be alright, won't he? He will recover, right? He will..?"

Bridger was cut off by a weak yet angered groan from Murdoch. "Y... You think some stupid f.. feathers will stop me?"

Sinah snickered a little glancing toward the relieved Bridger. "See."

Murdoch slowly and weakly got to all fours. "I... I won't d... disappoint my L... Lord. You... You can't stop me. Nobody can!"

Bridger's expression went from relief to confusion hearing loud bone cracking sounds coming from Murdoch's body. "What's going on?"

The top of Murdoch's battle suit suddenly ripped to shreds as black narrow bones pierced through the sides of his arms. They looked very similar to the blades Fallen drew from his fingertips as weapons except without the red spots. Similar yet smaller ones pierced through his back down his spine. Thick black sharpened claws overlapped and replaced Murdoch's regular fingernails. His skin seemed to almost pull inwards tightening as close to his muscles as they could. Each and every one of his wounds produced a sizzling and bubbling sound as if they were being boiled to heal.

Bridger's eye darted to Murdoch's feet as his Combat boots ripped open. Murdoch's socks were obliterated as the balls of his feet widened and his toes became larger. Thick black sharpened claws exactly like his fingernails grew then replaced his toenails. The arches of his feet lifted upwards and became elongated almost like an animal. Murdoch's ears sharpened and began to grow. As they did, they shifted sideways then backward. All of Murdoch's hair fell out and was replaced with by reddish-black fine fuzz.

Bridger couldn't help but to giggle as two small almost cute looking red and black wings popped out of his back. They appeared more like decoration then purposeful. Murdoch snarled an animalistic snarl as he slowly got to his feet. Murdoch, who now stood on the pads of his feet, stood much taller than he once did. His once built and bulky frame was now a solid lean one. Murdoch snarled again exposing his teeth which had become sharpened points. Murdoch looked more like a beast rather than his normal male form of a D Helix.

Bridger smiled seeing Murdoch's hands. They were exactly like his, only red. "Hey, you have them too."

Murdoch's fully blackened eyes shifted to Bridger. As Bridger tried to step forward, Sinah spoke. "Hang on a minute, Bridger. Since I've forced

Murdoch into his true form, his mind hasn't yet caught up with the sudden change of his body."

Bridger didn't shift his attention from him. "Is he going to attack us?"

"No, not unless he feels like doesn't have any other choice. He can sense that both of you are now equal in every way, so fighting you would be pointless. I'm his only real danger and he knows against me, it would be a losing battle."

"So then what do we do?"

Sinah smile slightly. "As he waited for your recovery, we will wait for his."

Bridger barely nodded noticing that Murdoch was studying him.

Seventy-One

Ownership of the World

The Director slammed his hands on his large desk. The force caused one of his piles of papers to topple over. "Answer me Lucifer!"

Fallen's throat released a quiet chuckle. "My days of answering to a lowly worthless human have ended."

The Director's lips were instantly consumed by a full frown. "If it wasn't for us lowly useless humans you wouldn't even be standing there! You wouldn't even exist!"

Fallen chuckled again shaking his head. "…The foolishness of humanity. Sinah and I would have breathed life with or without you. Do you honestly believe my creation was a simple accident?"

The Director hissed almost instantly. "Where is God?!"

Fallen glanced around at the many soldiers, all of them had their weapons aimed at his head. "She is where she needs to be."

The Director snarled snatching up his metal walking stick and sweeping it across his desk. As all the papers went flying, he hissed again. "Answer me!"

Fallen turned his attention back to the Director. "I already did."

"You killed her didn't you?!"

Before Fallen could answer, the Director hissed for the third time. "You destroyed our only chance at a better world! You killed the only hope we had in saving our-!"

Fallen wasn't hesitant to cut the Director with a scoff. "Our? You talk as if you were going to let everyone have an opinion on this so called better world. We both know that's far from the truth. It was going to become the perfect world in your eyes. A world created where you would have full say and full control. Where you would rule like an unworthy God."

Fallen's eyebrows lowered as a full frown took his lips. A wave of intimidation spread rapidly throughout the office. As the soldiers cautiously took a few steps back from him, he continued. "Sinah is the one and only God. I won't let anyone stand in her way nor will I let anyone manipulate her for their own selfish human whims. I will protect my beloved from those unworthy to even look upon her."

The Director's expression shifted to not only shock but disbelief. "Y... Your beloved?"

Fallen clenched his fists. "The world belongs to us. Nothing and nobody will stand in our way to take what is rightfully ours. If it has to become ours through blood shed..."

An ugly cold smile spilled across Fallen's lips as he finished his sentence. "..So be it."

Before the Director could give a response, the computer made an urgent beeping noise. Four screens suddenly appeared above his desk in front of him. The Director's expression shifted to confusion as his eyes scanned the information that was appearing on the screens. "Building Seven is under attack?"

Fallen's ugly smile shifted to an amused smirk. "As I said, she is where she needs to be."

The Director's eyes shifted beyond the green screens at Fallen. Before he could question, a frantic looking solider appeared on the screen. "Director Hart, the perpetrators have sealed themselves in cell 6 on the experimental floors!"

The Director's expression shifted to bewilderment as he looked at the soldier. "Sealed, with what? All Combat equipment except for the Helix soldiers guarding the building or the emergency military should have been deactivated."

The soldier shook his head in disbelief. "I... I think they're feathers. Also Lead ADGL Tech Revin Minta has been attacked. He's alive but appears to be suffering. ...Orders Director?"

A slight grin touched at Fallen's lips. "And she will do what needs to be done."

The Director shifted his eyes back to Fallen before he spoke. "Has an ADGL Tech been called for Revin?"

The soldier nodded before the green screen flickered and a live feed showing Revin appeared. Any time the ADGL Tech tried to touch Revin, they would get a nasty electrical shock.

Fallen chuckled watching Revin twist and squirm in agony and terror. "That shock is probably the same voltage that bastard uses to subdue his experiments."

The Director released a defeated sigh as he closed his eyes. "If this is God's judgement upon him then there's nothing we can do."

The Director opened his eyes as his expression shifted to firm. "Cut your losses and leave him. Focus all your attention on breaking through that seal. I don't care what means you have to use, just break it! More than likely God is beyond that wall and I want her in custody and brought to my office ASAP! She is top priority and no unnecessary force is to be used with her."

The soldier gave a quick 'Yes Sir' before the green screens vanished. The Director's eyes sharpened toward Fallen. "We both know she will be captured and brought to me. She will see things my way Lucifer and all your disobedience will end."

Fallen chuckled quietly shaking his head. "We'll see Director, we'll see."

Seventy-Two

Upgrade

Sinah didn't shift her eyes from Murdoch hearing rapid gunfire hit the feather seal. Bridger swallowed looked toward the blocked entrance. "Will it hold?"

Sinah gave the slightest nod. "Yes, we're completely safe."

As Bridger turned to take a few steps toward the cell doorway, Murdoch snatched his wrist. His expression was a combination of confusion yet slight recognition. His eyebrows furrowed a little as he reached his second hand toward Bridger's face.

Right before contact, Bridger snickered. "You're not going to kiss me are you?"

Murdoch scoffed cuffing Bridger upside the head. "I don't want to have to burn my lips off."

Bridger chuckled as Murdoch let him go. "Glad to see you're okay Mean Helix."

Murdoch looked at his hands then at his newly changed form. "We're equal in strength now."

Bridger gave him an arm nudge as he smirked. "Yeah, but I'm better looking and trust me, that's all that really matters."

Bridger hooked one of his wings around Murdoch. "And have you seen these? I'm telling you, I'm gorgeous."

Murdoch couldn't help but to snicker. His amusement vanished shifting his attention to Sinah. As Murdoch stepped away from him toward her, Bridger protectively moved in front of Sinah. "I won't let you harm her Mean Helix. Equal or not, I will win that fight."

Murdoch glanced toward Bridger then looked beyond him at Sinah. "I don't want to hurt her Bridger, I want to thank her."

Bridger's expression shifted to shock with traces of mistrust. "Thank her?"

Murdoch gave a slight nod. Once Bridger did the same, he moved out of his way. Despite Murdoch's slight frown toward her, he respectfully kneeled then bowed his head. "Thank you for helping me fully change into my developed form, my Lady."

Before Sinah could respond, Murdoch continued. "And forgive the trespasses I've committed against you in the past. I only wanted and still want what's best for my Lord."

Sinah smiled softly. "…As do I."

Bridger couldn't help but to smile at her soft smile. Sinah turned to the feather seal. "First thing we need to do is get out of here. Bridger, don't set off the bombs until I tell you, alright?"

"Yes my Lady."

Murdoch's eyes darted from Sinah to Bridger as he stood up. "You can set them off by will alone?"

Bridger flexed his muscles. "Of course I can Mean Helix, bombs are my specialty."

"But for you to able to set them off by will alone is-"

Sianh cut Murdoch off. "The weapon you preferred to use during your developing stages has massively improved in your true form."

Murdoch looked at his hands. "I preferred a gun."

Sinah shrugged. "So use your hands like a gun."

Murdoch gave Sinah an irritated look. "Use my hands like a gun? What? Like this?"

Murdoch lifted his fist then pointed out his index finger and lifted his thumb. Bridger chuckled looking at his finger gun. "Now make those fake gun sounds children make. Pew! Pew!"

Murdoch tossed Bridger a full frown. Sinah looked at Murdoch's finger gun herself then shrugged. "If that's how you want to use it then-"

Murdoch cut her off opening his hand and thrusting it toward the wall below the feather covered window. "What I want is-!"

Murdoch stopped short as red laser bullets suddenly shot out from the red glowing crystalized circular jewel like vein pools on the tips of his fingers. The laser bullets zipped clean through the wall like a hot knife through butter. "W... What the..?"

Bridger smiled as his eyes lit up. "Neat! Now that's not something you can do with those stupid Combat gloves!"

Murdoch looked at his hands in confusion. "These are my weapons?"

Sinah nodded. "I forced both of you into your true forms. While all of your capabilities at their best, you never got a chance to develop with them to fully understand them."

Bridger waved his hand dismissively. "Don't worry about that my Lady, we're fast learners."

Murdoch quickly nodded in agreement. "We'll hold our own. You don't have to worry about us."

Bridger approached Murdoch with a slight smirk. "What I want to know is..."

Bridger snatched one of Murdoch's wings as he giggled. "What are these adorable things for?"

Murdoch hissed trying to push Bridger back from him. "What the hell are you doing?!"

Bridger pinched the other then pulled them open and upwards. "Look at these cute little things! They're so tiny! Can you even fly with them?"

Murdoch hissed again until Sinah spoke. "They aid and increase in his speed. They cut through any wind resistance and make his movements unregistered to both human and Helix vision."

Bridger made a childish sound forcing them to flap. "These cute things make him invisible?"

Sinah smiled and shrugged. "Well, not exactly but…"

Murdoch growled elbowing Bridger across the jaw forcing him to let him go. "No you Idiot Angel, it means I can move so fast people don't see me move."

Bridger chuckled rubbing his sore jaw. "Like you're invisible like I said."

Murdoch rolled his eyes. "Yeah fine, can we get going already?"

Sinah stepped forward and placed her hand on Bridger's chest. Bridger gave her a confused look until two of his feathers shifted from his wings onto his shoulders. Bridger's eyes darted to them as the feathers melted down the sides of his chest and became suspenders. Bringer smiled as much as he could as his eyes lit up. "Suspenders!"

Sinah smiled lifting her hand. "Your new found capabilities have some small but useful skills."

Bridger hooked his thumbs under his suspenders holding his smile. "A very useful skill, now I don't feel so naked."

Bridger glanced toward Murdoch's tattered Combat suit. "You might want to see if you can straighten yourself up a bit too. The last thing you want to do is present your new form to our Lord looking like a slob."

Murdoch frowned a little until he glanced down at himself. Bridger couldn't help but to smile as he gave a slight nod.

Once Murdoch made a very tight almost second skin material form over his body, Sinah turned her hand toward the feather seal and gave a slight wave. All the feathers turned black then became ash. Once the doorway was open, the soldiers rushed into the cell with their weapons drawn ready to shoot.

Seventy-Three

Evacuation

Thanks to the incident in building Seven, the majority of the soldiers were D Helixes and the rest were human. All of the D Helix soldiers stared at Murdoch in absolute awe while all the humans stared at him in absolute terror. Sinah spoke turning toward them. "D Helixes, I-"

The D Helixes didn't wait for her to get far into her sentence before they opened fire on the human soldiers. Without hesitation, Bridger stepped protectively in front of Sinah and moved into his combat stance. Sinah quickly shook her head stepping out from behind him. "No, no! Stop! They're not your enemies!"

Once the last human soldier was dead, one of the D Helix soldiers spoke. "They were threatening you God."

Bridger glanced toward Murdoch as he gave them a slight nod. Sinah, who noticed, frowned a little. "They weren't our enemies."

Murdoch gave an indifferent shrug. "As my fellow D Helixes said, they were threatening you. Besides, just because you're God my Lady, doesn't mean the human soldiers were going to listen to you. They only take orders from the Director."

Sinah held her slight frown. "I won't have any unnecessary deaths Murdoch."

Murdoch gave Sinah the slightest nod before he turned his attention to the D Helix soldiers. "Understood my Lady."

All D Helix soldiers locked their eyes upon Murdoch as he began to give his orders. "Building Seven needs to be evacuated ASAP. All soldiers, ADGL Techs and anyone suffering experimentation are to be removed from the building. Be forceful without any excessive force. If you get too much resistance, just drag them out of here."

Instead of stepping into his soldier awaiting a command stance, he stood like a high ranking soldier giving the commands. "Ignore any and all of those Synthetic wastes of life. They are to be left to rot and die with the destruction of building Seven. There's also another ADGL Lab in building 5 that deals with Synthetics as well. Go wipe them out then destroy the Lab. Are my orders clear?"

All the D Helix soldiers gave an instant nod. Murdoch glanced toward Sinah. "…Anything to add my Lady?"

Sinah gave a slight shake of her head. "This is a rescue evacuation mission, not a slaughter, everyone is to remain unharmed."

The D Helix soldiers nodded again. Having only a split moment of time pass, Murdoch suddenly snapped at them. "You've been given an order! Go!"

The D Helix soldiers frantically raced out of the room. Bridger couldn't help but to chuckle. "I think your new form has made you crankier then before Mean Helix."

Murdoch tossed him a slight frown. "I just want to get to my Lord."

Sinah motioned her hand toward the open doorway. "Then let's go."

The minute Bridger left the cell, his eyes darted to Revin. His expression weakened as his shocked eyes filled with sympathy. "…My Lady?"

Sinah glanced at Bridger then Revin. "He's experiencing the pain he caused every Helix he's experimented on."

Bridger barely nodded. "…Oh."

Murdoch frowned toward Bridger. "You actually have sympathy for that prick?!"

Bridger hesitantly gave a weak shrug. "Well... No... Not really."

Sinah placed her hand on Bridger's arm. "The choice is yours. I can simply end his life now or he can lose it when the building is destroyed, it's up to you."

Bridger approached then knelt down beside Revin. He studied his agony filled expression for a few moments before he questioned. "Can he hear me my Lady?"

Sinah shook her head. "Not unless you remove the feathers from his ears."

Bridger glanced back at her. "May I, my Lady?"

Sinah gave a slight nod, while Murdoch snorted. "We're taking too much time! I need to be in the presence of my-!"

Sinah lifted her hand cutting him off. Whether Murdoch wanted to or not, his voice fell silent. Bridger released a quiet sigh. "Sorry Murdoch, I just need a moment."

Murdoch's anger and hostility quickly began to calm. "...Okay."

Bridger grabbed both of the feathers from Revin's ears and pulled them out. Despite actually being in his flesh, no wound or blood was left behind. Revin quickly turned his head back and forth hearing the blaring sounds of building Seven's emergency systems. He tried to scream for help but no sound escaped his voice box.

Bridger leaned close to his ear and whispered. "You didn't break me."

Revin's head shot toward Bridger. A cold expression unfamiliar to Bridger's demeanor took his features. As he stood up, he spoke in a tone matching his expression. "It was kind of my Lady to show you mercy. I would have just beaten you within an inch of your life and left you to die."

Murdoch couldn't help but to grin at Bridger's words. The second he turned back to Sinah and Murdoch, his cheerful disposition instantly returned. "Sorry that I took so long, I'm ready to go."

Sinah's features weakened a little. "Are you alright?"

Bridger gave his usual happy smile, chipper tone. "Of course I am, my Lady."

Sinah gave a slight nod before she turned and began to walk down the hallway. As Bridger passed, Murdoch placed his hand on his shoulder. "Wait."

Bridger looked toward him with a slight smile. His smile increased as Murdoch pulled out the romance novel from his back pocket. "Thanks. Do you still want to read it when I'm done?"

Murdoch chuckled. "Come on, our Lady is waiting."

Seventy-Four

Obstacle

Once the elevator doors they were waiting on opened, a loud gasp was heard from the person inside. Without hesitation, both Bridger and Murdoch stepped into their combat stances. The person in the elevator was Emma. Her eyes were transfixed on Sinah. "G... God?! You've recovered!"

Before Sinah could say anything, Murdoch spoke. "Don't stand in our way Emma."

Emma didn't shift her locked attention from Sinah. "You need to come with me God. I need to do a full status check on you."

Sinah shook her head. "I'm fine, now if you will please…"

"I understand that you might think you are, but until we do a thorough check, we can't…"

Murdoch snarled cutting her off. His snarl sounded somewhat animalistic and very threatening. "Get out of our way Emma!"

Emma's eyes darted then widened in absolute terror staring at Murdoch. "W... What..?"

Murdoch snarled again. Bridger smiled placing his hand on Murdoch's shoulder. "He speaks for both of us."

Terrified sweat beads began to form on Emma's entire body as she stared traumatized at Murdoch. Bridger's tone of voice suddenly became firm. "Our Lady isn't going to be touched by the likes of you."

Murdoch growled so loud that Emma flinched. "Humans are unworthy to even look upon her!"

Sinah smiled shaking her head. "Sorry about them, they just want to keep me safe. Now, if you'll please excuse us, we need to get to Fallen."

Despite every inch of her self-preservation telling her to get out of their way and run for her life, she shook her head. "I… I can't. Any and all double Helixes must be thoroughly checked out. Through samples and experimentation we're able to learn-"

Bridger cut her off. "The Creator isn't something anyone should learn about."

Murdoch clenched his fists. "Get out of our way, lowly human!"

Bridger glanced at the brimming with hostility Murdoch. "Aren't you her friend?"

Murdoch's lips touched at a cold frown similar to Fallen's. "I serve under the Lord and the Lady. My only friends are my fellow Helixes that do the same."

Bridger chuckled a little. "Remind me never to rebel. You'll probably hunt me down."

Murdoch mumbled. "And drag you back to where you belong."

Emma slowly shook her head. "I'm sorry God but I can't just-"

Sinah cut Emma off. "Building Seven is going to be destroyed"

Bridger went flush snapping his fingers. "Oh shoot!"

Murdoch couldn't help but to snicker as Bridger began to run up and down the hallways pressing his hands against the walls setting the bombs. "Even in his true form, his basic lazy irresponsible self, remains the same."

Murdoch suddenly snarled and within a blink of the eye, he snatched his hand around Emma's throat. As he effortlessly lifted her off of her feet, he snarled again. "Anyone who stands in our way will be killed!"

Emma released a loud cry of panic as she grabbed his wrist with both hands. Sinah calmly spoke, shaking her head. "I highly suggest you evacuate or help in the evacuation."

Emma struggled for breath as she tried to speak. "B... But all the… re... research we… we..."

"Now that Fallen and I have become what we were meant to, the need for human interference has ended. We don't care what you do with the past knowledge but you must understand something..."

A strong wave of strength and purity washed over both of them. Murdoch made a sound of discomfort, while all the pain Emma was experiencing, vanished. Sinah closed her eyes. "I won't allow any Synthetic creature to exist in our world. If you chose to continue to create them…"

Emma's pain instantly returned and increased. "You will be our enemy and I will forget my overwhelming natural instincts to show mercy."

Murdoch carelessly dropped Emma to the floor. "You've been warned."

Emma got to all fours coughing and rubbing her throat. Sinah closed her eyes and whispered. "Bridger, we're leaving."

Bridger, who was quite the distance from the elevator, suddenly lifted his head then ran toward them. As they stepped into the elevator, Emma spoke. "Why do you want to stop our work? We can learn so much from you and the double Helixes."

Sinah closed her eyes. "The focus now should be on healing the world. Your kin and ours have suffered long enough."

Sinah opened her eyes but didn't look toward Bridger as he passed her into the elevator. "I suggest you leave building Seven as soon as possible."

Emma barely nodded as she slowly stood up. "Y... Yes God."

"Also there's a man in the hallway outside of the cell where Bridger was kept captive."

Murdoch was quick to pipe up. "It's that sadistic bastard Revin."

Sinah gave a slight nod. "Leave him where he is. He's getting what he deserves."

Murdoch began to tap his foot filling with impatience. "Can we go now, my Lady?"

Sinah smiled and gave another slight nod. As Murdoch pressed the floor button, Emma spoke. "God, I don't think everyone needs to be saved. The World of the Lost Souls should just be wiped out."

Sinah was silent as the elevator doors closed.

Seventy-Five

Lives in Their Hands

Once the elevator door opened for each floor, Bridger ran up and down the hallways installing bombs. Simply avoiding the frantic chaos of the Helix soldiers trying to evacuate everyone in the building, he remained focused on his task at hand.

Murdoch held the doors open and discouraged anyone from trying to get into the elevator. Any time an ADGL Tech would stop panicking and actually look at Murdoch, they would instantly start screaming and run away from him. Murdoch couldn't help but to snicker every time this happened.

Sinah looked into the hall at the scared and discombobulated ADGL Techs. "You've been out in the World of the Lost Souls more than I have Murdoch. My visits began with many unpleasant memories and ended with a few very precious ones. Do… Do you think Fallen and I should forsake them?"

Murdoch's eyes darted back to her. "You're questioning yourself, my Lady?"

Sinah hesitantly shrugged as a slightly upset look took her features. "I know Fallen wants to end all of humanity. I can feel his desire for their massacre as strongly as I feel the world's pain and suffering. But if he simply wipes them all out, he'll be destroying the power he needs to maintain his true form."

Bridger interrupted their conversation as he raced back into the elevator. "I don't get why people are freaking out. Just leave the building, how hard."

Murdoch didn't shift his attention from Sinah as he pressed the button for the next floor down. Once the doors opened and Bridger ran out again, Sinah released a weak sigh. "I'm sorry, I know this isn't the time or place to have such a conversation."

Murdoch looked toward Sinah for a few moments before he spoke. "My Lady, I will follow and obey you and my Lord onto my last dying breath. Whatever decision is made for their souls, will be the right one. Whether they live or die, I will without question, accept their fate."

Sinah weakly nodded until Murdoch continued. "My Lady, don't burden yourself with this, it shouldn't be just yours or just the Lord's decision. The world belongs to both of you."

Sinah responded with a weak almost inaudible 'yeah.'

Murdoch studied Sinah's slightly upset demeanor for a few seconds before he spoke. "We Helixes will stand behind both of you whatever is decided. To us, there isn't a right decision or a wrong one, there is just whatever our Lords want and it shall be done."

Sinah closed her eyes lowering her head. "We are deciding the fate of a world that doesn't even need us, a world that has adapted on its own without us. What gives us the right to decide if they should live or die?"

Before Murdoch could answer Bridger raced back into the elevator. "All done, this building will be nothing but tiny bits of rubble when my bombs go off!"

Sinah opened her eyes and forced a smile toward him. "Then let's go to the Director's office."

Bridger smiled, until he noticed Murdoch just staring at Sinah. His expression shifted to confusion, until he felt a dull pain in his chest. It was the same emotional pain, Dante had felt. "My Lady, are you alright?"

Sinah quickly nodded holding her forced smile. "It's nothing Bridger. Don't worry about it."

Murdoch glanced toward Bridger before he pressed the elevator floor button. Bridger placed his hand on Sinah's shoulder. "Your pain is our pain, my Lady. Please let me take some of the suffering from you."

Sinah's features weakened and her forced smile cracked a little. "L... Let's just get to Fallen."

Once the elevator doors opened, Murdoch raced down the hallway and within a blink of the eye, he was gone. Bridger chuckled stepping out of the elevator after Sinah. "Well, it's a good thing he doesn't have to lead the way."

Sinah smiled. "He'll probably just wait beyond the security booth for us."

"Tapping his foot and mumbling how slow we move."

Sinah gave a short snicker as they walked down another hallway. "You're probably right."

After a few moments of them walking in silence, Sinah spoke. "I asked Murdoch if Fallen and I should forsake humanity."

Bridger barely nodded. "So, that's what was going on."

Sinah barely nodded herself. "It is a pressing issue. Many lives are at stake. Murdoch says I shouldn't make this decision alone and that the Helixes will follow either way."

Bridger turned down another hallway with Sinah. "He's right about both. The world belongs to you and the Lord. Our purpose is protect and serve anyway we can, whatever is decided."

Sinah gave a slight nod. "Yeah, I know."

Bridger crossed his arms behind his head. "But if you ask me, I say save them. Sure, they've managed to survive and scratch out some sort of existence without either of you, but in what way really? Life shouldn't just be about surviving and existing. Where's the fun in that? I think that's why there's so much negativity in the world. Humans have just forgotten that life can be happy."

Sinah stopped in her tracks and turned quick to Bridger. Not expecting it, he gasped almost bashing into her. Once he saw her shocked expression, he awkwardly scratched the back of his head. "But then again, what do I know? I could be way off."

Sinah smiled placing her hands softly on his chest. "No, I think you're completely right. Even if there is only a flicker of good in the world then it's our responsibility to nurture it and help in grow. Thank you Bridger, you have no idea how much this has helped me."

Bridger removed his hand from the back of his head and placed it on the side of her cheek. "I'm always here for you my Lady. If I can help you in any way at any time, I'll always do my best."

Sinah smiled as much as she could as she removed her hands from him. "Thank you Bridger."

As Bridger smiled and removed his hand from her cheek, Sinah spoke. "Now let's go save my husband."

Bridger's shocked eyes darted to Sinah as she raced down the hallway. "…Husband?"

Bridger suddenly giggled before giving chase. "Awww! sooo cute!!"

Seventy-Six

Hell Hath No Fury

Both Bridger and Murdoch stared up at the outside of the 6th building. Murdoch crossed his arms and frowned. "And what was wrong with just kicking down his office doors?"

Sinah smiled slightly with a shrug. "You're welcome to do it that way if you want. It won't have much impact with us being up there already."

Bridger spoke in a mocking tone. "Yeah Mean Helix if you want to do it the lazy way, go right ahead we're not gonna stop you."

Murdoch frowned as much as he could before he scoffed. "Just try and keep up."

And with that, Murdoch zipped over to the building and slammed his clawed hands and feet into the side into the wall. Bridger chuckled watching him begin to scale building 6. "He sure likes doing things the hard way, doesn't he?"

Bridger turned his attention to Sinah. "Shall we, my lady?"

Sinah nodded with a smile as she approached him and wrapped her arms around his neck. Bridger wrapped his arm around her waist then smiled. "Okay, hold on tight."

Sinah snickered a little. "You don't have to worry about me Bridger. Even if you drop me, I'll-"

Bridger cut her off. "I promise I won't drop you!"

Sinah snickered again. "It will be okay."

Bridger took in a large amount of air as he opened his wings widely. “Okay, let’s give this whole flying thing a shot. I really hope it’s not like flying a helicopter.”

“Just relax. Don’t think too much about it. All you have to do is flap your wings and you’ll be fine.”

Bridger glanced up at Murdoch. He had almost reached the half way point on the 11 floor building. “I can’t let him beat us!”

Bridger’s confidence only waivered a little, as he slowly lifted and lowered his wings. After a few moments of his unsure movements, he suddenly smiled. “Okay, I think I can do this now.”

Sinah smiled gripping him tighter. “I know you can. Now let’s get up there.”

Bridger lifted his wings upward as high as they could go. He then suddenly swung them downward. The force of he used and the strength of his wings thrusted them high into the sky. So high, they zipped clean passed the 6th building far above the protective dome.

The air current Bridger’s wings had kicked up aggressively slammed into Murdoch. He panicked a little almost being ripped clean off the side of the building. He locked all of his muscles and tried his best to flatten himself against the wall hoping to stay put. The amount of air thrusted against him, stole his breath and made his eyes water. Murdoch squeezed his eyes shut and held on for dear life. As the current began to dissipate and calm, Murdoch could hear childish giggles from the sky.

Bridger looked down at the facility giggling. “Oops.”

Sinah looked around at the bird’s eye view of the desolate world. “I told you they were strong.”

Bridger looked toward the protective dome that covered all the buildings and areas except buildings 5, 6 and Seven. “Do you think if we were under that barrier thing, we would have smashed right through it?”

Sinah snickered with a nod. “And you would have had a nasty headache afterwards.”

Bridger giggled again before he glanced at the view himself. “It sounds silly, but I never realized how much of the world there actually is. It’s a lot bigger than I thought.”

Sinah glanced up at the eclipsed sun and moon. “I’m sure a lot of people think it's really small. It's not like anyone really gets to see it from this high of a view."

Bridger slowly flapped his wings lowering them. Once he was aligned with the Director's office ceiling to floor windows, he called out. "Murdoch, are you okay?!"

Murdoch, who was three quarters of the way up, hissed. "You almost blew me off the building!"

Bridger went a little flush. "Sorry!"

Ignoring Murdoch's hisses toward him, Bridger turned his attention to Sinah. "Are you sure about this, my Lady?"

Sinah moved one of her hands away from Bridger and raised it into the air. The large golden circle appeared behind her back then shifted below them. "Let's save Fallen."

Bridger gave a confident nod before he let her go. "Yes, my Lady."

Sinah fell from Bridger and dropped into the golden circle. He couldn't help but to smile as she and the golden circle vanished.

Fallen's eyes darted to one of the ceiling to floor windows as the golden circle rapidly began to form. Once it fully did, Sinah leapt through the circle, landed on the floor then rolled herself to her feet. The second she stood completely upright, every one of the Director's windows shattered.

The Director and any soldier standing too close to the windows were hit by the spray of glass shards. Luckily for the Director, his leather bound chair took the brunt of the damage.

Fallen wasn't hesitant to use this chaotic opportunity to end the lives of the human soldiers on either side of him. He turned his palms upward and sent two silver blades with red spots into their lower jaws. The blades zipped clean through their mouths and out the top of their heads, instantly killing them. He then sent a wave of blades at the soldiers, killing only the human ones.

The second Murdoch climbed over the window cell into the office and Bridger calmly flew inside, Sinah looked toward the Director and said. "You will release my husband."

Seventy-Seven

The Human Plight

At first the Director merely stared at Sinah in absolute shock. His focus was quickly regained hearing the Helix soldiers lower their weapons. Each and every one of them had their attentions locked on their respective Lord. Those with lower level Helixes kept glancing toward either Murdoch or Bridger in absolute awe.

The Director released a defeated yet relieved sigh. "I can't express just how happy I am that you have recovered God. Mind you, it wasn't necessary to make such an entrance. You wouldn't have been denied into my office."

Sinah's lips touched at a frown. "Necessary or not, my way was better."

Bridger couldn't help but to chime in with a snicker. "And fun."

An ugly sneer took Fallen's lips. "You see worthless human, she is where she needs to be."

The Director ignored Fallen and kept his attention locked on Sinah. He placed his hand on his chest and gave a slight respectful bow. "My dearest God, I am more than honored that you're finally here. Many have doubted that you were ever going to make an appearance, much less recover."

Sinah gave a slight nod. "Yes, it was thanks to Fallen, that-"

The Director cut her off continuing his train of thought. "You have kept us trapped in this world of suffering for far too long."

Sinah's features weakened a little until Murdoch said. "All that matters is that the Lord and the Lady are here now. The past is in the past, where it should be."

The Director nodded in agreement. "He's right, the past is in the past and it's about time for those unworthy of our future, in our world, to be punished. It's time for them to pay for the sins they have committed."

Both Murdoch and Bridger began to frown. Glancing toward Murdoch, Bridger gave a sound of disbelief. "Did he just call it our future, in our world?"

Murdoch's eyes sharpened toward the Director. "As if HE has some sort of ownership to it."

Sinah calmly lifted her hand silencing their conversation. "Are you saying all those who have sinned, should be simply wiped out?"

Fallen chuckled, crossing his arms. "Your hands are far from clean Director Hart. Are you willing to have judgement cast upon you as well?"

The Director confidently nodded with a smile. "I did what was necessary to create a better world. Even if it had to be through blood shed, through agony and destruction, God has finally breathed life. The world has begun to breathe life. I have taken the first steps toward our perfect Utopia and now that God is finally here, she can take the final ones. She can end all the pain and suffering in the world. She can destroy all the evil and darkness that have ruled in her absence. That has plagued our world."

The Director turned his attention to Fallen. "She can finally put an end to the mistakes that don't have any more use to me."

All the A and D Helix soldiers glanced toward one another in confusion. Before Fallen or Murdoch had a chance to hiss, Bridger spoke. "You've gone mad with power."

The Director turned on Bridger with a snarl. "I am doing what's best for the world!"

Murdoch returned the snarl with a growl. "The hell you are! You're doing what's best for you!"

Bridger couldn't nod fast enough. "You're trying to create the perfect world in your eyes and yours alone. Only the Lord and Lady can decide perfection. The fate of the world is in their hands, not some human's."

The Director leaned down and snatched up his metal walking stick. It had fallen to the floor during Sinah, Murdoch and Bridger's destructive entrance. "God and his Angels, Lucifer and his Demons left our world. They abandoned us to basically fend for ourselves. We survived! We recreated what we had lost! We created each and every one of you! We simple lowly, apparently unworthy humans created all of you! We, in a sense are YOUR Gods! If it wasn't for us, none of you would even be here!"

While everyone began to fume and voice their angered disagreement, Sinah calmly spoke. "I wasn't."

The Director's eyes darted to her. "What?"

Sinah shook her head. "I wasn't created in a Lab. I wasn't created at all. I was born to this world. I breathed life in the World of the Lost Souls, the place I was truly needed. If there wasn't any Labs creating life at that exact same moment on that exact same day, Fallen would have been born where we was truly needed also."

The Director's eyes brows went from angered to questioning. "Are you saying if we did nothing, the both of you would still be alive?"

Bridger chuckled a little. "Did you really think the creation of the ultimate beings would be left in some human's hands?"

The Director shook his head in disbelief. "But I... But we... we created Lucifer. I... I..."

Fallen smiled looking toward Sinah. "If my creation was even a micro second too early or too late, I would have been born elsewhere."

The Director frantically shook his head. It was as if what they were saying didn't make any sense. "Then why did they give us their blood to begin with?! Why did they tell us to recreate them?! Why the hell did they grant me and my fellow scientist's immortality?!"

Bridger's eyes darted to the Director. "You're immortal?"

Murdoch stepped into his demon soldier at ease stance. "It sounds to me like the past Lords gave those gifts as a test to your human souls. A final gift that will grant humanity one last chance to fight as hard as they can to keep a dying world alive."

Bridger looked toward Murdoch. "Or maybe to create Angels and Demons for when our Lords decide the humans have worked hard enough to earn back their blessings?

Murdoch shrugged. "Maybe, who knows? Our Lords aren't copies of the past Lords so none of us would know for sure. Dante would have a better theory on this."

Bridger scratched the back of his head. "Yeah, all I'm feeling is confused."

Fallen gave a slight nod. "You're right Murdoch we're not merely copies of the past."

Fallen turned his attention to the Director. "So your belief that Sinah will end my life merely because I'm Lucifer and good is obligated to destroy evil is wrong."

Fallen couldn't help but to chuckle. "There goes your desire for your perfect Utopia."

The Director closed his eyes and flopped down into his leather bound chair. "..No, no! We can't have done all this for nothing! This wasn't how things were supposed to go. I... I worked so hard for… nothing?"

Sinah shook her head. "No, not for nothing, if you didn't do anything with their gifts, the world would have continued to rot away with humanity rotting alongside it. Eventually, your kind would have simply just died out. In your plight to create Helixes, you humans have gained the knowledge to make fully functioning facilities and Labs. Places that can provide food, shelter and safety. In your goals to create a better world, a different one developed. Sure, it moves with great difficulty but it still manages. As humans with or without sin, good or evil, all you humans have proven your worth to me."

Fallen's eyes darted toward Sinah. The Director's distraught expression softened and calmed as he looked toward Sinah. "Dear merciful God, I am-"

Sinah cut the Director off with a hiss. "However, I cannot and will not forgive those who tamper with the power of Creation."

Sinah lifted her hand. "Bridger, end it."

Bridger smiled then closed his eyes. After a few seconds of concentration, building Seven was obliterated to nothing but ash.

Seventy-Eight

Punishment

The Director sprang to his feet in a panic hearing the roar of the explosion. His eyes widened feeling the aftermath vibrations rush against building 6. As he hobbled as fast as he could over to the shattered ceiling to floor windows, tons of green screens appeared above his desk. All were panicked, shocked and confused reports on the destruction of building Seven. The Director's mouth dropped staring in disbelief in the direction the building once stood. A large crowd of people had formed around the charred smoking crater in the ground.

Bridger, who was looking in the same direction, beamed with pride. "Now that was a masterful Angel bomb."

Murdoch glanced out the windows before giving a slightly impressed nod. "Not a single speck of debris. It looks like you're not as lazy as I think you are."

Bridger chuckled a little. "Yeah, but I kinda miss all the remnants falling from the sky. It was like a fun and dangerous shower."

Murdoch couldn't help but to chuckle himself. "You really are a lazy and crazy Angel Helix."

Sinah calmly spoke walking toward Fallen. Any A or D Helix soldier in her path quickly bowed their heads then moved aside. "I won't allow anymore souls to suffer."

The Director seemed to be locked in a state of permanent shock. All he seemed to do was stare wide eyed and mouth gapped. As Sinah took Fallen's hand, she spoke again. "And those without souls will finally be set free and put to rest."

Murdoch glanced toward Bridger. "I think when they're not needed for experimentation they're kept in building 2."

Bridger turned his attention to Sinah. "My Lady, should I head over to building 2 and deal with them?"

Sinah shook her head lifting her hand. "That won't be necessary Bridger. Now that I've awakened and the power of Creation has begun to flow again, the soulless can't maintain life. They are dying out as we speak. Eventually, the empty vessels in this Lab and anywhere else in the world will be gone."

Sinah placed her second hand on the side of Fallen's smiling face. After a quick yet gentle kiss, Sinah smiled herself. Before she had a chance to speak again, the Director muttered. "All of our research, all of our work, all of it, gone. We've spent so many years trying to truly understand the true potential of the Helix. And, and now it's all gone."

Fallen's eyebrows lowered as he shifted his attention to the Director. "Humans know too much about things they shouldn't as it is."

The Director closed his eyes and slowly shook his head. "Forgive us God for trying to reach too far beyond our limits."

As Sinah opened her mouth to say something, the Director spoke again. "Surely, surely you understand it's in a human's nature to be curious."

"Also to destroy what you don't understand."

Fallen tightened his grip on Sinah's hand as he growled. "This world needs to be wiped clean of all of you worthless humans. This should be the beginning of the new world of only Helixes."

Sinah's eyes darted to Fallen. "But-"

The Director shook his head turning toward them. "You're wasting your time arguing with evil, God. If you truly want to save humanity, you need to end Lucifer's life."

Everyone's eyes darted toward Sinah and Fallen. Just the thought of their Lords being against one another made all the Helix soldiers fill with panic and anxiousness. Fallen released a quiet chuckle. "Light cannot exist without Dark. Good cannot exist without Evil. You, yourself have taught me as such."

Sinah placed her second hand on their holding hands. As soon as Fallen relaxed his grip a little, she spoke. "I won't harm my husband."

A wave of relief washed over the Helix soldiers until Bridger made a coo sound. "...Awww."

Murdoch couldn't help but to roll his eyes. As a few of the Helix soldiers snickered a little, Murdoch snapped at them. "Shut it all of you!"

The Director hissed hobbling toward Sinah and Fallen. "Again, you call him your husband! He is not your husband! The two of you are not bound by the marriage contract or even by love. Lucifer is a manipulative monster. He knows that you are the only one that can destroy him. He knows he has to keep you under his control for his own safety."

A frown took Fallen's lips as the Director continued. "He's using your kind compassionate nature to trick you into thinking his emotions are genuine. Love isn't something the Devil has even the slightest understanding about."

As Sinah began to shake her head, the Director's expression shifted to pleading. "God, I beg of you, end his life! If you can't, then banish him! Banish him and all of his D Helixes!"

The Director gripped his metal walking stick with both hands like he was begging. "Evil doesn't have a place in our world anymore. Right now it needs desperately to heal from the damage it has suffered. Destroy or banish what shouldn't be. Just like the soulless, get rid of the evil that casts only sins upon us."

Sinah eyebrows lowered. "Fallen and the D Helixes are not sins upon the world and I will not harm my husband."

Fallen's frown shifted into a smug smirk. Before he had a chance to say something matching his demeanor, both he and Sinah suddenly lifted their heads. Sinah wasn't hesitant to speak. "They're here."

Fallen gave the slightest nod. "There are more than a few Helixes with them."

Sinah's lips touched at a frown. "There are also more than a few Synthetic creations as well."

Fallen turned his attention to the A and D Helix soldiers. "Head over to the Launch Pad area and wait for commands."

Without hesitation the Helix soldiers gripped their weapons and raced toward the office doors. Fallen shifted his attention toward Bridger and Murdoch. "Prepare for war."

Both nodded and followed after the soldiers. As both Fallen and Sinah turned to leave, the Director snatched Sinah's wrist. "God, I-!"

Without hesitation, Fallen snatched his hand around the Director's throat and slammed him clean through his large desk. Papers and wood pieces crashed down upon him as Fallen hissed. "Don't you dare lay one of your filthy human hands upon my wife!"

Sinah shook her head placing her hand upon his arm. "Forget about him, we need to go."

Fallen gave a quick nod before he followed Sinah out of the office.

After a few moments of merely trying to get his sore body to move, the Director called out. "…Computer!"

The computer made a sound of acknowledgement before the Director called out again. "Send an emergency report to all human military. Under my order, tell them to gather in the lobby of building 6 and wait for my commands."

The computer again made another sound of acknowledgement. As the Director slowly got to his feet, he groaned in pain. "Don't worry God. I will free you and your Helixes from Lucifer's grip."

Seventy-Nine

A Prelude to War

Only four of the remaining Labs had taken the Directors invitation and threat seriously. All of them, including their Helix soldiers and Synthetic creations, stood in the Launch Pad area with slight frowns on their faces. Bridger, who was standing just inside one of the large hangars, continued to watch them. Seeing their expressions, he couldn't tell if they were annoyed that nobody was there to greet them or the fact they were there to begin with.

After a quick glance over all the Helix soldiers, Fallen spoke in a commanding tone. "…All eyes on me."

Everyone, even the Helix mechanics eyes locked on Fallen. Fallen's lips touched at a frown. "Forcing all of you into your true forms will take too long and most of you aren't ready for it. Unfortunately, that means you need to rely upon the Combat equipment."

Murdoch stepped into his demon soldier awaiting a command stance. "My Lord, for the higher leveled Helixes, the Combat equipment tends to act up."

Fallen gave the slightest nod. "For those whose Combat gloves fail, fall back. Nobody should be killed because of a human made device. Let the lower levels handle it."

One of the higher level D Helix soldiers frowned. "We have to do nothing while all the lower levels fight? We're supposed to be stronger than them!"

Any lower level Helix soldier in the group tossed him a frown. Sinah, who noticed, shook her head. "All of you are equal in strength. You are just at different stages of development. In the end, you will-"

The annoyed D Helix soldier cut her off with a hiss. "So we just let the less developed handle this?!"

Without hesitation, Murdoch slapped him upside the head. Even though the force was very light, the D Helix soldier still stumbled forward. Murdoch raised his hand to cuff him again as he frowned. "Show your respect! Our Lords are making sure none of you are just sitting ducks waiting to get picked off. Lower or higher, we all need to work together."

Murdoch sharpened his eyes as he lowered his hand into a clenched fist. "Stop acting selfish and fall in line! We are a team and we will obey our Lords even onto death!"

Murdoch shared his frown with all the other soldiers "Got it!"

The D Helix soldier and all the other soldiers instantly nodded then bowed. Many apologies spilled from the group toward Sinah. Shaking her head, Sinah's expression shifted to sympathetic. "Apologies aren't necessary. I know this is hard, especially for those on the cusp of a physical change. For the time being, we need to use what we have, not what we're waiting for."

Fallen wasn't hesitant in agreeing with Sinah. "She's right. Now nobody opens fire until I give the command, is that understood?"

While all the Helix soldiers nodded, Sinah released a weakened sigh. Hearing her, Fallen's eyes darted in her direction. "...Sinah?"

Sinah closed her eyes and released another. "We're approaching them as if we are already prepared for war. The Helixes out there are only following orders. We shouldn't punish them because-"

"Sinah, we can't force a Helix to obey his or her natural instincts. If they choose to stand alongside humanity then they will die alongside them."

Sinah opened her eyes as her features weakened. "But Fallen..."

Bridger gasped feeling an aggressive emotional numb pain strike him in his chest. His features weakened as well before he looked toward Sinah. Seeing her saddened expression, the pain increased. "...My Lady?"

Sinah's eyes darted to him. Seeing his mirroring expression, she slowly shook her head. "It's alright Bridger. The Synthetics are our enemies not our kin."

Before Fallen had a chance to respond, Sinah did turning her attention to the A Helix soldiers. "Focus solely on the Synthetics. Should a Helix from another Lab get in your way, respond passively, subdue rather than kill."

Bridger wasn't hesitant to speak up. "Anyone having trouble with that, just give me a shout, I'll knock those idiots too stupid to know where their loyalty should lay, back on track."

Fallen lips touched at a smile. "Her command is for all of you, subdue rather than kill."

Sinah's eyes darted to Fallen in shock. As he softly brushed his knuckles against her cheek, he continued on his train of thought. "But for those Helixes that insist on resisting-"

Sinah's features weakened a little as he continued. "Murdoch, end them."

Murdoch instantly bowed his head. "It will be done, my Lord."

Fallen took Sinah's hand. "Please forgive my cruelty."

Sinah slowly shook her head. "It's in your basic nature, just like mercy is in mine."

Looking at Sinah's slightly upset disposition merely for a few moments, he spoke. "Murdoch, for those who choose to resist, end them quickly. Don't let any of them suffer."

Sinah's eyes darted to Fallen's sunglasses. "But... ...But why?"

Fallen softly touched his lips to hers. Once he lifted his lips, he whispered. "I love you Sinah and I will do whatever it takes to make you happy."

Sinah returned his smile with her own smile. "I love you too Fallen and all I want is for those Synthetics to know true pain."

Fallen's lips curled into a full smile. "Then it will be done."

Bridger couldn't help but to coo placing his hand on his chest. "... Awww so sweet. The pain is completely gone. It's like my heart has been warmed up."

Murdoch rolled his eyes. "...Idiot Angel."

Fallen turned to the Helix soldiers. “Let those Synthetic creatures learn why this is our world. Let the lesson be taught in bloodshed.”

All of the Helix soldiers nodded and gripped their weapons in anticipation. Fallen turned his attention to Sinah with a smile. “Shall we go introduce ourselves?”

Sinah smiled gripping his hand. “It would be rude of us not to say ‘hello’ before we begin our attack.’”

Once Fallen and Sinah left the large hangar hand in hand, both Murdoch and Bridger glanced at their fellow soldiers then followed after.

Eighty

Introductions Aside

The second the Directors caught sight of Fallen, a wave of nervousness washed over them. Despite wanting to hide that fact, their dispositions became more apparent the closer he approached. As if responding to their Director's nerves, the Helix soldiers gripped their weapons and took aim. The many Synthetic creations on the other hand, only snickered and chuckled as if neither Fallen nor Sinah were a threat.

Fallen's lips touched at a frown recognizing one of the Directors. It was Carl Courtier. He was the Director from the now destroyed Lab 6. He was also the Director responsible for the now destroyed Synthetic Creation Lab underground better known as 'The Lost Souls Lab.'

Once Fallen and Sinah stepped in front of the Directors, all their A and D Helix soldiers fell in line behind them. All had their weapons ready for combat. Once Bridger and Murdoch took their places beside their Lords, the Directors gasped. Bridger's expression shifted to confusion seeing their shock aimed directly toward him.

Bridger couldn't help but to awkwardly scratch the back of his head. "Uh… Hi?"

One of the Directors stepped forward. He had dark hair and one dark brown eye exposed. The other was covered with an eye patch. He placed his hand on his chest and respectfully bowed. "God, we are honored that you grace us with your presence. My name is Director Chris Fa-"

Bridger cut the Director basically known as Director Chris off with a shocked loud voice. "You think I'M God?!"

Murdoch glanced beyond the Directors at the A and D Helix soldiers. All of their eyes were transfixed upon their respective Lords. Their once tightened grip on their weapons had relaxed and all of their expressions suggested they weren't sure about their next course of action. Murdoch shifted his eyes back to the Directors. "You should pay attention to your Helix soldiers."

Director Courtier glanced back at them then the Synthetics. The Synthetics stared back at him as if nothing was amiss. The Helix soldiers however, never once shifted their gazes from Sinah and Fallen. Seeing their focused expressions, Director Courtier's expression shifted to slight confusion. As he looked back at Sinah and Fallen, he suddenly snapped his fingers. "Now I recognize you!"

Fallen's lips touched at a frown as Director Courtier rudely pointed at Sinah. "You're that girl who stupidly stood beside Lucifer when he attacked my Lab."

Director Courtier's lips touched at a frown as he finished with. "And then blew it up."

Before Fallen or Murdoch could snap, Sinah calmly responded. "I'm also the girl who was killed by one of your Synthetic creatures in your underground Lab."

Director Courtier shook his head in confusion. "I don't understand, if you were killed, then how-?"

Director Chris cut him off in shock. "Oh my god, SHE'S God!"

Director Courtier's eyes darted from Director Chris to Sinah. "She's... This girl's God?"

Both Bridger and Murdoch frowned. Bridger was first to speak up. "Hey! Watch your tone with our Lady!"

Murdoch quickly followed after. "Show some respect human!"

Director Courtier shook his head in disbelief. "This is nonsense! She's just one of Lucifer's soldiers. There is no way that this girl is the high and mighty God."

Sinah shook her head. "It doesn't matter what you think or believe. You are one of the people responsible for using the power of Creation to create innocent A Helixes, just to turn around and end their precious lives to create these Synthetic abominations. You, and all of them, will burn for what you have done."

All the Director's eyes darted to Sinah. Director Courtier went flush stumbling over his words. "Th… The Synthetics... They... they are-"

Sinah frowned finishing his sentence. "…Sins against us."

Fallen gave a slight nod. "And they will not exist in our world."

A few of the Synthetics chuckled and boldly said. "Those pathetic A Helixes died to create something better."

Another agreed. "Yeah, something that doesn't have the restrictions or limitations of being under some worthless Lord."

Another chuckled. "That's right. We don't need Helixes or Lords in our world. We've evolved beyond your weak, pointless selves."

All the Synthetics began to snicker and joke about the lack of value the Helixes had to anything and anyone. Sinah frowned and released Fallen's hand. Before he could question, Sinah ran through the crowd and snatched the mouthiest Synthetic's wrist.

The Synthetic only continued to laugh until Sinah quickly twisted his arm behind his back. As she snatched the other and did the same, the Synthetic hissed. "You're wasting your time trying to stop us."

Sinah hopped upward and hooked her knees onto his upper back. "I'm not trying to stop you I'm going to kill you."

With an aggressive thrust of her knees and a forceful tug on his wrists, the Synthetic's arms were ripped clean out of their sockets and the back of his rib cage was shattered. Reddy grey blood gushed from his arm holes and mouth. As he fell forward, Sinah did a back flip off his falling body. Landing on her feet, she could hear the Synthetic begin to produce an animalistic growl. Any other being, be it human or Helix would have been easily killed by her actions. The Synthetic on the other hand, appeared only to be severely wounded.

Sinah calmly pointed her palm downward at him. The large golden circle appeared behind her and began to spin releasing tons of feathers. Within seconds, the Synthetic was rapidly ripped into nothing. Before any other Synthetic could react, Director Courtier yelled out. "Stop!"

Defensively lifting his hands, he yelled out again. "Please stop! There isn't any need for violence! God, I promise you, the Synthetic may be mouthy but they're not a threat to any of you."

Fallen raised his hand into the air. All the A and D Helix soldier's gripped their weapons and took aim. "The audacity of humanity thinking they can control something much stronger than themselves. All you Directors are deluded and think the exact same way."

Sinah eyes glanced over the Synthetics. While human and Helix alike had varying personalities and appearances, all the Synthetics looked like copies of one another. There wasn't a single thing remarkable about the dark hair dark eyed Synthetic creations. Each and every one of them could blend seamlessly in a crowd of humans or Helixes completely unnoticed.

Sinah turned her attention to the Directors. "This is out of your hands now. Run if you don't want to face the consequences of your actions. Understand this though, if you have created any type of Synthetic creation, your punishment will be at hand. It will only be a matter of time before we hunt you down."

Two out of the four Directors high tailed it toward the vehicles they arrived in. They didn't once think about the Helix soldiers they had left behind as they burned rubber out of the Launch Pad area.

Fallen snatched his sunglasses off his face. As he crushed them in his palm and tossed them aside, he spoke. "Judgement is upon them."

Sinah's eyebrows lowered as she spoke in a calm yet direct voice. "Judgement is upon them all."

Fallen suddenly dropped his raised hand and yelled out. "Kill them!"

Eighty-One

Death From Above

At first the A and D Helix soldiers from the other Labs lifted their weapons preparing to fire back. Once they realized all the gunfire was directed solely upon the Synthetics, most simply lowered their weapons while others joined in on the fight.

Though Director Courtier and Director Chris had run for cover, both stared at the battlefield dumbfounded. It was as if they couldn't understand the events that were unfolding. The more flesh that was shot off the Synthetic's humanoid looking bodies, the more their true forms began to reveal itself. Each new bullet exposed a greyish red skin that was quickly covered by a reddish grey fluid.

Murdoch hissed slashing his claw like nails across one of the Synthetic's throats removing his head. "How much of this wretched human skin do we need to rip off before we can actually do damage?!"

Bridger, who had just finished tossing another bomb, responded. "I have an idea."

Murdoch glanced toward Sinah and Fallen. Despite the fact they were attacking separate Synthetics, neither strayed too far from the other. As his attention shifted back to Bridger, he spoke. "Need help?"

Bridger couldn't help but to chuckle as he took flight. "Yeah Mean Helix, run for cover."

Murdoch smirked until the neck hole of the synthetic he had just decapitated, filled then over flowed with a black acidic liquid. It began to sizzle as it melted the rest of the flesh off its human shell. Murdoch shifted into his combat stance preparing for the Synthetics true form to reveal itself. "Whatever you're going to do Bridger, make it snappy."

Bridger, who was far too high above the battlefield to hear him, closed his eyes. "Alright Angel Bridger, let's just see what this new form can do."

Bridger opened his hands just in front of chest and turned his palms upward. It looked like he was going to receive an item from the sky. His wings turned inward and closed around him. Even though he had stopped flapping his wings, he didn't fall nor begin to descend toward the ground. Bridger's eyebrows lowered as he began to concentrate as hard as he could.

As Sinah effortlessly tossed one Synthetic into another, her eyes darted up to Bridger. A smile couldn't help but to touch at her lips as she raised her hand. All the A Helix soldiers instantly stopped their attacks feeling a strong calming warmth envelope them. Those A Helix soldiers that hadn't joined in on the Synthetic attack felt a slight sadness in the protective light. All of them filled with shame and regret as if they had disappointed their Lord.

Hearing the decline in gunfire, Fallen turned his attention to Sinah. Seeing her smile and raised hand, he shifted his attention skyward. Once he saw Bridger, a slight smile touched at his lips as he turned his palm toward the ground.

Murdoch, as well all the other D Helix soldiers jumped, as many black blades with red spots shot up from the ground around them. The blades quickly interlocked and encased them in a closed safety. The D Helix soldiers that chose not to enter the fight felt something much different in the cold protective darkness. Instead of a slight sadness, they were slammed with a wave of anger and hostility. It was as if Fallen was giving them a single warning, 'fall in line or be slaughtered.'

Director Courtier and Director Chris stared wide eyed at the two different ways they were protected. The A Helix soldiers still had a full view of their surroundings and while they didn't have a need to react, they could if a situation came up. The D Helix soldiers on the other hand, were completely sealed up and unaware of anything. Not even sounds could reach their ears. If something did occur that required their assistance, Fallen himself would have to lower their protection.

A few of the Synthetics attempted to use their human shells to simply punch the Helix soldiers. Those who tried to attack the A Helix soldiers screeched as their arms were burnt to nothing by Sinah's protective golden light. Those who attacked Fallen's impenetrable protective shell quickly became frustrated not causing any damage what so ever.

Bridger's determined eyes snapped open as did his wings. Many golden sparkling bombs rapidly began to form just in front of him. As he opened his wings wider and the bombs encircled him, a quiet chuckle caught his throat. "Let the fun begin."

The second he finished his sentence, Bridger nosedived wildly toward the battlefield. Upon contact, a massive explosion was set off. Chunks of cement, Synthetics and any vehicle in the area were effortlessly thrown and destroyed in the impact. Both Directors were carelessly tossed from the battlefield by the wind current Bridger's explosion produced.

As the smoke began to clear and the rubble began to settle, loud childish giggles could clearly be heard. As Bridger stood up completely unharmed, he raised his fist in triumph. "Yet another masterful bomb by the one and only champion Angel, Bridger!"

Sinah and Fallen, who were completely unaffected by Bridger's attack, lowered their protection on their Helixes. The golden protective light simply faded while the shells became ash and fell to the ground.

Murdoch's eyes darted to the destruction in both shock and surprise. Hearing Bridger's giggles, he couldn't help but to chuckle himself. "... Idiot Angel."

Murdoch's amusement instantly vanished seeing a few of the high level A and D Helix soldiers clutch their chests, drop their weapons and collapse to their knees. The expressions on their faces reflected absolute agony.

Fallen didn't hesitate to call out. "Murdoch! Bridger! Our protective energy has caused a forcible change into their true forms. Get them into the safety of the hangars!"

Both gave a quick 'Yes my Lord' then sprang into action. Within a blink of an eye, Murdoch was helping one of the D Helixes to their feet. Bridger on the other hand, took flight and scooped up two A Helix soldiers as he flew by them. As he passed Murdoch, he snickered. "I thought you were supposed to be the fastest Helix."

Murdoch chuckled hooking the D Helix soldier's arm over his shoulders. "Just try and keep up."

Bridger snickered again as Murdoch zipped passed him then put him in his dust.

Fallen shifted his attention from the Helix soldiers toward Sinah. She hadn't once shifted her sharpened eyes from the destruction. She had a full frown on her face and her fists were clenched. Before Fallen could question, loud growling, snarling and condescending chuckles spilled from the wreckage.

Eighty-Two

Broken Shells

Thanks to Bridger's bomb, all of the human skin that once hid the Synthetic's true forms had been completely ripped from their bodies exposing their greyish red flesh and eyes. Even though the basic process of the Synthetic creation was the same, it was obvious that each Lab tried to add their own twist on the production. Despite such attempts to make them differ from one another, all looked like they belonged to the same bloodline.

Most had the appearance of being a failed or flawed Synthetic creation. Sharp bones protruded from odd locations and at odd angles. Some bones had even pierced through vital areas such as organs and through the skull. They had teeth too large for their jaws which caused them to excessively drip an acidic black tar like substance similar to drool. They made godawful clicking and scraping sounds as they moved. It was almost as if their bones had relocated and were rubbing together. With so many flaws and imperfections, it was unbelievable that these Synthetic creations were even alive to begin with. They appeared more like broken mutated variations of Murdoch's true form rather than fully functioning beings.

The more successful Synthetics had sharp bones protruding from more useable locations. They had them in the arms or hands or anywhere else where they could utilize them as a weapon. They moved normally and were obviously the greater threat.

Sinah didn't once shift her eyes from the six larger Synthetics. Each of them had the upper half of a human form and the lower half was only made up of tentacles. This was the type of Synthetic that had ended her life.

Many flawed variations stood near them. They had the sharp protruding bones like the others but also tentacles that grew from sporadic locations. From the center of the forehead to the top of the foot, nothing about their true forms made sense.

Even though the ones with the correct protruding bone locations didn't move anywhere near as fast as Murdoch, they were first to rush and attack the A and D Helix soldiers. Without hesitation, Fallen yelled out. "Attack! No survivors!"

All of the A and D Helix soldiers shot their weapons as fast as they could pull the triggers. Without a single word spoken, Sinah walked toward the six large Synthetics.

As Bridger stepped out of one of the hangars, he heard a low rumble from above. Turning his head skyward, he noticed a few more dark grey clouds rapidly begin to form. A wave of panic instantly rushed over his senses as his eyes darted toward the battlefield in search of his Lady. Once he caught sight of Sinah, he called out. "Murdoch! I need you to grab the rest of the changing A Helixes."

Murdoch, who had just stepped out of the hangar, gave him a confused yet concerned look. "Why? What's going on?"

Bridger spoke as he took flight. "I have a chance to fix a mistake I made."

Murdoch's eyes darted to the aggressive fighting. Once he saw Sinah himself, he gave a quick nod. "Protect our Lady."

Bridger flew as fast as he could toward the large Synthetics. The wind current his strong wings produced knocked a few flawed Synthetics as well as his fellow lower level Helixes over.

All six Synthetics frowned focusing their attention upon Sinah. As they circled around her, one of them growled. "We know you! You killed one of our fellow Synthetics, Kadin!"

Sinah gripped two feathers in each of her hands. "He took my life so with my last dying breath, I took his."

Another of the six snarled. "This time we'll make sure you stay dead!"

As all of them shot tentacles toward her, Sinah quickly shifted into a combat stance ready to fight. Before Sinah a chance to strike, Bridger zipped right passed their line of attack. As his wings brushed by them, they effortlessly slashed through their tentacles like a hot knife through butter. As the pieces fell to the ground, Bridger looped back and landed next to her. "There is no way in Heaven I'm going to let you die again, my Lady."

A soft smile took Sinah's lips as she glanced toward him. "It was necessary."

A firm masculine voice spoke from behind them. "Necessary or not, I forbid it."

Sinah smiled even more but didn't glance back, Bridger however did. The voice belonged to Fallen. As he walked toward them, he effortlessly lifted one of the large Synthetics and tossed it into another. "I'm surprised these wastes of tainted Helix blood even know the meaning of the word camaraderie."

Within a blink of the eye, Murdoch joined them. As he passed by one of the six, he slashed the side of it. Ignoring the black acidic blood that was gushing out, he spoke. "Mission complete, my Lord."

As he took his place beside Fallen, Bridger snickered. "What took you so long?"

Murdoch chuckled before his eyebrows lowered and he shifted into an aggressive stance. Sinah's smile faded as the tentacles and the slash wounds began to rapidly regrow and heal. "No survivors."

Both Murdoch and Bridger gave an instant nod and a 'Yes, my Lady.'

Fallen placed his hand on Sinah's shoulder. "They will know true pain."

Sinah softly placed her hand on his. "Let's show them the true wrath of the Gods."

Eighty-Three

Idle Chat

Director Courtier groaned as he slowly regained consciousness. "Ugh... God..."

He muttered placing his hand on his very sore head. His mangled body was covered in many bleeding cuts and bruises. The damage his body sustained suggested that if he were any closer to the impact of Bridger's bomb, he'd be dead. As he slowly sat up, a hand was offered in front of his face. "Need a little help, Carl?"

Director Courtier's expression shifted from pain to confusion as he looked up to see who the voice belonged to. A frown instantly took his lips seeing the smiling Director Hart. As he cuffed his hand away, he noticed the condition of Director Chris. He was lying still on the ground, blood was gushing from his temple and his arm looked twisted and dislocated.

Director Courtier crawled as fast as he could over to him in a panic. "Chris! Chris!"

The Director watched as Director Courtier began to rattle the limp body of Director Chris. "Chris! Wake up goddamn it! Wake up!!"

A weak groan escaped Director Chris' throat as he slowly opened his eyes. "Ugh... Oh hell, I'm still alive?"

Director Courtier made a sound of relief before he snickered. "Yeah, sorry about that."

The Director glanced back at his many human soldiers. "Med Techs."

Two Med Techs raced toward the wounded Directors. Neither resisted as they quickly began to patch up their injuries.

The Director turned his attention to the battlefield. He watched the Synthetics bodies rapidly heal from every bullet wound they sustained. The only ones doing any real damage were Fallen, Sinah, Murdoch and Bridger. The Director leaned on his walking stick watching Sinah slash through any tentacle that came anywhere near her group. "I'm impressed you managed to create successful Synthetics. Their presence obviously pisses off God but it's still rather impressive nonetheless."

Director Courtier's lips touched at a frown. "Then it's safe to say, this butcher shop hasn't been successful in creating any?"

"No, every attempt has resulted in a mercy killing."

Director Chris instantly responded with a disgruntled scoff. "You wouldn't know mercy even if it slapped you across the face."

Director Courtier watched as the Med Tech sprayed a healing spray on his wounds. "Is this why you asked us here Walter, just so we can be slaughtered? Lucifer and his men have already destroyed two of my Labs. I'm completely out of any samples. So what is it that you want? When is enough, enough?"

Director Chris made a loud sound of discomfort as the Med Tech snapped and popped his arm back into place. In a sympathetic tone the Med Tech apologized then began to spray his injuries with the Med spray. Director Chris gave a slight dismissive nod before he turned his attention to the Director. "You knew this was going to be a warzone. I should have listened to Isadora and ignored your request."

The Director chuckled, shaking his head. "Actually, this is far from what I was expecting. God is pure, gentle, merciful and innocent and yet..."

The Director paused to watch one of the flawed Synthetics leap toward Sinah. Without hesitation, Fallen snatched him out of the air and without any real effort ripped him clean in half. "And yet, I don't understand God's rage. Why would something manmade cause her so much anger and not just simple annoyance?"

Director Courtier looked toward the ground but said nothing. Director Chris glanced toward him momentarily before he spoke. "All hell has broken out anyway you might as well tell him the truth."

The Director didn't shift his eyes from the ruthless fight. "What truth?"

Director Courtier's expression became awkward as he closed his eyes. "They're not exactly manmade. For a successful Synthetic to be created, a soul needs to be used or rather offered."

"...A human one?"

"...No, a successful A Helix soul."

The Director's eyes darted back to Director Courtier in shock. "You sacrificed a pure A Helix to create a Synthetic?"

Director Courtier released a defeated sigh as he opened his eyes. "When the A Helix is in its developing stages, we introduce then flood the system with Synthetic D. Since the soul is one of an A Helix, it will do its best to protect itself. Of course, at that stage of development, it's too weak to stand even the slightest chance. All side effects are removed and the Synthetic essentially consumes the A Helix and its soul. The method has yet to fail. Those messed up ones out there are the results of other Labs attempting to improve on perfection."

The Director shook his head as he weakly chuckled. "For us scientists, that's one hell of a step in the evolutionary progress. For God, that's one hell of a sin against her. You've used the power of Creation to destroy."

Director Courtier frowned almost instantly. "None of us, not even you, thought any of us would be successful in creating God! How the hell you managed to create Lucifer is beyond me."

Director Chris was quick to chime in. "You act like he gave any of us a real chance to create God. With him sending Lucifer and his men out to steal the pure samples, our priority became to protect ourselves. Synthetics became necessary thanks to him."

The Director chuckled under his breath. "Your hands are just as bloody as mine gentlemen. The only difference is I have a chance for forgiveness and redemption. I may have indirectly caused you to create them but as I said before, our Lab hasn't been successful. We haven't sinned against God nor have we violated Creation."

Both Directors instantly frowned as the Director turned his attention to his human soldiers. "Assist the Helix soldiers but don't interfere with God's battle. Let Lucifer and his men deal with it."

All the soldiers nodded before they raced toward the battlefield ready for combat. Director Chris shook his head. "Have you lost your mind? What the hell are bunch of humans going to do? This is a battle between Angels, Demons, Gods and the Synthetics. This isn't some disagreement or nonsense humans fight about."

The Director smiled slightly watching his re-enforcements join in on the battle. "If God sees that we are willing to risk our human lives to rid our world of the Synthetics, she may see us as allies. She might even see that we are worth saving. My actions could very well save humanity."

Director Chris scoffed. "Or agitate her with your pointless interference."

The Director held his smile. "We'll see."

Both Directors glanced toward one another before they shook their heads in disbelief.

Eighty-Four

Arch Angel in Safety

It had been hours since Dante and the A Helixes evacuated everyone from Residential. Almost all of them had never been anywhere near the outside of the protection of the facility. The whole journey into safety was one of many questions, anxiousness and nervous energy. Fortunately, for Dante and the A Helixes, who were slowly but surely becoming agitated, a gentle calm fell over them the second they stepped into the house. Even Dante and his fellow A Helixes had the comforting warmth wash over them when they entered. The presence of Sinah still lingered upon the air.

Although, the large amount of people mostly sat in the living room, Dante still had enough room to pace. Alex, who was frantically working on Dante's laptop, released a frustrated sigh. "All systems have been put under the emergency lock down system, Dante. Try all I like, there's nothing I can do."

Dante didn't react nor respond. He only continued to pace. Violet, on the other hand, panicked. "You can't see through any of the cameras?!"

"No, I'm sorry."

As if a switch was triggered, Violet hissed. "You're sorry?! You're sorry?! Our daughter could be in-!"

Amos cut Violet off placing his hand upon hers. "We know you're trying your very best."

Violet ignored his attempt to try and disarm her anger. "If he was trying his best, we would be able to see what's going on! We'd be able to know that Kid is safe! What type of A Helix are you anyway?"

Never having dealt with such an overbearing personality before, Alex had gone flush. An awkward nervous laugh caught his throat before he responded. "Umm… I'm not one. I'm a Lab Tech. Well, I... I used to be a Lab Tech."

A full frown couldn't consume Violet's lips fast enough. "You're a simple Lab Tech?!"

All the Lab Techs in the room were quick to toss Violet a frown and a glare. Before Alex had a chance to meekly defend himself and the other Lab Techs, Violet spoke again. "Why is a simple Lab Tech even attempting to deal with something so complicated? Obviously this would be way too hard for you to understand. Shouldn't an ADGL Lab Tech be handling this? Or better yet the Commander's-"

Dante cut Violet off as he stopped pacing, turned on her and hissed. "Shut the hell up!!"

Everyone, even the two A Helixes that remained in the house were caught off guard by Dante's outburst. Dante placed his hand on his temple, closing his eyes and releasing a defeated sigh. "When the emergency system has been activated, it's next to impossible to access anything. Only the Director can override the lock down."

Violet's expression weakened a little. "But Kid could be-"

Dante cut her off again as his eyes snapped open and to her. "You think I don't know that! My Lady could be in danger right now and I'm here wasting my time watching over a bunch of stupid humans!"

Before anyone could voice their disapproval of Dante's words, he slowly shook his head. "I'm sorry. I didn't mean to make it sound like humans are useless or anything."

Dante closed his eyes. "I'm just frustrated that's all. I feel like there's nothing I can do to help her."

As the room began to calm, Dante glanced toward his mother. She was the one he was most worried about bringing into the World of the Lost Souls. Even though, she hadn't once complained and only continued knitting, he could tell she was upset. "…Mom?"

Dante's mother glanced up at him with a slight smile and gave a pleasant sound of acknowledgement. Dante approached and knelt down in front of her. He placed his hands on her knees before he whispered. "Are you okay?"

Dante's mother smiled even more as she placed her knitting needles onto her lap. "I'm fine. You have more important things to worry about than me."

Placing her hands upon his, she continued. "You need to figure out a way to help those you need to help."

Dante sighed lowering his head slightly. "If I knew how to do that, I would have done it by now."

Dante's mother gave his hands a quick pat. "You'll figure this out Dante. You're very smart. Your Father and I..."

Dante's mother paused for a split second before she spoke. Her voice had minute traces of sadness in it. "We raised a clever boy."

Dante barely nodded as he stood up. "Thanks Mom."

As he began to pace the room again, he glanced toward Alex. The minute Alex glanced back, Dante stopped. "Wait a minute! Is there anything in the Hangars that we can use?"

Alex's expression shifted to a confused curious. "...In the Hangars?"

Dante nodded then shrugged. "Anything, It's just a thought."

Alex smiled as he began to type on the laptop keys. "Actually, that's a really good thought. There are a few tools that have camera attachments. We use them to do a more thorough diagnostic on the vehicles and helicopters. It makes locating a problem easier. They run on external batteries so they shouldn't be affected by the emergency shut down system."

Violet gave Alex a confused look. "How do you know all this? I thought you were a Lab Tech."

Alex continued to work. "I got fried so I transferred and I-"

Alex gasped in shock and delight. "Oh my God, it worked!"

Dante raced over to the laptop and looked at the screen. The surveillance that was being displayed was at an odd angle. It showed mostly the ground and thanks to all the other tools around it, the view was obstructed. Dante could only barely make out one of his fellow Helixes foot. "You can't move it can you?"

Alex shook his head. "No, but I might be able to access another tool. Maybe we can get a better view."

Dante released a defeated and frustrated sigh. "Or we could get another peek into nothing. All of them could be getting killed as we speak and all we can do it try to catch glimpses."

Violet's expression shifted to worry. "…Oh no, Kid."

Amos gripped his wife's hand. "She is God. We have to remember that."

Dante looked toward them before he gave a confident nod. "That's right, my Lady is God and I'm one of her Arch Angel's."

Dante closed his eyes and placed his hand on the top of the laptop. "I am her Data, Surveillance and Information Angel. A human anything, shouldn't stand a chance against my intelligence."

Alex, as well as everyone else's eyes darted to Dante in awe. Many beautiful flashes of gold sparkling lights appeared all around him. Alex's eyes darted to the laptop as tons of information began to rapidly appear. He never got a chance to read a single word or code before Dante moved onto the next phase of unlocking the emergency systems.

The glowing blue veins that were exactly like Bridger's slowly began to crawl along his hands down his fingertips. Dante's eyes suddenly snapped open as two medium sized pale bluey white feathered with gold tipped wings popped out the sides of his head near his ears. They were very similar to the plume of feathers Sinah had by her ears when she was in her true form.

Before Dante could touch or even question having them, Alex spoke in excitement. "You broke through the emergency systems! We have surveillance into the Launch Pad area!"

As Dante opened his mouth to say something, the A Helix that was keeping guard outside, busted into the house. "Sir, we have a situation!"

Dante raced toward him then onto the porch. His eyes widened seeing a huge crowd of Lost Souls standing by the vehicles.

Eighty-Five

Sheep without a Shephard

In almost every Lost Soul's hand was some sort of weapon. Some had simple hand guns while others had makeshift clubs, spears and other items of violence. Dante frowned quickly regaining his composure. "Listen here, Lost souls, that supply truck and those jeeps are ours! We're not giving them up!"

A few of the Lost Souls glanced toward one another in confusion, while most just kept their attention locked on him. Dante glanced back at the A Helix. "Go inside and join the other two. We need to protect those from Residential."

The A Helix's eyes darted to Dante. "But Sir, you could be in danger out here! I can't just leave you to deal with them alone!"

Dante clenched his fists, looking toward the Lost Souls again. "Protecting everyone inside is our priority. Our Lady gave us our orders, we can't let her down. I'll deal with the Lost Souls."

Despite the A Helix's strong urge to disregard Dante's orders, he gave a slight nod. "Yes Sir, please be careful and don't hesitate to call out if you need help."

Dante swallowed heavily before he forced a confident demeanor and walked off the porch. Once he heard the A Helix close the front door, he spoke. "We have no intention on fighting or hurting anyone here. But we'll do what we must to keep our vehicles. If left without any other choice, we will resort to violence."

The Lost Souls didn't move from their spots. They only simply continued to stare at Dante. A slight frown couldn't help but to touch at his lips. "Is anyone even listening to me? You're wasting your time! We're not going to-"

Dante suddenly stopped short as one of his wings opened widely then cupped around his ear. As he reached his hand toward it in confusion, faint whispering sounds could be heard. The second his fingertips touched the cupped wing, the whispers became crystal clear. Dante's shocked eyes widened hearing some of the conversations amongst the Lost Souls.

Within the large crowd, one Lost Soul said. "So that's what an Angel looks like. It's a lot stranger than I thought. It sort of looks like us but not really."

Another Lost Soul said. "Why would it think we're here to fight? This is sacred land."

Another said. "I think it's confused. It looks confused."

Dante lifted his fingertips from his wing. The minute he did, the wing opened and returned to its proper location. Dante gave the Lost Souls a slightly untrusting look. "So... What do you want?"

One of the Lost Souls nervously stepped forward away from the crowd. She gave a slight yet respectful bow before she spoke. "Angel, we have done a lot of bad things. Some for survival, others for greed and others just to make someone else suffer our same pain. None of us are proud of what we have done or the paths we choose to take. Nothing we can say or do can justify all the sins we have committed against God. We can only fall to our knees and beg for God's mercy."

Dante's expression shifted to shock. "You're looking for forgiveness."

Almost every single Lost Soul in the crowd nodded their head. The Lost Soul spoke again. "We were told that God has finally been born. That God has finally come to save us. Our salvation is at hand."

Dante gave the slightest nod. "Word really does travel fast. I guess that family told anyone who would listen."

The Lost Soul turned her attention up the dark grey cloud above them.

"Once we felt the air move and saw the mark God left upon the sky, it was impossible not to believe it."

Dante glanced up at the cloud himself and whispered. "I wonder if every time Sinah uses her power, a piece of heaven gets restored."

Dante's expression weakened a little. "Does that mean once it's completely rebuilt, the A Helixes will have to leave this place? I don't want to leave my mom or Murdoch or the Command... No, he is my Lord now. I just made a human friend and... I don't want to leave any of them behind."

Dante's expression weakened even more. "Is that why she cried? It's not just the pain and suffering in the world but also the fact she'll have to leave everyone here. She'll have to return to the heavens leaving my Lord, her love behind."

Dante looked back toward the Lost Souls. All of them were staring at back at him with hurt yet panic filled expressions. The Lost Soul quickly questioned. "God's going to leave us?! Why?! Why would God abandon us?! Are we really condemned for all eternity?! Please Angel, please, tell us what to do to be saved by God!"

Dante awkwardly smiled as he dismissively waved his hand. "Um... Don't worry about what I said I was just talking to myself."

Dante blindly motioned his hand behind himself. "My Lady was here but now she's-"

The Lost Soul cut Dante off with a nod. "We know but we were hoping God would come back. We're worried and think God is in danger."

"What makes you think that, Human intuition?"

"No, we felt this strong comforting warmth suddenly touch us. It made us feel peaceful, happy and positive. All the good emotions most of us forgot we had. But as fast as it appeared, it was gone. It's been a really long time since we felt that and haven't felt it again. We thought God was beginning to heal the world, then-"

Dante gave a quick nod. "Of course! My Lady just like my Lord needs to draw upon an outside source to step into their true forms. She must have forced what little positive emotions that were left in the world to the surface to assist her."

Dante's expression suddenly shifted to determined, locking eyes with as many Lost Souls as he could see. "...Everyone, stay here."

As he turned heel, the Lost shook her head. "But we-"

Dante eyes darted back to her as he frowned. “I said, stay here.”

The Lost Soul quickly recoiled and gave a meek. “Okay.”

The second Dante raced into the house, all three A Helixes weren't hesitant in showing their concern. One quickly questioned. “Sir, are you alright?”

Dante gave the fastest nod before he spoke. “Alex, what's the status on our facility?”

Both Violet and Amos were sitting beside Alex on the couch staring wide eyed at the laptop screen. Violet's expression was weakened and her hands were covering her mouth in worry.

Seeing her, Dante barely nodded. “Not so good.”

Despite Sinah's parent's looks of worry, Alex's expression was one of confusion. “I'm not sure what everyone is fighting. They look like really messed up Helixes.”

Dante snatched the top of the laptop and turned it toward him. A full frown instantly consumed his lips seeing the Synthetics. “Those are the murderous bastards that killed our brethren and our Lady.”

Once Dante caught sight of Sinah and the others fighting, he confidently nodded. “I have a plan. I need two of you A Helixes to stay here and protect this house and everyone from Residential.”

Before any of the A Helixes could question, Violet did. “What do you mean ‘stay here’? Where are you going?”

Dante's lips touched at a frown. “I may not be an Arch Angel meant for fighting but I'm sure as hell going to help them. I'm heading back to the facility.”

As Violet opened her mouth to say something, Dante rudely pointed his index finger toward her. “No! You and everyone else are going to stay here.”

Violet frowned. As she opened her mouth to protest, Dante hissed. “What part of ‘no!’ did you not understand? The only assistance that the Lord and Lady need at this moment is the Lost Souls.”

Eighty-Six

A Helping Hand

The shock and confusion on everyone's face was more than apparent. One of the A Helixes couldn't help but to speak up. "The Lost Souls, those useless savage humans out there?"

As Dante began to nod, another of the A Helixes spoke. "Um... Sir, we don't mean to question a higher ranking officer, in fact we dislike it altogether. I just don't understand what the Lost Souls could possibly have to offer our Lords. Well, besides general annoyance."

Dante smiled glancing out the open front door at the crowd of Lost Souls. They merely stared back at him with slightly confused expressions. "They can provide an outside power source."

Everyone stared at Dante in confusion. Glancing back and seeing their expressions, Dante couldn't help but to chuckle a little. "Our Lord and Lady need an outside power source to draw upon to change into their true forms. It's something only humans can provide."

Dante paused for a split second before he frowned. "It's called something. I can't think of the word for it. Damn it! I swear it's on the tip of my tongue. It's when you think highly of someone and believe in them and..."

Alex cut Dante off still holding his look of confusion. "Are you talking about faith?"

Dante snapped his fingers and pointed at Alex with a full smile.

"That's it! Faith! The power of the soul! In all of the ancient texts most of us had to read, they spoke about the Gods being worshipped. They needed followers to spread their words of wisdom. What if the faith of humanity is what provided them the strength they needed?"

Alex barely nodded. "That would explain why they left this world to begin with. Maybe the past Gods couldn't get enough faith to maintain their existence here."

Dante gave a slight shrug. "That's what I'm thinking but obviously it's just a theory. Without hearing it directly from the past Gods, we won't know what really happened."

"That's true but it's a very good theory, one that actually makes a lot of sense. Maybe they didn't leave this world because they wanted to. Maybe it was simply for survival, like they didn't have a choice in the matter."

Alex's expression suddenly shifted to slight panic. "Doesn't that mean God and the Commander are in danger of abandoning us too? There isn't much faith in the world right now."

Dante glanced back at the Lost Souls with a slight smile. "There may not be much but even the smallest amount will help them. Besides, as I've said before our Lord and Lady aren't just reproductions of the past."

Dante turned his attention to the A Helixes. "Start loading as many Lost Souls as you can into the supply truck. Once I join you, we'll drive as fast as we can to the facility. Once everyone has been unloaded, you drive back here and pick up more. The more Lost Souls we have with us, the better."

Violet gave Dante a confused yet slightly angered look. "Why are you bringing them back to the Lab and not us?"

Dante's lips couldn't help but to touch at a frown. "Were you just not listening or something? Our Lord and Lady need an outside source to-"

"So you think dragging a bunch of humans into a fight with things that are obviously very dangerous, will help them?" Violet pointed at the laptop screen displaying the battle at hand as she continued. "Have you lost your mind?! They won't stand a chance! Look, even the Helix soldiers are having a hard time with them!"

Dante placed his hand on his forehead, closed his eyes and released a frustrated sigh. It was as if Violet was giving him a massive headache. "I'm not going to send them directly into battle. All the group has to do is be close enough to the battlefield that our Lords can sense them. Right now, our Lord and Lady are in the middle of combat. Neither have the time to step back and drawn upon the power of faith. If I bring the power source directly to them-"

Alex smile finishing his thought. "Then they can instantly draw upon that strength. That's really smart."

Dante awkwardly smiled looking toward him. "Well, I am the Arch Angel of Data, Information and Surveillance."

Alex's smile faded. "But wait a minute wouldn't it only be a one sided power source?"

Dante's awkward disposition faded. "You mean because all of them are currently seeking the Lady at the moment?"

"Yeah, wouldn't that mean she'll be the only one that gets the boost?"

Dante shook his head. "Humans at their base core are completely neutral, neither Good nor evil. During their development, they are influenced by other humans and even environment. This causes them to begin to lean one way or the other. Despite the side they favor, the other will always be there. That's why good cannot exist without evil and vice versa. It's the balance of humanity, the balance of the soul. I suppose in a sense the whole world."

Dante glanced toward one of the A Helixes. "Load them up and let's move out!"

The A Helix barely nodded. "Um... Sir, what exactly do I say to them?"

Alex smile standing up from the couch. "I'll go with you and talk to them."

Dante's eyes darted to Alex in confusion. "Alex?"

Alex held his smile. "It might be easier for them hearing it from another human. I don't think they'll react positively to hearing 'Get in the truck Lost Souls.' It could either anger them or scare them."

"What are you going to say?"

Alex smiled. "I'll introduce myself, explain the situation and ask if they would like to help our Gods."

Dante smiled. "Then helping our Gods won't be a forced action. It will be by their free will. Thanks Alex."

Alex gave a quick nod before he left the house with one of the A Helixes.

Dante approached then knelt down in front of his mother again. "I have to go Mom. I'll be back as soon as I can."

Dante's mother placed one of her hands on the side of his cheek. "Be careful out there, Dante. I couldn't handle losing someone else I love."

Dante's expression weakened a little. "You won't. Alex will take care of things here. If you want to know what's happening, just ask him. He'll be watching the surveillance on my laptop."

Dante's mother barely nodded as he stood up and left the house. As she began to knit again, she glanced toward Amos and Violet. "It's so hard when it's our child."

Amos weakly nodded. "They're strong we need to keep believing that."

Dante's mother closed her eyes before she whispered. "My clever boy is strong."

Eighty-Seven

Back on the Battlefield

Sinah lifted her hands and sent a blast of feathers toward one of the large Synthetics. As its flesh was slashed off of its body, another sent a wave of tentacles toward her. As if sensing them, she did a few quick back flips easily avoiding their strikes. As Sinah lifted her hands to send out another attack, a few loud agony filled screams flooded the area.

An instant expression of worry took Sinah's features as her eyes darted to the A and D Helix soldiers. Both the A and D were still shooting as many Synthetics as they possibly could. Sinah's expression shifted to confusion until she noticed the human military the Director had sent in to assist them.

The Synthetics flawed or not had locked their attentions on the human soldiers and were wiping them out. Not a single sign of mercy was given as their lives were stolen. Bones were broken and ripped from their bodies. Limbs were mutilated and left to dangle barely hanging onto the flesh. Innards were pulled out and carelessly splattered onto the ground turning it red from the bloodshed. It was an absolutely horrific sight not meant for anyone to view upon. Yet every single Synthetic basked in their agony and they looked almost amused at such a brutal slaughter.

As Sinah stepped toward them, Bridger snatched her off the ground and took flight. Sinah eyes darted up to him in confusion until she looked back down at the battlefield. Two of the large Synthetics had sent waves of tentacles toward her. If Bridger hadn't scooped her up when he did, she would have been hit.

Bridger awkwardly chuckled. "Sorry to just grab you like that, my Lady."

Sinah quickly shook her head. "That's alright, Bridger. I really should have been paying better attention to my surroundings. I was just a little caught off guard. Why are there humans on the battlefield?"

Bridger's eyes darted downward to the warzone on confusion. "You mean like human Soldiers?"

Sinah didn't have to respond before Bridger noticed the three Directors standing in safety. "I'm guessing the Director sent them in thinking they could help us."

Sinah closed her eyes as her features weakened a little. "That foolish man just sent them directly to their deaths. What a sad and unnecessary waste of Human life."

Bridger's expression weakened as the sky produced a very low rumble. "I'm sorry, my Lady. If I would have noticed humans on the battlefield I would have done my best to protect them."

Sinah slowly shook her head, opening her eyes. "They shouldn't have been there to begin with. Unfortunately, there's nothing we can do for them now."

Bridger weakly nodded until Sinah said. "We must get rid of these damn Synthetics before more lives are taken!"

Bridger confidently smiled as he flapped his wings a little. "That won't be a problem, my Lady. With my strong and gorgeous new form, they won't stand a chance. Did I happen to mention how beautiful my wings are?"

Sinah couldn't help but to laugh. "...A few times."

Bridger smiled even more. "I'm betting it's all anyone ever talks about anymore."

Sinah wrapped her arms around Bridger's neck. His amused disposition instantly shifted to confusion as he hesitantly placed his hands on her back. "U... Um… My Lady?"

Sinah's golden circle appeared above and below them. A bright ray of light poured out of the circles covering both of them. As feathers began to appear and float around them, Sinah spoke. "Bridger I need you to start creating bombs."

Bridger nodded lifting his one hand from her. "Oh! Yeah! Um… I meant 'Yes my Lady.'"

The second a bomb was created, one of the feathers would attach itself to it then move to the edge of the light. As more and more feathers became explosive, Sinah spoke. "As soon as you're ready, we're going to fly straight through one of those insults to Creation."

Bridger flapped his wings a little as he finished creating his final bomb. "Just leave it to me and my razor sharp wings. Did I happen to mention how beautiful they are?"

Sinah couldn't help but to snicker. "Maybe once or twice."

Bridger glanced down at the battlefield toward Murdoch as he snickered. Murdoch was killing off as many flawed Synthetics as he could. While killing them, he was defending himself against the larger Synthetics attacks. He shot his laser like weapons at any tentacle that was sent his way. Murdoch's expression just screamed annoyance rather than combat hardened.

Bridger's eyes shifted to Fallen. Despite being in mid combat with one of the larger Synthetics, he repetitively glanced up a Sinah. Once his eyes shifted to Bridger, he tossed him a full frown.

Bridger snickered a little shaking his head. "He's has always had a jealous side for you my Lady."

Sinah's eyes darted to Bridger then down to Fallen. Seeing his frown, she began to smile. "Let's get back down there before he gets really mad."

Bridger flapped his wings a little. "Thank you for granting me this form, my Lady. I feel like there isn't a limit on how much strength I have to serve and protect both you and the Lord."

Bridger chuckled a little. "And did I happen to mention how beautiful my wings are?"

Sinah snickered again as he flew as fast as he could toward one of the larger Synthetics. As the wind current whipped passed them, many golden feathers rapidly began to form and cover them.

Fallen shoulder checked one of the larger Synthetics back from him before he turned his attention back to the sky. Fallen's eyes darted toward the mass of feathers charging toward the battlefield. A slight smile couldn't help but to take his lips as it slammed into one of the larger Synthetics.

As Bridger and Sinah effortlessly tore through the Synthetic's body, the bomb equipped feathers shot and attached to anything and everything they could. Once they were free from its flesh, the remaining feathers ripped Bridger away from Sinah and tossed him back into the sky.

Bridger franticly flapped his wings desperately trying to overpower the force. Try all he liked, he just couldn't manage to counter it. Once the feathers finally passed him and he got control, his eyes darted down to Sinah. She was on the ground trying to remove all of the Synthetics black acidic blood from her body. Whilst the two of them had successfully passed through the Synthetics body, Sinah's feathers had only protected Bridger from the dangerous effects of the Synthetic's blood.

Bridger's eyes widened in panic seeing some of her skin burn and begin to bleed. As he flew back toward her, he noticed both Fallen and Murdoch were rushing to her aid. Even with Murdoch's unparalleled and unmatched speed, neither he, nor anyone else, was able to get close enough before the larger Synthetic blew up.

Eighty-Eight

Blood Frenzy

Fallen didn't even glance toward Murdoch as the blast of the bombs sent him flying away from the area. Nor did he glance up at Bridger, who was tossed even higher into the sky. He only continued to run in the direction that Sinah was before the explosion. Thanks to all the heavy smoke, he had to close his eyes and rely on his other senses to pinpoint her exact location.

Once Fallen was in Sinah's range, he opened his eyes. The second he did, his eyes darted to a Synthetics racing toward her. This wasn't a flawed Synthetic. It was one that had all the bone protruding from the right locations. Before Sinah had a chance to react, the Synthetic slammed its blade like bone into her shoulder and out her back. As it ripped its weapon from her flesh, Fallen slammed his hand clean through its skull. With a quick twist of his fist, Fallen had beheaded the Synthetic.

As the Synthetic fell dead and Fallen tossed his head aside, he spoke. "Sinah, are you alright?!"

Sinah placed her hand over her wound. "Thanks for the help."

Fallen frowned, glancing down at the dead Synthetic. "I should have got here a tad sooner."

Sinah shook her head lifting her hand from her now completely healed wound. "It was just a minor injury."

Sinah frowned removing a black rock-like chunk from her skin. "It's the Synthetic's blood that's the problem."

Fallen studied the black chunks that were burning into her flesh. "It looks like the blood has somehow solidified."

Sinah frowned even more. "Well, whatever it did, the pain went from a wide range, to a specific point pain. The damn things feel like they're digging into my skin."

Fallen snatched and began to rip each and every piece off of her. Each one he removed, Sinah made a sound of discomfort. Once the last was pulled off, he whispered. "Please forgive me Sinah."

Sinah smiled softly rubbing one of the sore spots that had almost healed completely. "That's alright at least they're off of me."

Right before Bridger landed, Murdoch stepped right in front of them "Are you okay, my Lady?!"

Bridger chimed in right after. "My Lady, are you hurt?! I didn't think my own bombs could hurt me. I mean I made them after all and they are a part of me. So I don't get how-"

Sinah lifted her hand with a smile, shaking her head. "I'm fine, don't worry. It was thanks to my feathers that your bombs were amplified. That's why I tried to push you out of harm's way into safety."

As Sinah lowered her hand, a few blood drops fell from her fingertips. The second they hit the ground, loud ear piercing screeches were heard from the battlefield. Everyone's eyes darted to the still lingering heavy smoke.

Murdoch frowned as the screeching continued. "What the hell is that noise?!"

Sinah glanced up at Bridger. "You know those beautiful wings you never mention."

Bridger chuckled glancing toward her. "…Yeah?"

Sinah pointed toward the smoke. "They can easily clear this away."

As Bridger opened his wings widely, Murdoch scoffed. "You should have thought of that lazy Angel."

Bridger couldn't help but to chuckle. All it took was one strong flap of his wings to clear every inch of the battlefield. Having an unobstructed view, everyone's expression shifted to confusion. The flawed Synthetics were cowering on the ground making these absolutely wretched traumatized screeches. The ones that weren't flawed were cautiously moving toward Sinah and the others.

Fallen's eyes darted down to the blood dripping from Sinah's hand. "It's your blood."

Sinah's eyes darted to Fallen then to her hand as well. "Maybe the flawed ones weren't able to destroy the A Helixes soul completely. Maybe it's hurting them from within or at least scaring them."

Fallen lifted his hand. As one of his silver blades with red spots lifted from his palm, he spoke "If your blood is inducing fear, then my blood might render them useless."

Fallen slashed his blade across his wrist. As the blood began to run down his fingers, Sinah lovingly placed her hand softly upon his arm as her expression weakened. "I'm sorry you have to hurt yourself, my beloved."

Smiling softly toward her, Fallen spoke. "If we can at least put an end to the flawed ones, then this nothing pain will be worth it."

Sinah's sympathetic expression didn't waver as Fallen softly kissed her forehead. "You never have to worry about me, Sinah."

As Sinah looked up at Fallen, Bridger clasped his hands together and pressed them against the side of his face. "...Tch. Aww."

As Murdoch rolled his eyes, Fallen flicked his blood toward the ground. Different from Sinah's blood which seemed to have a fear effect upon the Synthetics, his blood seemed to awaken a rage. Even the flawed ones, who were still screeching, seemed to turn savage and began violently attacking the A and D Helix soldiers. It was almost as if Fallen's blood had not only provided them with a boost of energy but aggression as well.

The fully functioning Synthetics that were once cautiously approaching now didn't show any sign of hesitation in their attacks toward Sinah and the others. Sinah leap back avoiding one of the Synthetics slash from its blade like bone. As she avoided another, she glanced toward the A and D Helix soldiers. Some were doing perfectly fine holding their own, while others were trying their best to merely stay alive.

As Sinah lifted her hand to summon her golden circle, tentacles were shot toward her. Sinah gasped as she leapt out of the way narrowly avoiding being hit. Before she could even think about counter attacking, one of the fully functioning Synthetics body checked her to the ground.

As Sinah began to get to her feet, she heard Fallen, Bridger and

Murdoch yell out to her in concern. A full frown took her lips as she dismissively waved her hand. “I’m fine! Alright, you damn bastards I’ve had enough playing around.”

Chuckles were shared from a few more fully functioning Synthetics, as they circled around her. Their chuckles were instantly silenced as Sinah punched one of them in the chest. The Synthetic couldn’t help but to laugh at the minimal pain it caused. “Is that the best you have God? You really are weak.”

Sinah smirked pulling her fist back. The Synthetic’s expression sifted to confusion as a few feathers fell from her knuckles. Before it could question, feathers filled then overflowed its mouth, ears and eye sockets. Sinah held her smirk as the feathers suddenly burst free from its body, obliterating him. Without hesitation, Sinah swiped her hand toward another Synthetic. The feathers that were falling toward the ground instantly changed direction and slashed through that Synthetic like a hot knife through butter.

As Sinah turned on another to fight, a sudden pain hit her in the chest. Her eyes instantly filled with tears feeling the deaths of a few of her A Helixes. Fallen placed his hand on his chest as the exact same pain hit him as a few of his D Helixes took their last breaths as well.

Eight-Nine

Loss

Without even thinking twice, both Sinah and Fallen sent out a powerful blast of energy that aggressively forced any Synthetic near them, out of their way. The pain from the loss of their kin became almost unbearable as they raced toward their fallen A and D Helixes. Any Synthetic that decided to try and stop them, were instantly burned to death by either Fallen's hellfire or Sinah's golden light.

As Sinah approached one of the dead A Helixes, her features weakened and a few tears escaped her eyes. The second she collapsed to her knees, the other A Helix soldiers closed around her trying their best to protect her from any attacks.

Despite Fallen's lowered eyebrows and hostel demeanor, traces of loss reflected in his eyes. As he stepped closer to one of the D Helixes bodies, the other D Helix soldiers closed around him in a protective manner as well.

Sinah ignored the rapid gunfire and sounds of destruction as she placed one of her hands softly on the A Helixes cold face. A few more tears fell as she whispered. "I'm so sorry."

The features of the A Helixes near her couldn't help but to weaken, feeling her pain. Before any of them could offer her any words of solace, Fallen hissed. "This shouldn't have happened!"

The D Helixes near him nervously swallowed feeling his angered pain. Fallen snarled, looking toward Sinah. "This shouldn't have happened!!"

Hearing his snarl and feeling his anger, Sinah's eyes darted up to his. The second he saw the tears streaming down her face, he frowned as much as he could. Clenching his fists, he snarled again. "Those wretched Synthetics will pay for killing our kin!"

As Sinah's expression weakened and she got to her feet, Fallen snapped at the D Helixes standing protectively around him. "Get the hell out of my way! Obviously, none of you can handle a simple task, so I-"

Fallen stopped short as the ground below him suddenly cracked open and a rush of boiling hot air shot out. Fallen glanced downward only for a split second before he slowly lifted his angered expression toward the Synthetics.

Murdoch's eyes darted to the ground as it began to rumble and shake. They quickly filled with panic as parts of the cement spilt open like an overly ripe piece of fruit. Murdoch shoved the Synthetic he was fighting with back from himself as he yelled out. "My Lord, Stop!"

Bridger, who was attacking the Synthetics in flight, didn't feel the quake. Hearing Murdoch yell out however, his eyes darted to him then to Fallen. Panic also filled his eyes seeing the tears in the ground. "Oh no!"

Many pieces of the ground cracked and opened releasing more and more unbearable heat around Fallen. Not being fully formed D Helixes, the burning air escaping the ground was far too much for them to handle. For their own safety, they nervously moved away from him in a slight panic.

As Fallen began to raise his hand, his wrist was snatched. Fallen's eyes darted to the person who had grabbed him. The crimson ring encompassing his pitch black iris had bled into his silver eyes. Having been the one that snatched his wrist, Sinah's grip loosened seeing the hellfire that courses through his veins.

Even though Sinah spoke in whisper, her expression looked very serious. "Fallen, you can't release that place here. You will kill more than just the Synthetics."

Fallen's angry demeanor didn't wavier. "Are you saying I can't control hell?! Are you saying that I can't control my own world?!"

Sinah placed his hand upon her chest then placed her hand over his.

Fallen's eyebrows furrowed in confusion until Sinah locked her gaze with his. As the gold points began to form in her eyes, she whispered again. "THIS is your world, OUR world. If you release Hell without being in your true form, it will run wild and destroy everything. Fallen, my love, please... Please don't destroy our world."

Fallen blinked a couple of times, returning to his senses. The crimson red color rapidly returned to its ring around his pitch black pupil. As expression weakened slightly, he placed his hand on the side of her face. "Sinah, I... I'm so sorry. I shouldn't have snapped at you like that."

As Sinah's eyes returned to normal, she didn't glance toward the ground hearing the splits, cracks and tears close. "We can easily kill the Synthetics by releasing Heaven or Hell upon this world but we'll kill everyone else in the process."

Fallen closed his eyes as his brows furrowed. "That desire to destroy everything was overwhelming."

Sinah glanced toward her fighting A Helix soldiers. "It's the loss of our kin, it cries out to our true selves."

Fallen's eyebrows lowered as he looked toward the fully functioning Synthetics. "We're much stronger than them! Killing all of them shouldn't be taking this damn long!"

Sinah released a soft yet slightly upset sigh. "Our A and D Helixes aren't strong enough to fight without those human made weapons. The Synthetics themselves are human made, so recovering from the attacks is like second nature. With only you, Bridger, Murdoch and I doing damage, it's only a matter of time before-"

Sinah stopped short as both her and Fallen's eyes darted to the large hangars. Without hesitation, Fallen yelled out. "A and D Helix soldiers fall back! Fall back!"

The A and D Helix soldier's expressions shifted to confusion but they didn't stop fighting.

Sinah glanced up at the fighting Bridger as she called out. "Bridger! Murdoch!"

Within a blink of the eye, Murdoch was at Fallen and Sinah's side. A few moments later, Bridger landed beside them. Even though Murdoch's expression still showed signs of panic, he kept his tone of voice calm. "My Lord, are you alright?"

Fallen waved his hand toward the other soldiers. "There's no time for questions! The A and D Helix soldiers need coverage while they escape the battlefield into the hangars."

Bridger glanced toward the hangars before he gasped. Only a spilt second later, Murdoch did the same. Sinah couldn't help but to smile at their reactions. "We need to get our Helixes into safety. Let our newly awakened Angels and Demons handle things from here."

As they gave a nod, the A and D Helixes Murdoch and Bridger had evacuated from the battlefield earlier, rushed out of the hangars in their true forms as Angels and Demons.

Ninety

Reinforcements

Both Fallen and Sinah smiled proudly as each and every one of their Angels and Demons bowed before them, before stepping into battle.

Every time an Angel would pass by Bridger, he would either smirk or snicker. Murdoch, who heard him, questioned. "What's so funny?"

Bridger effortlessly hooked a few A Helix soldiers behind himself with his wings. "Head to the hangars, our Lords have given the order."

As soon as they made a run for it, Bridger glanced toward Murdoch. "Look at the Angels."

Murdoch glanced toward them. All had pale bluey white feathered wings with gold tips and veins that were glowing blue on their bodies. Most shot small bursts of blue energy from their palms similar to gunfire at the Synthetics. While others fought in the hand to hand combat style. Every time they threw a punch or a kick, a wide blue band would appear causing more of a wallop.

Murdoch blindly waved his hand behind himself at a few more D Helix soldiers. "...Head to the hangars."

As a few more D Helix soldiers escaped, Murdoch gave a quick shrug. "What about them? Our Lady said the weapon we mastered as we were changing would be our-"

Bridger cut him off. "Not that! Look at their wings."

Murdoch rolled his eyes as a frown touched at his lips. "I'm not going to say yours are the most beautiful or whatever else you want me to say."

Bridger chuckled shooing a few more A Helix soldiers away from the battlefield. "That's not what I'm talking about. Look at their wings."

Murdoch released an irritated sigh as he looked at the Angels again. All of their wings sizes ended just above their hips. Even though a few were flapping their wings, they could only hover a few feet off the ground. None seemed to have Bridger's ability to fly. Even though some had used bombs during their development, none had mastered the skill because of the dangers when dealing with them. Since it wasn't their attack of choice, they completely lost the ability to use them in their new forms.

Murdoch's eyes darted to the Demons. Their demonic appearances were very similar to his, except none of them had his wings. Like the Angels, they shot bursts of energy from their palms. Theirs however, were red. None seemed to have Murdoch's laser gun skill nor did they move anywhere near as fast as him.

Murdoch's eyes darted back to Bridger. "They're different from us. But that doesn't make sense. We're all Angels and Demons. Besides our weapon choices, shouldn't we all be the same?"

Bridger's lips curled into a full smile. "I'm thinking we're the stronger ones."

Murdoch's lips touched at a slight smile as he glanced toward Sinah and Fallen. Both had re-entered the battle. "Only we have been entrusted to protect our Lord and Lady."

"And with such an honor, we're never allowed to fail them."

Before Murdoch could agree and return to battle, Bridger spoke again. "And my wings are the most beautiful of all the Angels."

Murdoch chuckled until Bridger giggled. "And yours are the cutest of all the Demons."

As Murdoch frowned, Bridger giggled again and took flight. A slight snicker caught Murdoch's throat as he raced into battle and rejoined the fight.

As Sinah sent out a wave of feathers into one of the larger Synthetics, she glanced toward the fighting Angels and Demons with a smile. Despite the fact there wasn't many of them, they were easily holding their own. Synthetics had to band together to try and get the upper hand. The only time both her and Fallen felt their panic was when some of the Synthetics acid blood sprayed on them. Without missing a beat however, the other Angels and Demons would quickly rush to their aid.

As Sinah turned her head back toward the large Synthetic, it sent a wave of tentacles toward her. Without hesitation, she snatched two of her feathers in her hands and used them as blades to effortlessly cut through the attack.

As each tentacle healed and reformed, the large Synthetic laughed. "How long do you think you and your pathetic little Helixes will last? We Synthetics don't ever get exhausted. Do you really think any of them have enough strength to actually kill us?"

The Synthetic laughed even louder sending out more tentacles. "Face it, I can attack you endlessly and all you can do is try your best to defend yourself."

Sinah only continued to slash the attacks sent toward her. The Synthetic's laugh shifted into a smug snicker. "The only thing those Helixes are good for is food for our creation. Besides that, they are just mistakes in a Lab."

Sinah snapped her hands shut destroying the feathers. "No, you insult to Creation, you and the other Synthetics are the mistakes."

The Synthetic cackled almost instantly. "We are the evolution of the flawed Helixes. We are the perfection humans seek. We may have been born from the cast off blood of some past Angels but we have destroyed and evolved beyond their imperfections. We are the only creations that were born in a Lab that are worthy of this world."

Sinah's eyebrows lowered. "I wasn't born in a Lab. I was born to this world and you and the other Synthetics will die in it."

Before the Synthetic had a chance to respond, a blinding gold light wrapped around Sinah. It was so bright that it was impossible to see her standing in the glare. All the Angel's eyes darted to the sky in a panic as a few dark grey clouds began to rapidly form above her.

Sinah suddenly lifted her hand releasing a brilliant blast of gold energy. It slammed then tore straight through the Synthetic's body rendering it into dust. Another large Synthetic, who was simply in the path of the blast, screeched as half of its body was ripped off. As it flailed its wounded body about in pain and panic, the golden light faded. Once it faded around Sinah, she flopped to the ground like a rag doll.

Within a blink of an eye, Murdoch was kneeling beside her. "...My Lady!"

Sinah weakly muttered with a slight smile. "..I know, I know, it was stupid of me to use the strength of my true form."

Murdoch glanced toward Fallen who was running toward them. Right before he made it in range to speak, tentacles snapped around him and pulled him back. Murdoch's eyes instantly filled with panic. "...My Lord!"

Sinah barely managed to move her hand to wave it dismissively. "..Go Murdoch. Help him."

Murdoch's eyes darted to Sinah. "But my Lady..!"

Sinah closed her eyes. "Go."

Murdoch gave a hesitant slight nod before he rushed over to the large Synthetic that had grabbed Fallen.

As Sinah slowly opened her eyes, she heard a chuckle a few feet in front of her. "Well that wasn't very smart of him leaving you all alone. It looks like I'll be the one that gets to kill the pointless God."

Ninety-One

A Weakened State

Sinah's tired eyes shifted to the approaching Synthetic, the voice belonged to. It was one of the fully functioning Synthetics with all the protruding bones in the correct spots. As he lifted his bone like blade to strike her down, a large pale bluey white feathered with gold tipped wing slashed through its waist.

As his upper body fell from the lower, Bridger stepped out from behind him. "Actually, it looks like you're dead."

As Bridger approached Sinah, he repetitively waved his wing that he had used as a weapon. Any feather that had the Synthetics acidic black blood on it was released and vanished before it hit the ground. As he knelt down to Sinah, he protectively cupped his one wing around her. "My Lady, are you alright?"

Bridger's expression shifted to slightly awkward as he spoke again. "I know I shouldn't question your actions or anything but-"

Sinah gave a weak snicker. "..I know. I just put myself directly into danger."

Bridger couldn't help but to snicker himself. "Well my Lady, I always thought you were a tad combat crazy, like me."

Sinah weakly snickered again before she turned her attention to Murdoch and Fallen. Murdoch was easily avoiding the tentacle strikes while shooting his laser blasts into the large Synthetic. Fallen, on the other hand, was still trying to free himself from the tentacles.

As Fallen flexed his muscles destroying most of them, more tentacles were shot and snapped around him, enforcing its grip. Ignoring Murdoch's attack, the Synthetic lifted its human like form up to Fallen. It snickered wrapping its hands around Fallen's neck. "Now that I think about it, isn't this how the other was killed?"

Fallen's eyebrows lowered. "Do you really think your pathetic speck of existence can end my life?"

The Synthetic tightened his grip cutting off Fallen's oxygen supply. "Oh I know I can."

The Synthetic glanced down at Murdoch as he continued. "And there's nothing anyone can do. That little pest down there is too stupid to realize that I heal instantly. His feeble attempts to save you are pointless."

The Synthetic frowned as it shifted its attention back to Fallen. "You and that girl are pointless. This world doesn't need Gods, it needs us."

Fallen opened his palms. Many silver blades with red spots slashed through the tentacles. As more began to wrap around him, Fallen spoke in a strained voice. "Do you really think the humans will just accept a disgusting octopod freak like you?!"

The Synthetic tightened its grip again. "Humans are easily manipulated into believing whatever you want them to believe. All we have to do is convince a few and the others will follow suit. Their mass way of thinking will always be their downfall. Having them accept us in our hidden forms will be a snap."

The Synthetic chuckled a little. "Look how easy it was for us to convince the humans that created us that we are harmless. Such trusting and foolish things these humans are. These fools even gave us full knowledge on the method of Synthetic creation."

The Synthetic grinned. "We don't need them anymore. After we get the humans to do whatever we please of them, we won't need them anymore either. We will take and eat all of your worthless resources and turn this world into what we want. This is only the beginning of our new world, one run and ruled by only Synthetics."

A cold smile took Fallen's lips as an opaque black darkness slowly began to form from behind him. "This world belongs to Sinah and I, and nobody will take it from us."

The black darkness suddenly changed into the shape of two large hands and closed around Fallen. The darkness he was enveloped in was so dark, not even the brightest shine of light could scratch its surface. The Synthetic didn't even get a chance to react before the darkness quickly began to engulf him.

Murdoch leapt back in confusion as the Synthetic completely vanished in the darkness. Though it appeared only like a heavy veil of simple shadows, screams of absolute terror and torture echoed from within.

Once Fallen was released from the Synthetics grip, he fell to the ground. Once he landed on his feet, he instantly took a knee. His features were one of utter exhaustion.

Murdoch held his look of confusion as the screams came to an abrupt stop and the darkness around the Synthetic began to fade. All of its flesh, tentacles and bones had evaporated within the darkness and only its black acidic blood remained. As it fell like a waterfall, Murdoch raced over to Fallen. Quickly wrapping his arm around Fallen's waist, he pulled him into safety then over to Sinah and Bridger.

Bridger released a loud sound of relief. "Thank your Lord for giving you that speed Murdoch! A few more seconds and both of you would have been caught up in it."

Murdoch glanced back at the black acidic blood sizzling on the ground. "That was too damn close. I could feel the heat from the acid on my heels."

As Murdoch slowly helped Fallen kneel next to Sinah, a chuckle caught Fallen's throat. "We've both made a huge mistake."

Sinah weakly smiled. "Yeah, but on the bright side, we did kill two more of them."

Fallen closed his eyes. "It's going to take us a long time to recover our strengths. Tapping into our true from without releasing Heaven or Hell leaves us vulnerable."

Murdoch's eyes darted cautiously around the battlefield. "Don't worry about that my Lord and Lady. We'll use every last bit of our strength to protect you."

Bridger nodded glancing around himself. "You can count on us."

Sinah smiled softly before she looked back at Fallen. Not only did he look exhausted but also very annoyed. Despite it taking a lot of effort to do so, Sinah shifted closer to him and gently placed her hand on his. "We need to place our trust on our Angels and Demons now."

"They can't even draw upon our strength for assistance. We're useless to them."

Both Murdoch and Bridger's eyes darted to Fallen in shock until Sinah slowly shook her head. "No, we've given them a reason to fight harder. They need us just as much as we need them."

Fallen closed his eyes as he released an agitated sound. "Just as much as we need those wretched humans."

"Just as much as they need us."

Fallen opened his eyes as his eyebrows lowered. "For every sin they have committed, all of them should be wiped clean from our world!"

Sinah smiled softly. "Forgiveness is my burden not yours. If you want to hate them for as long as they draw breath, so be it."

"If I were to simply kill them all, we'd never be able to fully step into our true forms. Anytime we'd have to access that strength we'd be left like this after we use it."

Sinah gave a slight nod until she noticed small golden sparkles rising up from her golden circle below her. Fallen's expression shifted to confusion until dark almost transparent shadows began to rise from the ground from the pitch black darkness below him.

Both Murdoch and Bridger's expression went from shock to confusion hearing loud boisterous screams and cheers from the outskirts of the battlefield.

Ninety-Two

In All Their Glory

Murdoch's expression had become one of utter disbelief seeing all the Lost Souls raising their makeshift weapons and cheering their hearts out. "…Lost Souls?"

A full smile took Bridger's lips seeing that the ring leader of the group was Dante. He was cheering as loud as he could alongside them. "Aw wasn't that nice of our Data, Info, Surveillance and tough guy solider. He brought us an audience."

Murdoch smiled as his eyes darted back to Sinah and Fallen. "No, he bought the outside source that our Lords need to draw upon."

Bridger held his full smile feeling Sinah's warm pure strength gently push his wing back from her. "Leave it to Dante to think of something so smart."

Without resisting in the slightest, both Murdoch and Bridger were both pushed back by a powerful wave of energy from their Lords as they got to their feet. Any Synthetics near them backed away feeling the overwhelming and ultimate power their bodies were producing.

Sinah smiled softly at Fallen as she released his hand. "I hope you like my true form."

Fallen chuckled, looking toward her. "I know I will. My eyes will be unworthy to gaze upon such a beautiful image of light."

Sinah's cheeks couldn't help but to touch at a blush. "I'm excited to see your true form of darkness."

Fallen closed his eyes. "I hope it doesn't bring you discomfort"

Sinah smiled slightly before she whispered. "It will be utter perfection, my love."

Fallen's lips touched at a momentary smile before he whispered. "Shall we then?"

A bright blinding golden light covered Sinah's body. Any Synthetics watching her, screeched as their eye burned out of their heads. Bridger snickered glancing toward them. "Serves you right for looking at our-"

Bridger stopped short hearing a loud rumble from above them. Both his and Murdoch's eyes darted skyward. Dark grey clouds rapidly began to form covering the sky completely. The only thing that the clouds didn't cover was the eclipsed sun and moon. Being in the brightly lit Launch Pad area, neither Bridger nor Murdoch could tell if the dim blue light that covered the world was affected by the cloud coverage.

As the brilliant blinding gold light faded around Sinah, everyone could see her in her true ethereal heavenly form. Despite being in mid combat, both the Angels and Demons took a brief moment to gaze upon their Lady's beauty. The second the Angels did, they felt a very warm and powerful boost of strength wield up from within their chests. All of them knew it was the unparalleled power of God. Drawing upon the new strength, the Angel's began to fight more aggressively.

The two large opaque hands slowly closed around Fallen. From within the darkness, the sounds of disembodied souls wailed and howled in sheer agony. Any Synthetic within his range shuddered at the wave of terror that Fallen's change was producing.

As the hands slowly opened, Fallen stood dominate in his true cold hellish form. Overlapping shards of a slightly shiny black substance adorned Fallen's body. They had the appearance of pieces of black glass similar to his finger nails. Each piece complimented his body perfectly and looked very much like armor. The angle and edges on the armor suggested that every part of him had become razor sharp. A long slightly transparent cloak draped behind him. Even though it had the appearance of a sheer material, it looked more like shadows and darkness. Fallen's hair had become silver and the tips of his ears had sharpened. A crown made of black spikes with silver accents tore through his forehead.

Different from the delicate swirls of glowing golden veins that complimented Sinah's facial beauty, Fallen's black veins were sharp and crisp. Despite them complimenting his ghost white skin, they made him look even more menacing. The crimson ring around his pitch black pupil had covered the silver in his eyes and the rage of hell itself burned within his cold gaze.

In comparison to one another, Sinah appeared delicate, understanding, gentle and loving. Something most would assume God would be. Fallen, on the other hand, appeared dangerous, hostile, destructive and cruel. Something most would assume Lucifer would be.

The Demons smiled feeling the unparalleled strength of Lucifer burn within them. After a quick glance at their impressive intimidating warrior Lord, they drew upon the new strength and began to fight more aggressively.

Bridger smiled nudging the awe stricken Murdoch in the arm. "Wow! Check out our Lord! I wasn't expecting anything that like."

Murdoch smiled feeling his own strength massively increase. "He's much more powerful than I could have ever imagined."

Bridger smiled watching Sinah softly place her hand upon Fallen's cheek. "Well, let's not waste the power our Lords have blessed us with. Let's kill these Synthetics already."

Without hesitation, both Murdoch and Bridger turned their attentions to the larger Synthetics and returned to battle.

Sinah smiled softly as her golden eyes curiously explored Fallen's appearance. "Absolutely utter perfection."

Fallen gently placed his hand upon her waist. "You stole the words right out of my mouth, my sweet salvation."

A slightly upset sigh escaped Sinah's lips. "Fallen, about the humans, I know you want to rid our world of them but-"

Fallen cut her off gently slipping his free hand into her hair. He made sure not a single one of her strands was cut by his overlapping jagged black glass like nails. "If it grants me even a mere moment to gaze upon you in this holy form, I will tolerate them."

Sinah smiled softly as her eyes locked with his. "Thank you. I'm glad this won't be the last time I get to see my handsome beloved dark form of perfection."

Fallen closed his eyes and gently touched his lips to hers. Sinah closed her eyes and returned the desire. Though they had kissed many times before, a sigh and a wave of love at its upmost level of happiness, washed over them. It was as if in their true forms, their hearts and souls were laid bare and fully exposed to the other.

As their lips parted Fallen's expression shifted to firm. "Let's finally rid our world of these worthless abominations."

Stepping back from his touch, Sinah offered her hand to him with a smile. "Shall we?"

Fallen took her hand and smile. "...With pleasure."

Ninety-Three

The Wrath of Heaven and Hell

Murdoch raced toward one of the fully functioning Synthetics and body checked it high into the air. Without hesitation, Bridger zipped across the sky passed the Synthetic slashing it clean in half with his razor sharp wings. Any feather that was touched by the black acidic blood was instantly expelled. Any Angel or Demon below the downpour of blood instinctively moved out of the path of danger.

Murdoch couldn't help but to smile at the efficiency of the Angels and Demons attacks. Every energy blast or combat strike was dead on target, dead on point. Even their spirits seemed to have been lifted. Instead of being hardened soldiers ready to battle in a grueling uphill war, they appeared much more happy and calm. It was as if they were just goofing around in one of the Combat simulators.

Right before a fully functioning Synthetic attacked Murdoch, Bridger smashed his body into it knocking both of them to the ground. Though the Synthetic was aggressively struggling, Bridger still managed to pin its back and shoulders to the ground. "You're getting lazy Mean Demon."

Murdoch scoffed as he watched Bridger open his wings widely then slam the tips of them into the Synthetics throat. The force he used caused the tips to poke through its neck then jab into the cement below. Bridger gave a little chuckle as he tried to pull them free. "This new form keeps surprising me on how strong it is."

Once the tips were out, he opened his wings widely tearing the Synthetic's throat apart decapitating it. As Bridger's wings abandoned the black acidic blood covered feathers, he stood up. Turning to Murdoch, he snickered. "I swear Mean Demon, if I wasn't here to save y-"

Murdoch suddenly lifted his index finger and shot one of his lasers toward Bridger. Bridger didn't even flinch as it zipped very close to his face into a Synthetic behind him.

Murdoch lowered his hand releasing a scoff. "Not paying attention to your surroundings? Who's the lazy one now Angel."

Bridger stuck out his tongue. "Nyah! In the words of my Demon brother, shut it!"

Murdoch couldn't help but to snicker as Bridger took flight. His amusement quickly began to dissipate as he glanced toward Sinah and Fallen.

Sinah closed her eyes and raised her hand toward the sky. Fallen did the same, only he directed his hand toward the ground. The sky began to rumble and make sounds as if something very large was moving beyond the dark grey clouds.

The screaming and cheering Lost Souls all began to fill with fear as their panicked eyes darted skyward. The second Dante noticed the encouragement begin to dwindle, he yelled out. "Don't give up now! Our Lords need our strength! Nothing bad is going to happen to any of you, I promise! Just don't give up!"

Though the Lost Souls were hesitant and many of their voices wavered, they began to cheer again. Every time Dante would yell out 'We can do this!' the more confident they became. Seeing golden lightening sudden rapidly race across the clouds, their confidence vanished again.

Dante gasped as his eyes darted to the sky. He placed his hand upon his chest feeling God's strength wield up from within him. "Heaven has been opened."

Before any Lost Soul could question, Dante clenched his fists and yelled out. "Don't give up! We can do this! We can help them! Come on! Don't give up!"

Though the Lost Soul's eyes were darting around in absolute terror and their voices shook, they still cheered and screamed out their encouragement.

The ground silently began to open in many locations. Black almost transparent shadows of small hands connected to very long arms began to crawl out from the openings. Each shadowy hand had long menacing razor sharp claws and began to reach upward toward the sky.

Both Fallen and Sinah's eyes suddenly snapped open. As Sinah turned her hand downward, Fallen turned his hand upward. Thick blasts of golden lightening aggressively began to strike the Synthetics on the battlefield. Any of them struck with a direct hit had their flesh melted off of their bones. Those who only got grazed by the attack stumbled from the force and caught a blaze. As they ran around frantically trying to extinguish the flames, one or many of the shadow hands would grab hold of them.

Any Synthetics that they did get a hold of, either were slashed to bits by the razor sharp claws or had their bodies eviscerated by the hands. Being such a horrific and gruesome action, many Lost Souls had to turn their heads. Almost all of them were utterly disgusted and a few couldn't contain their need to vomit.

In mere moments, the Synthetics were either stuck down by God's wrath or cut to shreds by Lucifer's. Not a single one of their rapid healing capabilities were able to recover from the superior powers of God and Lucifer.

Once the final Synthetic fell, Fallen snapped his hand shut pulling the shadow hands back into the opening in the ground. As the ground began to close, the Synthetic corpses, bones, acidic blood and any other traces of them were burned to ash by silver flames.

As the flames began to die down, Sinah looked toward the sky with a soft smile. Once she closed her eyes, rain began to pour down onto the battlefield cleansing all of the destruction.

Ninety-Four

United

The second the rainwater hit the Lost Souls, an instant panic fell over them. Most screamed in sheer terror and scattered from the group in absolute horror. Others fell to the ground, curled up in the fetal position and began to rock back and forth whimpering. A few more couldn't take the shock at what was happening and simply fainted. A few of the more brave Lost Souls nervously cupped their hands together in a scared confusion. As the clear water filled their palms, their fears began to fade.

Dante, who was frantically trying to calm the Lost Souls down, noticed one of them take a sip of the water. Once the liquid passed her tongue and went down her throat, a full smile took her lips. "It's water."

She happily yelled out to the other Lost Souls. "Don't be afraid! It's water! Taste it! Taste it! It doesn't taste bad like the other waters! It's good! It tastes clean!"

Those, who were trying to escape, but were still close enough in range to hear her, stopped short. A few nervously tilted their heads back and opened their mouths to taste the rain. Those, who weren't brave enough to try it, anxiously watched on in anticipation. Once their eyes lit up from the refreshing taste of the heavily falling rain, others began to taste it as well.

Dante's lips touched at a smile watching their fears and nerves quickly turn to joy. The Lost Souls happily drank and played in the rapidly forming puddles. The filth and grunge that normally coated the Lost Soul's hair, skin and clothes quickly began to wash away. Though it didn't seem possible, the Lost Souls became even happier feeling clean and refreshed.

Dante's smile faded as the wing on his head suddenly opened then cupped around his ear. He could clearly hear Bridger's voice. "Just keep looking at the Lost Souls. Just keep looking at the Lost Souls."

Dante suddenly flopped to the ground, narrowly avoiding Bridger, who zipped over him. As the strong wind current his wings produced hit him, he could hear Bridger's childish giggles. "Hey! How did you know I was coming after you?!"

Dante frowned getting to his feet. As he looked up at Bridger in the sky, he hissed. "Have you lost your mind?! What the heck are you doing flying at me to begin with?!"

Murdoch, who had rushed up next to Dante, scoffed. "…Idiot Angel."

Dante, who hadn't heard him, released a girlish surprised screech as he jumped and turned quick to Murdoch. "What the hell?!"

Murdoch couldn't help but to chuckle. "You really should pay attention to your surroundings, Dante."

Bridger chuckled, landing next to them. "So… Did you miss me?"

Dante's eyes darted back to Bridger. As his smile softened a little, Dante's expression couldn't help but to weaken. Whether he wanted to or not, a few tears wielded up in his eyes. The second one ran down his cheek, he made a snort sound unbefitting of an Angel and wiped it away. "No! I knew you'd be fine!"

Bridger flapped his wings a little holding his soft smile. "I missed you."

A few more tears escaped Dante's eyes. He hissed slapping them off of his face. "Sh… Shut up!"

Bridger moved closer to Dante. "I'm so sorry I made you worry."

Dante suddenly turned his head toward the Lost Souls trying his best to regain control over his emotions. All of the Lost Souls were staring at both Bridger and Murdoch in shock and awe. Dante swallowed heavily trying his best to fight his tears. "Y... You didn't, it's fine. I knew you'd be fine."

Bridger moved even closer to Dante. "I'm also sorry I took all the blame, but I just couldn't let you get hurt."

Dante shrugged until Bridger snatched one of the wings on the side of his head and giggled. "…Ooo! Check these out!"

Dante released a loud 'Ow!' sound as Bridger pulled on it a little. "These are so cute! Both you and Murdoch have the cutest wings!"

Murdoch rolled his eyes before he shook his head. "He said 'ow' you know, that usually means, stop."

Bridger gently opened the wing widely. "He just said 'ow' because he wasn't expecting it, right Dante?"

Dante hissed frantically waving his arms. "Will you let me go?! I knew you had to be up to something! Leave my wings be!"

Bridger chuckled releasing them. "…Alright, alright, I really did miss you though."

Dante only tossed him a frown until Bridger gave an upward nod at his head wings. "They really are neat."

Dante gave an indifferent shrug. "I'm still getting used to them. They don't feel quite like mine yet."

Bridger glanced toward the Lost Souls staring back at him. "All it takes is time. So... do they increase your hearing or something?"

Murdoch chuckled stepping into his demon at ease stance. "He's only asking because he can't figure out how you managed to counterattack his surprise attack."

Bridger chuckled putting his index finger to his lips. "Shh! You're not supposed to tell him!"

Dante gave another shrug. "I heard your thoughts."

Both Murdoch and Bridger's eyes darted to him in shock. Murdoch was quick to question. "You heard his thoughts?"

Bridger chimed in right after. "You heard my thoughts?"

Dante confidently nodded. "Just keep looking at the Lost Souls. Just keep looking at the Lost Souls."

Bridger instantly went flush while Murdoch snickered seeing his reaction. "I'm guessing he got it right."

"Yeah, that's exactly what I was thinking. I'm going to have to start watching what I say… I mean think."

"That's definitely a useful skill to have in battle. You'll always know exactly what your enemy's next move will be."

Dante shook his head. "I don't quite have control over it. I think right now it's only reacting to dangers or situations where I need immediate information."

Bridger awkwardly laughed scratching the back of his head. "Murdoch's right, it's a very useful skill. Just do me a favor, once you get control over it don't read my thoughts. Especially, when I'm reading those books where the man is shirtless and the woman is about to take off her pretty dress."

Dante cheeks instantly went bright red until the heavy rain abruptly stopped. Both Murdoch and Bridger's eyes darted to Sinah and Fallen. Bridger spoke, opening his wings widely. "Dante, can I fly you to our Lords?"

Dante didn't hesitate to nod in agreement. "Yes, of course."

Sinah opened her eyes as a gentle wind blew through the battlefield. Though the breeze barely moved the long strands of hair by her face, the Angels, Demons, Fallen and herself became completely dry in seconds. A slight smile took her lips as Bridger and Dante landed a few feet ahead of them.

Once Bridger placed Dante on the ground, they both instantly knelt. Once Murdoch followed suit, all the Angels and Demons lined up behind them and did the same. Fallen looked beyond them at the hangars as the A and D Helixes ran toward the Angels and Demons and also knelt down.

Sinah's eyes darted to the dripping wet Lost Souls as they timidly stepped onto the battlefield and knelt before them as well. Sinah smiled as the gentle breeze blew toward them and dried them as well. All looked shocked and surprised but none of them lifted their heads. They, as well as the others, kept their heads respectfully lowered.

Ninety-Five

Where We Belong

Sinah smiled softly at those kneeling before them. She gracefully picked up the side of the skirt part of her elegant dress and gave slight curtesy. "Thank you everyone so very much for fighting with everything you got. You've made both Fallen and I very proud."

Fallen glanced toward her, seeing her smile, he smiled slightly himself. "All of you did very well. We may have lost a few lives but I knew we would succeed in destroying our enemies."

Sinah released Fallen's hand and approached Murdoch, Bridger and Dante. As she bent down to Dante, she smiled even more. "And Dante, we are especially thankful to you. If it wasn't for your quick thinking Fallen and I would never have been able to draw upon our true forms."

Dante's cheeks touched at a red in embarrassment but he still didn't raise his head. "I just had to help, my Lady."

Sinah slipped her hand delicately under his chin and lifted his head. Once they made eye contact, she spoke. "I'm glad I can rely on one of my Arch Angels even when I send them away."

Dante smiled as much as he could while beaming with pride. "You can always count on us, my Lady."

As Sinah stood up straight, she looked toward Murdoch and Bridger. "All three of you have done so much for us. I can't even begin to thank you enough."

Fallen gave an assertive nod of agreement. "Murdoch, Bridger and Dante, the three of you have more than earned your places as our Arch's."

All three men couldn't help but to smile. Sinah glanced toward Fallen only for a split second, before she turned her attention to the Lost Souls. Fallen locked and unlocked his jaw keeping his attention solely locked upon her as she walked toward them.

A noticeable wave of nervousness emanated from their bodies as Sinah approached. The second she stopped right in front of them, the nervousness increased. Whether they wanted to or not, a few made quiet sounds of fear. Others couldn't contain their minor tremors of panic and worry. Sinah smiled softly as she raised her hand. A soft calming wave of warmth quickly washed over all of them. Their nerves, fears and panic were instantly soothed and replaced with a relaxing comfort.

As Sinah lowered her hand, she spoke. "Lost Souls... No, Humans of our World, thank you for helping us as well. Without your strength and determination to help save our suffering world, we wouldn't have been able to step into our true forms."

One of the Humans spoke, not lifting her head. "God, are you going to abandon us and go to Heaven?"

Sinah glanced up at the sky. The dark grey clouds had lightened to a greyish white. "No, this is our world too. We will cherish and care for it alongside all of you. We belong here."

Many relieved and happy sighs and whispers spilled from the Humans. As Fallen approached Sinah, he spoke. "We won't make the same mistakes the last Lords made. We won't simply rely upon blind faith."

Sinah smiled toward Fallen as he took her hand and continued. "It will take a great deal of hard work to rebuild and heal our damaged world."

Nodding and gripping his hand, Sinah spoke in a positive tone. "But we can do it. Together with everyone's help, I know it can be done."

Fallen gave the slightest nod. "Humans of our World, God has been kind enough to forgive all your sins and spare you from punishment."

Fallen's lips touched at a frown as his hellfire reflecting crimson eyes scanned the humans. "Never forget this generous gift she has bestowed upon you."

Fallen's eyebrows lowered. Despite the calm Sinah had placed upon them, a few felt his air of intimidation as he firmly spoke. "And never ever make her regret her choice."

All the Humans didn't hesitate to nod. Sinah placed her second hand on Fallen's chest as she spoke. "I would like to ask one more thing of the Humans of our World."

As the Humans nervously looked up at Sinah, she softly smiled. Seeing her soft smile, the calmness returned. "Please tell any other Human that wasn't here today that our World will be changing for the better. That both of us..."

Sinah glanced toward Fallen. Once he gave a nod, she continued. "That both of us want to put an end to our world's suffering."

Fallen gave another nod before he turned a full frown toward the Humans. "And if you dare oppose us, then you will truly understand the word pain."

The Humans instantly went flush until one of them yelled out. "You heard God! Spread the word! Make it known!"

As the Humans began to get their feet, Sinah waved her hand at a couple of the Angels and Demons. "The Humans need a ride back to the World of Lost... No, it's not called that anymore." Sinah smiled. "They need a ride home."

Two Angels and Demons instantly got to their feet. After a quick bow, they approached the Humans. As they were led toward the hangars, many of the Humans respectfully bowed at Sinah and Fallen before they went on their way.

As Sinah turned her attention back to Fallen, loud clapping sounds could be heard. Fallen's eyebrows instantly lowered as his eyes darted in the direction the clapping was coming from.

Ninety-Six

Final Comeuppance

The Director was clapping as loud as he could as he walked toward Sinah and Fallen. Without hesitation, Murdoch, Bridger and Dante sprang to their feet and stepped in his way. The Director chuckled as he defensively lifted his hands. "This isn't necessary gentlemen. I only want to congratulate them on winning their battle."

Sinah's lips touched at a frown. "It wasn't just our battle. It was a battle for the future of our world."

The Director smiled looking beyond the men blocking his path. "If I never would have seen it with my own eyes, I never would have believed it. God, you truly are worthy enough to rule over this world."

Fallen frowned as much as he could, before he had a chance to vent his anger, Sinah spoke. "All of us are worthy enough to watch over our world. Only the Synthetics mean to do it harm."

Director Courtier shook his head, hearing what she had said. "No, you're wrong!"

Both Sinah and Fallen frowned toward Director Courtier and Director Chris as they approached. Without hesitation, Bridger opened his wing to block their path to his Lords. Director Courtier's eyes darted to him in confusion as Bridger snickered a little. "Did you really think I'd let you just pass by us?"

Director Courtier released a slightly frustrated sigh before he tried to look beyond Bridger's wing at Sinah. "God, the Synthetics are manmade gifts to this world. They can help in so many ways. The only reason you had trouble with them here was because you wanted to fight them."

Sinah hissed almost instantly. Responding to her anger, there was a loud crash of thunder from beyond the clouds. "Are you saying they were only defending themselves?!"

As Director Courtier began to nod, Sinah released Fallen's hand and hissed again. "Are you telling me those creatures that want us, our Angels, Demons, Helixes and the Humans dead, should be allowed to live in our world?!"

Before Director Courtier could speak, Sinah hissed for the third time. "Those things that killed our kin, killed all those innocent A Helixes should live?!"

As Director Courtier opened his mouth again, Sinah snarled advancing forward. "You and everyone else that have repetitively violated the pure power of Creation, my power, will not be allowed life upon our world. You and all the Synthetics are parasites that only want to destroy."

Director Courtier shook his head as fast as he could. "No, no God, you don't understand."

Director Courtier placed his hand on Bridger's wing trying to push it out of his way. The minute his fingertips touched the feathers, they split open. Director Courtier drew his hand back in confusion. As he looked at the bleeding cuts, Bridger chuckled a little. "Obviously you weren't watching the battle. If you were, you'd know how dangerous my beautiful wings are."

Director Courtier lowered his hand as he turned his attention back to Sinah. "God, the Synthetics are our creations. They are like our children."

Sinah's eyebrows lowered. "Your children are alive at the cost of our A Helixes lives. Tell me, whose are more important. Their lives that are created through death or ours that are created through life. The answer is more than obvious."

Director Courtier sighed, shaking his head. "I'm sorry that you're A Helixes had to die but the Synthetics-"

Sinah closed her eyes finishing his sentence. "Will be wiped out and anyone who stands by them will suffer the same fate."

Before Director Courtier could protest anymore, Sinah suddenly raised her hand. An aggressive blast of golden lightening shot down from the clouds and slammed into him. Both Bridger and Murdoch leapt back avoiding the attack. Before Dante had a chance to react, Bridger snatched his arm and pulled him into safety.

The force of the strike knocked both Directors to the ground. As they began to get to their feet, Director Chris looked in the direction Director Courtier once stood. He was now only a pile of ash. Getting to his knees and clasped his hands together, Director Chris spoke in a pleading manner. "Oh please merciful God, I beg of you, please, please don't kill me!"

As Fallen approached Sinah's side, he spoke. "If you want to be spared his punishment or my version of the punishment you deserve, you will tell our Data, Information and Surveillance Arch Angel, the other Lab locations."

Before Director Chris had a chance to nod, Murdoch raced over to him and snatched him off the ground by his throat. "And don't even dare try to lie to him!"

As Dante walked toward them, Bridger spoke. "He can read minds so it really is pointless."

Director Chris tried to swallow but Murdoch's grip was too tight. "I... I won't betray you. I promise you God and Lucifer, I will help you rid the world of the Synthetics. I will devote the rest of my human life to your mission."

Fallen shifted his attention to the Director hearing him snicker. "I never would have thought my fellow scientists would have become so pathetic over the years."

Fallen's lips touched at a frown as he waved his hand at Murdoch. "He's trying to save his own skin. Something I wouldn't expect you to do."

Once Murdoch released Director Chris, he and Dante took a few steps away from everyone else. Despite Director Chris' glare tossed toward him, the Director chuckled again. "My life is in the hands of God and Lucifer, not yours."

Sinah smiled slightly as a wave of comfort washed over the Director. As he smiled toward her, she spoke. "Fallen, my love, you have my blessings to punish him or spare him. The choice is now yours."

Without hesitation, Fallen raised his hand. The ground right below the Director suddenly split open. Before the Director could react, many of the clawed shadow hands snatched hold of him. The Director's eyes widened as he frantically struggled in their grip. "You're going to kill me?! Me?! If it wasn't for me, most of those A and D Helixes wouldn't even be alive!"

Both Sinah and Fallen watched his expression overflow with an angered panic as he hissed. "If it wasn't for me the Labs wouldn't have the technology to provide food or water or-"

Fallen's lips touched at a cold cruel smile. "And we are thankful for the great strides you made to pieces of our world. We'll take it from here and help the rest."

The Director hissed again struggling as hard as he could. "You can't do this to me!"

The Director's panicked eyes darted to Sinah. "God! God, please help me!"

Sinah smiled taking Fallen's free hand. "He is only removing someone who could potentially cause us trouble in our new world. You have your vision of how our world should be. We have a similar one, only ours involves the equality of the Angels, Demons and Humans alike."

The Director squeezed his eyes shut screaming. "No!! No! This isn't how this is supposed to go! I was supposed to help rule over the world with you! I began all of this! I deserve Utopia! I deserve-!"

Fallen snapped his hand shut as he finished his sentence. "Everything you're going to get."

The Director screeched as he was pulled into the ground. Sounds of agony were heard only for a split second before the ground snapped shut.

Sinah smiled as Fallen turned to her with a smile. "His death is my gift to our new world."

Sinah gently touched her lips to his. Once she lifted them, she whispered. "This is the ending of a dying world. Let's celebrate the beginning of our new world filled only with peace and happiness."

Epilogue

In the twenty-eight months that passed, the world went through many drastic positive changes. Those against Fallen and Sinah's rule and protection quickly changed their tune seeing all the good they had brought forth. The once barren desolate wasteland of a mere couple of years ago had blossomed and bloomed with life. Lush green grass coated the valleys, fields and everywhere else there was natural ground. The tall bare trees that were once only considered firewood grew leaves and bore fruit. The rivers, lakes, streams and oceans that were once only stagnant pools of filthy water, now began to flow and grow aquatic life. The once dead air never had a chance to return before a gentle breeze would whisk it away. The world itself had become such a place of unparalleled beauty that the memories of the past were only considered a nightmare.

Though the wind pushed the clouds in the sky along, never once did they vanish. Nor did they cover the eclipsed sun and moon. In the past, the Humans would only see the eclipsed sun and moon as a constant reminder of their punishment. A badge of their failure and the choice their Lords made to abandon them. Now whenever one of them would gaze upon it, a smile would take their lips. The eclipsed sun and moon had become a symbol of hope and happiness. To them, it meant God and Lucifer was still watching over and protecting the world.

The designated day and night cycles that anyone from a Lab grew up with remained the same. The clouds would drastically darken at night and drastically lighten during the day. A normal sleep schedule seemed to massively lower the violence amongst the Humans and genuinely make them happier.

The life and death cycle had begun again, only it had limitations. Simply rotting in one's flesh was a disgusting thing of the past. Once a Human would pass away, his or her life would simply and painlessly leave their body. The power of Creation only allowed one child per human female. After that, the female and male, who created that life, would again return to barren. Not having the capability to create life to begin with, nobody questioned God's choice in the birthing restrictions.

Lab 1, the Lab that was once ruled by Director Walter Hart had become God and Lucifer's home. Though the Angels and Demons throughout the world had pooled there as well, Humans were welcome to visit whenever they liked. All were treated with kindness and respect. This Lab was also where plans were formed and strategies were developed in the struggling war to rid the world of the Synthetics.

The Human once known as Director Chris had kept his word and joined forces with God, Lucifer and their Angels and Demons. Slowly but surely, he rose in the ranks and became a Commander under Murdoch. Alex did the same and became one under Dante. Bridger was usually ordered to stay at the Lab and make sure everything ran smoothly. Being so kind and friendly, it just made sense to have him protect their home. Anytime he was needed elsewhere however, he never hesitated in helping out.

Bridger smiled tossing a baby high into the air on the out skirts of the Launch Pad area. Her brilliant forest green eyes with gold and red flecks beamed with happiness. Each time Bridger tossed her, she'd open her hands widely. Every time she did this, small purple flowers would fall from her palms. The second they touched the ground, they would take root. Bridger, who would giggle anytime one would fall on him, spoke in a fake annoyed tone. "Hey! Don't turn me into a flower."

The baby happily squealed and directed her hands toward him. Many different types of colored flowers shot from her palms. Bridger squeezed his eyes shut and made a fake scream noise. "Oh no! Help me! It's happening!"

The baby happily kicked her legs and waved her arms at his reaction. Collapsing to his knees, Bridger released another fake scream. After gently placing the baby amongst the flowers to sit, he fell onto his side. Making fake sounds of worry and distress, he rolled around. "Oh no! I'm becoming a flower! Baby, Baby you're turning me into a flower! Help me! Someone help me!"

The baby giggled and squealed loudly watching his fake display of torture. After a few more moments of pretending, Bridger suddenly sat up in front of her. "You would have just watched me become a flower without helping me? How cruel. You get that from your Father, you know."

The baby made a soft soothing coo sound toward Bridger. She picked one of the flowers beside her and offered it to him. Bridger elaborately gasped placing his hand on his chest. "Is that for me?"

The baby smiled softly as she shook it a little. Bridger smiled taking it. "Well, thank you. You get that kindness from your mother."

Bridger hooked the flower over his ear as he spoke. "Can you make more flowers appear?"

The baby closed her eyes and a wave of energy escaped her body. As the energy ran along the ground, many pink, white and purple flowers popped up and bloomed. Bridger clapped his hands happily scooping the baby up and getting to his feet. "Wow! That was amazing!"

The baby squealed in excitement until they heard a soft voice speak. "These are beautiful."

Both Bridger and the baby looked toward the person the voice belonged to it. It was Sinah. She smiled approaching them with Violet and Amos. Bridger looked down at the baby. "My Lady and your Mama's here!"

The baby instantly filled with excitement as Bridger carried her over to Sinah. "My Lady, your little one says all these flowers are for you."

Sinah smiled softly as she took the baby from his arms. As the baby cuddled her, she spoke. "You made all these flowers for me?"

The baby happily looked up at Sinah with her matching smile. Sinah gave a slight nod. "Thank you. They really are beautiful."

The baby made happy cooing sounds at Sinah. Holding her soft smile, she spoke. "Have you been keeping Bridger out of trouble?"

Both Bridger and the baby shook their heads. Sinah snickered a little until she suddenly turned her head away from them. It took Bridger only a few moments to sense what she had sensed and did the same. In the distance, they could see a hummer driving toward the Launch Pad area. Sinah turned her attention back down to the baby. "I need you to stay here with your grandparents, alright?"

The baby didn't resist as Sinah placed the baby in Violet's arms. "I'll be back in a few moments."

Violet smiled down at the baby. "Don't worry about us, we'll be fine."

Sinah gave the baby a soft kiss before, her and Bridger walked toward the approaching vehicle. Violet gently rocked the baby back and forth. "I still can't believe it."

Amos gently ran his hand over the baby's head. "Are you talking about the fact our daughter is God and can speak? Or the fact our daughter and Lucifer created Nature."

Violet glanced up at Fallen as he climbed out of the driver's side and approached Sinah. As they embraced, Violet shook her head. "Both, I never thought I'd ever hear her speak. And I definitely never thought I'd accept Lucifer as her husband."

Violet looked back down at the baby. "From what we've read in ancient texts, it makes sense that Nature would be created from both good and evil and that's exactly what this little girl is, she's born from both."

Amos smiled. "And she's adorable."

The baby smiled, opening her hands, sending flowers toward him. Amos couldn't help but to smile even more. "Very adorable."

As Fallen released Sinah from his grip, she spoke. "How did it go?"

Once Dante and Murdoch climbed out of the vehicle, Dante answered. "We might have a line on another Synthetic Lab. We're not sure. Those sneaky bastards are getting good at hiding. I'll have to do some checking into the information we collected today."

Fallen gave a slight nod. "We've left the two Commanders Chris and Alex at the Lab to handle the cleanup. With the help of the team of Angels and Demons that are with them, it shouldn't be a problem."

Sinah barely nodded. "Were there many Synthetics created there?"

"This was an animal Synthetic Lab. Most were mutated and undeveloped. They appeared to be suffering more than anything else."

Sinah's expression weakened as she closed her eyes. "…Mercy killings."

Fallen gently ran his hand down her arm with a smile. "You have blessed our world with animal life Sinah. Those Synthetics that shouldn't have been created to begin with are better off."

Sinah looked up at Fallen. "If they would have survived, I'm sure their thoughts would have been the same as the other Synthetics. Destroy and consume our world's resources and give nothing in return. The Humans will just become servants then food to them and we'll have much more unnecessary blood upon our hands."

As Fallen began to nod, Sinah shook her head. "Let's stop talking about this unpleasantness. Our daughter has been missing her father."

Fallen's lips touched at a smile as Sinah took his hand. "I've missed both of you very much."

Sinah smiled as she led Fallen away from the others toward her parents. Dante released a loud yawn as he leaned against the front of the hummer. "Man, I'm exhausted."

Murdoch glanced toward Bridger as he stepped into his demon at ease stance. "How about next time we send out the lazy Angel to deal with things?"

Dante snickered until the wing on the side of his head opened and cupped around his ear. After listening only for a few seconds, Dante shook his head. "I wouldn't do that if I were you Bridger."

Bridger couldn't help but to chuckle as he moved closer to Murdoch. "Do what? I'm not going to do anything."

Murdoch's eyes sharpened as he tossed Bridger a frown. "I swear now that he knows you can read his thoughts all he does is spend his time bothering me."

Bridger chuckled. "But you're so much more fun to bother. I guess the crankier the better."

Murdoch frowned as much as he could. "What the hell is he going to do Dante?"

Before Dante could answer, Bridger removed the flower from his ear and hooked it onto Murdoch's. Bridger giggled running away from him. "There, now you look as cute as your wings."

Murdoch scoffed removing the flower and carelessly tossing it to the cement. "Idiot Angel, I can catch you with my eyes closed."

Dante's eyes suddenly darted to the baby in Sinah's arms. As he opened his mouth to say something, Murdoch rushed after Bridger.

Right before he caught up, a flower covered vine shot up from the ground and snapped around his ankle. As Murdoch stumbled forward, Bridger took flight. Murdoch's expression shifted to confusion as his eyes darted down to what had stopped him. Once he saw the vine, he looked toward the baby. She was happily squealing up at Bridger. Once Bridger noticed what happened, he elaborately waved and called out. "Thanks Nature!"

As Murdoch began to free himself, he hissed. "I'll get you yet Idiot Angel!"

Bridger chuckled flapping his wings a little. "Not if me and the baby can help it Mean Demon!"

Sinah smiled up at Bridger. "We have to win this war Fallen. Their happiness and everyone else's in our world depends upon it. All of them need to forget all the pain and suffering they once knew."

Fallen gently ran his knuckles against her lower cheek. "As long as we both live and breathe Sinah, we will fight this war and we will win. As their Lords we won't fail them."

Sinah turned her smile toward Fallen as he gave a confident nod. She smiled even more as the baby made excitable happy sounds toward her parents.

Acknowledgements

To those who traveled this long journey with me: Thank you kindly from the bottom of my heart for your encouraging words and support. Thanks for all the laughs, love and sarcasm.

And to all the many musical talents that have kept me sane: Much appreciated!

Also a special thank you to my best friend Riri: Thank you kindly for being a strong voice when my words fall silent. You'll always be my ride and die!

And Finally, Thank you Michael Anthony. You will be forever missed and never forgotten. Rest in Peace.

Printed in the United States
By Bookmasters